The Eldritch Affair of the Cosmic Ne'er-do-wells: A Roustabouts Brouhaha

Alex De-Gruchy

FIRST PRINTING, March 2022.
Harry Markos, Director.

Paperback: ISBN 978-1-914926-86-0
eBook: ISBN 978-1-914926-87-7

Book design by: Ian Sharman

www.markosia.com

First Edition

For Mam and Dad, for everything.

The Widowing of Edwina Elbert

Newmuck, capital city of England. 1880.

Morris Elbert ran frantically along the cellar's dark hallway, stumbling and slipping on the damp stone floor, unaware he was racing towards his own very messy doom.

He had known that robbing his workplace was a risky idea given that Cecil Burgess would sooner see a thief sink to the bottom of the Brazenbrook than be handed over to the police, but Morris was a gambler – and not a good one – who owed a lot of money to some bad men, and the pittance he earned working eleven-hour shifts at the cannery was never going to settle his debt. Burgess being as rich as he was, Morris was confident he could find a stash of money or some things worth stealing inside the cannery.

So earlier that night he had ignored his wife Edwina's latest complaints about him throwing away money they didn't have, left the single rented room that was their home, and headed for the cannery. He snuck past the guards patrolling the yard and slipped into the main building through a ground-floor window he had propped open with a small metal wedge at the end of that day's shift.

The cannery interior had been still and silent, and in the darkness Morris crept past rows of bulky pressure-canners, slinked around tall columns of wooden packing crates, smelled the salty aroma of the storage tanks full of brine and blood-water, and felt the chill as he passed the vast cold-room in which thousands of pilchards, tuna, sardines, salmon, cod, mackerels, herrings, anchovies, mussels, whelks, eels, crabs, and shrimp waited, dead and staring, to be washed, decapitated, gutted, boned, shelled, cleaned, smoked, cooked, filleted, dried, or whatever other preparations they might require before being sealed into their respective Burgess Canning Company-branded cans.

Morris had ignored the spacious, high-ceilinged room that took up a large part of the building as he knew there was nothing worth stealing amongst its bloodstained chopping tables, tool-racks and stinking barrels used to transport skin, viscera, heads and bones to the solid waste room. The valuable PulpMaster 1000 pulping machine recently purchased by the cannery was the exception, but the hulking contraption must have weighed well over a ton.

Morris had thought the offices on the second floor – one for the elder Burgess and another, smaller one for his pansy son – were a better bet but he combed the latter and emerged with only a few fancy pieces of stationery and some loose change. As for the former, the three locks built into the door of Cecil Burgess' office must have been worth the money because Morris couldn't pick a single one of them. The door itself was too sturdy to break down and the office's large window that overlooked the Brazenbrook was dozens of feet above the ground outside.

That had left the cellar, which only the two Burgesses were ever allowed to enter. The entrance was a solid metal door tucked away inside a ground-floor storeroom, one always kept locked – except tonight, Morris found to his surprise. He pushed open the door and descended the rough stone steps on the other side, using his lighter to illuminate the complete darkness around him.

That lighter lay forgotten now, Morris having dropped it when he opened the door at the end of the cellar hallway and been confronted with the nightmarish figures coming the other way.

Please, God, let me get out of here, Morris prayed as he scrambled back up the steps on his hands and feet then stumbled into the storeroom. *Please, I won't drink or gamble or steal again.*

He was right about that.

Behind him, from the cellar below, he could hear hurried footsteps and urgent voices. Those things were coming for him. He ran.

Morris bounced off a wall and got turned around but kept moving, the ease with which he had navigated the cannery's dark spaces gone now, his surroundings suddenly a confusing blur of alien shapes and threatening shadows. He came to some metal steps and didn't think about where he was going as he bounded up them two treads at a time, his heart pounding. He reached the top of the stairs and sprinted along the rickety metal catwalk affixed high up on one wall of the main room.

One of Morris' shoes came down on an oil-slick section of catwalk and he slipped and fell into the waist-high railing at his side, the length of rusty metal snapping with the impact, Morris tumbling off the catwalk and into open air.

Morris screamed but only briefly. It wasn't a long fall into the open chute of the PulpMaster 1000.

The PulpMaster 1000 was designed for one task: whatever you fed into the top chute of the machine would quickly emerge from the bottom chute as lumpy paste. With sales of Burgess Economy Unnamed Sea-Based Lifeform Sandwich Spread having steadily risen in recent years, the machine was an efficient method of meeting demand.

It also activated automatically when something was fed into it, so as Morris plunged into its gaping, blood-spattered maw, the PulpMaster 1000 roared into life and the numerous cutters, hammers and grinders inside got to work. Several seconds later the lumpy paste which had been Morris Elbert was deposited into a metal container at the base of the machine and the PulpMaster 1000 sputtered and went quiet again.

The five robed figures who Morris had encountered in the cellar gathered around the machine, looking at what had become of Morris Elbert through the eyeholes of their grotesque masks. One of them turned aside as vomit exploded from beneath his mask, which he hurriedly removed.

Cecil Burgess glared at his son with undisguised contempt and, in a voice that could melt the ink from the pages of a children's storybook if he ever read one aloud, said, "Pull yourself together, Oliver."

Arthur Blacklock's smile couldn't be seen beneath his mask, but the mocking amusement was clear in his voice as he looked at Oliver Burgess and said, "You've got sick on your Old One."

Oliver used a sleeve to wipe his face then his mask, a representation of the monstrous cosmic entity known as Saucy Kenneth, the Winking Blasphemy. "Sorry, father." His eyes moved between the three other men. "Sorry."

Oliver reluctantly glanced at the container in which Morris Elbert rested. "What should we do with… that?"

"It's edible," Cecil said flatly. "Can it."

Amidst Whelks, a Discovery

"*Twat!*" Bryn shouted as he twatted the twat in the face, beer and blood and teeth spraying through the air like confetti at a Viking wedding.

The twat flew backwards and across a table before coming to rest on the floor, unconscious. A cheer rose from the other drinkers in the pub: the Welshman had been in the right throwing the punch, the unconscious man having insulted Mrs. Clubber, the little old lady who sold bits of felt over on Finney Street. Everyone loved Mrs. Clubber.

Bryn walked back to his chair and sat down, rejoining his fellow Roustabouts at the same scratched, stained and chipped wooden table they had been drinking at for years. Their suit jackets hung on the backs of their chairs, some of them wearing waistcoats over their shirts while the others wore braces, the soot-blackened fireplace keeping the pub warm on this brisk spring afternoon.

Henry gave Bryn a nod of approval. "Nice job."

"Imagine that," Ambrose said, "saying Mrs. Clubber smells like a bag of damp beetroot."

Talbot tutted and shook his head. He paused. "I mean, she does."

"Yeah, but you don't *say* that, do you."

A lit cigarette between his lips, Digby looked towards the bar then nudged Bryn with an elbow. "I don't think quite everyone approves, Bryn."

Annie was striding towards their table, a cleaning rag in hand and a disapproving look on her face. Her long blonde hair was tied back and she wore a stained apron over her long skirt and blouse, her sleeves rolled up.

"Bugger," Bryn said.

Annie Radcliffe had been the landlady of The Bewigged Pig for six years and although not physically imposing, the regulars knew her as someone not to be trifled with. She didn't miss a beat as she approached the Roustabouts' table and threw her rag into the face of the bearded, barrel-chested Bryn.

"You know I don't like fighting in here," Annie said as Bryn peeled the cleaning rag off his face with a sticky, distinctly unclean sound.

"Sorry, Annie," Bryn said.

Annie looked over the other Roustabouts with a commanding gaze that would have made her a fortune if she could bottle it and sell it to substitute teachers. "And that goes for the rest of you as well."

"Yes, Annie," said the four men in unison.

Henry Alabaster, Bryn Williams, Digby Grimble, Talbot Ashmole, Ambrose Parish: each man alone had fought his share of fights and overcome his share of obstacles, and together as the Roustabouts the five of them had fought and overcome plenty more – like when they beat the bejesus out of the Werewolf King who had been pissing on the vegetables in the allotment owned by Ambrose's grandfather, now *that* was a Christmas Day to remember – but before the slim, five-foot-four frame and cool blue eyes of Annie Radcliffe they were little boys again. Only with more impressive facial hair.

Annie's hand darted out and snatched the half-full pint of Haunted Weasel that Bryn had been raising to his lips. "No more cider for you until you throw that idiot out and clean up the mess you made."

For at least as long as Henry had been alive, the general consensus in Britain was that women were fragile, lesser creatures compared to men and were treated thusly by society. And while the situation had improved to a degree – women being allowed to play certain sports, some universities admitting women on equal terms with men – Henry had always disagreed with that consensus and continued to do so now as he marvelled at Annie's power: he had once seen a man snatch a pint out of Bryn's hand and that man had to breathe through his eyes now.

"Be fair, Annie, you heard what he said about Mrs. Clubber," Bryn said.

"I don't care," Annie said firmly. "Go on, get to it."

Bryn sighed, stood up and, cleaning rag in hand, walked towards the unconscious customer.

"Any chance of some service?" George called from his stool at the bar. "A man could die of thirst 'round here."

"The pox'll get you before thirst does," Murray said from his stool next to George.

"Shut your sauce-box."

Taking Bryn's drink with her, Annie headed back behind the bar to pour George another pint. She didn't need to ask what he wanted as George and Murray had been regulars at The Bewigged Pig since before Annie inherited the pub from her uncle Ewan, and the two men had one simple rule: lager when the sun was out, gin when the moon was out. A few years ago there was a solar eclipse, that had really thrown them.

George was loosely employed at a confectionery factory, the irregular nature of the work meaning that only the better hands were given permanent hours. George was not one of the better hands but always managed to find money for drink, and now he rooted around inside his ragged coat for coins as Annie poured his lager from one of the taps that lined the bar.

As for Murray, he and his wife had their own small business manufacturing umbrellas at home and supplying them to local shops. They had recently experimented with some novelty models, although Murray admitted their dog-hair umbrella wasn't really taking off like they had hoped.

Henry took a swallow of his Flank's lager, wiped foam off his moustache and looked around the room. Situated about halfway along Mulligan Avenue, The Bewigged Pig was one of the oldest pubs in Newmuck, a place where people came to drink and laugh and talk and forget their troubles for a time. The pub bore its name in large painted letters on the front wall outside, and on a hanging wooden sign attached to the same wall. Centuries ago, when a much larger percentage of the population was illiterate, a picture was more useful than words in identifying a pub, so it made sense that The Bewigged Pig's hanging sign portrayed a fat, pink pig standing alone in a muddy pen, staring blankly into the distance while resting atop its head was a fabulous, bouffant, blonde wig, an elaborate construction that stood almost three feet tall. Annie claimed to have no idea as to the origin of the pub's name, and Ewan had always said the same before her. And so, as with how Odd Reg had managed to eat that entire chest of drawers without dying, it remained a local mystery no one could explain.

The barstools and tables were mostly occupied by men but there were a few women present as well, as although many of the city's drinking establishments followed social etiquette in refusing to allow women to enter public bars, The Bewigged Pig was not one of those places. Nor was it one of Newmuck's many dangerous back-alley drinking establishments where you might enter with a smile on your lips but leave with a knife between your ribs. Here everyone was welcome and new customers tended to either fit right in or, as in the case of the stranger who had insulted Mrs. Clubber, display unwelcome attitudes which were quickly readjusted.

Pedestrians and the occasional carriage or wagon passed by in the street outside, the traffic only noisy shadows if seen through the small coloured panes of the partially stained-glass windows. Hanging on one of the wood-panelled walls was a hole-riddled dartboard and next to this was a battered piano which Henry was confident Talbot would end up playing before the night was over, a few drinks and a little encouragement usually being all it took. Talbot may have had large, sinewy hands that could crush an ape – not that he ever would, that would be horrific – but those thick fingers could dance across piano keys with surprising grace. Talbot could have everyone in the pub singing along and lifting their drinks to songs such as *Excelsior* and *Come Into the Garden, Maud*, with the later hours of the evening often involving bawdier numbers such as *My Tent Stands Firm Amidst the Boldest of Breezes* and *The Baker's Wife Knows Her Way Around a Pastry*.

Henry drew in a deep, satisfied breath. It seemed like you couldn't throw a stone in Newmuck without hitting a pub, and there were some good ones, but they weren't The Bewigged Pig. This was the Roustabouts' *local*.

Henry had a pint in his hand, money in his pocket, a group of friends who stood with him through thick and thin, and a weekend to spend doing nothing but carousing. Life was good. And it got even better when he remembered that it wasn't his round next. He drained his pint then set down his glass. "Ambrose, your round."

Ambrose and Digby drank what remained of their lagers while Talbot polished off his Beggar's Belief bitter.

"Do me a favour," Talbot said to Ambrose, "grab me a tin of Burgess whelks and a tin-opener while you're at the bar."

"No problem," Ambrose said as he collected the empty glasses.

"Oh, and some vinegar. Can't eat whelks without vinegar."

"That's funny," Digby said as he smoothed his black horseshoe moustache with a thumb and index finger, "I can't eat whelks without vomiting."

Ambrose made his way to the bar, Henry noticing the admiring glances he received from a couple of female customers as he went, Ambrose himself oblivious to them. His impressive physique, blue-green eyes, neat pencil moustache and flowing blonde hair often turned heads and led to cases of the lady-swoons, as Henry believed the medical term to be.

Bryn had thrown the unconscious man out onto the street and was now down on one knee, wiping up beer and blood. When he saw Ambrose going to the bar, he quickened his speed.

Henry turned to Digby. "How are your giggleberries?"

Generally it wasn't a question you asked a bloke, but given the knee Digby had taken to his crotch the previous evening, Henry felt the interest was warranted.

Digby frowned and shifted in his seat as he stubbed out his cigarette butt in the ashtray. "Better than last night, but still tender."

"That'll teach you to invite a lass back to your flat for a look at your special French illustrated pamphlets," Talbot said.

"It's worth it for when it works," Digby said, smiling that rakish smile which had gotten him into many situations both pleasurable and dangerous – sometimes both at once – over the years.

"Your optimism is a constant source of inspiration, Digby," Henry said. "You remind me of that bloke a few years back who vowed to swim the Brazenbrook in a full suit of armour."

"But he drowned."

"Yeah, immediately."

Ambrose appeared carrying a tin of whelks, a tin-opener, a bottle of vinegar and five pint glasses filled to the brim with not a drop spilled, each of the Roustabouts having had years of experience carrying a round of five pints. Bryn had finished cleaning the floor and was now standing at the bar, downing what remained of his Haunted Weasel, Annie having returned his pint.

"Bryn, I've got your next one here," Ambrose called out as he set the drinks on the table, and Bryn gave him a thumbs-up as he drank.

Talbot used the tin-opener to open the whelks then pulled back the lid to reveal the lumpy, moist, sickly-coloured contents. He held out the tin. "Anyone fancy a whelk?"

Henry, Digby and Ambrose made distasteful expressions and shook their heads, Bryn doing the same as he returned to the table.

"Suit yourselves," Talbot said as he sprinkled some vinegar into the tin. Then he dug in with his fingers and began to eat.

"You know, Bryn," Digby said, "since you're a cleaner now, you can pop 'round and clean my floors over the weekend if you like."

"I'll use you as the bloody rag," Bryn said.

"Henry?" Talbot said.

"Mm?" Henry replied distractedly. He was staring at the two-foot-by-four-foot nude painting of Ewan Radcliffe which hung on the wall behind the bar, a stipulation in the former landlord's will stating that the painting could never be taken down. Henry always wondered how the painter had made it so that the nipples seemed to follow you around the room.

"Henry," Talbot said again.

Henry blinked. "Sorry, I was miles away. What is it?"

"What would you say *that* is?"

Henry studied the object which Talbot was holding up in the slick fingers of his right hand. After a few seconds he came to a conclusion and, confident in it, said, "What you've got there is a nose."

Talbot looked at the severed human nose he had found inside his tin of whelks and nodded. "I thought so."

Digby, Ambrose and Bryn were all looking at the grey, wrinkled lump of cartilage now as well.

"Maybe it's a prize," Bryn suggested. "You know, like last year when Dillard's put free socks inside some of their cans of oxtail soup?"

"That only happened because Willard Dillard lost his marbles," Digby said. "They found him dancing naked in Saint Alan's Cathedral not long after that."

"I paid good money for this tin of whelks," Talbot said.

"Actually, I paid for them," Ambrose said, "you haven't given me the –"

"*Good. Money.*"

The Burgess cannery was only about a thirty-minute walk away, over in the riverside district of Bryanferry, so Henry downed his pint and adjusted his braces. "Drink up, lads."

"What's the rush?" Ambrose asked.

"We're going to pay a visit to Burgess Canning Company. Whelks may be revolting slime fit only for foul, bottom-feeding creatures but Talbot enjoys them and that's what counts, so I won't stand by while he has his pub snack ruined by an unwanted nose."

"To the cannery!" Bryn said enthusiastically, and he, Talbot, Digby and Ambrose drained their pints.

Talbot placed the nose back into the tin of whelks, pressed the loose lid down onto the contents and held it in one hand. The Roustabouts took their suit jackets from their chairs and carried their glasses to the bar.

"Where you off to?" Annie asked.

"To get satisfaction," Talbot said.

Murray turned to the Roustabouts and frowned. "I thought Madam Rutt's didn't open until five? Uh, not that I'd know, obviously…"

The Streets of Newmuck or: The Terrible Accuracy of the Truthful Sculptor

"Do you get it?" Ambrose asked.

"Yes," Henry said, "we get it."

"See, I know whelks aren't fish, but they're a kind of seafood, aren't they? So, 'something smells fishy about this' still works –"

Digby groaned.

"You lot just don't appreciate good comedy," Ambrose said.

"I'd appreciate the sweet release of death if we have to listen to any more of your jokes," Digby said.

The Roustabouts walked along Hobbin Way, heading in the direction of Bryanferry, the sky blanketed with grey clouds. They were in the heart of Newmuck and the area beat with a fitting, chaotic vitality, the streets alive with sights, sounds and most definitely smells as the people of the overcrowded capital city went about their day.

Posters advertising entertainments and products from travelling circuses to soap were plastered on fences and walls while multi-chimneyed houses with patterned brickwork and intricate roofs of shingle or slate stood separated from the pavements by iron railings, their bay windows looking out onto the streets. Rising above these rooftops and jutting up all across the Newmuck skyline were the spires of numerous churches, cathedrals and other Gothic-style buildings.

Newmuck had its share of distinct districts – no wealthy gentleman would saunter through the grim alleys of Gristle after dark, while in the upmarket Fondle Green the city's elite were known to fire spare servants out of cannons when bored – but here the Roustabouts walked amongst the rich and the poor, the young and the old, the law-abiding and the criminal, and the ugly and the beautiful alike, most of the upper-class looking down on those upstarts the middle-class while most of the middle-class looked down on those ghastly oiks the working-class.

For those who could afford it, fashion had become a major concern, there were even fashion magazines available to those eager to follow the latest trends. Middle- and upper-class women wore tight corsets, choker necklaces, layers of petticoats, large bows at their lower backs, and skirts that exaggerated their backsides to a degree that you could lay out a three-course meal on them, while men of similar status were dressed in Ascot ties, three-piece suits, restrictive frock coats, and shirts whose collars had been pressed into upstanding wings that could have someone's eye out if you weren't careful.

And then there were the various hats, from modest bowlers to towering top hats on the men, and small bonnets to flowered and plumed monstrosities on the women. Ambrose glimpsed one woman with an entire exotic bird perched on her head, the creature either stuffed or very well-trained. None of the Roustabouts ever really bothered with hats, and none of the fancy clothing on display looked particularly comfortable to Ambrose, but then he knew it wasn't about comfort but showing off the fact you could afford to dress uncomfortably.

A costermonger pushed his wooden wheelbarrow along the pavement, shouting about the fruit and vegetables piled up in it, smoothly weaving around a pair of uniformed nurses and a muscular builder carrying a hod of bricks over one shoulder. On the other side of the street a dung cart slowly rolled along next to the pavement, a team of three men collecting horse droppings from the road, while the owner of a newsstand held aloft a newspaper and called out the prominent headlines of the day, including the lurid-sounding poisoning of a well-to-do merchant by his mistress.

The Roustabouts came to a traffic light and waited for the policeman standing at its base to turn the crank that switched the light of the gas lamp at the top of the column from green to red. The stream of horse-drawn vehicles on the road came to a stop, the more impatient drivers grumbling as the Roustabouts and other pedestrians had the nerve to want to cross the street without being mown down, a danger which had grown alongside the number of carriages, wagons, omnibuses and horse-trams on Newmuck's roads.

Alongside the traffic lights, another welcome transport development was the tarmacking of many roads, which meant more comfortable carriage journeys, although naturally the city's budget for this hadn't stretched to the poorer districts – except where slums were demolished due to being in the way, their inhabitants displaced – whose old cobblestone roads could still shake your teeth loose if you were riding in a carriage with poor suspension.

Although you couldn't even fit a carriage inside the worst of Newmuck's slums, which were overcrowded, poorly constructed, unsanitary warrens of narrow streets and unlit alleys where children walked barefoot, a dozen people might live in one squalid room, diseases such as tuberculosis and rickets were rife, and some men and women drank and squabbled and wallowed in filth while others struggled for a better life that remained beyond their reach no matter how hard they worked. It was a world apart but sometimes only streets away.

Newmuck had long ago sloughed off its modest origins, having been founded almost two-thousand years ago by a Roman farmer and his family when they left the old patch of muck on which they lived for a new, slightly nicer patch of muck next to the Brazenbrook. A town sprang up and, despite occasional invasions over the centuries by Saxons, Vikings, Danes, a really nasty and ambitious Spanish badger, and anyone else who fancied having a go – not to mention that much of the city had burned down at one point or another only to be rebuilt – Newmuck grew in both size and population, swallowing farmland as it expanded outwards around the Brazenbrook until earlier this century it officially became the largest city in the world.

And it wasn't just Newmuck: the nineteenth century had seen the British Empire become the largest in history, ruling over hundreds of millions of people and millions of square miles of land across the globe via its numerous territories and dominions, Great Britain boasting a real aptitude for barging into other countries and telling the people who lived there what to do. Even those countries not under its umbrella had to recognise its dominance of much of world trade. Britain still considered nations such as France and Russia enemies but the Royal Navy ruled the waves, international cable lines supplied a worldwide communication network, imperial expansion was the national policy, and on the whole the country was utterly self-assured in its superiority.

And the capital city of Newmuck was the tacky gold tooth in the smug, punchable grin that was nineteenth-century Britain.

Ambrose, Henry and Digby had been born and raised in Newmuck, the place as much a part of them as Ambrose's luxuriant hair, Henry's luxuriant chest hair and the lump on Digby's leg that he could swear was getting bigger. Bryn and Talbot were the exceptions, Bryn being Welsh and Talbot having been born in Yorkshire, but both men were practically natives and knew Newmuck as well as their fellow Roustabouts. Talbot's parents had moved their family to the city when he was six years old whereas Bryn had arrived in Newmuck at the age of thirteen, alone and with nothing but a bindle full of meat and a beard full of dreams.

The Roustabouts turned onto Marlowe Street, passing the open expanse of Sunderland Square and the statue of the late Queen Jeff that stood on a plinth in its centre. The controversial fifteen-foot-tall statue was made of bronze, its head and shoulders spattered with pigeon-shit, and had been erected during the reign of Queen Jeff, a reign which ended abruptly when people finally realised that the "queen" was actually a very poor female impersonator, specifically a six-foot-three, seventeen-stone, middle-aged bricklayer from Newcastle.

The current Queen of the United Kingdom of Great Britain and Ireland, Trixie, was outwardly far more feminine and, judging by her six children, definitely a woman.

Ambrose looked at the statue of Queen Jeff and shook his head. "Honestly, you'd have thought the beard would've been a dead giveaway."

Bryn glanced at a particular part of the statue then quickly looked away. "That or the scrotum."

The Roustabouts passed gin palaces, pubs, restaurants and hotels; tailors, haberdashers and barbers; greengrocers, bakers and butchers; tobacconists, sweet shops and chemists; theatres such as The City Pride and The Old Darren, the latter currently host to "bad boy of naturalism" Graham Kellogg's controversial show detailing his theory that human beings had evolved from grapes; and grand structures such as the Newmuck Historical Museum, Saint Alan's Cathedral and Chipman's End railway station, the busiest and oldest station in Newmuck, with an incredibly ornate entrance façade.

Amongst all of these, further modern advancements could be seen in the form of photography studios, the news wire agency which reported on global events with incredible speed, Newmuck's first telephone exchange, international mail-order businesses, huge retail chains, and the slew of railway lines which had come to crisscross the city both overground and underground. Ambrose had even heard that a milk-powered flying contraption was being developed which would allow a man to soar distances of up to twenty feet with only an eighty-five percent chance of bursting into flames. Incredible.

The Roustabouts' surroundings became increasingly industrial as they neared Bryanferry on the south bank of the Brazenbrook, smaller businesses such as cabinetmakers, upholsterers, cutlers and stables nestled between large factories churning out tiles, varnish, railway sleepers, guns, and more. The area's residents acted as cheap labour for these industries and the nearby riverfront, creating a dizzying array of products and components which Newmuck manufactured in huge numbers and which all contributed to the flow of lifeblood that kept the heart of the British Empire beating.

The Roustabouts passed beneath Hooley Viaduct, emerging from the arch to see a group of four young children in frayed, dark-coloured clothes playing at the side of the road, two laughing as they leapt in and out of puddles while the other two were playing some kind of game. Ambrose wasn't sure as to the details of the game but it seemed to be called "String" and involved a lot of punching and kicking in an effort to be the one to hold a piece of string, which was marked by a cry of "I've got the string!" followed by more punching and kicking.

"Shouldn't you be in school?" Ambrose asked the children.

The boy currently holding the string turned to him and said triumphantly, "I've got the string!"

A moment later his opponent, a girl who couldn't have been more than eight, delivered a vicious punch to his kidneys. As the boy crumpled to the ground, she snatched the string from his hand, thrust it towards Ambrose and, with a frightening intensity, screamed, *"I've got the striiiing!"*

The moaning boy didn't look to be getting up anytime soon so Ambrose guessed that made the girl the winner.

The low, constant drone of riverside industries came into hearing, wharves taking up sizeable swaths of the Brazenbrook, the docklands having built up and expanded to accommodate the growth of the British

Empire and the accompanying growth of industries which relied on sea-carried cargoes, the entire Port of Newmuck now receiving millions of tons of goods ever year while also being connected to the national railways, the larger riverside business premises covering acres of ground.

Tall chimneys belched plumes of black smoke up into the sky, contributing to the smoky pall that so often hung over the city as a result of both industry and the huge number of domestic fires. It had gotten bad enough that some types of tree and flower refused to grow in the most polluted areas, many buildings were blackened with soot, and even just walking the streets in certain districts for long enough could see a person coated in fine dirt.

The Brazenbrook, that great river which ran through much of southern England and connected Newmuck to the North Sea came into view, its waters flowing through the heart of the city, although it was only a couple of decades ago that those waters had slowed to a disgusting crawl after centuries of the Brazenbrook being used as an open sewer for all kinds of waste, leading to a constant stench for miles around the river as well as outbreaks of cholera and other diseases. The building of an extensive sewer system beneath Newmuck's streets had done a good job of cleaning up the river, the fish that swam in it didn't even scream anymore.

Many barges, clippers and other vessels both small and large, powered by sail or steam – the latter outnumbering the former – sailed along the Brazenbrook, its span still wide here even with the docklands crowding the river on both sides and the hundreds of ships moored along the quays as they unloaded or took on cargo with the aid of swarms of dockers and hydraulically-operated cranes. Road bridges, railway bridges and footbridges crossed the Brazenbrook, linking the north and south ends of Newmuck, although these were all upstream of Bryanferry and so offered no obstruction to the huge cargo ships and luxury liners that used this part of the river.

Ambrose noticed Talbot staring out across the water, his brown mutton-chops flanking a wistful smile. It was no surprise given his love of the sea, Talbot having told them all many times about the eighteen months he spent serving onboard a prawning vessel. Talbot insisted that the dangers of whaling were nothing compared to hunting prawns, with one particular species being so notoriously cruel that Talbot had seen one fellow crewman who fell overboard choose to eat his own head rather than be taken alive by the crustaceans.

In Bryanferry the Roustabouts made their way through streets of sullen, underpaid transport and warehouse workers while scattered prostitutes lounged against walls and made half-hearted advances to passing men, the daytime trade generally slow except for the occasional sailor on shore leave.

Burgess Canning Company stood apart from its riverside neighbours, a gasworks on one side and a shipbuilders on the other, the opposite side of the street lined with smaller businesses such as a ship chandler and leathermaker. The rear of the cannery faced the Brazenbrook, allowing easy access to the ships which moored there. The main building was an imposing, three-storey brick structure, the company name painted in dirty-white letters on the front wall. Directly below the name was the main entrance, its tall, wooden double-doors standing open. Attached to one side of the main building was a two-storey wooden warehouse which, judging by what could be seen of its interior, was used as a machine shop and a storage space for cans, labels and equipment, other buildings around the cobblestone yard including a privy and a brick shed. Men in dirty work clothes moved around the yard and in and out of the buildings as they went about their work, largely in grim silence.

The Roustabouts stopped before the front gate set into the spiked iron fence surrounding the property, the smell which wafted from inside the cannery strong even at this distance. The gate was open but blocking the way was a tall, stocky man standing with his arms crossed. He had a shaved head, a wide jaw, an upper body that strained against his shirt, and a solid-looking cosh hanging from his belt. Ambrose tried to give people the benefit of the doubt but this man had that nasty glint which Ambrose had seen in the eyes of many bullies, thugs and killers.

"Afternoon," Henry said. "We'd like to speak to the man in charge."

"Piss off," growled the guard. "Mr. Burgess don't see unwanted visitors."

"Let's try this one more time," Henry said patiently. He glanced at Talbot. "My friend found an unwanted item inside a tin of whelks from this cannery, one he paid for with his own money."

"Actually –" Ambrose began.

"So now we'd like a word with your employer about it."

The guard stepped forward and prodded Henry in the chest with his right index finger. "I said *piss off.*"

Henry sighed. "I hope that's not your nose-picking finger."

"Eh?"

The guard may not have deserved the benefit of the doubt after all, but even so Ambrose still winced inwardly at the snapping sound that followed.

Buyer's Remorse for Cecil Burgess

Oliver Burgess paused as he heard the cry of agony outside the front of the cannery, the noise cutting through the din of men and machines at work.

He had just descended from the blessed solitude of his office to the busy main room, which he had always found gloomy and oppressive despite its size, the wall-mounted gas lights turned off most of the time, the open double-doors and high windows doing little to brighten the interior when it was cloudy outside, as it was now. He needed to talk to the foreman about some incorrectly labelled crates, a task he had been putting off as even mild conflict could make his throat tighten and his left ear turn red. He had been assistant manager at the cannery for almost ten years but never became comfortable dealing with the workforce. Not that they ever gave him any trouble, although he knew that wasn't out of respect for him but rather fear of his father.

Oliver looked through the main entrance and saw a group of five men walking across the yard, towards the main building. Behind them, Larry, one of the more vicious and ill-tempered guards on his father's payroll, was on his knees, his right hand cradled in his left.

Oliver looked around but none of the nearby workers appeared interested, merely glancing at the five men before returning their attention to their work. He couldn't blame them, considering how his father treated them. Cecil Burgess was displeased by many things including the creation of bank holidays, the legally enforced reduction of work hours per day, and any mandatory wage increase. Oliver was grateful that the cannery employees hadn't tried forming a trade union yet as he could imagine what his father's reaction would be to that.

Oliver stood frozen to the spot as the five men caught his eye and made a beeline for him. Apart from Larry, there were no other guards in sight.

Typical, Oliver thought. Even his father would have been a welcome sight at that point, and that was saying something.

Not that the strangers appeared particularly threatening, their general size notwithstanding. They weren't armed and didn't look angry, instead giving off an air of calm self-assurance as they strode confidently into the building. Oliver wondered what that felt like, to stride confidently. He didn't think he had ever stridden in his life. He was more of a shuffler.

As the men approached Oliver, the one at the head of the group – broad-shouldered, with side-parted black hair and a neatly trimmed moustache – smiled and said, "I take it you're in charge?"

"Why do you say that?" Oliver asked hesitantly.

"Well, you're the only bloke I can see wearing a suit, holding papers and who hasn't got fish blood on his shoes."

Oliver looked down at the paperwork in his hands as if for confirmation. "Yes, right, I'm –"

"My name's Henry Alabaster and these are my friends" – Henry gestured to the other men in turn – "Bryn, Digby, Talbot and Ambrose. Talbot would like to make a complaint. I'll let him explain."

Oliver watched as Talbot held up a tin of Burgess whelks, pulled open the already loose lid, reached inside and withdrew some kind of wrinkled, grey lump. "It's a nose," Talbot said.

Oliver leaned in a little closer. The big man was right. It *was* a nose.

"I found it inside this tin of whelks," Talbot said. "Now, I've travelled, I'm open-minded when it comes to new cuisine –"

"Like the time you ate that buttered emu," Bryn chipped in.

"Like the time I ate that buttered emu. But you have to draw the line somewhere, and the only time I'm ever going to chew on some bugger's nose is if we're in a fight to the death and my arms and legs are tied."

"Like the time you fought that furious emu farmer," Bryn chipped in.

"Like the time I fought that furious emu farmer. So, I'd like reimbursement for these whelks, let's say ten free tins on top of that, and the cost of a round of drinks for me and my mates. I reckon that's fair."

Oliver's eyes moved to the severed nose again. How on Earth did a human nose end up –

Oh God, Oliver thought. *Morris Elbert.*

His stomach lurched and his throat went dry. Were these men police? They didn't look like police.

"Are you alright?" Henry asked. "Your left ear just turned red."

Oliver's mind filled with images of the kind of life a man like him could look forward to in prison and none appealed. He had always known his father's obsession would land them in trouble eventually and now it seemed that day had come. Despite the risk of incurring his father's wrath, he had secretly thrown away the foul paste which was all that remained of that poor worker, unable to stomach the thought of human remains being canned and sold to some unsuspecting man, woman or child, but even so it was the only explanation for the nose.

The five men were looking at Oliver expectantly. He had to do something. "Daddy," he squeaked.

Henry raised an eyebrow.

Oliver cleared his throat. "That is, um, my father. My father's in charge of the company. You should speak to him about your... issue."

Before Oliver knew what was happening, Henry clapped him on the shoulder, turned him around and began walking him across the room in a friendly but firm manner. "Bang up the elephant," Henry said.

"I'm sorry?" Oliver said.

"It means 'perfect'. Lead the way."

Simultaneously swept along and leading the way, Oliver looked around at the sea creatures being decapitated, skinned, boned, shelled and disembowelled, and saw no brighter future for himself. He led the five men through a doorway and into the stairwell beyond. They climbed the steps to the second floor, the old wooden stairs creaking beneath their weight, dust motes drifting lazily in the dim afternoon light that entered through the grimy glass of a small window. Oliver knew his father wasn't going to be happy about this but given what was at stake, he also knew his father would want to handle the situation himself. His father and happiness went together like sliced lemons and open wounds anyway.

Oliver led the visitors along the second-floor hallway, passing a small storeroom and his own office before stopping outside the thick oak door of his father's office.

"Is this it?" Henry asked.

"Yes," Oliver said, "my –"

"Righto."

Henry opened the door and the six men entered Cecil Burgess' office, the atmosphere inside like that of a tomb but with less *joie de vivre*. The room was spacious but largely bare, containing a desk, two leather armchairs, a wide set of bookshelves, a grandfather clock, a tall cabinet, and a coat-stand from which hung a black top hat, cutaway dress coat and gloves. The floor was made up of bare wooden boards and the walls were painted a sombre grey, nothing breaking up the dullness besides a couple of gas lights and a framed painting of what appeared to be haphazard splashes and streaks of paint, a mess of black and red and several queasy shades of yellow and green. A large fireplace was built into a wall, unlit and filled with cold ash. A wide window flanked by thin curtains looked out onto the Brazenbrook but dust motes didn't drift lazily in the dim afternoon light in here. They wouldn't dare.

Unlike the doughy Oliver, Cecil Burgess was thin and severe, a sixty-year-old man of lines and angles in a creaseless waistcoat, shirt and tie. Beneath a head of short, receding white hair was a narrow, cleanshaven face with cold blue eyes and a thin-lipped mouth. Cecil was sitting behind his large mahogany desk with a pen in one hand, having been writing on a sheet of paper, but now he stopped and looked at each of the five strangers in turn before his gaze settled on his son with an expression as disapproving as if Oliver had burst naked into the room, called his father a wanker and showered him with a bucket of manure.

Oliver swallowed. "Father, these… gentlemen would like to speak with you."

Talbot repeated the story of the nose as Cecil listened in stony silence, his expression unchanging even when the severed nose in question slipped from Talbot's fingers and landed on the desk with a wet plop, Talbot then placing the opened can of whelks next to it.

After Talbot finished there was a moment of silence during which Oliver nervously waited for his father's explosion of rage. But to his surprise, instead his father reached inside his waistcoat, took out his wallet – which would have cried out if it had eyes, unused to daylight as it was – and withdrew from it a banknote which he placed on the desk and slid towards Talbot.

"I don't know how much you usually pay for a 'round of drinks' but I assume that covers it," Cecil said.

Talbot picked up the banknote and looked at it, pleasantly surprised. "Aye, more than enough. Ta very much."

"Oliver, take these men back downstairs and provide them with eleven cans of whelks, then see them to the front gate."

Oliver nodded weakly, stunned.

"As for the nose, gentlemen, my apologies," Cecil said. "I'll look into the matter. Now, if there's nothing else, I have pressing business to attend to."

Talbot pocketed Cecil's money then Oliver escorted the five men out of the office and back down the stairs.

"Nice man," Henry said as they descended, and his friends murmured and nodded agreement.

Oliver tried to remember if he had ever heard those words said in connection with his father and all he came up with was, "Everyone knows Cecil Burgess had that nice man killed."

On the ground floor, Oliver led the visitors past an archway, the constant hiss of numerous industrial-size steam-cookers coming from the room beyond, then they passed the entrance to the cold-room as a pair of miserable-looking workers emerged from within, their breath misting from their mouths, one rubbing his upper arms with gloved hands while the other carried a crate filled with ice and dead mackerel.

Oliver showed the men to the stockroom, where Talbot helped himself to eleven tins of whelks, cramming some into his trouser pockets, then they walked to the front gate, where there was no sign of Larry now. Talbot shook Oliver's hand with a grip that Oliver thought he might still be feeling tomorrow then the five men walked off down the street.

Oliver returned to his father's office, where he found his father standing before his painting, staring at it, his hands held together behind his back. He had paid a small fortune for the centuries-old work due to it being painted by an obscure artist who went mad creating art inspired by the Old Ones, but Oliver saw no cosmic truth in the painting, just an unpleasant mess.

Oliver looked at the whelks and severed nose on the desk. "Should I get rid of –"

"When you convinced me to purchase the PulpMaster 1000," Cecil said, "did you mention that, should an employee in the process of trying to rob me happen to fall into the machine, his nose might fly off and land in a pile of whelks which would then be canned and sold and eventually bring a gang of thugs to my door?"

"Um, no."

"Just like how you didn't manage the very simple task of locking the cellar door behind us that evening, which allowed said employee to enter and witness us in our garments of worship, which in turn led to his death and our current situation."

"I just forgot. Sorry. Again." Oliver shifted his feet and looked down at the floor. "You were very fair in dealing with those men, I thought."

Cecil turned around and glared at his son. "I'll placate them for now with whelks and pocket change if necessary but I haven't finished with them. I want to know who they are, what they know and what they really want. And you're going to find out for me. *Discreetly*. I don't want to tip our hand should action be necessary. The Order meets at the house tomorrow evening, I expect you to have something by then."

Oliver didn't like the sound of all this. "They didn't seem to know anything about… you know, the Old Ones and all that. I think they just wanted the whelks and the money like they said, they seemed happy when they left. Frankly they struck me as very… *capable* men. Have you considered perhaps we should just leave them alone?"

"Perhaps they are as ignorant as they seem. But I will leave *nothing* to chance and that includes those men who had the gall to threaten me."

"They didn't really threaten…"

Cecil bared his crooked, yellow teeth and his eyes took on that fervent glint which made Oliver even more nervous than usual. "You *know* what's at stake, Oliver. You *know* how close I am to achieving the destiny I have worked for all these years. Soon the planets will align, The Order of the Void and the Abyss-Dwellers will gather to perform the Ritual of Suth-G'nar, and the Old Ones will be free to reward me with the godhood which is rightfully mine! *And nothing is going to stop me!*"

Silence hung in the room.

Oliver slowly backed away, heading for the door. "I'm going to fetch a sandwich from down the street. Would you like one?"

"Get out."

"Scotch egg?"

"*Out!*"

So a Woman Walks into a Bar…

Talbot wasn't sure what time it was but Bryn was standing on their table in only his long-johns, downing a yard of Haunted Weasel while everyone in the pub chanted "*Down it! Down it! Down it!*", so he knew they must have been drinking for a while.

It was dark outside, the interior of The Bewigged Pig illuminated by the fireplace and the gas lights dotted around the barroom, the pub packed and rowdy as men and women drank and laughed and talked and drank and played darts and stumbled and drank, the night in full swing, the place usually doing good business at weekends, the clean, cold water of the public water fountain across the street being a blessing for dry-mouthed hangover-sufferers on Saturday and Sunday mornings.

Behind the bar, Annie was rushed off her feet, taking orders and pouring all manner of pints and spirits. She had taken on extra staff once but the little bastard turned out to be skimming from the till so Annie sent him packing with a concussion. She hadn't hired anyone else since then despite how busy the pub could get, refusing to admit that it could sometimes be a struggle doing everything alone.

The final dregs of the cider disappeared into Bryn's mouth and he raised the empty yard glass above his head with a triumphant grin as cheering filled the room. With impeccable timing, the flap of Bryn's long-johns chose that moment to pop open, revealing his arse. Some onlookers turned away in disgust, others cheered even louder, and Murray laughed so hard he snorted gin out of his nose.

Bryn climbed down from the table, leaned the yard glass against it, rebuttoned the flap of his long-johns and sat in his chair, rejoining Talbot, Henry and Ambrose. He had a pouch of tobacco and a pack of cigarette papers on the table and he began rolling himself a cigarette, his beard glistening with beads of cider like amber dew in a bristly brown glade.

"For God's sake, Bryn, buy some long-johns with a more secure flap," Talbot said. "None of us needed to see that."

"I wonder if Annie's got any bleach I can pour into my eyes," Henry said.

"You should take that arse back to the shop, it's got a crack in it," Ambrose said, and the other Roustabouts chuckled. That was pretty good by Ambrose's standards.

Talbot's smile fell as his stomach gurgled loudly. He winced and placed a hand on his gut. Eleven empty tins of whelks and an almost empty bottle of vinegar were spread out before him as damning evidence.

Bryn looked around, frowning. "Where the hell did I put my clothes?"

Talbot, Henry and Ambrose shrugged, none of them able to recall exactly when Bryn had stripped down to his long-johns or why. It was just shaping up to be one of those nights.

As for Digby, he was at the bar chatting up a young woman whose male companion had gotten drunk and passed out at a corner table, Digby not one for wasting time when it came to the ladies, bellswagger that he was. Talbot watched Digby and the girl talk, leaning in close to each other to make themselves heard over the noise. Digby whispered something into the girl's ear. She looked momentarily shocked but there was a smile in it, and this was followed by some furtive glancing around before she whispered something into Digby's ear in return. Whatever it was caused Digby to grin wickedly.

Talbot recognised some familiar faces who occasionally drank at The Bewigged Pig, including the woman who manned the counter at the post office and the strange bloke who worked at the greyhound track and who loved nothing more than startling women with the grubby artificial hare he kept inside his coat, although Annie had warned him against doing that in the pub.

Other customers Talbot knew by name, such as retired hangman Joe "Dangle" Chatterton; Ras Ghosh, an immigrant and the owner of a successful Indian restaurant where Talbot had devoured many a chicken bhuna; Birdie Bolton, a skilled forger who specialised in banknotes but who knew to behave herself in The Bewigged Pig; and Gambro, the bearded, rotund life of the party who spent his days and nights roaming Newmuck's pubs, beer houses and gin palaces, telling tales and spreading cheer with unfailing and infectious enthusiasm.

Talbot suddenly realised that Henry and Bryn were having a disagreement about something.

"The idea of giving them the vote is ridiculous," Henry said. "We're naturally superior to them, it's just how things are, how they've always been."

"Some of them can surprise you," Bryn said, smoke rising from his cigarette.

"Look, they're too emotional, they don't have the intelligence and things are best when they know their place."

"What are you talking about?" Talbot asked.

Henry nodded in Bryn's direction. "This fool thinks horses should be allowed to vote."

"I'm just saying you shouldn't underestimate them," Bryn said. "They're smart creatures, and I'm not talking about those trick horses third-rate magicians parade around onstage, pretending they're psychic."

The Roustabouts had long ago said their piece on the increasingly prominent issue of women receiving the vote. While many men stamped their feet, shook their jowls and harrumphed disapprovingly at the very idea, the Roustabouts didn't see the problem. It wasn't as if women could balls things up any worse than men already did.

Talbot drank what remained of his bitter and was about to get another round in when the front door of the pub was thrown open, slamming against the wall and drawing everyone's attention to the distraught woman standing in the doorway.

"Please, someone help!" the woman cried to the room at large. "My husband, he's being attacked!"

"Go fetch a bobby!" a man called from the crowd.

"There aren't any policemen out there! Please, he's just down the street!"

The woman looked to be in her late twenties, with brown hair that was parted and tied back. She wore a skirt and blouse and around her shoulders was a shawl, the ends clasped together in one hand held before her chest. Her eyes darted around the room, desperate and pleading.

"I would do, love," George said sheepishly from his barstool, "but it's this wooden lung of mine, see." He rapped his knuckles against his chest. "I'm not to exert myself. Doctor's orders."

Talbot sighed and thought, *First the nose, now this.*

Henry, Ambrose, Bryn and Talbot stood up, Bryn stubbing out his cigarette in the ashtray.

Talbot rose gingerly, his stomach protesting angrily. "Do we have to do this?" he groaned. "Those whelks are *not* sitting well."

"You heard the lady," Henry said.

"I know, I know. Bloody hell."

Talbot, Ambrose, Bryn and Henry walked towards the front door, the crowd parting for them.

Digby winked at the woman he had been chatting up and said, "Back in a minute." He joined the other Roustabouts as they approached the distraught woman.

"You'd better show us the way, Missus," Henry said.

She looked them over uncertainly, her gaze lingering on Bryn.

"Just be glad he had his long-johns on under his clothes," Digby said.

The woman hurried back outside and the Roustabouts followed her into the chilly night, where the moon was partially hidden by clouds and a fine mist hung in the air, each end of Mulligan Avenue disappearing into a dark haze apart from where streetlights and windows glowed, surrounded by soft coronas of light. Generally it was later in the year that Newmuck's fog became so thick you could almost spread it on your toast.

About a third of the properties that lined the street were homes while the rest were businesses including a dry goods store, a draper, a cobbler, and a firm of solicitors – the cheapest solicitors in Newmuck for very good reason – all closed for the night. The pavements were quiet, the only people in sight being a middle-aged couple drunkenly weaving along arm-in-arm and a beggar slumped at the mouth of an alley. Talbot wasn't surprised the woman hadn't been able to find help, the streets of Newmuck at night weren't exactly bustling with Good Samaritans.

And like she said, there was no sign of a policeman. It was common for an officer to linger at a pub at night and accept a few free drinks – reluctantly given by an annoyed landlord – in return for throwing out any troublemakers who might be affecting trade, but none of the local bobbies had tried that on at The Bewigged Pig since it was made clear that Annie didn't usually need help throwing out nuisance drunks, and if she did, the Roustabouts were often on hand.

The woman turned right and ran along the street and the Roustabouts followed, keeping pace with her.

"What's your name?" Henry asked.

"Beatrix!" the woman said. "Beatrix Sowerby! My husband Randolph owns the barn at the end of the street, he bought it a few weeks ago!"

"The carriage shed?" Ambrose asked.

"Yes! Randolph was late coming home, I got worried and went to check on him! When I got there I saw him inside with five men, they were pushing him around and threatening him, so I ran to get help!"

They came to the old wooden barn that stood on a dirt lot at the end of Mulligan Avenue. Talbot hadn't been down this end of the street for a little while so the fact that a new business had moved in was news to him, and he saw the wooden sign which had been attached to the wall above the large double-doors of the front entrance: "R. Sowerby Transport". Light coming from inside the barn was visible through gaps in the timber boards and around the edges of the doors.

Henry placed a hand on one of Beatrix's shoulders. Despite the darkness, Talbot could see tears glistening at the corners of her eyes.

"Stay here, Mrs. Sowerby," Henry said. "We'll go and check on your husband."

Beatrix glanced nervously towards the barn then nodded. The Roustabouts began walking across the dirt yard, heading for the front entrance.

"Watch out for –" Ambrose began, but before he could finish there was a squishing sound familiar to anyone who has lived long enough in a place with a huge horse population.

Bryn stopped, looked down and made a disgusted noise as he wiped his bare right foot on the ground. "The *one* time I'm out without my shoes…"

The Roustabouts pushed open the double-doors and entered the barn. It was a one-room structure with a regular-size door in the rear wall and four horse stalls, two on each side of the barn, half of them empty while two horses occupied the others. A workbench and accompanying tools stood against one wall, a horse trough against another, and in one corner was a large pile of hay, pieces of which were strewn across the dirt floor. Hanging from a nail hammered into one of the wooden columns supporting the roof were a top hat and tailcoat. Parked at the rear of the barn was a Clarence carriage which, although recently painted, still bore faint traces of its previous owner's coat of arms on its sides.

Standing with his back against the door of one of the empty stalls was a dark-haired, twentysomething man in simple working clothes, blood running from his nostrils, a few drops on the collar of his shirt. Surrounding him were five hard-faced, rough-looking men, four of whom brandished thick wooden clubs while the fifth held a knife in one hand and the scruff of the bleeding man's shirt in the other. All of them turned to look at the Roustabouts, their eyes lingering on one in particular.

"Yes, I'm in my long-johns," Bryn said impatiently, "let's just move past that, shall we?"

"Trot along," said the thug holding the knife. "We're closed."

Henry looked at the bleeding man. "Randolph, I assume?"

"Are you deaf?" the knifeman said. "You don't want no part of this. This is your last cha–"

"Sorry to interrupt you being all intimidating," Digby said, "but can we get on with this? Only I've got a lady-friend waiting back at the pub."

The knifeman released Randolph's shirt and the five thugs stood in a row, facing the Roustabouts. Randolph remained where he was, afraid to move.

"Don't say I didn't warn you," the knifeman said, pointing his weapon at the Roustabouts. "You got no idea who you're dealing with. I'm gonna cut you into tiny pi–"

A furious, chaotic gurgling echoed throughout the barn. In the silence that followed, everyone looked at Talbot, who placed a hand on his stomach. "Pardon me."

"*Kill 'em!*" the knifeman growled, and the thugs and the Roustabouts rushed at each other as Randolph leapt into the empty stall behind him.

Ignoring his grumbling stomach, Talbot focused on the thug coming at him, not worrying about the other attackers as he knew that Henry, Ambrose, Digby and Bryn would deal with them, each of the Roustabouts having complete faith in the others when it came to a brouhaha of any size or severity. Talbot disarmed the thug, pulling the club from his hands and swinging it down onto his head twice, hard enough to leave a dent in his skull, the man going limp and collapsing.

The knifeman slashed at Henry's face but Henry dodged then clamped one hand around the wrist of the knife arm and slammed his other fist into his opponent's ribs, breaking several. He yanked down the knife arm and snapped it across his knee, the weapon falling to the floor, the knifeman screaming as his arm bent at a horrible angle. Henry silenced him with a punch to the face, caving in his nose and knocking out four teeth, then he released his grip on the knifeman's wrist, the thug unconscious before he hit the floor.

To the credit of the man who faced Bryn, he didn't flinch when confronted with a large, roaring Welshman in long-johns with a horseshit-smeared right foot. He swung his club with both hands and Bryn took the blow on his thick upper left arm before bringing his right arm around in a punch that snapped back the thug's head with enough force that his neck broke, killing him instantly.

Ambrose didn't fall for the feint that his opponent made with his club, so when the real blow came the weapon swung harmlessly through empty air as Ambrose ducked. He rose quickly, driving his right fist into the stomach of the thug, whose eyes bulged and mouth gaped. Ambrose followed that with a left-right combination of punches to the man's face before grabbing him by his hair and slamming his face into a nearby column. He slid to the ground, his pulped face leaving a trail of blood on the wood.

Keen to bring the fight to a rapid close, Digby dealt with the man who charged at him with a simple kick to the testicles and a headbutt.

The Roustabouts looked around at the fallen thugs, all unconscious or dead, then Henry turned his attention to Randolph, who was hesitantly peering over the top of the stall door, and said, "You can come out now."

Randolph slowly emerged from the stall, looking at the thugs then at the Roustabouts. "Who *are* you?"

"Friends of your wife," Ambrose said, smiling.

"What?"

"Randolph!" Beatrix cried with relief as she rushed into the barn and over to Randolph, glancing at the thugs as she stepped around them. She embraced her husband tightly. "Oh, thank God." She pulled back and looked at Randolph's face with concern. "Your poor face…"

"It's nothing," Randolph said, wiping away blood with his shirtsleeve. "What are you doing here?"

"I came by and saw those men hurting you so I went to get help."

"Are the girls alright?"

Beatrix nodded. "I told Rachel to read Sadie's book to her until I came back."

Randolph and Beatrix turned to face the Roustabouts, keeping one arm around each other. "They say they're friends of yours," Randolph said doubtfully.

"They were in the pub up the road," Beatrix said, then she gave the Roustabouts a grateful smile. "No one else would help, but they did."

"Oh, someone else would've if we hadn't," Ambrose said. "Eventually. Maybe."

"Thank you," Randolph said. "I'm in your debt."

Henry nodded at a nearby thug. "Who are they?"

"They said they work for someone called Offal Cromwell."

Digby shook his head, his bitter laugh no more than a snort of air.

"You know him?" Randolph asked.

"Long-time Newmuck villain," Talbot said.

Henry turned to Digby. "Do you recognise any of them?"

"No," Digby said.

"So who exactly is this man?" Beatrix asked.

"Offal Cromwell deals in prostitution, protection, stolen goods, robbery, murder," Henry said. "He has his fingers in a lot of nasty pies."

"Protection money, that's what these men wanted," Randolph said. "They came the first time about a week after I opened for business. When I refused, they said they'd be back. I didn't see them again until tonight."

Beatrix frowned at her husband. "You never told me about this."

"I didn't want to worry you," Randolph said apologetically.

Beatrix gave him a slap on the shoulder. "Stupid man."

"Sorry, sweetheart."

"Cromwell has run his nasty little empire from over in Shinglesgate for years but he knows to leave Wealdbury alone," Henry said. "Or he did. If he sent this lot here then maybe he's getting ideas."

"As grateful as I am to you lads," Randolph said, "isn't what happened here tonight going to make this Cromwell bloke, well, angry?"

"Furious, I imagine. But he'll hear who did it and that'll give him pause. If he gives you any more trouble, you can usually find us at The Bewigged Pig. Do you live around here?"

"We're renting a small place on Carpenter Street, it's about ten minutes away. We moved in when I bought the business. Beatrix thought I was a fool, what with the trams and the Burrows becoming as popular as they are, but I reckon there's still plenty of life in the carriage business if a man plays his cards right. And Beatrix has her job at the brush-making factory."

Digby clapped his hands together. "As fun as this has been, I've got the jammiest bit of jam waiting for me in the pub, so I'm off. Who's coming?"

"Me," Talbot said. "I need to drown some whelks who won't shut up."

"Before you go, is there some way I can repay you for what you did?" Randolph asked. "We don't have much in the way of money, but... well, how about free carriage rides for all of you, whenever you need it? As long as I haven't got a customer at the time, of course. If you need to get somewhere, I'm your man."

"Very kind of you, Randolph," Henry said. "Do you two fancy joining us for a drink?"

"We've got two young girls at home so we best get back," Beatrix said. "By the way, what are your names?"

The Roustabouts introduced themselves then bid the Sowerbys goodnight. They had left the barn and were crossing the yard when behind them Randolph called out, "Hang on a second."

The Roustabouts turned to face Randolph and Beatrix, who were standing in the barn's front entrance. Randolph gestured towards the thugs behind him. "What should we do with them?"

"Take any money and valuables they've got on them then dump them in the road," Henry said.

"Oh, we couldn't do that," Randolph said.

"You could just dump them in the road, but if you don't take what they've got, someone else soon will."

Randolph and Beatrix looked at each other.

"He makes a good point," Beatrix said.

"And our anniversary *is* coming up," Randolph said.

"You check their pockets, I'll fetch the wheelbarrow."

Troubling Reflections and Sweet Tea

It was Saturday morning and a light drizzle was falling as Oliver Burgess sat inside a hansom cab heading in the direction of Renley Street.

He fidgeted, adjusting his top hat, tie and gloves. He looked out of the window, trying to distract himself with the scenery, but soon gave up and sat back with a sigh. He found it hard to relax when set a task by his father, who always wanted results as soon as possible but would never be satisfied no matter how quick or impressive those results were.

It had been like this as long as Oliver could remember. Not that he had many early memories of his father. His mother, Lydia – Oliver would later learn his father only married his mother to gain control over the property and money left to her by her wealthy parents, treating her poorly in the few years they spent together – had died in childbirth but that didn't lead to his father taking a more prominent role in raising him. Quite the opposite, in fact, with Cecil leaving all of that to the hired help.

After some miserable years at home followed by more miserable years at boarding school, Oliver didn't spend any significant time with his father until he was eighteen, when Cecil reluctantly took him on as Assistant Manager at the cannery, a largely meaningless position as almost all of Oliver's suggestions were ignored and no decisions were made without Cecil's approval. Still, he didn't mind paperwork and was able to spend most of his day sitting alone in his office, so it wasn't all bad. Although working at the cannery had put him right off seafood, even just passing a fish 'n' chip shop made his stomach turn.

And he had never been able to look at marine life the same way again since meeting the Abyss-Dwellers.

Cecil had initially wanted Oliver to apply for a position in the Indian Civil Service like many young men were doing as they sought a promising career overseas but still within the umbrella of the British Empire, Oliver well aware that his father was just trying to get him far, far out of the way. But the prospect terrified Oliver so he complained persistently enough that eventually his father relented and employed him at the cannery, a rare victory for Oliver. But the hollowness of that victory had been clear for a long time. It had been ten years since he started working at the cannery, a decade gone in the blink of an eye. Many other men of his age and standing were already husbands and fathers and successful in their own right, building lives for themselves, making their mark on the world. He didn't even own an unusual pet.

Although Cecil deciding six years ago to bring about the end of the world had certainly livened things up, at least until Oliver realised that not much had changed: his father had always been a spiteful, ruthless misanthrope, now he was just a spiteful, ruthless misanthrope who worshipped the Old Ones, ancient cosmic entities who he believed would make him a god if he summoned them into our reality, causing insanity and death on a global scale in the process.

Cecil Burgess had been born into circumstances that were comfortable if not wealthy, but he always had a head for business and thus became a successful industrialist relatively young via the application of sharp intelligence, shrewd negotiation and a complete lack of ethics. He came to focus on food, specifically the canning of it, a process which for decades was done slowly and sloppily in unsanitary conditions by numerous small canneries. Cecil invested in making the canning process faster and more hygienic, not because he cared about customers potentially being poisoned by contaminated cans but because he knew people wanted cheap food they could consistently trust, and if his company offered that then those people would soon part with their money. And they did, making Burgess Canning Company one of the most successful canners of vegetables, meats and seafood in England, seafood becoming the company's focus after Cecil's purchase of the Bryanferry property which had been his main place of business ever since, the cannery packing thousands of cases of seafood every year for the catering and retail trades.

This business with the Old Ones started when Cecil sailed to South America on a business trip and returned months later with stories of forbidden knowledge he had inadvertently uncovered: monstrous gods inhabiting a reality beyond our own, eldritch rituals, arcane artefacts, and the Abyss-Dwellers, a race of aquatic humanoids who lived in the blackest depths of the oceans and who had worshipped and served these gods, the Old Ones, for millennia. Cecil had never been a man given to flights of fancy so Oliver assumed his father had suffered a head injury or been stricken by some sickness of the brain during his trip.

But the more evidence Cecil presented, the more Oliver began to realise that while his father was obsessed, he wasn't deluded. And when Oliver came face-to-face with an Abyss-Dweller for the first time – the pale, clammy flesh and bulging eyes, the stinking breath and rows of pointed teeth, the scraping, guttural language – he had no more doubts.

Cecil was eager to gather as many writings and artefacts connected to the Old Ones as possible, but given how rare and hard to locate such items were, it was a process that required a great deal of money and influence, and while Cecil was a man of both, his resources and reach were not infinite. So he reluctantly formed The Order of the Void, a small cult consisting of himself, Oliver and three other rich and powerful men: Arthur Blacklock, who made his money in silk manufacturing and tenement housing; Thomas Sugarfoot, a partner in one of Britain's largest railway firms; and Frederick Orchardson, a successful veteran of the banking industry.

Cecil knew Blacklock, Sugarfoot and Orchardson thanks to their shared membership of The Apollo Club, a very exclusive dining club consisting of men who had made a fortune in their respective fields. And while Cecil didn't like or particularly trust the three men, he trusted they would serve their purpose, Cecil having convinced them that by joining him they would share in the power he intended to claim from the Old Ones. Although Oliver doubted his father had any intention of sharing with anyone in the end, including his own son.

Even so, Oliver had gone along with the whole thing, doing what he always did: what he was told. The Order of the Void spent massive amounts of time and money gathering as many materials on the Old Ones as they could, prioritising those required for the Ritual of Suth-G'nar, the method by which the cult would achieve godhood. And finally the time was nigh: the planets would align in the correct manner, the ritual would be performed and Suth-G'nar, the Mad Walker of the Halls, would hear the call and lead his fellow Old Ones across the void and into this reality. The world as humanity knew it would end and be replaced with a new reality of infinite horror and insanity ruled over by the Old Ones and those loyal to them.

This new reality didn't sound particularly pleasant to Oliver, and the nightmarish, faded drawings he had seen of some Old Ones and the number of eyeballs, tentacles, teeth, mouths and general orifices on display certainly didn't help convince him otherwise. There was also one Old One who looked like a screaming, winged lemur wearing goggles, he wasn't sure what was going on there. And the Old Ones were certainly numerous, Oliver having the names and titles of many drilled into his head over the years, including Rh'und, the Lady of the Spores; Ayhogloth, the Conductor of Veins; Cr'eme Bon, the Private Dancer; The Silent King; Gub Nubbins, the Toucher of Stuff; Harold; and many more.

Truth be told, Oliver found the whole thing rather silly, not that he would dream of telling his father that. And while he certainly felt guilty about playing a part in bringing about the apocalypse, if it was a choice between that or disobeying his father, the horrors of the former were vague enough while those of the latter were very easy to visualise.

Oliver's cab slowed to a stop. The driver, positioned on his seat at the back of the two-wheeled carriage, pulled the lever that opened the door and Oliver stepped out of the passenger compartment and onto the pavement. The driver moved the lever again, closing the door, as Oliver withdrew his wallet then handed over the fee.

The driver was a middle-aged Irishman who seemed pleasant enough, even if he had driven a little fast for Oliver's liking. Cecil didn't like the Irish. Or the Scottish or the Welsh or even the English for that matter. Or the French, the Germans, the Chinese, Christians, Jews, women, children, animals... the list went on. Holding that much hatred in your heart seemed exhausting and wasteful to Oliver, it certainly hadn't brought his father any joy.

The driver smiled and tipped his weathered hat. "Thank you, sir." He cracked his whip, the horse began to move and the carriage rolled away down the street.

Located in the heart of the fairly affluent district of Elmswick, Renley Street was bustling with men in smart suits and women in fine dresses, the buildings a mixture of upmarket businesses, townhouses owned by wealthy families whose main residences were out in the country, and properties divided up into flats. 84 Renley Street was one such property, and on a panel next to the front door were three numbered doorbell buttons representing the flats into which the three-storey terraced building was split. Oliver pressed the button for flat 3.

He had initially planned to head out yesterday evening and get started right away on learning what he could about the five men who visited the cannery, but then it occurred to him that wandering the streets of Newmuck at night might not be conducive to his health, so he decided to not only wait until this morning but also to hire a professional to do the job for him. He hadn't told his father, hoping that as long as he got results then his father wouldn't care how he had done so.

Oliver was about to ring the doorbell again when the front door opened to reveal an old woman of Oriental descent. Just shy of five feet tall, she was dressed in a dark-green, intricately patterned matching set of silk trousers and long-sleeve blouse. Her long white hair was tied back and her deeply lined face was placid as she looked up at Oliver.

"Oh, hello," Oliver said. "I'm looking for Dulcet Jones?"

The old woman nodded, turned around and walked back the way she had come. Oliver stepped through the doorway, closed the door behind him and followed the woman as she shuffled along the ground-floor hallway, passing the front door of flat 1 on her way to a staircase that doubled back on itself as it ascended to the upper floors. They slowly climbed the steps as Oliver tried to make small talk by complimenting the lovely wainscoting, but the woman said nothing.

On the third floor a short hallway ended in the front door of flat 3, and the old woman led Oliver through the entrance and into the parlour beyond. She gestured for him to wait, so he stood and watched as she disappeared into one of two adjoining rooms.

Two tall windows flanked by heavy curtains let plenty of natural light into the parlour, and the décor spoke to its owner being a man of culture and at least some wealth, the carpeting and wallpaper tastefully coloured and designed, an ornate light fixture hanging from the centre of the embossed-wallpaper ceiling. A large set of bookshelves was crammed with volumes on military history, medicine, engineering, various sciences, law, and a few novels and plays. There was a chest of drawers, a desk on which papers and more books were neatly placed, a detailed globe, and in one corner a small, potted palm tree. Attached to the walls were an array of ornaments, furnishings and paintings as well as a large mirror, a clock, a hanging scroll with what Oliver assumed was Japanese or Chinese writing on it, and, each resting on its own mount, a pistol and a slightly curved sword inside a scabbard. A small fire was burning in the fireplace, the crackling of the flames mixing with the ticking of the clock and the muffled sounds of the street outside.

"Do you roller-skate?" asked the man who entered the parlour through the doorway the old woman had passed through. He was dark-skinned, average height, with an athletic build, blue eyes and short black hair. His trousers, shirt and patterned waistcoat were clean and neat.

"I'm sorry?" Oliver said.

"I visited a roller-skating rink for the first time recently," the man said. "Interesting experience. Balance is the key, of course."

"I see." That was a lie.

"Mrs. Miyazaki took me."

Oliver hesitated. "The woman who let me in?"

"She's very good at it."

Through his confusion, Oliver remembered he was still wearing his hat and gloves, so took them off. "Um, are you Dulcet Jones?"

"I am," Dulcet Jones said. "And you're Oliver Burgess, son of Cecil Burgess and Assistant Manager of Burgess Canning Company. Tea?"

Mrs. Miyazaki appeared from behind Dulcet carrying a tray, on which were two saucers, mugs and teaspoons, a teapot, a bowl of sugar and a small jug of milk.

"Yes, please," Oliver said, glad to be back on more familiar ground.

As Mrs. Miyazaki placed the tray on a tea table, Dulcet gave her a small bow. "Thank you."

Still without uttering a word, Mrs. Miyazaki left the parlour again. Dulcet gestured towards the two armchairs that faced each other across the tea table. "Have a seat."

Oliver sat, placing his hat and gloves on the tea table while Dulcet sat opposite him and began pouring the tea.

"Milk and sugar?" Dulcet asked.

"Please," Oliver said. "Two sugars. So, how did you know who I am?"

"It's my job to know things, Mr. Burgess. And your father is a prominent Newmuck businessman, after all."

"You have quite the reputation yourself, Mr. Jones. You're the most renowned detective in the city. I read about some of your famous cases in the newspaper: The Adventure of the Warm Tongs, The Mysterious Mystery of the Puzzling Enigma –"

"Journalists do enjoy their colourful titles," Dulcet interrupted as he passed Oliver his tea. "Whatever sells more papers."

"But… you are as good as people say."

"In a business such as mine, an undeserved reputation can kill you as quickly as any bullet or poison." Dulcet sipped his tea. "And I'm not dead yet."

"Right." Oliver sipped his tea and glanced towards the doorway through which Mrs. Miyazaki had passed. "Your maid is… interesting."

"Mrs. Miyazaki is a lot more than my maid, she's acted as my valuable assistant on more than one of my cases. Not only does she possess a keen intelligence but she's also a master of stealth and four distinct martial arts. I once saw her stop an assassin's heart simply by prodding a particular spot on his left buttock."

"Good lord. I don't remember seeing mention of her in any of the newspaper stories."

Dulcet smiled thinly. "Mr. Burgess, the fact that the newspapers are willing to celebrate the achievements of a coloured gentleman is a welcome sign of progress, but lauding the efforts of a woman at the same time, and a foreign one at that? Unfortunately we've yet to reach that point."

"Well, Mr. Jones, I'm here because I'd like to hire you."

"Are you representing yourself, your father or your business?"

"Myself," Oliver lied. "It's a personal matter." His father wouldn't appreciate any unnecessary attention being drawn to him, especially at such a critical time.

"And why do you need a detective?"

"I'm looking for information on a group of five men. I'd like you to find out everything you can about them as quickly as possible. In fact, I'm willing to pay more if you can have anything for me by this evening."

"You're in quite the rush. Who are these men to you?"

Oliver unconsciously adjusted the collar of his shirt. "As I said, it's a personal matter. Private. If you don't mind."

"Depending on the circumstances, Mr. Burgess, I might. I don't take on every case I'm offered, you understand. Describe these men for me."

Oliver described the five men as best he could, including what he could remember of their names, unable to recall them all in full.

Dulcet regarded him in silence for a moment then said, "You've convinced me, Mr. Burgess. I'll take the case."

"I have?" Oliver said. "Excellent. Thank you."

"My fee is two pounds and fifty pence per day, the first day payable upfront, in cash."

Oliver set down his tea and took out his wallet. He counted out the fee, placed the money on the tea table and slid it towards Dulcet. "When do you think you'll have something?"

Dulcet sipped his tea. "The five men are Henry Alabaster, Bryn Williams, Digby Grimble, Talbot Ashmole, and Ambrose Parish. Collectively they're known by many as the Roustabouts, although it's not a name they self-ascribe and I've never been able to ascertain where it originated. Their ages range from thirty-five to thirty-nine years old and all but two of them were born in Newmuck. They reside in the district of Wealdbury and each man lives alone with the exception of Parish, who shares a house with his grandparents. None of them currently hold down regular employment but their former occupations include construction worker, apprentice butcher, sailor, soldier, millworker, night watchman, and knocker-upper. They spend a large portion of their time together, often at a pub named The Bewigged Pig, and all of them have been arrested at least once, their crimes including drunk and disorderly behaviour, gross indecency, assault, public disturbance, affray, and the unauthorised distribution of government property and funds. They all share a reputation for being fearless, extremely capable when it comes to violence, and generally being men not to be trifled with, although at the same time they're highly regarded by many in their local community. They seem to attract trouble, often of a common enough nature, while some incidents in which they've been involved possess more... *unusual* overtones." Dulcet set down his teacup, picked up Oliver's money and slipped it into his waistcoat pocket. "I believe that concludes our business."

Oliver stared at Dulcet, dumbfounded. "So you know them, then," he said eventually.

"It was a pleasure working for you, Mr. Burgess. I trust you're satisfied with the results."

Oliver supposed Dulcet had given him what he paid for. He didn't *feel* like he had been cheated, although he knew that might be the problem. "I suppose," he said uncertainly.

"Then I'll bid you good day. You'll forgive me if I don't stand, I've been taking an obscure but quite potent poison with my tea over the past week in order to build up a tolerance for it, so I'm afraid I currently have no feeling in the lower half of my body. The effect should wear off within the hour. Mrs. Miyazaki will see you out."

Big Wheel, Little Man

Henry awoke to a knocking at his front door and a pounding inside his head.

He half-opened bleary, sleep-encrusted eyes. Why was the world sideways? Oh, he was lying on his side. Made sense. Apparently he had made it to bed. He rubbed his eyes and gingerly sat up, planting his feet on the bare wooden floor, the inside of his mouth sour and dry. He ran a hand through his hair, looked towards his bedroom window and winced, the daylight dull but still too bright for him at the moment.

Whoever was outside his door knocked again. Henry took a deep breath and stood up. He was barefoot and shirtless but still had on his long-johns and trousers, his braces hanging at his sides.

Henry's flat consisted of three rooms – bedroom, bathroom, open-plan living room and kitchen – on the second floor of a shared house. It was big enough for him, and the other occupants of the house – Mrs. Reynolds, a widowed schoolteacher, and the Kiers, a middle-aged German couple – were nice people. Besides, Newmuck was so overcrowded that Henry was happy not to be living inside a paper bag with a family of seventeen. He walked into the adjoining living room and opened the front door.

Standing in the hallway, Dulcet Jones looked Henry up and down. "Late night?"

"Your powers of deduction never cease to amaze me, Dulcet," Henry said as he turned and walked towards the sink. Dulcet entered the flat and closed the front door.

Henry reached into a ceramic pitcher, cupped some lukewarm water in his hand and splashed it onto his face and neck. He rinsed inside his mouth and swallowed. It *had* been a late night, although he couldn't recall how late. There had been a lock-in involved, with the Roustabouts and a handful of other regulars staying to carry on drinking after Annie kicked out everyone else and locked the front door, but there were only flashes after that, including Talbot betting he could balance a barstool on his chin (a bet he won, surprisingly) and Digby creating an eye-wateringly powerful cocktail he named "Wicked Tingler".

"Sorry if I woke you," Dulcet said as he took off his hat and held it down at his side.

"I should think so," Henry said, wiping his face with a tea-towel. "Knocking on a man's door at this hour."

"It's half past one in the afternoon."

"Fair enough."

Dulcet wandered past the fireplace and over to the window, a cane held in one hand. Henry had never seen him use the cane to walk but had seen him use it to batter two armed thugs unconscious, the detective being skilled in the cane-focused martial art *canne de combat*, which he had picked up during his time in Paris. Dulcet looked through the glass at the dirty alley alongside the house and the crumbling wall of the building opposite.

"Don't take this the wrong way, Henry," Dulcet said, "but I sometimes wonder why the five of you don't live in more comfortable circumstances given your means."

His brain demanding he lie down and go back to sleep, Henry compromised by leaning on the back of one of the living room's two armchairs. "That money from the Wells business was a lot but probably not as much as you think, and we split it between five of us," he said, referring to that strange, rain-soaked visit to the distant and isolated Wells estate back in 1878 which had ended with the curse of the Wells bloodline lifted and the Roustabouts with enough money that they wouldn't need to worry about it for some time. "It's not going to last forever. Besides, Wealdbury's our home, we're all happy where we are."

Dulcet turned away from the window. "So I take it The Bewigged Pig enjoyed a profitable evening," he said as Henry entered the bedroom.

"The lads and I believe in supporting local businesses," Henry said as he opened his wardrobe and rooted around inside, Dulcet watching him through the doorway.

"One significantly more than others."

"The pub is the heart of Britain, Dulcet. Cavemen were sitting around making and drinking booze ten-thousand years ago. Progress is all well and good but some things never change."

"There's half a steak-and-kidney pie sticking out of your back pocket."

Henry reached for the seat of his trousers and found Dulcet was right. He looked at the flaky pastry, congealed gravy and sinewy chunks of meat and his stomach churned. He placed the half-eaten pie on his bedside cabinet. "I'll save it for later."

Henry withdrew a white shirt and a pair of black socks from the wardrobe and pulled his shoes out from under the bed. "I assume you didn't come here just to dig me out. What's going on?"

"I had a visitor this –" Dulcet began.

"Actually, hang on," Henry interrupted as he pulled on his socks. "You can tell me when we get there."

"Get where?"

Henry began putting on his shirt. "My head feels like someone crammed a church organ inside it. Where do you think we're going?"

"Well, I haven't had lunch yet, and while choking down a pack of pork shavings at The Bewigged Pig is certainly an experience, how about we go somewhere with a slightly more appetising menu?"

Dulcet made his suggestion, Henry agreed and they set off.

As tempted as he was to suggest jumping on an omnibus rather than walking, Henry chose the latter just the same, a little exercise would do him good. Dulcet didn't object, like the Roustabouts he chose to travel on foot where he could, agreeing that you could miss a lot when on public transport and not in the thick of things. Henry regretted his decision briefly when a tram glided past in the road, the high-pitched screeching of metal on metal as it moved along its steel rails cutting right through his throbbing skull. The shoe-black they passed could have buffed his customer's shoes a little more quietly too, Henry thought.

Ambrose's house was on the way so they gave him a knock. Henry tried to appear less hungover than he felt for Ambrose's grandmother, Beryl, a sweet old woman who liked all of the Roustabouts, especially Digby, who flirted with her shamelessly. Ambrose's grandfather, Wilbur, was at the allotment where he spent much of his time. Henry wasn't surprised to find that Ambrose, being one of those people who rarely got a hangover, wasn't suffering any effects from the previous night's drinking. Bastard.

When Henry, Ambrose and Dulcet arrived at Valerie's, Henry wondered if he had made a mistake agreeing to Dulcet's suggestion, his stomach roiling at the air inside the café, which was thick with the smell of bacon, fried eggs, sausages, fried bread, and other oil-soaked foods.

Valerie's was the most popular café in Wealdbury, a no-nonsense greasy spoon that served good portions at decent prices and where the Roustabouts had eaten many times over the years. French cuisine may have been all the rage, but as far as Henry was concerned you could keep that under-portioned, overpriced stuff. Almost all of the tables in the main room were occupied, the place filled with conversation as customers talked about the news, sport, work, family, and their plans for the weekend, while a few sat in silence as they read their newspapers – "MOON MEN STOLE MY SHOEHORN" declared the front page of one publication – and ate.

Valerie Grocer, the owner, served customers and shouted through the open doorway to the kitchen and the cook, Greasy Tim. Valerie was dressed in a skirt and blouse, a tea-towel slung over one shoulder, her greying hair tied back. She had a handsome face and a warm smile that emphasised the crow's feet at the corners of her eyes. She greeted Henry, Ambrose and Dulcet and pointed them to an empty table at the back of the room, where they sat and she took their orders.

Henry kept his breathing slow and even, his stomach alternating between churning in horror and rumbling hungrily. When his tea came he put in three spoonfuls of sugar, and the three men drank tea and made small talk until Valerie returned again with Henry's double-sausage-and-egg sandwich, Ambrose's full English breakfast and Dulcet's scrambled eggs on toast, Dulcet removing his hat from the table to make room for the plates. Henry grappled with his sandwich, drops of oil, butter and egg yolk spilling from between the bread and plopping onto his plate. He took a bite, swallowed, and felt relief when it seemed he was going to keep the food down.

"So, why the visit?" Henry asked Dulcet.

As they ate, Dulcet told Henry and Ambrose about Oliver Burgess' visit that morning. When he was done, Henry frowned and said, "Nice of you to take the job and tell him all about us."

"Come now, Henry," Dulcet said. "I only told him what any half-competent detective could find out easily enough. And I'm here telling you this now, aren't I?"

"I suppose."

"Do either of you have any idea why Burgess has an interest in you?"

Henry and Ambrose told Dulcet about the previous day's incident with the whelks and the severed nose and the visit to Burgess Canning Company.

"I thought things were settled when we left the cannery," Ambrose said.

"Apparently not," Dulcet said. "Although I wouldn't look to Oliver Burgess as the true interested party but his father, Cecil. From what I know, Oliver has little to no influence on the family business whereas Cecil Burgess has long enjoyed a reputation as a formidable and ruthless man willing to do anything to achieve his goals, even murder if certain rumours are to be believed. The fact he gave in to your demands so easily – your imposing physical presence notwithstanding – goes against everything I've heard of the man. Perhaps he wasn't being weak but patient, and he has something planned for you. His son approaching me suggests so. Your unexpected attention has bothered him. Which of course makes me wonder what he has to hide. The nose in the whelks raises many questions, after all."

"It's certainly nothing to be sniffed at," Ambrose said. Henry and Dulcet looked at him. He lowered his eyes and sliced off a piece of fried egg. "Sorry."

"If Cecil Burgess wants to have a pop at us, he's welcome to try," Henry said. "We've handled a lot worse than some old businessman who smells of cod."

"You shouldn't underestimate the threat of big business, Henry," Dulcet said. "The world is changing. A man can do a lot of damage with a pen and a piece of paper."

"He's got a point," Ambrose said to Henry before a dark expression appeared on his face and he stared ahead, lost in a troubling memory. "A bloke came at me with a pencil-sharpener once. That got very ugly very quickly."

"I could take a closer look at the Burgesses if you like. Although it wouldn't be for a few days, I have some business outside Newmuck first."

"It's fine," Henry said. "Let Burgess poke around all he wants. If he decides to start a ruckus, people will be finding pieces of *him* inside their whelks."

As the three of them finished their food, Ambrose asked Dulcet if he was working on any interesting new cases. Dulcet revealed that the business requiring him to leave the city was a train journey to Brighton that evening, having been invited by a wealthy landowner to investigate the suspicious death of his great aunt, whose corpse had been found in a room locked from the inside next to a slipper containing a jade aubergine and a note containing the message, "The blind milkman sees better at night." A most puzzling mystery.

Henry had never had the patience for puzzles or mysteries. When he was a boy he received a shifting wooden cube puzzle as a gift, the goal being to move the cube's various connected parts in the correct way so as to form complete images on its faces. After five minutes spent trying to solve it, Henry called it a bastard and threw it into the fire.

When they were done, Dulcet reached for his wallet but Henry insisted on paying as thanks for the news on Oliver Burgess. He paid the whole bill, telling Ambrose to just buy him a pint in return, then the three of them thanked Valerie and Greasy Tim and left the café.

Outside on the pavement, Dulcet placed his hat on his head. "Gentlemen, a pleasure as always."

"Can you hear that?" Ambrose asked, looking around with a frown.

Henry and Dulcet listened but all Henry could hear was the usual buzz of the city: the garbled chatter of the crowds, the rumble of vehicle wheels, the clacking of horses' hooves, the hammering and drilling and general noise of workmen going about their trades…

Then he heard it. A chaotic chorus of high-pitched bell rings, distant but growing louder as they approached. "Oh, not those wankers," Henry said.

They appeared from around a corner up the street, heading in the direction of Valerie's, and even if they hadn't been ringing their bells it was impossible to miss the Penny Dreadfuls as the enormous penny-farthings they rode ensured they could be seen above the heads of any crowd not made up of especially tall giraffes. There were five of them, all dressed in flat caps, Norfolk jackets, bow ties and tweed breeches. When the rider at the head of the group spotted Henry, Ambrose and Dulcet, an arrogant smile appeared on his narrow face and he raised one hand in a signal to the riders behind him, the group slowing to a stop in the road outside the café, looking down from a height of almost twenty feet. Henry couldn't stand the Penny Dreadfuls but he had to give them one thing: the bastards could balance.

"Well, well, well," the lead rider said, "if it isn't two of the five apes who escaped from the zoo." He sneered at Dulcet. "Oh, and they've got a new friend."

"Afternoon, Bollock," Henry said.

"That's *Pollock!*" the lead rider said angrily. "*Winthrop Pollock-Seymour,* you uncouth swine!"

The son of a very wealthy, landowning earl, Winthrop Pollock-Seymour was the leader of the Penny Dreadfuls penny-farthing "gang", a group of five young, rich, spoilt sons of nobility who for the past few months had been riding around Newmuck on their expensive toys, hassling poor people while looking down on them both figuratively and literally. The Roustabouts had had two previous run-ins with them and were waiting for Winthrop and his lackeys to get bored and move onto some other distraction, but that had yet to happen and the Roustabouts' patience had worn thin.

Ambrose looked at Winthrop's penny-farthing, the bicycle sleeker, shinier and a foot taller than those of his fellow riders. "Isn't that a different boneshaker to the one you were riding last time?"

"*Boneshaker?*" Winthrop said, offended. "This is a Volonté Mark-6, the tallest and most expensive penny-farthing in the world! I had it shipped over from Italy last week! Only six of them were made!"

"Were they not very good?"

"What? No, it –"

"You know," Dulcet said, "it could be said that a man who feels the need for such a large vehicle might be overcompensating for something."

"Jones, isn't it?" Winthrop said. "The 'detective'? I've seen your photograph in the newspapers. They'll let your kind do anything nowadays, won't they? Tell you what, I'll do you a favour: if the detective thing doesn't work out, you can sign on as one of the help at my manor. I'm sure you'll be much happier in your proper place."

Winthrop and the other Penny Dreadfuls chuckled.

Dulcet smiled pleasantly. "You mean your father's manor. I'll keep your offer in mind, thank you. I hear your sister does an excellent job keeping the male members of your family's staff entertained."

The smile fell from Winthrop's face. "What's that supposed to mean?"

"Especially while your father is holidaying at his property in Scotland after that unpleasantness. How *is* his syphilis, by the way?"

"That was just gossip! It was all lies!"

"Bollock, I was just starting to get over a hangover but now here you are making my head ache again," Henry said. "I suggest you and your little chums move along before I pull you down from there and shove that bike so far up your arse that the bell will ring against the silver spoon in your mouth."

Winthrop glared at Henry. "You horrible commoner, how *dare* you talk to me like that!" He cleared his throat and glanced over one shoulder at his companions. "Luckily for you we have more important things to do than waste our time in this grotty little slum. But mark my words: we'll meet again."

"You should honestly hope we don't."

Winthrop rang his bell several times and gave his fellow riders a hand signal. "Onward, Penny Dreadfuls!"

They all rang their bells as they rode off down the street at speed, forcing a man who had been crossing the road with a crate of vegetables to hurry out of their way, cursing them as carrots and potatoes fell to the ground.

"Wankers," Henry said, because it bore repeating. Ambrose and Dulcet nodded in agreement.

Dulcet smiled and tipped his hat. "Well, until next time."

"Good luck with the aubergine thing," Ambrose said.

"Before you go, have you heard any news on Offal Cromwell recently?" Henry asked. "Maybe him making a move on Wealdbury?"

"I heard there were attacks on two of his operations," Dulcet said. "A gambling den and a warehouse filled with stolen goods. The details were few and far between but apparently both locations were thoroughly destroyed and there were some fatalities, mostly Cromwell's men but a couple of civilians as well. Nasty business. But nothing involving Wealdbury as far as I know. Why do you ask?"

"We caught a bunch of his goons roughing up a businessowner on Mulligan Avenue last night. They were after protection money."

"That seems unwise, he knows how the five of you would feel about that. Maybe his ambition is outweighing his prudence. Or he could be looking to send some kind of message."

"Maybe. Anyway, all that can wait." Henry turned to Ambrose. "Pint?"

Out of Order

The iron gate at the front of Cecil Burgess' property clanged shut behind Oliver and he walked up the drive, the hard-faced guard who had let him in remaining at his post.

Gravel crunched beneath Oliver's shoes as he adjusted the collar of his coat against the chill in the night air. The old, large house, as grim and unwelcoming as its owner, loomed ahead in the darkness, the curtains closed in most of its windows, smoke rising from one of the chimneys that jutted from its slate roof. The smoke was coming from the fireplace in the second-floor study, light shining from its two windows that overlooked the front of the property.

Cecil Burgess' house stood on a plot of land on Isaac Street, at the edge of a patch of woodland on the outskirts of Fondle Green, the front of the property set back slightly from the road. The lawns and gardens were neglected and overgrown, and surrounding the property was a tall brick wall topped with iron spikes. Oliver had grown up here but the bare, silent rooms and draughty hallways had never been filled with warmth or love so the place never felt like home to him and now he only visited when necessary. He was far happier where he lived now, in a more modest but comfortable house at the opposite end of Fondle Green.

Oliver saw another guard off to one side of the house, leaning against a wall with a lit paraffin lamp in one hand and a shotgun in the other, and he knew there would be another man at the rear of the property, his father having become increasingly concerned with security in recent years.

Parked near a corner of the house was Blacklock's private brougham, and sitting in the driver's seat, in boots, trousers and a topcoat, was Blacklock's man, Quinn. Oliver only glanced in his direction but he could feel Quinn watching him, silent and expressionless as ever, those cold blue eyes never missing a thing. Orchardson and Sugarfoot had their drivers drop them off for Order meetings and return later, but Blacklock preferred to keep Quinn around.

Oliver climbed the steps of the stone dais outside the main entrance, opened the heavy wooden door and stepped through into the lobby. The interior of the house was almost as cold as outside and didn't have the whistling of the breeze, rustling of foliage or distant sounds of the city to break up the silence. A few wall lights glowed feebly in the gloom that dominated the spacious, high-ceilinged room.

Oliver followed a thin, frayed rug to the foot of the wide staircase that led up to the second-floor balcony that circled the lobby. Like the gardens, the condition of the house had seen a steady decline as Cecil gradually fired almost all of his household staff, his fear of servants possibly snooping around and learning things they shouldn't overriding his desire to keep a well-maintained household. Only a butler, cook and two maids remained and only for minimum hours during the day, while the armed guards were a nightly expense.

Oliver climbed the stairs, walked along the balcony and into an adjoining hallway. He passed his childhood bedroom, glancing towards the closed door even though there were precious few fond memories on the other side. He came to another door and knocked on it.

"Come in," Cecil Burgess said.

Oliver entered the study, closed the door and removed his overcoat, gloves and top hat, adding them to those already hanging from the coat-stand next to the door. A fire burned behind the metal grate of the large fireplace, a nearby desk lamp adding to the room's light. Above the fireplace, the stuffed head of a stag watched over the room with glassy black eyes, the trophy a disquieting presence during Oliver's youth. He used to wonder who killed the animal – his father was no hunter – and what its final moments were like, but the stag wasn't telling. Two wide bookshelves contained dozens of books on a range of subjects, most connected to Cecil's obsession with the Old Ones in some way: geography, history, religion, folklore. The rare, forbidden texts that dealt directly with the Old Ones, those yellowed tomes and scrolls that made Oliver's hairs stand on end, were kept hidden away under lock and key in the cellar.

Near the centre of the room stood a short, circular table, on which sat a half-empty glass decanter of brandy and a folded newspaper. Oliver bought a newspaper every day himself, although really only for the comic strip on the back page. Oh, Stumpy Persimmons, how could one leprosy-riddled ten-year-old boy get into so much mischief?

Sitting around the table in high-backed, leather-padded armchairs, each man wearing a suit – Blacklock's clothing being less stuffy and plain than the others – and holding a glass of brandy, were Cecil Burgess, Arthur Blacklock, Thomas Sugarfoot and Frederick Orchardson, four fifths of The Order of the Void.

Like Oliver's father, Blacklock, Sugarfoot and Orchardson were prominent businessmen who didn't let things like ethics or legalities stand in their way. Also like Cecil, none of them were really family men: Blacklock had no wife or children, Sugarfoot was unmarried – although there was talk of an illegitimate son – and Orchardson was a widower with an estranged daughter.

Blacklock was fifty years old with a slim figure and swept-back, black hair greying at the temples. He had inherited his father's already successful textile business and gone on to specialise in silk. The silk industry had generally been on the downturn over the past few decades, but although this had meant lower wages and unemployment for many, a few of the larger manufacturers such as Blacklock Silk Weavers flourished. Blacklock also earned a tidy sum from his tenements, which he had allowed to become slum housing due to lack of maintenance.

In his mid-sixties, Sugarfoot was the oldest member of the Order, his dozens of pounds of extra weight and reddish nose attesting to him also being the one with the largest appetite for food and alcohol. His lazy eyes were in danger of being consumed by his fabulously bushy white eyebrows and he had a shock of chaotic white hair to match. Sugarfoot had made his money in one of the biggest things to have come out of the nineteenth century to date: the railways. In his younger days he made investments that paid off massively as the number of new railway companies and railway lines in Newmuck and beyond exploded, the industry becoming powerful enough to steamroll any interference from the formerly vital canal companies and even the government. Sugarfoot's wealth grew alongside the railways, from the creation of the Burrows underground system to luxury rail cars travelling between Newmuck and other parts of England. For the past several years he had served as Chairman of Great Newmuck Railway, a high-paying position with very few actual responsibilities.

A few years older than Blacklock, Orchardson was bald and wore spectacles and was the most serious and joyless man Oliver had ever met, more so than even his father, who at least exhibited some emotions, even if they were all negative. Newmuck was the financial centre of the world and Orchardson, who occupied a seat on the board of directors of Bowers Bank, one of the largest banks in the country, was one of the many men in control of the money that made it so, the majority of the world's trade being financed in pounds sterling. Orchardson knew everything there was to know about banking, banknotes, cheques, stocks, bonds, investments, insurance, currency, and both national and international finance in general, his expertise helping to offset the huge costs incurred by the Order in its work.

Like Oliver, the other members of The Order of the Void each wore an identical ring, a gold band engraved with the Sign of Xysh-Lon, an ancient symbol of the Old One named Xysh-Lon, the Thing That Quibbles Needlessly, Cecil having had the rings made to mark them as worshippers of the Old Ones.

"Hello, everyone," Oliver said as he walked across the carpet to the empty chair at the table and sat down. No one replied but he hadn't expected them to. He may have met with Blacklock, Sugarfoot and Orchardson regularly for several years but they had never been his friends, the three men having as much respect and affection for him as his own father did.

Oliver ignored the brandy, very rarely drinking alcohol of any kind. He had only gotten drunk once in his life, when he was seventeen, which had involved three glasses of red wine, a blackout, and waking up in a stranger's garden wearing a novelty hat that bore the message "Kiss Me I'm Turgid". Never again.

"I've informed everyone of yesterday's incident at the cannery," Cecil said. "What have you learned about those men?"

Without explaining where he got the information, Oliver revealed what Dulcet Jones had told him. The four men listened in silence, although Blacklock only seemed half-interested, looking around the room as he sipped his drink, exhibiting his usual self-assuredness, as if he already knew everything Oliver was going to say.

Oliver concluded by saying, "It seems to me these 'Roustabouts' really are no threat to us. I think we should just leave them alone."

Blacklock finished the brandy in his glass and set it down on the table.

"That's because you're meek," Cecil said. "If you had your way you'd do nothing but cower in a hole and hope things turn out for the best even as your betters are burying you. If all men were like you, Oliver, mankind would've never dared to walk upright. And yet here we few stand on the precipice of godhood, mere days away from reshaping reality as we know –"

Blacklock picked up the decanter of brandy by the neck and smashed it across Cecil's face, the vessel exploding in a shower of glass shards and golden-brown liquid, Cecil and his chair toppling sideways to the floor.

Oliver sat frozen, staring open-mouthed at his father as Blacklock stood up, dropped the broken neck of the decanter, took a handkerchief from the pocket of his waistcoat and wiped brandy from his hand. He looked at Cecil. "God, I've been wanting to do that for years."

Cecil shifted and groaned on the floor, conscious but stunned. His head and shoulders were wet with brandy, which mixed with the blood running from where shards of glass had pierced his face.

"I say, Arthur, a trifle much, don't you think?" Sugarfoot said, frowning.

"You could've warned us," Orchardson said flatly as he brushed at drops of brandy which had splashed onto his trousers.

"A spur-of-the-moment indulgence," Blacklock said, smiling as he adjusted the cuffs of his shirtsleeves. "You'll humour me, of course. Besides, with Oliver here, why waste any more time?"

Oliver blinked. That hadn't just happened, had it? He knew he should say or do something but his mind was blank, his body numb.

"Arthur," Cecil mumbled, one eye open, the other covered in blood.

"You're a sorry example of potential godhood, Cecil," Blacklock said. "Did you really think that your true intentions of manipulating us and claiming the power of the Old Ones for yourself weren't completely transparent? I knew it was only a matter of time until you betrayed us, and Frederick and Thomas were wise enough to heed me."

Blacklock paced the carpet, speaking and gesticulating confidently. "We are kings ruling over the greatest city of the greatest empire in the world, the lands and seas ours to do with as we please even as we continue to push and push, climbing the tallest mountains, delving into the deepest jungles.

Other nations bow to our control while at home we prosper, making advancements with dizzying speed. Medicine is helping people live longer, education is making them more intelligent, horseless carriages reach speeds of up to eight miles an hour, alienists explore the boundaries of the human mind, and science promises us domination of the skies even as the building blocks of *life itself* are revealed to us." Blacklock paused for effect. "Still, we remain human, and our weaknesses remain with us. Crime is at an all-time high. Branches of Christianity argue amongst themselves even as they argue with other religions, all of whom argue with those freethinkers who've cast off the notion of religion altogether. The politicians are no better, squabbling like children even as they fret over phantom foreign threats." Blacklock smiled, clearly relishing the moment. "But we know the truth. We know how meaningless it all is, that *true* power lies in the unseen, beyond this petty reality, up there amongst the infinite void. That power is not for you, Cecil. You may have brought us together, but we've surpassed you. I expertly played the part of the obedient accomplice while it was necessary, but with the Ritual of Suth-G'nar at hand, the time has come for the masks to fall. As the great playwright Percival Comb said…"

Blacklock stared across the room. "He said…"

Oliver waited. Sugarfoot and Orchardson looked at each other.

"*Shit!*" Blacklock shouted angrily, his previous composure vanishing. "*Shit, damn it all, I had it!*"

Sugarfoot leaned forward in his chair. "He said that?"

"No, it – it doesn't matter."

"So what *did* he say?" Orchardson asked.

"*I said it doesn't matter!*" Blacklock shouted. He sighed. "The moment's gone."

Blacklock looked down at Cecil. "Cecil, you and your son are going to die and the three of us are going to carry out the Ritual of Suth-G'nar ourselves and become gods." Blacklock turned to Sugarfoot and Orchardson. "There, happy now? Neither of you have any flair for the dramatic, do you?"

Oliver heard the door handle turn and he looked towards it. *My father's guards*, he thought hopefully. *They heard the noise and have come to help. They'll save me.*

"Ah, they're here," Blacklock said.

The door opened and when Oliver saw the figures who came through it he felt his hopes melt like butter on the Devil's arse. He didn't know why they were here, but he did know that the Abyss-Dwellers could never represent any kind of salvation.

There were five of them, around five feet in height with squat, solid bodies, webbed claws for hands and feet, short fins running along their spines, and gills on each side of their short, thick necks. Their pale skin was rubbery and hairless and they were naked – Oliver was grateful for the fact that wherever Abyss-Dwellers kept their genitals, it was out of sight – except for the long, ragged, hooded capes they wore when they needed to move around on land, a flimsy disguise but one that sufficed with enough distance and darkness. Some wore necklaces, bracelets or belts of shells and coral tied together with seaweed. One carried a harpoon while two others held crudely fashioned machetes, the weapons rusty and partially encrusted with barnacles. The Abyss-Dwellers' eyes were two large, staring orbs, their noses stubby snouts, their mouths filled with short but sharp teeth, two rows on their upper jaw and two on their lower jaw. Their breath stank of fish and wet rot and they spoke in a harsh and utterly alien tongue.

Oliver generally found it difficult to tell Abyss-Dwellers apart, although he recognised the one at the front of this group: Gerald was the only Abyss-Dweller Oliver knew of who wore spectacles. They were the kind with a string of beads connecting the frames, the string resting across the back of Gerald's neck, the frames resting on his snout. He also wore a seaweed bandolier across his torso, attached to which was a large conch shell.

One of the other Abyss-Dwellers had been carrying something in his claw, which he now tossed towards the men. The object sailed through the air, hit the table with a wet thump and came to rest on the floor. Oliver recognised it as the head of the guard from the front gate. He looked surprised.

Sugarfoot and Orchardson leaned away from the severed head with disgusted expressions while Blacklock smiled and said, "See, now *there's* a flair for the dramatic."

"Good evening, everyone," Gerald said, his voice guttural but his tone pleasant. As well as being the only one to wear spectacles, Gerald was also the only Abyss-Dweller Oliver had heard speak English.

While it was uncommon for Abyss-Dwellers to converse with human beings, they had done so at times over the millennia when it was in service of the Old Ones. Initially the language barrier was a problem so the Abyss-Dwellers decided that some of their number should learn those human languages necessary for their dealings and act as ambassadors, even adopting human names for the sake of convenience. Gerald was one of these ambassadors, going by many human names and becoming fluent in many human languages over the centuries. Oliver had to admit that Gerald's English was certainly better than Oliver's Abyss-Dweller. Beyond vague mention of "elders", Oliver didn't know who among Abyss-Dweller society Gerald reported to directly and frankly he didn't want to know, he already found the creatures terrifying enough without learning the ins and outs of their system of government, although he imagined it must be a nightmare trying to keep paperwork dry at the bottom of the sea.

Cecil had propped himself up on one forearm and now looked at Gerald through one narrowed eye while gesturing towards Blacklock, Sugarfoot and Orchardson with one shaking hand. "*Kill them!*" he shouted. "*They've betrayed us!*"

"No, Cecil, your colleagues have betrayed *you*," Gerald said. "Our cooperation with Arthur, Thomas and Frederick will continue after your death." Gerald glanced at Oliver. "And the death of your son, of course."

"You see, Gerald and I have been having our own private discussions for some time," Blacklock said to Cecil. "I convinced him of your selfish greed and how it endangered the ritual, and that I should take your place as head of the Order. He agreed. You never made much effort to hide your contempt of us, after all, our Abyss-Dweller allies included. Such ingratitude."

"*Bastards*," Cecil hissed through clenched teeth as he struggled to rise.

"Your eyes will not gaze upon the majesty of the Old Ones, Cecil," Gerald said. "For you there is only oblivion."

Gerald gave the harpoon-wielding Abyss-Dweller a nod. The creature walked over to Cecil, pinned him to the floor with one foot, raised his weapon in both claws and thrust it violently downwards into Cecil's back. Cecil cried out, shuddered, then lay still. The Abyss-Dweller pulled his harpoon free, the barbs slick with blood.

Gerald turned towards Oliver. "Now –"

With speed he didn't realise he possessed and no other thoughts beside escape, Oliver bolted out of his chair, sprinted across the room and leapt through one of the windows, shielding his head as glass exploded around him and he tumbled out into the night.

First-Time Customers

"I bid two fives," Digby said.

Talbot lifted his upturned cup slightly and glanced at the three remaining dice beneath it again. "Three sixes."

Digby stared at him for a moment. "Liar."

Talbot and Digby removed the cups that hid their dice, Digby with only one die left compared to Talbot's three. Digby had one six, Talbot had two sixes and a four.

Talbot smiled. "Bid is true. I win."

"Bastard," Digby said. "Sold me a dog there."

Talbot swept the coins from the centre of the table and shoved them into his trouser pocket. Digby had been the only other player left in the game, Henry, Ambrose and Bryn having already been eliminated. Talbot played a mean game of liar's dice. Good thing they only ever played for small amounts, more for fun than anything.

"Another game, lads?" Talbot asked.

"Aye, go on," Bryn said, and the Roustabouts collected their respective dice and dropped them back into their cups.

They sat around their table in The Bewigged Pig, the pub as full as the previous night but not quite as rowdy, although the night was still young. They were several pints into their day, any hangovers distant memories now.

Digby had ended up spending the night alone, the work he put into sweet-talking the girl at the bar going to waste when her drunk companion woke up, confronted them, vomited on the girl's dress then passed out again. Sort of spoiled the mood. She dragged the idiot out of there and that was the last Digby saw of her.

After parting ways with Dulcet Jones that afternoon, Henry and Ambrose had called at Bryn's flat then the three of them continued on to The Bewigged Pig, Digby and Talbot turning up soon afterwards. Henry and Ambrose brought Bryn, Talbot and Digby up to speed on what Dulcet told them about the Burgesses, but the Roustabouts were all equally unconcerned about the whole thing so it was quickly brushed aside.

Now, as they reached into their pockets for more coins, Bryn said, "I wish you lot would let me teach you how to play poker so it's not just liar's dice and blackjack all the time."

"I told you, I know how to play poker," Digby said.

"So do I," Ambrose said.

"You only know the boring, 'traditional' rulesets," Bryn said. "You need to learn 7-Card-Supper or Hold-Me-Bernard, those are proper types of poker."

"You tried explaining the rules of Hold-Me-Bernard to us once," Ambrose said. "I fell into a coma for three days, remember?"

"Look, it's simple. In Hold-Me-Bernard, twos act as nines unless it's a diamond, in which case you need three twos and a Jack to make a string. When a player makes a string, all of the clubs are put in the trough, unless the trough has been marked as unclean by an eight of spades. Now, six face-down spades make a Bernard, that goes without saying –"

Digby took a drink of his lager and tuned out Bryn, his attention turning to the front door as a familiar figure entered the pub. Oliver Burgess' clothes were damp and muddy, a leaf lodged in his tousled blonde hair, and he was holding his left arm against his torso with his right hand as if he had injured it. He was breathing heavily and looked scared, his eyes darting this way and that until eventually settling on Digby. He hesitated, then began limping towards the Roustabouts' table.

"Look what the cat dragged in," Digby said.

Henry, Bryn, Ambrose and Talbot looked at Oliver, who received curious glances from a few other customers as he passed them, looking back over his shoulder as if afraid something might be following him. He arrived at the Roustabouts' table and smiled nervously. "Good evening, gentlemen."

"Mr. Burgess," Henry said, looking him up and down. "What brings you here?"

Oliver glanced back over his shoulder again. "It's, um, rather a long story."

"In that case you better get a round in and pull yourself up a chair."

Oliver did as he was told, Henry insisting he order a whiskey for himself to calm his nerves, and the Roustabouts listened as he told them a somewhat condensed story about himself, his father, a host of godlike cosmic entities named the Old Ones, a race of aquatic humanoids named the Abyss-Dwellers who worshipped these entities, The Order of the Void and the strange gold ring he wore, an upcoming ritual to summon the Old Ones and end the world, the truth behind the severed nose in the tin of whelks, and how all of these things were connected. When pressed for details on the Old Ones, Oliver described some of them as best he could, both what was known about their natures as well as their physical appearances if certain drawings, paintings, sculptures and other artworks were to be believed. He added that a handful of writings claimed the Old Ones were in fact divided into separate groups of beings which included Inner Gods, Outer Gods, Lesser Inner Outer Gods and more. It could get quite convoluted if you believed everything you read and got tangled in the branches of that labyrinthine family tree, which Cecil had chosen not to do, instead following the generally accepted belief that the Old Ones were beyond any real hierarchies or familial relationships.

Oliver concluded with an account of what had happened at his father's house earlier that night, explaining that his fall from the second-floor window had been broken by an overgrown hydrangea bush and the decapitated corpse already lying in it. After that he had run through streets and alleys with no idea of where he was going. He considered taking the Burrows but didn't like the thought of being trapped underground if the Abyss-Dwellers caught up to him. He knew he couldn't go home because they would know to look for him there, he was just glad that his servant Mrs. Madsen was currently taking some time off as he would hate to put her in danger. Eventually he decided to find The Bewigged Pig and hopefully the Roustabouts, so he crossed the Brazenbrook, heading south towards Wealdbury, and after some searching managed to locate the pub.

"Sounds like quite a pickle," Henry said.

Oliver hesitated. "So you believe me? I understand it sounds insane…"

Talbot shrugged. "We've seen our share of weird. I've never heard of any Old Ones or Abyss-Dwellers but the world's an odd place."

"Yes, I suppose so. And none of you consider it blasphemous? The talk of the Old Ones as gods? I mean, it's very far from Christian teachings."

"None of us are exactly religious, Christianity or otherwise," Henry said.

"Tentacles are a bit of a theme with these Old Ones, aren't they," Digby pointed out.

"There are similarities in some of their forms, but they differ tremendously in other cases," Oliver said. Something apparently occurred to him. "One of them has a beard."

"Is it made of tentacles?"

Oliver frowned thoughtfully. "Actually, now that I think about it, yes." He winced and gingerly shifted his right arm. "I think my arm might be broken."

"I doubt it," Bryn said. "You don't strike me as a man with much experience of physical pain. If your arm was broken you'd probably be crying and screaming a lot more."

"Well… it still really hurts. I don't suppose anyone's got any aspirin? Or laudanum? I don't usually partake, it doesn't agree with me, but the pain is terrible."

"Drink your whiskey," Henry said. "So why come to us? Last we heard, you were trying to dig up information on us."

"Ah," Oliver said, looking guilty. "Sorry about that. It was my father's decision, I said we should leave you alone. How did you know? If you don't mind my asking."

"Dulcet Jones is a friend of ours," Ambrose said.

"I see," Oliver said. He sighed. "The truth is, I came to you because I didn't know where else to go. With my father gone, I have no family. I don't have any friends and I doubt the police will believe me. Although I don't suppose any of this really matters, what with the world ending in two days' time." Oliver sipped his whiskey and grimaced. "I am *not* looking forward to meeting that winged lemur in the goggles."

Before the Roustabouts could get to grips with that last sentence, the two windows at the front of the pub exploded as two cloaked and hooded figures came leaping through, men and women cursing and screaming in surprise. The two figures landed on their feet a moment before a powerful blow on the front door smashed it off its hinges and a third similar figure stepped into the pub. All three were armed, two carrying harpoons while one gripped a machete.

"Oh God," Oliver moaned as the Roustabouts rose to their feet. "It's them."

Digby noticed the webbed and clawed hands and feet a second before the three figures cast off their ragged disguises, fully revealing the monstrous forms beneath.

These'll be the Abyss-Dwellers, then, he thought.

The creature closest to the Roustabouts' table unleashed a gurgling howl that filled the room. Having been frozen in shock, the crowd now erupted in a frenzy of panicked movement and terrified screaming, men and women running and pushing and clambering to get away from the monsters, dropping glasses and knocking over barstools, chairs and tables as they surged towards the back of the room, where Annie herded them through the doorway that led to the adjoining hallway, at one end of which was the back door of the pub. Annie caught Digby's eye and gave him a nod which he understood: she would handle the crowd while the Roustabouts handled the intruders.

Digby looked away and briefly wondered where Oliver had gone until he heard something coming from beneath the table and found Oliver huddled on the floor down there, arms wrapped around himself and eyes squeezed shut, his voice terrified and miserable as he chanted, "No, no, no, no, no…"

Digby's attention turned to the Abyss-Dwellers as they rushed towards the Roustabouts' table with murderous expressions, Ambrose hurling his pint glass, one of the creatures cursing in pain as it shattered against his head. More armed Abyss-Dwellers were already swarming through the windows and front door, tearing off their hooded cloaks as they came.

"The temperance movement aren't messing around anymore, are they," Digby said, smiling.

The Roustabouts charged forward.

An Eyeful of Violence

The violence that erupted inside The Bewigged Pig reminded Oliver why he never went into pubs, although he knew he had brought this particular violence with him. From the floor beneath the table, he watched as the fighting between the Roustabouts and the Abyss-Dwellers raged. He wondered if he should have followed everyone else when they ran from the room but it was too late now, he certainly wasn't going to step out into the maelstrom around him.

As formidable as the Roustabouts had seemed, Oliver fully expected them to be quickly overpowered and murdered by the Abyss-Dwellers, who outnumbered the men roughly two to one. Then the Abyss-Dwellers would come for him and that would be the end of that. But instead the Roustabouts were holding their own against the creatures. Oliver would be the first to admit he knew nothing about fighting – he had been in one fight when he was eight years old, a couple of slaps and shoves followed by many tears – but it was obvious the Roustabouts did and that they were bloody good at it. The fact they were facing off against monstrosities from the ocean depths never gave them pause either.

The Roustabouts dodged the Abyss-Dwellers' weapons or blocked them with makeshift shields such as a chair or table or at one point a struggling Abyss-Dweller, who was inadvertently stabbed in the chest by one of his companions, thick, black blood pouring from the wound. Although the Roustabouts occasionally used a stolen harpoon, machete or sword, generally they seemed to prefer using their fists, not to mention their feet, knees, elbows, and heads. An impressive exception occurred when a harpoon was thrown at Talbot, who caught it in mid-air, spun around and hurled it back in one smooth motion, the harpoon slamming into its owner and pinning the Abyss-Dweller to the wall.

"Don't mess with an ex-sailor, you slippery bastards!" Talbot shouted before turning to face another attacker.

For powerful, solidly built brawlers, the Roustabouts' reflexes were sharp and they could be surprisingly fast, even Talbot and Bryn, the largest of the group, the five men fighting multiple opponents singlehandedly when forced to. And it was clear that, unlike the Abyss-Dwellers, the Roustabouts knew how to fight as a team. Even amidst the chaos they looked out for each other, such as when an Abyss-Dweller charged at Ambrose's back with a sword only for Henry to step in from the side and swing a barstool into the creature's face; or when Bryn had an Abyss-Dweller clinging onto his back, attempting to claw at his face, and Digby yanked the creature off and drove his head into a table.

The Abyss-Dwellers fought savagely and drew blood more than once, the Roustabouts receiving their share of cuts and knocks, but none of the injuries seemed serious and eventually it became clear the fight was turning in the Roustabouts' favour as they battered and killed one Abyss-Dweller after another: a long shard of window glass jammed into a throat, a spine snapped across a knee, a skull shattered against the bar, a body pummelled until it was a sack of broken bones and pulped flesh, a sword run through its owner's stomach while still gripped in the creature's hand.

One Abyss-Dweller upended a table on which sat several full pint glasses, causing a furious Bryn to shout, *"Now that's just a waste!"* then kick him into the fireplace. The Abyss-Dweller howled and thrashed as he rolled out of the flames and across the floor, his flesh blackened and smoking.

Overall the scene was a bloody, brutal and overwhelming spectacle of violence the likes of which Oliver had never seen. A small, primal part of his brain couldn't help but be awed and feel a flicker of an urge to revel in it, to unleash the savage beast that lurked deep within the heart of every man. Then an Abyss-Dweller's gouged-out eyeball hit the floor near him with a wet plop and he decided his savage beast was fine where it was. Oliver looked past the large, staring eyeball to see one of the two remaining Abyss-Dwellers collapsing to the floor, dead, one eye left in his head and a broken chair leg impaled in his chest.

This left a sole survivor, who snarled and jabbed his harpoon at the Roustabouts as they slowly advanced on him. Eventually the Abyss-Dweller threw the harpoon at Digby, who dodged it as the creature leapt onto a nearby table and then out through one of the broken windows. There was the receding sound of bare feet slapping against pavement, then silence.

The Roustabouts stood battered and bloody, although much of the blood on their hands, faces and torn clothes wasn't their own but the black blood of the Abyss-Dwellers. Getting their breath back, they looked around the room, the place a mess of broken furniture and glass, cracked and dented walls, pools and spatters of blood, and Abyss-Dweller corpses.

"*Oh, this is just fucking marvellous, this is!*" shouted a woman's voice, and Oliver looked to see the landlady standing in the doorway through which she and the other customers had fled earlier. He felt a tiny, illicit thrill at hearing a woman use the f-word, it was a first for him.

She entered the room, a disbelieving and furious expression on her face as she stepped around blood and bodies and debris, seemingly more fazed by the state of the room than the presence of the Abyss-Dwellers. "Look at this place! Look at it!"

Avoiding the rogue Abyss-Dweller eyeball, Oliver crawled out from beneath the table and rose to his feet.

"Sorry, Annie," Henry said. "No helping it. Did everyone get out alright?"

Annie surveyed the carnage with a frown. "What? Oh, yeah, as soon as they got to the alley out back you couldn't see them for dust."

Henry turned to Oliver. "I'm guessing these things followed you here from your father's house."

"I suppose so," Oliver said.

"Hang on," Annie said, and she glared at Oliver. "This is *your* fault?"

Annie's expression made Oliver wonder how quickly he could make it back under the table. "Um, well, I wouldn't exactly say that…"

"Don't kill him yet, Annie," Henry said. "We've got a use for him."

Oliver didn't fail to notice Henry's worrying use of "yet".

"You're going to take us to your father's house," Henry said to Oliver.

Oliver thought about the harpoon plunging into his father's back, the guard's severed head and the dark streets of Newmuck potentially crawling with murderous Abyss-Dwellers. "Why don't I just write down the address for you?" he suggested with a nervous smile.

"Oh no, you lot aren't swanning off and leaving me in the lurch!" Annie said. She nudged a dead Abyss-Dweller with one foot. "What am I supposed to do with these things?"

"Start selling fish sandwiches to pay for the damages?" Bryn suggested.

"That's it!" Ambrose said. "Well, not fish sandwiches, but… Annie, is there enough room in the cellar for all these bodies?"

"Yeah," Annie said, "but why in God's name –"

"I'll explain later. For now, just hide them in the cellar and don't tell anyone about them. Especially the police if they turn up."

"And what if more of these monsters turn up?"

"They only came here because they want *him*," Henry said, glancing at Oliver. "And he's coming with us. But just in case, a couple of us will stay here with you until the rest get back. Any volunteers?"

For a moment none of the Roustabouts said anything, apparently preferring another potential fight over clean-up duty.

Eventually, Digby sighed. "Fine, I'll do it. I can't say no to a damsel in distress."

"Call me a damsel one more time, Digby, and you're going to be the one in distress," Annie said.

"I'll stay as well," Bryn said.

"Don't worry about the cost of the damages," Henry said to Annie, "we can dangle Oliver here upside-down by his ankles and see what falls out of his pockets if it comes to it. Right now we need to get our hands on the bastards behind all this." He looked at his fellow Roustabouts, their expressions resolute. "No one smashes up our local and gets away with it."

Telling Porkies at The Bewigged Pig

The orange glow had been visible against the black sky from several streets away and its nature was unmistakeable, so when the carriage eventually turned onto Isaac Street, Henry wasn't surprised to see Cecil Burgess' house engulfed in flames.

Randolph Sowerby parked his Clarence across the street from the property. Oliver stepped out of the carriage and into the road, followed by Henry, Ambrose and Talbot, while Randolph remained in the driver's seat and his two horses snorted and shook their heads. The pavements of the upper-class street were dotted with small clusters of people watching the fire, mostly smartly-dressed local residents, although a few random passers-by had also stopped to gawp.

Henry assumed the fire brigade were on their way but it was clear there was no saving the house at this point as the inferno tore hungrily through it, the building would be nothing but a blackened husk by the time the flames were out. Some of the greenery surrounding the house had caught fire but the blaze didn't seem likely to spread beyond the boundaries of the property, at least.

"Looks like they were serious about covering their tracks," Ambrose said.

Henry looked over at Oliver, who stared at the burning house with a slightly stunned expression. "You alright?"

"I don't know," Oliver said, his eyes fixed on the conflagration. "I think so. That house and my father have always been in my life, but now…" He paused. "It's been quite a night."

There was a distant crash as some unseen part of the house's interior collapsed.

"Blacklock and the others must've looted the place first," Oliver said, "taken all of my father's writings and artefacts related to the Old Ones. Especially the items required for the Ritual of Suth-G'nar, they'd need those."

"Your Order friends, do you know where they live?" Henry asked.

"No. We never met outside of Order business, and that was always here or at the cannery."

"Alright, we best be off before the police arrive and take you in for questioning."

Oliver looked at Henry with a twinge of alarm. "Questioning? But I didn't do anything."

"How about trying to destroy the bloody world?" Talbot said.

"Fair point, I suppose," Oliver said. "But… what should I do now?"

"You're coming with us," Henry said. "You and your father and those other three started this mess then you brought us into it. So now you're going to help us clean it up."

Oliver looked over the three Roustabouts. "You mean you're going to try to stop the ritual and save the world?"

"Well, we're not going to sit on our arses and let these cosmic bastards come here and throw their weight around. So looks like we're saving the world."

As the four men walked back towards the carriage, Henry noticed Oliver remove the gold ring from his finger, the one engraved with the Sign of Xylophone or whatever he had called it, and toss it into a nearby drain without a word.

Randolph drove back the way they had come, heading for The Bewigged Pig. When they turned onto Mulligan Avenue, Henry stuck his head out of the window and looked up the street in the direction of the pub, where he saw a uniformed figure standing outside.

"Drop us off here," Henry called up to Randolph, who gave him a nod.

Henry ducked back inside the carriage and Ambrose, Talbot and Oliver looked at him questioningly as the vehicle slowed to a stop at the side of the road.

"There's a bobby outside the Pig," Henry said. "Maybe more inside. Oliver, we'll sneak you in through the back door and you can wait back there until we give you the all-clear."

"I'll take him," Ambrose said. "You and Talbot go in through the front."

The four men exited the carriage and Ambrose led Oliver into the mouth of a nearby unlit alley on The Bewigged Pig's side of the street, where the two men were quickly swallowed by the darkness.

Henry reached into his pocket and withdrew a twenty-pence coin, which he tossed up to Randolph. Randolph caught the coin and looked at it then shook his head. "I can't take this," he said. "I told you, you ride for free."

"You can take it in return for not saying a word about any of this to anyone," Henry said.

"Thank you. My lips are sealed."

Randolph drove off as Henry and Talbot began walking along the pavement, the hanging sign of The Bewigged Pig visible up ahead, the constable standing beneath it in his helmet and dark-blue uniform, hands clasped together behind his back. The handful of people moving along Mulligan Avenue cast curious glances at the bobby and the pub's damaged frontage.

"So what's our story for the police?" Talbot asked.

"Let's just play it by ear," Henry said.

The policeman was young and thin and stood blocking the pub's doorless front entrance, his truncheon hanging at his hip, his whistle dangling from a string around his neck. He watched Henry and Talbot approach.

"Can I help you?" the constable asked.

"This is our local," Henry said.

"Sorry, police business. No one's allowed inside until –"

"Let them in, constable," called a familiar voice from inside the pub.

"Yes, inspector," the constable said, and he stepped aside.

Henry and Talbot entered the pub. Broken glass and furniture still lay strewn around the barroom but the dead Abyss-Dwellers and their weapons were gone. There were still some bloodstains present but they had been scrubbed enough that you couldn't tell the blood had actually been black and not red. Bryn had lifted the front door off the floor and was leaning it against the wall while Digby added the broken remains of a barstool to some debris piled up in a corner, out of the way.

Annie was standing with Inspector Jeremy Alabaster, who frowned at Henry and Talbot as they approached him.

Jeremy was in plain clothes, wearing a suit beneath a knee-length overcoat, a bowler hat on his head. He was almost two years younger than his brother, around the same height but with a less muscular build, his brown eyes a lighter shade than Henry's. His hair and moustache were a similar colour to his eyes, although touches of grey had begun to appear at his temples. He carried a police-issue Myers & Pouch revolver in a holster on his right hip, his rank placing him among the small percentage of officers authorised to carry a firearm.

Henry gave his brother a nod. "Jeremy."

"Annie was just telling me what happened here," Jeremy said. "Why don't you tell me as well?"

Henry glanced at Annie, who gave an almost imperceptible shake of her head. "How would we know, we've only just arrived."

Jeremy looked over Henry's and Talbot's cuts and bruises and torn, bloody clothing. "So what happened to you two?"

"Dogs," Talbot said.

Jeremy raised his eyebrows. "Dogs."

"Strays. They jumped us on our way here. Do you want descriptions?"

Henry couldn't help smiling, and Jeremy gave him an annoyed glance. "Very funny," Jeremy said. "Where's Ambrose?"

"Probably helping his gran with something," Henry said. "He's good like that."

"I was telling the inspector how some troublemakers came in and started a ruckus but Digby and Bryn fought them off," Annie said.

Jeremy looked around the room with a frown. "Must've been quite the fight. There's a lot of blood here for a barroom brawl."

Annie shrugged. "They were big blokes, they probably had a lot of blood in them. Now if you don't mind, inspector, I've got a lot of cleaning up to do."

"You'll inform the police if these 'troublemakers' come back, of course."

"Of course. Talbot, will you give me a hand?"

Talbot followed Annie in the direction of the bar, leaving Henry and Jeremy alone.

"Isn't a simple pub fight a bit beneath the rank of inspector?" Henry asked.

"I came because I was in the area," Jeremy said.

"You came because you heard it was the Pig and you thought we'd be the ones causing the bother."

"It wouldn't be the first time."

"We don't cause any bother here, we just deal with it if it comes knocking. Trouble has a way of finding people."

"Some more than others."

Henry smiled. "Maybe me and the boys can get our faces up on your rogues gallery down at the station."

"This isn't a joke. You and your friends aren't above the law, Henry. I'm tired of having to remind you of that."

"And yet here you are."

Jeremy sighed in frustration as he and Henry looked away from each other. Henry didn't like that conversations between himself and his brother sometimes went this way, he might have ended up on the wrong side of the law more than once over the years but he knew the police had it tough in this city.

The Newmuck Police Force had come a long way since its humble beginnings: the force was more organised and efficient, there were more bobbies on the streets than ever (even if sometimes you still couldn't find one when you needed one, just ask Beatrix Sowerby), most of the drunks had been weeded out, less civilians hated the police, and advancements in science and technology allowed them to tackle crime using methods unheard of just a few decades ago. But the force remained understaffed in policing an extremely overpopulated city, out-of-touch higher-ups were more concerned with their careers than delivering justice, the crime rate continued to rise, corruption was a problem, and many newspapers stoked public fear and mistrust with sensationalist, factually incorrect headlines and articles.

Even in the face of all this, Jeremy had put in the time and graft to get where he was today, having walked a beat and risen through the ranks to become an inspector in the Criminal Investigation Department. He was a damn good policeman, he had even been awarded a Police Medal for Gallantry after saving a suspect's young daughter from drowning, an accolade which he insisted was unnecessary and which he didn't like to talk about.

He had also managed to balance his career with being a family man, having married Jane, a schoolteacher, the two of them going on to create two tiny humans who Henry would lay down his life for: Robert and Emily. Henry liked Jane, she was intelligent and passionate and had a sense of humour that offset Jeremy's tendency towards seriousness. The family had recently moved into a nice two-up two-down on the outskirts of the city and were happy there.

Henry couldn't have been prouder of his brother. Not that they ever spoke about that sort of thing.

Henry broke the brief silence that had fallen between them. "How are Jane and the children?"

"They're fine," Jeremy said. "Robert and Emily ask after you."

"I'll have to visit again soon."

"No drawing on Emily's face next time."

"She asked me to do it."

"That was strong ink in that pen! Our six-year-old daughter had to go to school with a moustache for three days before we finally managed to wash it off."

Henry remembered the wide, toothy grin on his niece's face when he showed her her reflection. "Well, *she* liked it," he said, smiling.

Jeremy took his pocket watch from the breast pocket of his suit jacket, flipped open the brass lid and checked the time. "I should be on my way, my shift ends soon. Although I'll be back at the station again by the time the sun's up."

"What are you working on?"

Jeremy put away his pocket watch. "Too many things. We're getting a lot of pressure on a case involving a duel between two rich, young idiots, one of whom ended up dead, and now his fiancé is screaming to the high heavens it was murder. Apparently she's the goddaughter of a good friend of our dear commissioner, so you can imagine how delightful he's making things for us. Still, the dead man's weapon of choice was the stuffed corpse of his beloved pet ferret, so that's a first at least." Jeremy took one last look around the room then turned back to Henry. "Take care of yourself, Henry. And try not to do anything foolish."

"Wouldn't dream of it."

Jeremy walked towards the front entrance. "Oh, and watch out for those dogs, won't you?" he said without looking back, then he stepped out onto the street and disappeared from view, the young constable following closely behind him.

How to Become a God

It was almost midnight by the time the Roustabouts got to sit down at their table – one of the few which had survived the brawl intact – inside The Bewigged Pig, joined by Annie and Oliver.

Ambrose and Oliver had shown their faces after Jeremy and the bobby left, and the seven of them tidied up the barroom as best they could for now, the debris collected into a pile in one corner while two loose tabletops were nailed into place across the shattered windows. The front door stood loose in its frame, kept in place by a table jammed up against it. At one point George and Murray appeared, returning to check on things, and Annie told them she didn't know when the pub would be open again. So, looking lost and distressingly sober, George and Murray left. Bryn could swear he heard Murray weeping softly as they went.

Eventually, when the tidying was done, Annie added some fresh logs to the fire, poured a round of drinks – pints for the Roustabouts, a large gin for herself and a half-pint of lager shandy for Oliver – and they took their seats at the table, using seven of the eight intact chairs left in the room.

As Digby and Bryn rolled themselves a cigarette each, Annie said, "So, who's going to tell me what in the name of the Pope's balls happened inside my pub tonight?"

Annie sipped her gin and listened as Oliver told her the same story he had told the Roustabouts earlier, this time concluding with the burning of his father's house. Afterwards, she sat in thoughtful silence for a moment then said, "What does 'antediluvian' mean?"

Bryn took a drink of cider, glad to not be the only one who didn't know.

"What?" Oliver said.

"You said 'occult carvings, objects and writings unearthed from deep, antediluvian tombs in hidden corners of foreign lands,'" Annie said. "What does that mean?"

"Oh. Um, I think it means something very old. To be honest I never looked it up, my father used to say it sometimes, I suppose I just picked it up. So, do you believe me? About everything?"

"I've got a pile of bodies in my cellar as proof, haven't I? I can't say I'm sure about all this Old Ones and end-of-the-world nonsense but if the boys think something needs to be done then there must be something in it. They might be idiots but they're not stupid."

"I think that's the sweetest thing you've ever said about us," Bryn said.

Henry nodded at Oliver's untouched shandy. "You not drinking?"

Oliver looked down at his glass. "I'm not much of a drinker." He made the effort to take a sip and looked pleasantly surprised. "That's quite nice, actually. Very refreshing."

"See, a little drink never hurt anyone."

"What about Stuart the tobacconist?" Digby said. "He passed out drunk on a railway track and a train came along and dragged him all the way to Liverpool. His legs have been the wrong way round ever since."

"Still," Bryn said, "our last Prime Minister tried to ban strong liquor in Newmuck and what happened to him?"

"He was eaten by bears," Ambrose said.

"*He was eaten by bears,*" Bryn said, tapping the table with an index finger for emphasis.

There was a pause.

"I don't think those two things were connected, though," Ambrose said.

Bryn sat back, satisfied. "My point stands."

"So how many of these Abyss-Dwellers are there?" Talbot asked Oliver.

"I'm not sure," Oliver said. "They must number in the thousands, I suppose. They live in two great cities, each built on the floor of a different ocean. They believe the Old Ones created them and placed them on Earth to serve their will. The Abyss-Dwellers live for a very long time and they're very patient. Apparently they've been on this planet even longer than we have."

"What about the ritual?" Ambrose asked. "What does that involve, exactly?"

"Every eight-hundred years the planets align in a specific way and this is when the barrier between this reality and that of the Old Ones is at its thinnest and most vulnerable, when it's possible to summon them into our world. Eight particular artefacts have to be brought together and the relevant rites performed, and if done properly the Old Ones will be called. The plan was for The Order of the Void to perform the ritual under the guidance of the Abyss-Dwellers."

"Quite the party," Digby said, looking at Oliver through the thin haze of smoke rising from his cigarette. "Why don't the Abyss-Dwellers just do it themselves? Why do they need you lot?"

"Abyss-Dwellers can only survive outside of water for so long, Gerald said they learned early on it was useful to have human allies to help them with their work, men who could reach places on land the Abyss-Dwellers couldn't, move about in public, that sort of thing. Other Old One-worshipping cults worked with the Abyss-Dwellers before the Order did, some still exist around the world. Most are true believers, others only serve for the promise of great rewards. Men like my father, Blacklock, Sugarfoot and Orchardson. Gerald said the Abyss-Dwellers don't mind as long as they achieve their goals."

"What about the Old Ones?" Henry asked. "What do *they* want?"

"It's said the Old Ones are so far beyond us that the human mind isn't capable of truly comprehending their intentions. But everything points to their arrival unleashing madness, death and unimaginable horror across the entire planet."

"Even Wales?" Bryn said.

"I'm afraid so. Life as we know it would be over, replaced by whatever the Old Ones make of it."

"Are you sure these things even exist?" Digby asked.

Oliver looked down into his shandy with a troubled frown. "I may not have seen any of the Old Ones with my own eyes but I've seen enough proof of their existence. They're real."

Annie gave Oliver an accusing look. "And you were willing to destroy the world for them."

Oliver shifted in his seat, looking guilty and uncomfortable. "I never wanted to destroy the world. I accidentally sat on a spider last Christmas and couldn't eat my sprouts for the guilt." He sighed. "My father was a very… dominating presence all my life. When he started with all this I was to help him and that was that. My not doing so was never an option."

"You said your father served the Old Ones because he'd be rewarded, but if the ritual worked, wouldn't he be killing himself along with everyone else?"

"No, that's the thing, apparently those who carry out the ritual will be granted godhood by the Old Ones, them essentially being gods themselves. That's what my father wanted: to become a god. And that's the carrot he dangled in front of Blacklock, Sugarfoot and Orchardson when he created The Order of the Void. The Abyss-Dwellers already had some of the artefacts needed for the Ritual of Suth-G'nar, and the Order used its money and influence to find and gather the others. The Abyss-Dwellers never had everything they needed when previous alignments came around, but this time they do."

"And now them and your Order friends are still going to perform the ritual, just without you and your father?"

"That's what Blacklock said. But they can't do it before Monday night. Right around ten o'clock, that's when the planets will be in position. If the ritual's performed too early or too late, it won't work."

"Where's it happening?" Ambrose asked Oliver.

"Beneath the cannery," Oliver said. "A few years ago my father and the Abyss-Dwellers arranged for a tunnel to be dug connecting the cellar to a network of caves beneath the Brazenbrook. A lot are flooded and lead all the way out into the Atlantic Ocean, the Abyss-Dwellers use them to travel inland, but there's a dry cave down there where we usually held ceremonies and met with Gerald. That's where we were going to perform the ritual."

"At least we know where they'll be Monday night if we don't get our hands on them before then," Ambrose said.

Oliver shook his head, frowning. "I don't know. The door to the cellar is made of reinforced concrete and steel and my father had the only key. Blacklock and the others will need to get onto the property, into the main building and through that door. Although, if they took my father's keys…"

"I think it's more likely they won't use that place because they know *you* know about it," Henry said. "When that Abyss-Dweller who got away earlier tells them you're still alive, they might not want to risk using the cannery in case you send the police or someone else there to spoil the ritual. Chances are they'll pick somewhere new that you don't know about. If you don't know where they live, what *can* you tell us to help us find them?"

"I know Blacklock owns some silk-mills and tenements. Sugarfoot is Chairman of Great Newmuck Railway and Orchardson's a director at Bowers Bank."

"Banks will be closed on a Sunday," Bryn said. Not that he ever used a bank himself. He liked to know exactly where his money was and trusted himself to protect it better than any uppity git in a fancy suit. "Same as the silk factories and probably wherever Sugarfoot works. Why don't we ask Dulcet to find out their addresses?"

"He's out of town for a few days," Ambrose said.

Bryn took a final drag on his cigarette then blew out smoke as he stubbed out the butt in the ashtray and looked at Henry. "What about your brother?"

"He won't believe all this," Henry said. "Besides, he'd insist on letting the law handle it, and I don't think any of us are willing to take that chance."

Silence fell across the table as people drank and mental gears turned until eventually everyone else looked at Oliver at the same time.

"You don't need to raise your hand, Oliver," Henry said.

Oliver lowered his arm sheepishly. "Right. Um, there *was* something else. Well, a couple of things. Probably nothing."

"Spit it out," Digby said.

"Orchardson has a daughter. Elizabeth, I think. I've never met her but apparently she's some sort of artist. I heard she lives on Hiram Avenue. Maybe she can point you in the direction of her father."

"What's the other thing?" Henry asked.

"Most of the materials on the Old Ones that my father owned came from overseas, but two months ago some pages from an ancient book called the Yaroslav Manuscript found their way into the hands of a wealthy collector of curiosities here in Newmuck, a man who wasn't aware of the Old Ones or the pages' true relevance. My father offered to buy them but the owner wouldn't sell, so Blacklock arranged for them to be stolen instead. He didn't go into much detail about it but he did mention the name of a man involved, someone connected to the Newmuck underworld. Perhaps you might know him. Um, not that I'm casting aspersions on you or the people you associate with."

"What was the name?" Bryn asked.

"Cromwell. Offal Cromwell, I believe."

"Bloody Offal," Digby said, shaking his head.

"Gets around, doesn't he," Bryn said.

"So you do know this person?" Oliver asked.

"We know him," Henry said. "So Cromwell stole these pages for Blacklock?"

"I believe so. Blacklock didn't tell him anything about the Order, of course. Or that's what he told the rest of us, anyway. I'm afraid that's all I can think of. I wasn't really kept in the loop as much as everyone else."

"So we've got Orchardson's daughter and Cromwell. How about tomorrow we –"

"Hang on, hang on," Annie said, leaning forward and looking at Ambrose. "*You* still haven't told me why you wanted me to stash those bodies in the cellar."

"Ah, right," Ambrose said. "Professor Bracegirdle."

"That mad old scientist at the university?"

"He's always on the lookout for interesting scientific finds, and he's willing to pay good money for them."

"He didn't give me much for that flying, ten-legged cat I brought him," Talbot said disapprovingly.

"To be fair, Talbot, you just tied two cats to a duck, you should be glad he gave you anything," Ambrose said, then he turned back to Annie. "If we go to Bracegirdle with those Abyss-Dwellers, he'll flip his lid. You'll easily have enough to pay for the damages to the pub. We'll just get this end-of-the-world business sorted out first."

Annie sat back and thought about it for a moment. "Alright. But you better be right or *you're* getting rid of them."

"Fair enough."

"As I was saying," Henry said, "how about this: Bryn and Ambrose, you two take Oliver and find the Orchardson girl, see if you can get her to tell you where her father is. Me, Digby and Talbot will pay Cromwell a visit and see if he can point us towards Blacklock. If he knows anything useful, we'll get it out of him."

"Why do me and Ambrose have to babysit the rich boy while you three have all the fun?" Bryn asked.

"He's not going to last long on his own if the Order decide to have another crack at him, and we don't want him making a run for it either."

"Maybe I should just hide somewhere safe?" Oliver suggested.

"Maybe you should try to make up for what you've done," Annie said.

"That worker at your cannery *died* because of you and your precious Order."

"He *was* a thief," Oliver said half-heartedly.

"Oh, that makes it alright, then."

"I'm not saying that –"

"Enough," Henry interrupted.

"I'm going with them," Annie said, folding her arms.

"What?"

"Bryn and Ambrose and this one," Annie said, hooking a thumb in Oliver's direction. "The Orchardson girl might be more inclined to talk to three strange men turning up at her door if there's another woman with them." Annie looked at Oliver. "We'll make a stop at your house as well so you can fetch me some money to help pay for this place, just in case Ambrose's plan doesn't work. If it does then I'll use your money to pay for an exorcist to finally remove that curse from the privy instead."

"Annie –"

"Don't start, Henry. I'm getting something out of this fool before he runs off or gets himself killed. Besides, what do you think's safer, me being with Bryn and Ambrose or here on my own?"

Henry sighed. "Fine. Oliver, have you got cash at your place?"

"Some," Oliver said, "although I –"

"That's settled, then," Annie said.

"We'll meet back here afterwards and go from there," Henry said. "Any objections?" No one spoke. "Annie, is it alright with you if we all sleep here tonight? We'll head out in the morning but it'll be safer if we stick together for now. We can take turns standing watch in case any more Abyss-Dwellers turn up."

"You'll have to fight for the few spare sheets and pillows I've got," Annie said.

"Don't worry about me," Talbot said. "I once slept for fourteen hours straight on top of an upturned rake. Bastards never let me back into the garden centre after that."

Digby drank what remained of his pint and set down the empty glass. "I'll take first watch, I'm not tired."

Annie finished her gin and stood up. "I'm going to bed. You can all sleep in here, blankets and pillows are in the spare room upstairs. Keep the fire going, you'll need it with the draught." She started walking towards the doorway at the back of the room but then paused and turned around. "And *don't* think you can go helping yourselves to the bar, either."

"Um, will you be alright, miss?" Oliver asked Annie. "What with everything that's happened and your, um, delicate womanly disposition?"

The Roustabouts froze, waiting in hushed silence like a crowd waiting for the guillotine blade to drop.

Annie stared at Oliver for a moment then turned and continued towards the doorway. "If you run out of logs for the fire, throw him on there. I hear stupid burns nicely."

The Man Who Would Be Another

Blacklock awoke with tears in his eyes, an emptiness in his chest and a churning in his stomach, and knew it wasn't because of the spiced-tongue-and-apricot-jam pie he had eaten before retiring for the night.

The dream was always the same and never failed to leave him shaken.

The glare from the limelight on high and the footlights spanning the front of the stage was almost blindingly brilliant, the space beyond impossibly vast, countless seats stretching into infinity and all of them filled, not an empty one in the house. None of the figures had faces but Blacklock knew they were all focused on the stage. On him. But he wasn't intimidated. He was exactly where he belonged and what he was always supposed to be and he burned like a star for all the universe to see as he made the stage his own. He moved across the gleaming floorboards, the driving force of the action one minute only to be borne along on the rushing waters of fate the next, he was the hero, the villain, the king, the lover, the god, the peasant, the soldier, the fool, he was everything and anything, whatever he needed to be at that moment, and he gloried in it.

And then the dream would end and he would be wide awake with the crushing, overwhelming knowledge that in reality he wasn't what he was always supposed to be. And that knowledge made him feel sick and sad and angry.

Things could have been so different.

Blacklock had been born into money and privilege, to traditional, stuffy parents who expected him to follow in their traditional, stuffy footsteps. His father was no fool, his focus on textiles, the dominant industry of his day, having made him a wealthy man.

But Blacklock knew at an early age that such a conventional life was not for him. His parents never approved of or supported his dream, and his older brother, Archibald, mocked him mercilessly for it, but with his debut role as "Birch Tree No.2" in his school's production of the play *Mrs. Butterchurn's Woodland Birthday Delights*, the nine-year-old Blacklock knew what he was put on this Earth to be: an *actor*. He was destined to tread the boards of the grandest stages all over the world, playing all the great parts, a master of comedy and tragedy and everything in between, able to inspire the most intense of reactions within audiences. He could see it all so clearly.

Then when Blacklock was eighteen, his father died of a heart attack and control of the family business was handed over to his heirs. Blacklock couldn't care less about the company and was happy to leave all that to the much keener Archibald. Five months later, however, a drunken Archibald fell off a horse and broke his neck, leaving Blacklock as the sole inheritor of the business. Despite his young age, his mother convinced him to take charge on a temporary basis, just to ensure that the money continued to flow and the family name maintained its status. Blacklock reluctantly agreed on a period of no more than six months, enough time to keep the business on course while a more permanent solution could be arranged, then he could go back to focusing on acting. Maybe get around to appearing in a second play at some point.

It was a decision Blacklock had come to regret like no other. Because before he knew it those six months became a year, a year became two, and now here he was, a fifty-year-old man whose one dream was both a distant memory and yet, at times like these, so painfully fresh. How could he have let his purpose get away from him? Even after his mother died and he had made enough money that he didn't need to work another day in his life, he hadn't seized that freedom.

He had taken the easy option. Because the thing was, despite his complete lack of interest in the world of business, it all came easily to him nonetheless. He had not only kept the family company afloat but made it more successful than ever, changing it to Blacklock Silk Weavers after seeing how much money there was to be made in the silk industry. Even now, when the industry had been in decline for some time, mostly as a result of cheaper French silks, the company continued to make money hand over fist as the largest remaining manufacturer in Britain, the women who worked at the machine looms in Blacklock's three Newmuck factories

– unlike some industrialists, Blacklock was more than happy to employ women as he could pay them less than men for the same amount of work – churning out overpriced ribbons, shawls, handkerchiefs, parasols, slippers, dresses, and more.

Still, Blacklock knew a smart businessman didn't put all of his eggs in one basket even if that basket was lined with silk, so that was why he had bought several tenements on the outskirts of the grotty little district of Gristle. Because although there was money to be made from rich people wanting fine things, there was just as much to be made from poor people wanting a roof over their heads. Blacklock overfilled his flats, charged extortionate rates and only paid for the absolute bare minimum work necessary to meet public health acts as they came along. This inevitably meant his tenements deteriorated into filthy and dangerous slums, but this didn't lower the amount of money they generated for him so what did it matter?

Yes, business was easy. And that was what he had become: a businessman.

And so for years he had been an actor trapped in a single role, one he played day in and day out, a constricting straitjacket of a façade which he could not escape. At the same time, the world of theatre had become bigger than ever, with famous Newmuck venues such as The Royal Nook, The Newmuck Jewel and Saint Tomofumi's Theatre packing in crowds of thousands even as more and more theatres popped up all over the city. Blacklock didn't count those horrible, rowdy little music halls where prostitutes plied their trade and drunken patrons jeered at crude comedians and off-key singers. He didn't care for vaudeville, ballet or opera either. All that dancing and singing, and most of the operas weren't even in English. Or so he gathered, he had never actually been to see one. And the less said about the recent trend of plays dealing with actual social problems, the better. If he wanted to hear poor people complain he would visit one of his tenements.

No, he was talking about real theatres and real plays, those ornate venues where the great playwrights had their work performed, from Milton Booth-Booth's classic tragedy *A King Gets Stabbed* (the reworked version, in which the king doesn't get stabbed, was popular with those sensitive audiences who found the original text too distressing) to William Carnation's witty satire *The Softening of a Gentleman* to countless other dramas, melodramas, comedies and adventures.

Advances in stagecraft helped bring these tales to life – one play, using a system of levers and pulleys and a bucket of water, managed to recreate a 10,000-man naval battle – but of course it was the actors who were the lynchpins on which the entire endeavour relied. Without them it was all just meaningless words on paper left to collect dust on an empty stage.

Britain's acting royalty such as Peter Hunter, Terence Bates, Hilda Godolphin and Scorch Dinsdale were worshipped far and wide, all of them stars who captivated audiences and lit up the stages they graced. Although Blacklock found it a little crass that some of them also worked as directors, producers, writers and theatre managers, believing that such a dilution of focus sullied the purity of the actor's craft.

Blacklock had shelves filled with books and periodicals on acting, a few of which he had almost read in full: the theatre performers of ancient Greece, studies and theories of communication between the actor and audience, symbolism and meaning, different acting styles, physical and emotional expressivity, and something about the "semiotics of acting." He had meant to look up what that meant but hadn't gotten around to it. All of this knowledge was also being shared in theatre schools across Newmuck and it amused Blacklock to think of those vacant, ignorant youths struggling in vain to bring any kind of gravitas or truth to a role, the kind of things that only an artist and creator such as himself could summon.

It had been a long time coming but now the second chance that Blacklock had longed for all these years was within reach. It was why he agreed to join Cecil Burgess in the first place. Because things had to change. At first he believed Cecil to be mad with his talk of the Old Ones, but Blacklock couldn't deny the proof when it was put before him. And of course, the fact that being a member of The Order of the Void occasionally involved dressing up and reciting speeches appealed to the performer inside him.

As a god, Blacklock would play out every role there had ever been and countless yet to be imagined, reality itself would be his stage and humanity his eternal, captive, unblinking audience. He had been born to be a star. And his light would shine forever.

"Unpleasant dreams, Arthur?" croaked a voice from across the room.

"*Jesus Christ!*" Blacklock said as his heart leapt in his chest and he abruptly rose from his chair.

He was in his bedroom but hadn't made it to bed, instead falling asleep in the armchair near one of the windows. The curtains were open but the moon was obscured by clouds and did little to illuminate the darkness in the room. A squat figure came padding across the thick carpet, what little light there was catching the lenses of its spectacles.

"Gerald," Blacklock said, his shoulders sagging, tension draining. "Bloody hell."

Hurriedly wiping at the wet corners of his eyes, Blacklock switched on the lamp that stood on the table next to the armchair, although the corners of the large room remained dim. There was no light from the fireplace, the fire having died out while Blacklock slept.

The main bedroom was one of three bedrooms in the twelve-room, two-storey house. It wasn't the house which had been in his family for four generations, Blacklock had sold that for a handsome profit soon after his mother died, this was a more modern property in an equally upmarket district on the other side of Newmuck. Blacklock lived alone so the house was certainly too big for him, but money wasn't an issue, so why not?

At his feet Blacklock spotted an empty glass and a damp patch and remembered he had been cradling a Scotch before he fell asleep. He picked up the glass, placed it on the table and sat back down in his armchair. He wasn't sure of the time but it must have been the early hours of Sunday morning. He ran a hand over his hair and straightened his waistcoat.

Blacklock wouldn't bother to ask how Gerald had entered his house, he knew locked doors and windows gave the Abyss-Dwellers little trouble, but Gerald's presence still concerned him. He may have convinced Gerald to side with him over Cecil but he wasn't naïve enough to trust the Abyss-Dwellers. Still, he could keep up pretences, and there was no risk of Gerald being discovered: something on which Blacklock had agreed with Cecil was the wisdom of keeping only a small number of part-time servants to lessen the risk of people stumbling onto his secrets. Quinn didn't count, of course, but he wasn't currently at the house anyway, although he was only a phone call away.

"This is a surprise," Blacklock said.

"You were shifting in your sleep," Gerald said. "What were you dreaming of?"

Blacklock smiled. "I don't remember. Dreams are such nonsense anyway. Do Abyss-Dwellers dream?"

"We dream of the Old Ones."

Blacklock resisted rolling his eyes. The Abyss-Dwellers were a predictably single-minded bunch. "Of course."

"Although several decades ago I did have one dream in which a seahorse was giving me banjo lessons. I'm not sure what the significance of that was."

Blacklock poured himself a Scotch from the bottle on the table next to him, not offering Gerald the same, Abyss-Dwellers not drinking alcohol. "So, to what do I owe the pleasure? We only parted ways a few hours ago."

"Oliver Burgess remains alive."

Blacklock sipped his Scotch and listened as Gerald told him of what had occurred at The Bewigged Pig, the story having been relayed by the sole Abyss-Dweller to survive the incident. Blacklock knew how dangerous the creatures could be so was surprised to hear how they had been soundly defeated by five men. Were these the same men who visited Burgess Canning Company? The Roustabouts? It had to be. When Oliver presented his findings on them to the Order he mentioned The Bewigged Pig. But why flee there? For protection? Did he really tell the Order everything at Cecil's house? Was there some sort of connection between the Roustabouts and Oliver that he was hiding? Blacklock had difficulty picturing Oliver lying or manipulating to any real degree but knew he couldn't dismiss the possibility.

After Oliver had taken his surprising leap out of the window and run off into the night, it was Blacklock who suggested that Gerald send some Abyss-Dwellers after him, arguing that although Oliver was a feeble sponge of a man, they shouldn't let him roam free considering what he knew. Orchardson and Sugarfoot were unsure but Gerald agreed after Blacklock insisted they could afford a little boldness given the Ritual of Suth-G'nar was so imminent. Now it seemed his plan had backfired, and Blacklock didn't like looking incompetent. (Although he was still angrier at himself for forgetting the Percival Comb quote and spoiling the end of his speech, he had had it all planned out in his head). He had never expected Oliver to be any sort of problem. As for the Roustabouts, he had no idea what their game was, although if they had indeed butchered a group of Abyss-Dwellers then they were dangerous men if nothing else.

Then Blacklock realised this wasn't his fault after all. He had made the right suggestion, it was the Abyss-Dwellers who couldn't handle the simple task they were set.

"I didn't think your people would have trouble killing a weakling like Oliver," Blacklock said.

If the comment offended Gerald, he didn't show it. "Apparently the men who came to his aid were very powerful. Wurzel said he'd never seen humans fight with such strength or ferocity."

Blacklock blinked. "Wurzel?"

"The Abyss-Dweller who survived. I thought 'Wurzel' would be easier for you. His true name is Whuuur-sh 'Lah-rash Chatal Sahmahnanan Krip-krip Loth Granak."

"Well, my sympathies for your losses." One corner of Blacklock's mouth turned up in a hint of a smile. "Still, plenty more fish in the sea, eh?"

A small crease appeared in the centre of Gerald's brow. "My auntie was sliced in half."

"Oh. Sorry." Blacklock cleared his throat. "So, this is a potential problem. As I said, Oliver knows too much. Anyone he speaks to might not believe him but he could still cause trouble for us, especially if he's being protected."

"I confess to concern of my own. After all, if we'd never agreed to your suggestion of disposing of Cecil and Oliver and placing our faith in you, this never would've happened."

Blacklock frowned. "You're suggesting this is *my* fault."

"Merely an observation."

"I told you we didn't need the Burgesses and I was right. Cecil was arrogant and self-centred and intended to betray us, and Oliver is a worthless fool. And let's not forget, you don't need the Burgesses but you need *someone*, don't you? After all, if the Abyss-Dwellers could summon the Old Ones without the help of human beings, you'd have already done so."

"It's true." Gerald removed his spectacles and breathed on them, the lenses briefly fogging up, Blacklock hiding his disgust as he caught a whiff of the Abyss-Dweller's foul breath. Gerald placed the spectacles back on his snout. "We realised that allying with humans was a necessity in completing the preparations required for the Ritual of Suth-G'nar. The majority of the necessary relics were scattered across your world, not ours, and not only can we survive outside the water only for so long, your species growing and spreading in such vast numbers made it increasingly difficult for us to move around on land at all. When the planets aligned in the past, we were not ready. This time we will be. But we Abyss-Dwellers live very long lives, Arthur, and the Old Ones are eternal. Should the worst happen and the ritual is not performed tomorrow, we can wait another eight centuries. You're unable to say the same. We're relying on you having the wisdom to remember that."

Blacklock tensed but knew Gerald was right. This was his *one* chance to put things right, to become what he should have always been. But he hadn't crumbled under the pressure when bringing Birch Tree No.2 to life and he wouldn't do so now.

Blacklock poured himself another Scotch and gave Gerald a self-assured smile. "Neither of us has anything to worry about. With the remaining ritual relics we took from Cecil's house, we have everything we need. I was giving Oliver too much credit as a potential threat, as far as he's aware the ritual's still taking place beneath the cannery. The actual site is ready and secure, and you saw for yourself earlier tonight the relics are all safe there."

Even with Quinn left to guard the place, Blacklock hadn't been completely comfortable storing the relics where Gerald and the Abyss-Dwellers could get to them, but he was confident that as long as he had the Silent King idol all to himself, the Abyss-Dwellers wouldn't betray him. Also, even though he had never spoken of his true motivation, he believed Gerald recognised his determination to do whatever it took to see the ritual performed.

"All the relics except the Idol of the Silent King," Gerald pointed out. "You've yet to reveal where you've been keeping that."

One of Blacklock's tasks for The Order of the Void had been to locate and arrange for the retrieval of the Idol of the Silent King, one of the relics required for the Ritual of Suth-G'nar, and earlier this year, after a long and expensive search encompassing three countries, he did just that. Except the idol which Blacklock then handed over to Cecil wasn't the genuine relic but a forgery he had commissioned. Because Blacklock had never trusted Cecil and decided that holding back an essential ritual relic for himself was sensible insurance. And although Blacklock told Gerald, Sugarfoot and Orchardson of the forgery when convincing them to betray Cecil, he didn't tell them where the real idol was hidden, just in case they got any ideas about him not being needed any longer.

"The idol is safe," Blacklock said, doing his best not to think about the relic: the rough, clammy, unknown material from which it was carved, the way it made his head swim and eyes water if he looked at it for too long, and of course the horribly misshapen figure of the Silent King itself. "I'll be bringing it to the ritual personally. In the meantime, as you know, it remains in a very secure location to which only I have access, so if anything unfortunate should befall me before then, well... no ritual."

This last sentence was a lie that Blacklock had told before, but it wouldn't hurt to keep Gerald thinking it.

"I hope you realise you can trust us, Arthur," Gerald said. "Just as we've trusted you. Betraying you offers us no advantage, especially at this stage. We have no qualms about cooperating with humans as long as the ritual is performed and the Old Ones summoned."

And I'm sure you offered Cecil the same assurances, Blacklock thought.

"And you have my word your trust in me wasn't misplaced," Blacklock said. "As you'll see tomorrow when the Abyss-Dwellers and The Order of the Void summon the Old Ones and reshape the world."

"And what of Oliver and his protectors?" Gerald asked.

Blacklock knew his initial concern over Oliver and the Roustabouts had been a mistake, he shouldn't be displaying any doubt at such a critical time, he needed everyone to believe he had everything under control. He had to sell the performance.

It's not a performance, he thought. *You* do *have everything under control.*

Blacklock made a dismissive gesture with one hand. "These men were just defending themselves and Oliver, there's a big difference between that and actively interfering in things. As for Oliver himself, we can put plans in place to kill him if the opportunity presents itself, but there's no need to panic. I'll send word to Sugarfoot and Orchardson so they're up to speed."

Gerald's bulging, staring eyes gave no indication as to whether or not he believed in Blacklock's confidence. "What kind of plans did you have in mind?"

Blacklock swirled the Scotch in his glass. "I have an idea."

Far from the Tree

Hiram Avenue was a seven-days-a-week street market in a working-class part of Newmuck, a stretch of colour, activity and noise with numerous stalls crammed together on both sides of the street, the most forward of the traders thrusting goods at passers-by in displays of overly enthusiastic salesmanship.

Behind the stalls were two rows of buildings, a mixture of houses and small businesses including a second-hand clothing shop and a phrenologist's office whose dusty windows held signs such as "Your crippling mental afflictions diagnosed within ten minutes or a percentage of your money back!" and "I will touch your skull!" Pavements separated the buildings from the stalls but most people simply walked in the road, which saw little vehicle traffic.

One end of the street held all of the food and drink offerings while the rest of Hiram Avenue was a mishmash of stalls selling all kinds of goods including jewellery, postcards, clothing and accessories, homemade remedies, and even small dinosaur fossils, a popular collector's item.

As with many markets, however, *caveat emptor* was the order of the day as coloured glass masqueraded as precious stones, fake dresses were about as close to French high-end fashion as a garlic baguette, there was a good reason why some of the "dinosaur" skeletons looked suspiciously like those of rats and cats with extra bones glued on, and the treats offered by some of the more corrupt food-sellers consisted mostly of candle wax, sugar-sweepings, lice, animal hair, and paint.

A good ear was also important, at least if you wanted a chance of understanding the seemingly unintelligible shouting of some stall-owners, as exemplified when a stocky man with untamed ear hair bellowed, "*Punt straahhb tuh pen!*" which Ambrose translated for Oliver as, "A punnet of strawberries for two pence!"

It was a few minutes after nine on Sunday morning and Hiram Avenue was already packed, the weekend traditionally being its busiest period. Bryn, Ambrose, Oliver and Annie walked along the road, making their way through the crowd. They didn't have a specific address for Elizabeth Orchardson and Oliver was concerned she might not even live on this street anymore, it had been a while since he heard she did. He didn't want to incur the wrath of his new acquaintances, including Annie. Even if the world was going to end tomorrow night, he'd still rather not spend what little time he had left in any physical pain if he could avoid it. Although that had basically been his approach to life in general.

Despite the circumstances, Oliver had slept well. Of course he was last in line for any blankets or pillows so had to settle for just a musty towel beneath his head as he lay on the hard wooden floor of The Bewigged Pig, but he quickly fell asleep and didn't open his eyes until Annie threw a pint of water in his face when it was time to get up. Apparently there had been no sign of any Abyss-Dwellers during the night.

It hadn't taken Oliver long to realise why he enjoyed such a deep, peaceful sleep: because he was waking up to a world which no longer had his father in it. At first he felt a twinge of guilt at this realisation but that was quickly replaced by a feeling not of happiness or hope, he wouldn't go that far, but at least of relief, born of the knowledge that he would never again have to face his father's withering glare or cutting words. While etiquette decreed Oliver should wear a black hatband and suit as a sign of mourning, he would sooner wear a colourful banner emblazoned with the message, "I'm glad the bastard's dead." His relief dissipated, however, when he remembered that he wouldn't have much time to enjoy this new world before it was replaced by a much more unpleasant one.

After everyone had risen at The Bewigged Pig, they washed themselves then ate a quick, unhealthy breakfast of packaged bar nibbles, Talbot declaring he was swearing off the whelks for a while. They went over the plan again, Henry warning Oliver, Ambrose, Bryn and Annie to keep an eye out not only for Abyss-Dwellers but also the police as The Order of the Void knew where Oliver lived and the police might also have that information by now.

Oliver was still wearing the same clothes as when he had leapt through his father's window, so Annie dug around in her spare room and found a weathered bowler hat and simple sack coat to help him fit in a little better with her and the Roustabouts while they were out in public.

Henry, Digby and Talbot left for the cooperage which served as Offal Cromwell's headquarters while Oliver, Bryn, Ambrose and Annie hopped onto an omnibus heading in the direction of Hiram Avenue, the two groups agreeing to meet back at The Bewigged Pig later that morning.

It was the first time Oliver had travelled on an omnibus and he didn't much care for the experience, uncomfortably packed with both standing and sitting passengers as it was. At one point Ambrose gave the stranger pressed up against Oliver a hard look and said, "Put it back." Oliver then saw the stranger slip Oliver's wallet back into the trouser pocket from which he had lifted it, having pickpocketed Oliver without him even noticing. The would-be thief sheepishly apologised and hurriedly got off at the next stop while Oliver thanked Ambrose.

The four of them disembarked a few streets away from Hiram Avenue and walked the rest of the way, Annie checking with the men that they all had their story straight for Elizabeth Orchardson.

They were about two-thirds of the way along Hiram Avenue when Annie said, "I better ask someone or we'll be wandering around here all day."

Oliver, Ambrose and Bryn followed Annie as she walked to a nearby stall offering a selection of soaps, ladies' cosmetics and men's bathroom items such as straight razors and pomade. The short, middle-aged woman standing behind the stall's waist-high counter locked her eyes onto Annie and smiled as the younger woman approached.

"You there, sweetheart!" the stall-owner said, and she waved a hand over the products on display. "You look like you can spot a bargain! I've got everything you need right here to make you look and feel like a princess, all at prices so low you'll think I've gone daft!"

Annie and the three men stood before the stall, Oliver eyeing with a little concern some strange-looking face-masks.

"See, this one knows!" the stall-owner said, pointing at Oliver. "Why not treat yourself to one of these regenerating face-masks, sir? These'll cleanse impurities, deliver essential oils and aerate your fibulas! Leave one of these on overnight and you'll wake up looking and feeling ten years younger, guaranteed!"

"What are they made of?" Oliver asked.

The stall-owner winked. "Trade secret, I'm afraid."

"Only it looks like ham."

"We're not looking to buy, we were just wondering if you could help us," Annie said.

The stall-owner's smile fell as if its strings had been cut. "If you're not buying then clear out of the way for those who are."

"This'll only take a second. I'm looking for a friend of mine, I was told she lives on this street. Her name's Elizabeth Orchardson."

"What's she look like?"

"She's in her twenties. She's an artist. Maybe. Um…" Annie hesitated. "Alright, look, she's not my friend but it's very important I find her."

The smile returned to the stall-owner's face but it was a different kind of smile now. "I'm here every day rain or shine, I might know who you mean. But you know, her address escapes me without the proper incentive."

Annie nudged Oliver with an elbow. He looked at her then the older woman, both of whom were looking at him expectantly. "Ah," he said.

Oliver took a five-pence coin from his wallet and handed it to the stall-owner, who swiftly pocketed it.

"Where does she live?" Annie asked.

The stall-owner looked away with a frown and tapped her chin with an index finger. "Now where was it again? I've almost got it, I reckon I'm about halfway there."

Bryn planted his hands on the counter and leaned forward. "Don't push your luck, love. Where is she?"

The stall-owner took Bryn's advice. "I don't know her name but if it's the girl I'm thinking of, she's got rooms at number 73. Across the street, a little further up."

Annie gave her an insincere smile. "Very kind of you."

Oliver, Annie, Bryn and Ambrose turned and crossed the street, cutting through the flowing throng. They passed through the narrow gap between two stalls and stepped onto the pavement, the foot-traffic on the pavements a lot lighter than in the road. Keeping an eye on the numbers of the buildings they passed, they soon reached 73 Hiram Avenue, a drab two-storey house flanked on one side by a similar house and on the other by a haberdashery. The glass in the ground-floor windows was grimy and covered up from inside by yellowed newspapers. When Annie moved to knock on the front door she found it ajar, so the four of them stepped through the doorway and into a short, dusty hallway containing two doors and a set of stairs leading to the second floor.

After knocking on the two ground-floor doors and receiving no answer, they made their way upstairs and Annie knocked on the only door on the second-floor landing. From the other side of the door came a loud, metallic clatter and a woman's voice shouting, "*Oh, bloody, buggering, shitting hell!*"

Oliver, Annie, Bryn and Ambrose looked at each other, then a few seconds later the door opened inwards and standing there was a chubby, twenty-something woman with dark-brown eyes and long, black hair tied up in a messy bun, strands hanging around her face. She was barefoot and wore dark trousers with a loose-fitting shirt, the sleeves rolled up around her forearms, a simple silver necklace hanging around her neck. Spots of paint in a rainbow of colours were spattered across her clothing and bare skin.

"Yes?" the woman said.

"Sorry to bother you," Annie said, "but are you Elizabeth Orchardson?"

"Please, call me Lizzie," Lizzie Orchardson said with a friendly smile. "How can I help?"

"My friends and I are trying to find your father, we were wondering if you might be able to help. It's urgent."

Lizzie's smile melted away. "You must be desperate if you're coming to me." She sighed. "Alright, come in."

Lizzie turned and walked away and the four visitors followed her into the flat. "Excuse my language earlier, I'm just working on something," she said.

It was clear the second floor of the building had once been split into three smaller rooms but that the walls which separated them had all been knocked through, meaning the second floor was now just one large space, brightly lit thanks to its four windows, two overlooking Hiram Avenue and two overlooking the alley behind the building, the room's white walls adding to its open feel. A few frayed rugs covered little of the paint-spattered floorboards, and although the room contained other things that suggested someone lived there – a bed, a chair, a chest of drawers, a washstand, some clothing and books – it was largely bare except for the art.

A number of painted canvases were scattered around the edges of the room, none of them framed or attached to walls but carelessly discarded on the floor. Each canvas bore a different image but each was a jumble of colours brushed, smeared, flicked and stabbed onto the material seemingly at random in most cases, with few recognisable shapes and patterns in sight. A wooden easel stood in a corner of the room, paints and brushes and a jar of dirty water on a stool next to it.

Then there were the sculptures, over a dozen of them around the room, varying in size, the tallest over eight feet, a stepladder standing next to it. Like the paintings, the sculptures didn't seem intended to represent actual objects, instead their various parts twisted and pointed and looped and connected with no rhyme or reason, or at least none that Oliver could discern. Adding to their chaotic nature was the selection of materials they were made from: wood, metal, cloth, wire, paper, rubber, glass, slate, and in one case several rotting heads of cauliflower. Pieces of these materials and others lay strewn across the floor, along with a selection of tools.

"Oliver said you were an artist," Annie said uncertainly as she looked around. "Of a sort."

Lizzie came to a stop at the tallest sculpture and bent down to pick up a piece of metal tubing and a pot of glue with a small brush sticking out of it. "Oliver who?"

"Oh, I'm Oliver Burgess," Oliver said. "I… worked with your father for a time. I heard about you being an artist."

With the metal tubing in one hand and glue in the other, Lizzie climbed the stepladder and continued working on the sculpture, although Oliver couldn't see how you would be able to tell if it was finished or not.

"Not from Frederick you didn't, I'm sure," Lizzie said as she smeared glue onto one end of the tubing. "His daughter the troublesome embarrassment to his good name who simply won't do as she's told. I've never exactly been a point of pride for him."

Although Oliver could go on all day about disapproving fathers, he thought it best not to open that can of worms.

"You're not close, then?" Ambrose asked.

Lizzie barked a bitter laugh, jammed the glue-covered end of the metal tubing against a chunk of different metal near the top of the sculpture and held it in place as she looked down at Oliver, Annie, Bryn and Ambrose. "We haven't seen each other in years. I'd like to keep it that way and I'm certain he feels the same. He essentially disowned me a long time ago. Or I disowned him. Either way, neither of us wants anything to do with the other. It's probably the only thing we have in common. So no, we're not close. You know, you don't strike me as the kind of people my father would usually associate with." She looked at Oliver. "Except maybe you. Anyway, whatever business you have with Frederick, it's none of mine. But I might be able to point you in his direction."

"Are you sure you don't want to hear why we're looking for your dad?" Ambrose asked. "It's a good story." He grunted as Annie nudged him in the ribs.

"Can you give us your father's address?" Annie asked.

"42 Adler Lane, it's on the west end of Stowbrook Hill," Lizzie said. "At least that's where we were living when I left home. If he's moved since then, your guess is as good as mine."

"That's very helpful, thank you."

"He probably won't be there today, though."

"Why not?"

Lizzie studied the spot where she had glued the metal tubing to the sculpture then, apparently satisfied, released her grip and descended the stepladder. "Because I assume today Frederick will be at the Annual Newmuck Bankers Garden Party. They used to hold it on the same date every year and he never missed it. Not because he does anything as frivolous as have fun, it's all business for him, what with anyone who's anyone in the city's banking industry attending. It's a predictable, nauseating event filled with predictable, nauseating people. When I was eighteen and Frederick still held onto a tiny, vain hope of marrying me off, he made the mistake of insisting I accompany him to that year's party. I didn't see much appeal in becoming a man's property so I wasn't exactly receptive to the idea. Less than an hour after we arrived, he was furiously bundling me into a carriage and sending me home. One of my potential suitors had been arguing in favour of beating servants and I made my opposing argument by dunking his head in the punch bowl. My father didn't ask me to attend again."

"Where's this party taking place?" Ambrose asked.

"11 Envy Crescent, Fondle Green. It's a mansion owned by Richard Patmore, one of Newmuck's wealthiest bankers, at least according to my father. The one time I met him he certainly seemed to be one of the most boring. And he was up against some stiff competition. The party usually starts in the morning and it's a very exclusive, invitation-only event, I doubt the guards will let you past the gate."

"Don't you worry," Bryn said with a wink, "we've got a knack for dealing with guards."

Lizzie looked Bryn up and down, which could take some time if you were being particularly thorough, and smiled. "I'm sure you have. But you'll be outnumbered perhaps ten-to-one, they take security seriously there, although God knows why. Maybe they're terrified someone interesting will sneak in and mingle."

"Alright, thanks again for your help," Annie said.

"You're welcome."

Lizzie walked them to the door. Then, as they stepped out onto the landing, she said, "Wait, apart from Oliver here, I don't know your names."

Annie introduced herself then Bryn and Ambrose.

"It was a pleasure to meet you," Lizzie said. "Listen, I've got a new exhibition opening at Warblesworth Gallery next Friday, why don't you come along?"

The four visitors looked at each other uncertainly, making muttered, halting excuses.

"It's nice of you to offer," Annie said eventually, "but I don't think any of us know much about art."

"Neither do most of the critics in this city," Lizzie said with a conspiratorial smile. "Well, if you change your mind, feel free to pop in. There'll be plenty of food, all *gratis*."

"I don't think I've ever tried gratis before," Ambrose said. "Is it spicy?"

"No, it means the food is free."

"Will there be tiny sausages on sticks?" Bryn asked.

"Possibly," Lizzie said.

"*With* tiny blocks of cheese?"

"I don't see why not."

Bryn grinned. "Now, I may not know much about art but I know what I like, and I bloody love tiny sausages and cheese on sticks. I'll see *you* Friday."

Oliver, Annie, Bryn and Ambrose descended the stairs, exited the house and stood on the pavement outside.

"She's much nicer than her father," Oliver said.

"She wasn't trying to kill you, that's always a good start," Bryn said. "But yes, lovely woman."

"If Orchardson isn't likely to be at home then there's no point us wasting time going to his house," Ambrose said. "As for this garden party, we should probably speak to the others first, wait until they get back from Cromwell's place and see what they've found out."

"Agreed," Annie said. "We'll head to Oliver's house then back to the Pig."

Oliver groaned inwardly. He had been hoping Annie forgot about that. He didn't mind giving her money, he felt bad about what the Abyss-Dwellers had done to her pub, it was the danger inherent in fetching it that gave him pause. When it came to dying at home, Oliver liked to envision the scenario more as "Dying peacefully in your bed while surrounded by loved ones" than "Dying in agony in the pantry while surrounded by monsters poking you with pointy metal things."

Drinks on Steve

Flanked by Henry and Talbot, Digby knocked on the steel door and waited, tense, his hands clenched into fists down at his sides. He didn't like coming back to the old neighbourhood. Shinglesgate was a rough area but it wasn't the dangers of its poverty-stricken, crime-riddled streets that gave Digby pause. It was the memories.

The three men stood in an enclosed courtyard at the rear of Shinglesgate Cooperage, a two-storey brick building and the outwardly legitimate business which Cromwell had been running for years as a front for some of his numerous illegal dealings. To be fair, the coopers and hoopers he employed were good at their jobs and the barrels, kegs, casks, troughs, tubs, vats, and other containers the cooperage produced were of high quality, so the breweries and shipping companies that made up the majority of Cromwell's customer base didn't even need to be strong-armed into signing contracts. Most of the time, anyway.

Weeds sprouted from the dirt floor of the courtyard and the spike-topped brick walls that surrounded it were tall enough to keep out prying eyes. Digby, Henry and Talbot had entered through an iron gate that connected the courtyard to a system of narrow alleys that ran between the cooperage and several nearby factories. It was a private spot where you were unlikely to be disturbed, and Digby knew from experience that the dirt of the courtyard had soaked up a lot of blood over the years.

There was a rectangular slot cut into the steel door at head-height and now the steel plate that covered it slid open to reveal a pair of suspicious eyes that took in the Roustabouts, lingering on Digby.

"What do you want?" asked the man behind the door.

"Tell Offal we're here to see him, O'Driscoll," Digby said.

O'Driscoll hesitated then slid the steel plate back into place. Almost a minute passed before there came the sound of several locks being opened, then the hinges of the thick door screeched as it swung open, revealing the large figure and grim face of O'Driscoll.

"The boss says he'll see you," O'Driscoll said.

"Of course he'll see us," Henry said as he, Digby and Talbot entered the building.

Followed by O'Driscoll, they made their way along the gloomy, windowless hallway lit only by one bare ceiling bulb, the walls unpainted brickwork. From the front of the building came the muffled sounds of clattering wood and the hammering of metal on metal as the coopers and hoopers went about their work. The Roustabouts turned right into another, shorter hallway with two doors leading off it. They opened the one they wanted and entered the room beyond.

Like the adjoining hallway, Cromwell's office featured no windows but was brighter and cosier thanks to its wall-mounted lights and fireplace, its brick walls papered over and wood-panelled. Mounted on a rack on one wall was a police cutlass. A lot of people had asked Cromwell about that cutlass over the years but as far as Digby knew he had only told the story behind it to a handful of people, Digby being one of them.

Facing the door was Cromwell's wide wooden desk while a large metal safe and a liquor cabinet occupied the far corners of the room. There were three armchairs, two on opposite sides of the room and one behind the desk, and a coat-rack stood near the door. At one side of the room was a pool table, its surface scuffed and faded, a cue rack attached to the wall nearby.

Dressed in a shirt and braces, Cromwell sat behind his desk, a lit cigarette between his lips. He smiled at the Roustabouts. "Look who it is. Because you lads hadn't already brightened up my weekend enough."

Cromwell looked at O'Driscoll and motioned with his head and O'Driscoll left the room, closing the door behind him.

In the office were two men Digby didn't recognise. One, a wiry man in a scruffy suit with swept-back blonde hair, was playing pool alone. He held a cue in his hands and had been lining up a shot but now slowly rose to his full height as he glared at the Roustabouts. The second man appeared unconcerned as he sat in an armchair, idly twirling a matchstick between the fingers of one hand. His shoes, shirt, trousers, waistcoat and tie were clean and neat and a little on the flashy side. He was slim and looked to be in his twenties, with short, black hair, blue eyes and a clean-shaven face.

Cromwell sat back in his chair and took a drag on his cigarette. Strong and fast in his younger days, years of unhealthy living had taken their toll and he had gotten fat. He was pushing fifty now, his black hairs gradually being overwhelmed by the grey. But whatever his physical changes, Digby knew Cromwell remained the same ruthless, conniving, self-centred, crooked bastard he had always been.

"Digby, my boy," Cromwell said. "It's been too long. Always a pleasure to see your gigglemug."

"I was worried you might not be eating enough," Digby said. "Obviously I was wrong."

Cromwell smiled. "I'm not quite as spry as back in my old van-dragging days, I'll admit. You know, I think that sparkling wit is one of the things I miss most about you. I've always said it's a shame you lost your nerve."

"Go for the pistol you keep in your desk and I'll show you my nerve."

"Why would I do that to an old friend?" Cromwell leaned forward, his expression hard now. "Oh, that's right, maybe because you killed two of my boys on Friday night. And the ones who survived aren't gonna be much use anytime soon either."

"You sent those men into *our* neighbourhood, Offal," Henry said. "You pushed your luck and they paid for it."

"Plus they seemed like a bunch of arseholes," Talbot added.

The blonde man took a step towards them, gripping his pool cue tightly. "*Bastards!*" he hissed, his eyes fixed on Talbot.

Talbot shrugged. "Arseholes, bastards… you knew them better, I suppose."

"Settle down, Steve," Cromwell said to the blonde man before turning his attention back to the Roustabouts. "One of the blokes you killed was Steve's brother, so you can understand he's a little upset."

"Did he look like you only a bit shorter, with dark hair?" Talbot asked Steve.

"Yeah," Steve said. "Why?"

"It was me that killed him. Don't know my own strength sometimes."

"*I'll kill you!*" Steve growled as he came forward.

"I doubt that, lad."

"*Back off, Steve!*" Cromwell shouted, and Steve stopped in his tracks. "*Now!*"

Steve glared at Talbot for a few more seconds, his chest rising and falling, before reluctantly stepping back to the far side of the pool table. He looked at the smartly-dressed man, who was smirking, and said, "And *you* can wipe that smile off your face!"

"Remember who you're talking to, Steve," the other man said calmly, his smirk still firmly in place. "Or you'll be in a barrel at the bottom of the Brazenbrook before the sun goes down."

Looking at the Roustabouts, Cromwell nodded towards the man in the armchair. "I don't know if you've met: this is Caleb, my right hand as of a few weeks ago. He joined up with me last year and has done top-notch work since then. Boy's got a bright future."

"What happened to Barker?" Digby asked.

Cromwell shrugged. "He served me well for a long time but I had to let him go in the end."

"Out of a fourth-floor window, I'm guessing."

"It wasn't the fall that killed him," Caleb said, staring at Digby.

"Caleb," Cromwell said, "this is Digby, Henry and Talbot, three-fifths of the Roustabouts, the five pains in my arse I told you about who live over in Wealdbury. We go back a long way, don't we, lads?"

"So do me and gout, and I've got about as much affection for that," Talbot said.

"You lot have had a busy weekend all round from what I've heard. A little bird told me there was a big bust-up at The Bewigged Pig last night. Annie's alright, I hope. I'd hate to see a tasty bird like her get damaged."

"Because if anyone knows how to look after women, it's a pimp," Digby said.

"My girls are treated better than a lot in this city, you know that. The newspapers and the church can bang on about 'reclaiming fallen women' all they want, like they know anything about how the real world works."

Digby wasn't in the mood for this. He took a step towards Cromwell's desk. Steve tensed. Neither Cromwell nor Caleb twitched.

"Let's keep this simple," Digby said impatiently. "You're going to tell us what we want to know or we're going to tear this place down with you and all your goons still inside it."

"And what is it you'd like to know?" Cromwell asked.

"Why don't we start with why you tried extorting Randolph Sowerby," Henry said. "You know Wealdbury's off-limits. It's not like you to be foolish enough to get on our bad side, Offal."

Cromwell smiled. "Let's just call it misguided enthusiasm."

"Would that enthusiasm have anything to do with Arthur Blacklock?"

It was the slightest of reactions but Digby caught it. "Never heard of him," Cromwell said.

"You're lying," Digby said flatly.

"We know you've had dealings with Blacklock," Henry said. "So is that it? You start hobnobbing with Newmuck's rich and powerful and that gives you ideas about expansion? Because you're hitching your wagon to the wrong horse there."

"Say I did know this Blacklock," Cromwell said. "What's he to you?"

"We need to find him. Today. We know that a few months ago Blacklock wanted to get his hands on some pages from a certain book and you stole them for him. You may be an immoral, parasitic, lard-scented piece of gutter-filth –"

"I'll have you know that's *Larde for Men* by Swishums Dumas, it's eighty pence a bottle."

"–but you're not completely stupid. I don't believe for one second you'd have gone into business with Blacklock without finding out what you could about him first in case it might offer you some kind of advantage. So give us his home address and we'll be on our way."

"Any chance you'd tell me who's been talking to you about my business affairs?" Cromwell waited a moment. "I didn't think so. So what did Blacklock do to get your backs up?"

"You wouldn't believe us if we told you," Henry said. "But you can take our word for it that us finding him as soon as possible is in everyone's best interests, including yours."

"I am a man who likes to look after his interests. The Blacklock job wasn't easy but it got done, largely thanks to Caleb here. I only met Blacklock twice. After our first meeting, I had him followed. Like you said, I'm not stupid. He lives at 55 Wood Street, in Milner Park. Nice little place."

"Alright, then. If you go near the Sowerbys again or try to worm your way into Wealdbury in any other way, we'll be back and next time we won't knock. Behave yourself, Offal."

"Or don't," Digby said. "Give us an excuse."

Digby, Henry and Talbot turned to leave and that was when Steve charged at them, his pool cue raised. Digby spun around and stepped in close to Steve, who swung the cue, the two men close enough that the cue only caught Digby a glancing blow on his left shoulder. Digby yanked the cue out of Steve's hands, drove its bottom end into his gut, then dropped it and grabbed Steve by the lapels of his suit jacket. Digby threw him across the room, Steve scattering items off one side of Cromwell's desk as he tumbled across it before smashing into the liquor cabinet, splintering wood and shattering glass. Steve came to rest on the floor, bloody and dazed and soaked in alcohol.

Cromwell frowned at the mess then at the Roustabouts while Caleb twirled his matchstick with a flat expression.

"Your men aren't what they used to be, Offal," Digby said.

Cromwell stared at him. "Oh, I know."

The Importance of Brushing

Oliver turned the key in the lock and gently pushed open the door, expecting a trident to come hurtling through the air and for him to die looking like a sausage pinned by a fork. Bryn entered the house first, followed by Oliver, Annie and Ambrose. They stood in the hallway, listening, but the only sound was the ticking of the grandfather clock in the adjoining parlour.

"I think we're alright," Bryn said.

From a discreet distance they had watched Oliver's house and the small plot of land on which it stood and saw no signs of any police or Abyss-Dwellers. None of Oliver's neighbours were out in their gardens as Oliver, Annie, Bryn and Ambrose clambered over the short hedge that marked the rear boundary of the property and hurried to the back door, following a gravel path flanked by neat, close-cropped lawns, colourful flowerbeds and a rockery.

Although the interior of the house seemed as unguarded as the exterior, they didn't want to linger any longer than necessary, although Oliver certainly wished he could just curl up in his favourite armchair in front of the fire and forget the world outside with a soft blanket and a nice nap.

"Where do you keep your money?" Annie asked Oliver.

"Under my bed, upstairs," Oliver said.

Bryn smiled. "You can tell a bloke's rich when he keeps money under his bed and not mucky pamphlets."

Oliver, Annie and Ambrose all looked at him. His smile faltered.

"What?" Bryn said. "I mean, *I* don't, obviously. And anything Digby might tell you about him selling me any is a bloody lie."

The hallway split the ground floor of the house, the back door at one end and the front door at the other, and the group walked towards the stairs that led up to the second floor, passing ornament-filled shelves and paintings of pastoral scenes, the hallway's wooden floor polished to a shine. Bryn and Ambrose poked their heads into the rooms they passed – pantry, water closet, kitchen, parlour, dining room – but saw nothing out of the ordinary. The Roustabouts repeated the process on the second floor, checking the bathroom and two spare bedrooms before finally coming to the main bedroom, which Oliver, Annie and Bryn entered while Ambrose remained on the landing to keep watch.

"You said you've got someone who works for you?" Annie said to Oliver.

"Mrs. Madsen, yes," Oliver said.

"Just the one? Don't people like you usually have a team of servants waiting on them hand and foot?"

"Mrs. Madsen is very capable, she can do the work of three people. But she's not around at the moment, she gave birth last week and I told her to take as much time off as she needed. I'm afraid I don't give her much to do anyway, I like to cook and I don't mind seeing to my own clothes and keeping the place tidy."

The bedroom curtains were closed but enough daylight filtered through that the gloom wasn't deep, and Annie looked around at creaseless sheets on a four-poster bed, a fireplace without a speck of ash beyond the grate, and a wardrobe and other pieces of furniture with no trace of dust on them, everything clean and orderly.

"I can see that," Annie said.

Oliver knelt next to his bed and reached beneath the frilled valance that surrounded its base. He withdrew a leather satchel and stood up as Annie and Bryn came to stand at his sides. Oliver opened the satchel then turned it upside-down and hundreds of pounds in banknotes and coins of various denominations spilled onto the bed.

Oliver turned to Annie. "How much do you think –"

Annie took the satchel from his hands and began scooping the money – *all* of the money – back into it. But then she paused at the sound of the front door opening downstairs, accompanied by two voices.

"– saw something round the back, I'm sure of it." A young man, earnest and keen.

"My attention was focused on Mrs. Plipp's raspberry crumble." An older man, more jaded.

Oliver, Annie and Bryn looked over at Ambrose, who carefully leaned over the banister that ran along the landing, looked down at the ground floor, then turned and tiptoed into the main bedroom. He hooked a thumb back over his shoulder in the direction of the stairs.

"Police!" Ambrose whispered.

"Shit!" Annie whispered. "We have to hide."

"Bollocks to that," Bryn said.

The younger policeman had been talking but now stopped suddenly, and there was a moment of silence before he said, "Did you hear something?"

Annie glared at Bryn, who gave her an apologetic look. She looked around frantically until her eyes settled on the wide wardrobe standing against a wall. "In there."

"Really?" Ambrose said sceptically.

"Would you rather beat up a couple of innocent bobbies?" Annie whispered impatiently, already ushering the three men towards the wardrobe.

"Well, no –"

"Then shut up and get your arse in that wardrobe!"

The sound of two pairs of feet ascending the stairs could be heard as Oliver opened the double-doors of the wardrobe before being pushed inside alongside Bryn and Ambrose, Annie entering last and pulling the doors closed after her, cramming the four of them in amongst the shirts, trousers, waistcoats, coats, belts and ties, Bryn and Ambrose having to stoop to fit. Oliver had never been a slave to fashion and was glad of it now as the wardrobe struggled to contain the four of them and the modest amount of clothes he kept in there.

"The money!" Annie whispered suddenly.

She moved to open the doors again but then stopped as the two policemen stepped onto the landing, their voices louder now.

"I hope you realise my crumble's getting colder by the minute, Schilling," the older policeman said.

"We shouldn't have gone in there in the first place," the younger policeman, Schilling, argued. "We were supposed to be keeping watch on this house."

"And we did. For over two sodding hours, with no sign of this Burgess character. Very nice of the lady next door to invite us in for a cup of tea and a bowl of crumble, I thought. Trust me, lad, you've only been on the force a couple of months, stick with it and you'll soon see you're not going to get offers like that often. Most of the time you're more likely to be invited to kiss someone's arse as they run off in the other direction."

The wardrobe doors were solid wood so it was impossible to see through them but Oliver could hear the two policemen making their way towards the main bedroom. His heart was pounding, mostly due to the threat of discovery but also partly due to Annie being pressed up against him. He wasn't used to such close contact with the fairer sex. Thinking mild, inoffensive thoughts was nothing new to him but now he had to force himself to do so in order to ignore the feeling of Annie's shoulder against his chest, the smell of her hair in his nostrils, the soft sound of her breathing and oh God if this went on much longer his little gentleman was going to stand to attention.

"Mrs. Plipp was very nice but it's not right for an officer to leave his post," Schilling said. "We're just lucky I spotted movement at the back of this place through her parlour window."

"You didn't see anything outside and you didn't hear anything up here," the older officer said as the policemen entered the room. "Look, all I want –"

Silence.

Then two pairs of feet moving towards the bed, slowly.

More silence until eventually the older officer said, "That's a lot of money."

"Do you suppose Burgess is here?" Schilling asked, lowering his voice slightly. "Benchley, what are you doing?"

"Just… checking the money, that's all," Benchley said. "There might be a clue."

"Should we search the house for Burgess?"

"Well, what we *really* should do is take this money and leave. It's evidence, this. And evidence is absolutely vital in the policing game, oh yes."

"Right. What if I search the house and you look after the evidence?"

A man forcing himself not to grin generally doesn't make a sound, but if it did then the four people hiding inside the wardrobe would have heard it loud and clear now. "Fine idea, Schilling. *Fine* idea. You're going to go far on the force, I can tell."

Schilling sniffed the air. "Can you smell that?"

"Smell what?" Benchley asked over the sound of banknotes and coins being swept into a satchel.

"Smells like… fish."

It took a moment but then realisation dawned inside the wardrobe. Bryn and Ambrose flung open the doors and leapt out, followed by Oliver and Annie and various items of clothing.

Schilling and Benchley wore constable's uniforms and helmets, Schilling clean-shaven and barely in his twenties while Benchley had a black moustache and looked to be on the far side of forty. Each stood frozen, staring in shock at the four strangers who had burst from the wardrobe, Benchley leaning over the money on the bed with Oliver's satchel in one hand while Schilling stood nearby.

Behind them, out on the landing, was the source of the smell: Abyss-Dwellers. Moving stealthily, some were clambering up over the banister while others walked into view from the sides of the doorway, at least half a dozen that Oliver could see, all converging on the main bedroom, their pointed teeth bared, rusty weapons gripped in their webbed claws.

Oliver felt his legs go weak, his little gentleman definitely in no more danger of standing to attention. He didn't know where the Abyss-Dwellers had been hiding but clearly they were waiting for him and he walked right into their trap. He briefly considered another window-dive but doubted he would be so lucky a second time. Also, he felt guilty at the thought of abandoning Annie, Bryn and Ambrose. He was the one who had brought these monsters to their door in the first place, after all. He never liked to leave a mess, so he supposed it was only right he should do what he could to clean up the biggest mess he had ever created. Although he wondered if that would add up to anything more than crying, fouling himself and being horribly murdered.

Bryn grabbed a nearby footstool and hurled it towards the doorway, the constables ducking away from it, their eyes following the footstool as it sailed between them and slammed into the face of the Abyss-Dweller at the head of the group entering the room. The creature gave a pained croak and stumbled backwards, bouncing off one of his companions and falling to the floor.

Already in a state of shock, Schilling and Benchley found themselves even more shocked as they came face-to-face with the Abyss-Dwellers. Bryn and Ambrose rushed past the policemen and barrelled into the creatures, Bryn lifting one of them off his feet and using him as a shield as he ran out onto the landing, scattering the Abyss-Dwellers out there and taking some with him as he smashed through the landing railing, tumbling over the edge and out of sight.

"Bryn!" Annie called out.

An Abyss-Dweller inside the bedroom swung his machete only for Ambrose to steal the weapon and plunge the blade into the creature's throat, black blood spurting into the air and across Ambrose's shirt. Ambrose withdrew the machete and kicked the dying Abyss-Dweller away then turned to Oliver and Annie.

"Catch!" Ambrose said as he threw the weapon towards them, the blade pointing upwards.

Although part of Oliver instinctively wanted to catch the machete, he felt a stronger instinct to not risk losing any fingers, so he flinched away from the weapon, drawing his hands close to his chest. He felt a little stab of shame as Annie smoothly caught the machete by the handle then gave him a disapproving glance, but it was preferable to picking his severed digits up off the floor.

More Abyss-Dwellers appeared in the bedroom doorway but Ambrose was already on them, forcing them back out onto the landing.

"Come on or we'll be trapped in here!" Annie said to Oliver, who followed her as she hurried towards the doorway, pausing briefly to address Schilling and Benchley: "Those things want to kill us all, so get moving!"

Apparently in agreement that doing what the machete-wielding wardrobe-woman suggested was probably the best idea under the circumstances, Schilling and Benchley drew their truncheons and followed Annie and Oliver out onto the landing, Ambrose fighting several Abyss-Dwellers near the head of the stairs while from downstairs came the sounds of crashing furniture, monstrous growling and inventive Welsh cursing. Oliver had no idea how many Abyss-Dwellers were in the house but there seemed to be no shortage of them as another one leapt up off the stairs and onto the landing, separating Annie and Oliver from Schilling and Benchley. The creature jabbed a harpoon at the two constables, who stepped backwards while waving their truncheons.

Annie darted forward with a roar and plunged her machete into the Abyss-Dweller's back. The creature cried out, Annie losing her grip on her weapon as the Abyss-Dweller spun around and swung his harpoon, the metal shaft smacking Annie across her temple. She grunted and collapsed, unconscious, as Schilling and Benchley attacked the Abyss-Dweller from behind, battering him with their truncheons.

Frozen to the spot, Oliver watched all of this happen, aware he really should be doing something. Enjoying an extended holiday in Switzerland, perhaps.

"*Oliver!*" Ambrose shouted.

Oliver turned to see Ambrose drive his left fist into an Abyss-Dweller's gut then his right fist into his head, knocking him down. Two other Abyss-Dwellers already lay on the floor around Ambrose, one dead while the other appeared to be in enough pain that he wished he was. Even so, Oliver could see two more creatures coming up the stairs while another emerged from one of the spare bedrooms.

"Get Annie away from these bastards!" Ambrose said.

"*Where?*" Oliver asked frantically.

"I don't know, it's your house!"

As Ambrose dodged an incoming sword swing then punched his attacker in the mouth, Oliver squatted near Annie's head, slipped his arms beneath her armpits and lifted her upper body off the floor, her head dangling to one side. Moving backwards in an awkward crouch-walk, Annie's heels dragging across the floor, Oliver hurried towards the nearest doorway, which turned out to lead to the bathroom. He set Annie down on the tile floor, being careful with her head, then returned to the doorway to see an Abyss-Dweller running at him with a raised sword. Oliver screamed, slammed the door shut, slid the bolt into place then fell on his arse and scrambled away, his bowler hat falling from his head as the Abyss-Dweller charged into the door, rattling it in its frame.

When his panicked, half-blind scramble caused him to slam into the porcelain bath at the far end of the room, Oliver yelped then got to his feet and looked around frantically as the door shook again, the frame splintering near the lock with a sharp cracking sound that was loud against the background din of the ongoing fighting.

The window? No, he assumed that dropping an unconscious woman from a second-storey window was a stupid idea if you were trying to protect her.

Hide in the bath? No, that was stupid as well, just in a different way.

Drown himself in the washbasin before the Abyss-Dweller could kill him? Maybe.

Oliver realised there was nowhere to run or hide and that the washbasin had no water in it anyway. Another bang and the door finally flew open, the lock breaking off. Oliver's right hand shot out and grabbed something off the nearby washstand, he didn't even look at what it was, his attention focused on the Abyss-Dweller as the creature stepped into the bathroom.

"*Stay back!*" Oliver cried, his voice trembling, Annie lying between him and the Abyss-Dweller. Overcoming a very strong self-preservation instinct, Oliver took a step closer to her in a protective gesture. "I'm warning you! Don't make me use this!"

Oliver thrust the toothbrush out before him in both hands.

Oliver and the Abyss-Dweller looked at the toothbrush then back at each other.

"Oh, bugger," Oliver said.

The Abyss-Dweller howled in rage and raised his sword as Oliver screamed in terror and hurled his toothbrush.

He watched the toothbrush turn end over end, aware that as a man's final act of defiance it wasn't much. Then he saw the toothbrush enter the gaping mouth of the Abyss-Dweller and disappear. The creature's howl was abruptly cut off and his already bulging eyes bulged even further as he reached his free claw towards his throat and uttered a choking sound. He took a faltering step forward and dropped his sword to the tiles with a metallic clatter, both claws at his throat as he stumbled sideways and crashed into a wall-mounted mirror, glass shards falling as he gasped for air, his gills apparently useless in this situation. He sank to one knee, clawing desperately at his throat, his head shuddering as he stared at Oliver. One final, barely audible squeak escaped the Abyss-Dweller's mouth before he fell forward and hit the floor with a damp slap.

Oliver stared at the Abyss-Dweller. He had killed the creature. *Him.* Oliver Burgess. He had stood his ground, stared death in the face, killed the monster and saved Annie's life. *Him.*

Oliver came out of his daze with a start when another Abyss-Dweller, this one with a screaming, truncheon-swinging Schilling clinging onto his back, slammed face-first into the bathroom doorframe then spun away.

Oliver checked on Annie, who remained unconscious, then moved to the doorway, pausing to pick up a large shard of broken mirror from the floor. His heart was hammering in his chest and he could almost feel the blood surging through his veins, everything around him – smells, sights, sounds – standing out in vibrant detail as if his senses were suddenly supercharged, he was Oliver ruddy Burgess and he was *alive* and if those sea-dwelling bastards or Arthur Blacklock or anyone else thought they could stop him then they had another thing –

Darkness.

"–ess?" A voice.

The darkness began to slowly dissipate and with it came faint sounds and shapes. And pain.

"Burgess?" The same voice. A woman. Louder now.

More awareness, more pain. Oliver tried to retreat from it, back into sweet oblivion.

"Wake up, you useless git!" The woman was annoyed. And familiar.

There was no fighting it. Oliver groaned as the world swam into focus before his narrowed eyes, pinpricks of light floating across his vision. He was looking at Annie's upside-down face and beyond that the ceiling.

You're pretty, Oliver thought.

Annie raised an eyebrow. Wait, did he just say that out loud? His head felt fuzzy, it was hard to think straight. What had he been doing?

"Come on," Annie said as she moved Oliver into a sitting position, the fuzz inside his head gradually clearing, although the same couldn't be said for the painful throbbing. As Annie sat him against a wall and knelt next to him, he blinked a few times and looked around.

He was on his second-floor landing, which was a lot more damaged and blood-covered and corpse-filled than usual, with rusty weapons, dead Abyss-Dwellers and pieces of dead Abyss-Dwellers scattered around the landing and adjoining rooms, black blood pooling on floors, running down walls and even dripping from the ceiling. Oliver dazedly wondered if he should ask Mrs. Madsen to come back to work after all.

A large, bearded man with hands covered in black blood was holding a dead Abyss-Dweller by the seashell necklace the creature wore around his neck. The man released his grip and the Abyss-Dweller slumped to the floor.

The man looked at Oliver. "You're alive, then."

Bryn. That was it. It was all coming back to Oliver now. He recognised Ambrose as well and even the two constables, Schilling and Benchley. The four men stood around the landing, their clothing torn and bloody,

Schilling gripping his truncheon with both hands while Benchley held his truncheon in one hand and a stolen sword in the other. The policemen were staring at the carnage with wide eyes, Schilling's helmet cocked at a slight angle.

It was the first time an Abyss-Dweller had set foot inside Oliver's house, The Order of the Void's business with the creatures always being conducted elsewhere. He didn't even keep any materials related to the Old Ones, the Abyss-Dwellers or the Order at home, his father refusing to trust him with the responsibility even if Oliver wanted it, which he most certainly didn't.

Ambrose flicked a severed Abyss-Dweller finger off his shoulder and nodded towards Oliver's head. "Quite a bump you've got there."

Without thinking, Oliver lifted his right hand to his head and managed to poke the sore lump which had formed there, causing a bolt of pain to pinball around inside his skull. He squeezed his eyes shut and groaned.

"Idiot," Annie said.

Oliver took his hand away from his head, looked at it and saw blood. "Oh God, my head's broken open!"

"It took a bang but it's not broken. Look closer, you cut your hand."

Oliver only then noticed the gash running across his right palm and felt the pain radiating from it. The shard of glass from the broken mirror in the bathroom. He silently cursed himself for picking it up, not feeling any pain at the time. That electrifying, vital feeling of being so alive was already a distant memory, the pain Oliver now felt reminding him that being alive wasn't always what it was cracked up to be.

Oliver remembered grabbing the glass shard and heading for the door, then nothing. He looked at Annie. "What happened?"

"Annie didn't see it, she was unconscious in the bathroom," Ambrose said. "You came storming out of there with a piece of glass in your hand and this strange look in your eye. You know how you usually look nervous and uncomfortable?"

"I do?"

"Well, you looked different. But then you slipped in some blood, fell over and banged your head on the banister. Out like a light. Annie woke up as we were mopping up the last of the Abyss-Dwellers."

Annie. The toothbrush.

"I saved your life," Oliver said to Annie.

She didn't look convinced. "Was that when you were cutting your hand open or knocking yourself out?"

"In the bathroom. An Abyss-Dweller came in and was going to kill us but I threw my toothbrush at him and –"

"A toothbrush."

"Yes!"

"I think you hit your head harder than we thought."

"It's true!" Oliver looked to the other men for support. "One of you must have seen me do it!"

Ambrose shook his head and Bryn shrugged while Schilling and Benchley seemed to be in shock and barely listening.

Oliver turned back to Annie. "Look, if you go into the bathroom and reach into that Abyss-Dweller's mouth, you'll find my toothbrush in its throat, I swear."

Annie stood up, frowning. "Are you mental? I'm not doing that." Her expression softened slightly. "They said you did drag me into the bathroom to try to get me out of harm's way, though. So thanks for that." She nudged Oliver's leg with one foot. "Now come on, on your feet. You're not the only one with a headache."

It was only then that Oliver noticed the lump on Annie's temple, a moment before she walked into the main bedroom. Oliver gingerly placed one hand against his throbbing head and the other against the wall and slowly rose from the floor. Killing that Abyss-Dweller was the bravest thing he had ever done – alright, so luck may have played some part – and no one had seen it or believed him. Typical.

Bryn walked over to the dazed Schilling and Benchley, who looked at him as if seeing him for the first time.

"You boys did alright," Bryn said.

"What…" Schilling said, his truncheon loosely gesturing around the landing. "What are…"

Benchley cleared his throat. "It's alright, Schilling, I'll handle this," he said with as much authority as he could muster. He looked Bryn in the eyes then hesitantly glanced at the surrounding carnage. "What's all this, then?"

"Officers?" Annie said as she emerged from the main bedroom, carrying Oliver's satchel. "My friends and I understand you must have a lot of questions, but we're in a rush."

Annie came to a stop near the constables and held the satchel in a way that managed to be both casual and prominent. Oliver noticed Benchley's eyes flick towards it for an instant before Annie reached one hand into the satchel and withdrew a handful of banknotes.

"So, how about we offer you both something for your troubles," Annie said as she stuffed the banknotes into Benchley's breast pocket then repeated the process with Schilling, "we part ways as friends, and neither of you ever tells anyone what you saw here today. You were never here and neither were we."

Benchley placed his sword on the floor, thumbed through the banknotes in his pocket then looked at Annie. "Seems fair."

Schilling looked at his own payment then at the older constable. "Benchley, we can't. It's… well, it's not the done thing, is it."

"Now, Schilling, what did I tell you about turning down offers from helpful members of the public?"

"I know, but –"

"And they did save our lives, lad. Don't you think we owe them one?"

"I suppose," Schilling said doubtfully.

"That's settled, then," Annie said. She walked towards the head of the stairs, being careful to step around blood and corpses and slippery things which belonged on the inside of Abyss-Dwellers but which were now on the outside. Bryn and Ambrose followed her.

"So long," Ambrose said to the policemen.

Oliver followed the others but paused next to Schilling and Benchley. "I didn't kill my father."

He couldn't tell if they believed him or not. Probably not. He supposed it didn't matter either way but he had felt like he needed to say it.

Oliver entered the bathroom and picked up his bowler hat. He looked at the Abyss-Dweller lying dead on the tiles, a terrible dragon slain by the hand of the hero. *His* hand. Well, technically his toothbrush, but he had been holding that in his hand and that was close enough for him.

"*Move your arse, Burgess!*" Annie shouted from the bottom of the stairs.

Oliver sighed, placed his hat on his head and headed for the stairs, really not seeing the appeal in this hero business.

Bryn Makes a Wise Suggestion

"And you took care of all of them?" Henry asked.

"I think so," Ambrose said. There was a pregnant pause in which Henry sensed something terrible lurking. Ambrose grinned. "We gave them a battering."

And there it was.

Silence fell across the table.

"Like battered fish?" Ambrose offered helpfully. "Because the Abyss-Dwellers, they're from the sea and are a bit like –"

"*So*," Henry said, "we've all had a busy morning by the sounds of it."

They were sitting around their table in The Bewigged Pig, Henry, Digby and Talbot having returned before Bryn, Ambrose, Oliver and Annie, the pub untouched during their absence. Annie had changed into a clean skirt and blouse before rooting through the spare room for clean – or at least clean-*ish* – clothes for Bryn, Ambrose and Oliver. Finding a large enough shirt for Bryn proved difficult until Annie found one which had actually belonged to him until he forgot it there one drunken night last year after a "Who's got the hairiest chest in the pub" competition broke out. Bryn was disappointed to only make second place but couldn't argue with Mrs. Colosso's victory: it looked like an orangutan had been fired into her torso at two-hundred miles per hour.

The two groups had brought each other up to speed over drinks, Oliver grimacing with every sip of the large whiskey that Henry recommended for his pain. As they talked, someone would occasionally knock on the jammed-in-place front door or the barricaded windows and ask about getting a drink only to have Annie tell them to bugger off, they were closed.

Annie had bundled up some ice cubes in a tea-towel and was holding it to the spot on her temple where the Abyss-Dweller's harpoon had struck her, Oliver holding a similar bundle against the lump on his own head. His right hand had a bandage around it, Annie having cleaned and dressed the wound while reminding him he was an idiot. Oliver didn't disagree.

Bryn took a drink of cider then set down his glass. "At least the Abyss-Dwellers take a while to really start stinking when they're dead, I can't smell the ones down in the cellar."

"Probably because this place is so well bloody ventilated at the moment," Annie said, looking at the shattered windows and the barricades that were solid but not so solid that they didn't let in a draught. Oliver's satchel was on the table and Annie began to open it with her free hand. "Still, this should cover the repairs. I might even splash out, spruce the place up a little."

Henry's pint stopped halfway to his lips and he and the other Roustabouts looked at each other.

"Now, Annie," Henry said carefully, "you don't want to get carried away. We like The Bewigged Pig as it is. The place has always had a certain…"

"Stickiness," Bryn suggested.

"Yes. Well, no. Look, tradition is important and –"

Annie rolled her eyes. "Don't panic, I'm not talking about anything drastic."

The Roustabouts relaxed as Annie set down her bundle of ice, removed a handful of banknotes from inside the satchel and counted them out on the table.

"Here," Annie said as she slid the Roustabouts five identical amounts of money. "Considering the trouble Burgess has dragged you all into, it only seems fair you get a little something in return." Annie's eyes moved to Oliver. "That's not a problem, is it?" she asked with an expression and tone of voice which suggested the question mark at the end of that sentence was actually a very definitive full-stop in disguise.

Although Henry got the impression that Oliver wasn't a man with much experience of women, a man didn't need experience to know that flicking a rattlesnake's plums when it was giving you the evil eye was a bad idea. Not that Annie had plums. Did rattlesnakes have plums? Henry wasn't sure. He made a mental note to visit Newmuck Zoo.

"No, of course not," Oliver said. "No problem at all."

Annie closed the satchel again, keeping whatever remained inside for herself. "Hopefully we'll all live long enough to spend it."

It seemed to Henry that Oliver genuinely didn't mind Annie handing out his money, recent events had clearly left their mark on him and he seemed to be trying to make things right. He was still a spoiled, pudgy fool who had played a part in a plan to doom mankind, but even so he wasn't such a bad sort. Henry knew the modern English gentleman was widely expected to be blindly courageous and bold in the face of danger to the point of stupidity, it was a notion born of a delusional national sense of superiority and Henry wouldn't recommend it. But there was a big difference between that nonsense and simply standing by your friends when things got nasty. While they may not have been friends, Oliver had stood his ground alongside Bryn, Ambrose and Annie, and as far as Henry was concerned, that counted for something.

"I really *am* sorry about all this," Oliver said, looking around the table with a guilty expression. "I never wanted to hurt anyone. I should've never gone along with my father's plans. I know that might not mean much now, but… I hope you can all forgive me."

Oliver almost looked like he was about to cry, leading to an awkward silence, the Roustabouts shifting in their seats, taking long swallows of their pints, showing sudden interest in stains on the floor. A man getting all emotional and whatnot – and in a *pub* of all places – was rocky ground for them. The silence dragged on until, to Henry's relief, it was broken by Bryn clearing his throat.

"Uh, well, we all make mistakes, Oliver," Bryn said. "Christ, I got *married* once. The important thing is… uh…" He floundered for a moment. "Look, just don't be a twat, alright?"

Follow the Money

Bryn looked out through the window of the Clarence as the city rolled by, not reflecting on what might happen to Newmuck and its people if the Old Ones were summoned, because him and the boys weren't going to let that happen and that was the end of it.

It wouldn't be the first time the Roustabouts saved the city from some weird threat, like that time with the magic Scottish pirate and his fire-breathing owls. Not that they ever got a parade or statues or even a "Good job, lads!" in return, the people of Newmuck generally being blissfully ignorant of the strangeness that shambled, stalked, swooped and slurped through the city streets on a regular basis.

Bryn couldn't stand people like Cecil Burgess and his mates: rich, arrogant, greedy cowards who thought they were the centre of the universe and didn't care who they stepped on in getting what they wanted. And the Old Ones didn't sound much different, what with humanity apparently being utterly insignificant to them. As far as Bryn was concerned, being a timeless cosmic entity with the powers of a god whose true nature would shatter the human mind if comprehended was no excuse for being an arsehole.

"So, Bryn," Oliver said. "You said you were married once?"

Annie was at Bryn's side while Oliver sat across from them, Randolph Sowerby outside in the driver's seat as he drove towards Fondle Green and the Annual Newmuck Bankers Garden Party.

"Yeah, but not for long," Bryn said, his mind conjuring the bittersweet memory of Penelope's face. "We had some good times but she was dedicated to her work. When she rolled me up in a carpet and threw me off a bridge, I think we both knew it was over."

Oliver nodded slowly then looked away.

Bryn wondered what Penelope was up to now. Something for Queen and Country that was vital to the safeguarding of the British Empire, no doubt. He couldn't help but feel a little sympathy for anyone the government might set her loose on. Penelope McAllister wasn't someone you wanted as an enemy. Or a wife, if he was being honest.

Bryn shook off thoughts of the past and focused on the task at hand. They had decided at The Bewigged Pig that they should split into two groups again, one going to the party to grab Frederick Orchardson while the other visited the address Cromwell gave them for Arthur Blacklock, Annie once again insisting on coming along. When Henry suggested they stick to the same groups, Bryn said that Ambrose should go with Henry, Talbot and Digby instead as Blacklock was likely to be more trouble than Orchardson. Bryn was confident he could keep an eye on Annie and Oliver while handling a few posh bankers. What were they going to do, not let him open an account?

The Blacklock side of the plan was for Henry, Talbot, Digby and Ambrose to knock on his door, grab him and do whatever was necessary to make sure the Ritual of Suth-G'nar couldn't take place. If Blacklock wasn't at home... well, there was such a thing as too much planning.

As for Orchardson, that would require a little more subtlety – something Annie suggested the Roustabouts might not possess in droves – as it involved a more public situation, and Bryn wading in like a bull in a China shop might give Orchardson a chance to slip away. They also couldn't allow Oliver to be seen at the party in case Orchardson spotted him. Then Digby suggested that rather than try to gain entry to the party, why not have Orchardson come out to them instead?

Details were hashed out, Oliver provided physical descriptions of Orchardson and Blacklock, Annie hid Oliver's satchel of money in her bedroom, and Henry, Talbot, Digby and Ambrose flagged down a carriage while Bryn, Annie and Oliver walked to Randolph Sowerby's barn, Randolph being more than happy to drive them to Envy Crescent.

Bryn knew the truth would take too long to explain and would also make him sound like a complete lunatic, so he kept it simple and told Randolph that a lot of people were in danger and he, Annie and Oliver needed to get their hands on one of the men responsible. Randolph intended to live up to his offer of free rides but Bryn insisted on paying him due to Randolph having a family to support. Annie called Bryn a big softie, he called her a daft cow, she punched him in the arm, then they and Oliver climbed into Randolph's Clarence and were off.

Bryn returned his gaze to the window now as the carriage continued onwards, the dull afternoon daylight unchanging while the same couldn't be said of the scenery as they left behind dirty streets of shabby buildings and noisy crowds, the poorer parts of town gradually being replaced by cleaner and wider spaces, fresher paint, bigger houses, nicer clothes, smoother roads, and less shouting and shoving. They may have been found in the same city but places like Fondle Green or Stowbrook Hill might as well have been on the other side of the world to places like Wealdbury or Gristle or Bryanferry. The rich got richer and the poor got poorer and sicker and old before their time and dead. Not for the first time, Bryn wondered if rather than putting so much effort into spreading across the world, maybe the glorious British Empire should first think about what it was spreading.

Randolph knocked on the pane of glass that separated the driver's seat and the carriage interior, his signal that they were almost at their destination. Bryn drew the dark-red curtain across his side of the carriage and Annie did the same on her side, obscuring the windows and darkening the interior.

Bryn looked at Annie. "Remember, if something goes wrong, I'll –"

"I'll be fine," Annie said. "You just sit tight."

The Clarence rolled to a stop and Annie ran a hand through her hair and straightened the dress she had changed into before leaving The Bewigged Pig.

"Good luck," Oliver said with a nervous smile.

Annie gave him a nod, opened her door and stepped down from the carriage and onto the pavement outside.

Annie's door was only open for a moment but it was enough for Bryn to get a look at 11 Envy Crescent. Lizzie Orchardson had described it as a mansion and she wasn't wrong. The three-storey brick house stood on a large plot of land ringed by iron railings and boasting paved paths, a cherub-topped fountain and immaculate lawns, bushes and trees. Bryn couldn't see the rear of the property but doubted it would be any less impressive back there. He guessed the house contained at least a couple of dozen rooms, tall windows overlooking the grounds while ornate brick chimneys jutted up all around the roof.

Several grand barouches and some smaller but equally polished hansom cabs were parked at one corner of the house, their smartly-dressed drivers standing around nearby, chatting, an expected distance away from the men in expensive suits smoking cigars and drinking champagne on the concrete dais before the front entrance of the house – these men were guests and the drivers were just the help, after all. The large front door stood open, revealing figures and movement within, although Bryn couldn't make out any details, the distant sound of music drifting out from the house.

After Annie closed the door, Bryn sidled over to it and pushed the curtain aside just enough that he could peek out and watch her through the window, Oliver doing the same at his window.

Annie crossed the pavement confidently, heading for the open gate at the front of the Patmore property, where three men stood beneath a curving stone arch, two of them tall and solidly built guards standing at opposite ends of the arch in identical suits, their hands behind their backs. Bryn could see no other guards from where he sat but that didn't mean there weren't more around.

The third man at the gate looked like he would have trouble guarding the cake at a six-year-old's birthday party. Dressed in a more elaborate and colourful suit than the guards, he was short, pale and scrawny, with dark hair and a feeble moustache. He stood beneath the centre of the arch, a silver pen in one hand and a clipboard – the guest-list, Bryn assumed – in the other.

The three men watched Annie approach, the guards' faces flat while the guest-list man looked her up and down with suspicion and a trace of contempt.

"Yes?" the guest-list man said sceptically, his voice quiet to Bryn's ears because of the glass and distance.

"I've been sent to collect one of your guests, a Frederick Orchardson," Annie said firmly and in a slightly posher accent than normal. "Please inform him that Mr. Blacklock requires his presence immediately as a matter of the utmost urgency in regard to tomorrow night's festivities."

The guest-list man looked down at his clipboard. "Mr. Orchardson *is* in attendance today."

"Then I suggest you run along. Mr. Blacklock is not a man who likes to be kept waiting."

The guest-list man stiffened and forced a thin, insincere smile. "Please wait here. I shall only be a moment." He turned around and walked at a quick pace along the wide path that led from the front gate to the main entrance of the house.

"It's working," Oliver whispered.

"Just remember to stay out of the way," Bryn whispered. "Annie brings Orchardson to the door, I grab him, she jumps in and off we go."

The guards watched Annie as she waited and the guest-list man entered the house, disappearing from sight.

"Good party?" Annie asked, receiving a shrug from one guard and nothing at all from the other. Apparently they weren't being paid for their conversation skills.

Eventually the guest-list man re-emerged from the house following behind a bald, spectacled man in a severe black suit, his face thin, lined and humourless as he stared ahead. Frederick Orchardson, based on Oliver's description.

Lizzie must've gotten her looks from her mother, Bryn thought.

"Is that him?" Bryn whispered.

"Yes," Oliver whispered.

Orchardson and the guest-list man stopped beneath the arch.

"What's this about?" Orchardson asked Annie.

"As I told *him*," Annie said, glancing at the guest-list man, "Mr. Blacklock requires your presence urgently. It concerns your plans for tomorrow evening."

Orchardson stared at Annie for a moment. "And who are *you*, exactly? I don't recognise you."

"I doubt Mr. Blacklock sees a need for you to be familiar with everyone he employs."

Orchardson glanced at the carriage parked at the pavement. "And where are we going?"

"Mr. Blacklock's home in Milner Park."

Orchardson stared at Annie again, longer this time. Eventually his eyes narrowed and he said, "Arthur doesn't live in Milner Park."

All eyes at the front gate turned towards Randolph's carriage as Bryn threw open the door, leapt out and hit the pavement running.

"*Don't you move!*" Bryn shouted at Orchardson, who stared at him in slack-jawed shock for a second before turning and bolting towards the house like a startled rabbit.

Annie set off after him, the guest-list man letting out a yelp of surprise as she shoved him aside. One of the guards lunged at her but she sidestepped him and ran on while the second guard moved into the path of the oncoming Bryn.

Bryn dipped his shoulder and slammed into the guard, sending him sprawling. The other guard wrapped his meaty arms around Bryn's chest and upper arms from behind, trapping him in a bearhug. But other, stronger men – not to mention an actual bear – had tried to restrain Bryn like that before and none had succeeded for long. Bryn snapped his head backwards and the back of his skull crunched into the guard's nose. The guard grunted, his grip loosening, and Bryn broke free and spun around, his right fist coming around with him and connecting with the guard's chin, dropping him to the ground.

Bryn looked up to see Oliver running towards him with an expression that suggested he knew he was doing a very stupid thing by going towards trouble instead of away from it but was already committed now.

"*Bryn!*" Randolph called out, reins in hand. "*What do you want me to do?*"

"*Go!*" Bryn shouted, waving an arm down the street, not wanting Randolph to stick around and end up in trouble.

"*Are you sure?*"

"*Yes, go!*"

Bryn ran towards the house, Oliver following close behind him. Up ahead, Orchardson was making a beeline for the front door, Annie in pursuit. The group of men on the dais watched them in puzzlement then hurriedly moved out of the way as Orchardson vaulted the steps two at a time and ran into the house, followed by Annie, then Bryn and Oliver.

Bryn found himself inside a bright, high-ceilinged lobby that stretched from the front of the building to the rear. A vast, intricately patterned rug set in the centre of the room covered much of the polished granite floor while a huge, sparkling chandelier hung from the decorated ceiling and a number of gilt-framed paintings adorned a tripartite wall crowned by an elaborate cornice. A pair of staircases curved upwards to a second-floor landing, numerous doors leading off from the lobby on both floors. A pair of double-doors opened onto the garden behind the house and it was in this direction that Orchardson was fleeing.

The party was in full flow: glass-encased candles and lengths of bunting adorned the staircases and landing railing, uniformed waiters circulated with trays of champagne and cases of cigars, dozens of silver dishes of various foods were spread out along two long rows of tables, and in one corner of the lobby a circular stage had been set up and on it a group of musicians were playing cello, harp, violin and more. The lobby was packed with dozens of boring-looking men in expensive suits, many accompanied by their bored-looking wives in expensive dresses and jewellery, although heads turned and conversations stopped as Orchardson and Annie rushed through the lobby, waves of surprise, confusion and alarm following in their wake as they darted past those guests they could and shouldered aside those they couldn't.

A white-haired man with a drooping moustache raised his eyebrows in shock, causing his monocle to fall out and into his glass of champagne, because it was one of the few immutable rules of the universe that this had to happen in such situations.

Guards who had been positioned around the edges of the lobby were now converging on the chase, their progress slowed by the guests in their way. Meanwhile, the band, professionals that they were, played on.

Bryn gained ground on Orchardson and Annie as he followed the path through the crowd that they left behind them, then the blurred faces rushing past at his sides disappeared as he ran through the rear doorway and out onto the patio, where there were only a few scattered guests and waiters. Behind the house was a spread of lawns, paths, flowerbeds, trellises, trees, and even a tennis court, the rear boundary of the property ending in a waist-high concrete wall that Orchardson was sprinting towards. On the other side of the wall was a short stretch of grassland that sloped downwards and out of sight as it met a line of trees marking the edge of some woodland.

His lungs beginning to burn, Bryn spotted two running guards off to his left, far away but closing fast, while on his right side Oliver overtook him, panting and wide-eyed, seemingly propelled more by the fear of stopping than anything else.

A wooden bench stood against the rear wall and Orchardson clambered onto it and then over the wall, stumbling as he landed on the grass and fallen leaves on the other side before regaining his balance and running for the trees. Annie cleared the wall then Oliver did the same only far less gracefully.

Bryn could hear the two guards closing in behind him so after he vaulted over the wall he spun around, thrust out both hands and caught the guards by their throats as they landed from their own jumps, their eyes bulging before Bryn cracked their heads together. He released them and they fell to the ground, unconscious. He looked towards the house to see the patio now swarming with guests who had come out to watch the excitement while more guards ran towards the rear wall.

Bryn turned around to see Orchardson look back over his shoulder as he passed through the treeline only to lose his footing, cry out and tumble over the brow of the slope and out of sight. Annie skidded to a halt at the same spot, followed by Oliver, and the two of them looked down the slope.

"Oh, God!" Oliver said, putting a hand to his mouth, while Annie drew in a hissed breath.

Bryn arrived next to them, breathing heavily. He looked at their faces then followed their gaze. He winced. "Ooh, that's a nasty one."

The ground before them was made up of bare earth, tufts of grass, fallen leaves and scattered stones, and fell away at a sharp angle until it eventually evened out below at a shallow stream gently burbling its way through the woods, the ground rising again on the opposite bank.

Orchardson had tumbled down the slope but hadn't made it all the way to the bottom, instead hitting a tree and being impaled on a thick, wickedly pointed branch that pierced his right side just below his ribcage and emerged near his left collarbone. Orchardson's mouth hung open, blood running down his chin, and he had a pained, baffled expression on his face as he clawed weakly at the pointed end of the branch, moving like a man half-asleep. His arms soon fell away again, his head lolled, his right leg twitched, then the only thing of Orchardson's that moved was his blood as it ran down the branch and his body, spread across his clothes and dripped onto the ground.

Bryn didn't think he needed to check for a pulse to be certain that Frederick Orchardson had attended his last Annual Newmuck Bankers Garden Party.

Bryn looked back towards the house again and saw the chasing guards nearing the rear wall of the Patmore property. He turned to Annie and Oliver. "Come on, we'll lose them in these woods. We need to get to Milner Park."

"Why?" Oliver asked.

"You heard Orchardson earlier. Blacklock doesn't live in Milner Park. The boys might be walking into a trap."

Lo, Peanut!

"This is blatantly a trap," Digby said as Henry knocked on the front door.

"You think Cromwell lied to you?" Ambrose asked.

"He's always got an angle. We shouldn't have listened to him."

"A bit late to worry about that now," Henry said. "If Cromwell *is* messing us around, he'll get what's coming to him."

Talbot, Digby, Henry and Ambrose stood on the front porch of the detached, two-storey house that was 55 Wood Street. It was a nice enough place but Talbot had expected something grander for a man of Blacklock's supposed wealth and status. Outside the front of the house was an overgrown lawn while a gravel path ran along one side of the building, connecting the front of the property to the rear. Wood Street was located in a quiet, residential suburb in the middle-class Milner Park, the modest houses that lined both sides of the street built far enough apart so as to allow for plenty of privacy. There were few people moving along the pavements and even less traffic on the road.

No one answered, so Henry knocked again. Talbot looked at the window next to the front door but the embroidered net curtain on the other side of the glass made it impossible to see inside. The house was silent and still.

Talbot got tired of waiting. "I'll go round the back, see if –"

He was interrupted by the click of a key being turned in a lock. Then the handle turned and the front door opened inwards.

If the man standing in the doorway was Arthur Blacklock then Oliver's description had been way off. This man looked to be over twenty years older and half a foot shorter, thin rather than slim, and what remained of his thinning hair wasn't black and grey but pure white. A loose-fitting suit hung on his bony frame, the collar of his shirt leaving plenty of room for his scrawny neck. He leaned slightly to his right, the palm of his right hand resting on the rounded metal grip of a wooden cane. On his left index finger he wore a silver ring into which a large, glittering opal was set.

"Can I help you?" the old man asked politely.

"We're looking for Arthur Blacklock," Henry said doubtfully. "We were told he lives here."

The old man smiled, revealing crooked, yellow teeth. "Of course, Arthur should be back any minute." He stepped aside, opening the door wider. "Please, come in."

The Roustabouts entered a small, sombre lobby, the old man closing and locking the front door behind them. Limping slightly and supported by his cane, he led his visitors into the adjoining living room, which felt empty and lifeless, sparsely furnished and decorated as it was. An equally bare dining room could be seen through an open doorway while a staircase attached to one wall led up to the second floor. A door was built into the side of the staircase, Talbot assuming it led to a closet or cellar. The net curtains that covered the windows dulled the daylight, the atmosphere inside the room only made more dismal by the unlit wall-lights and the chill from the cold, ash-filled fireplace.

"Make yourselves comfortable," the old man said, indicating a scuffed leather armchair and simple wooden chair. "Sorry, we don't usually receive so many visitors at one time."

Talbot couldn't quite place his accent, it seemed to be English but with some kind of foreign twang.

"We'll stand," Digby said.

"So, you are…?" Henry prompted.

"Where are my manners?" the old man said. "My name is Mr. Lucan."

"And you live here. With Arthur Blacklock."

Lucan nodded. "Yes, he and I have known each other for some time."

Talbot and Digby shared a glance. Oliver had never said anything about Blacklock living with some old man.

"How exactly do you know him?" Henry asked.

Lucan limped over to the fireplace, the end of his cane tapping on the floorboards as he went. He used his free hand to lift something off the mantelpiece, and when he turned to face the Roustabouts, Talbot saw it looked like some kind of perfume bottle, a glass vial of liquid with a nozzle and squeezable rubber ball attached.

"Mm?" Lucan said distractedly as he released his grip on his cane, letting it rest against his hip as he stood slightly awkwardly to balance himself, holding the bottle with both hands.

"How do you know Blacklock?" Digby asked, an edge of impatience in his voice.

"We're friends. Good friends." Lucan held the bottle up at head-height and squeezed the rubber ball several times while moving the bottle in a horizontal arc so that the clouds of fine mist that sprayed from the nozzle gently blanketed the part of the room where the Roustabouts stood.

Talbot felt tiny droplets of moisture settle on his head and hands. "What the hell are you doing?"

Lucan lowered the bottle. "It's musty in here, I thought I'd freshen the air a little."

"By spraying perfume into it? What sort of idiot does that?"

"Mr. Lucan, it's very important we speak to Arthur," Ambrose said. "He's involved in some bad business and we need to find out where these pretty lights are coming from…"

As Ambrose trailed off, Talbot looked over at him. He had a dazed expression on his face, his eyes unfocused as he stared at nothing and swayed gently on his feet.

And it wasn't just Ambrose. Henry squeezed his eyes shut and pinched the bridge of his nose between a thumb and index finger while Digby took a step backwards and placed a hand on a nearby dresser to steady himself.

"What…" Digby said.

Talbot suddenly felt the floor lurch beneath his feet, and although his time at sea had taught him how to handle unsure footing, he couldn't find his balance now as the living room turned this way and that and spots of light popped before his eyes.

As steady as a rock, Lucan watched the Roustabouts with a small smile. *The spray*, Talbot thought. *Poison.*

He heard a thump, then another, and turned to see Ambrose and Henry lying unconscious on the floor. He was fairly certain it was them anyway, shapes and colours were beginning to shift and blur together, making it hard to tell.

"Told you," a voice muttered drunkenly. Talbot thought it sounded like Digby except it was coming from far, far away. "I bloody told y–"

Another thump.

Talbot turned towards where he thought Lucan was standing but then found he couldn't stop turning, everything was turning and turning and turning.

Then nothing was turning because everything went away.

For a time Talbot drifted in darkness, dreaming unpleasant dreams of being pissed on by a three-legged goblin.

"Guh," Talbot said as awareness returned.

He opened his eyes, his vision slowly focusing. His head swam, his thoughts as soft and fragmented as an exploded gerbil.

Then it all came flooding back. Blacklock's house. Lucan. The spray bottle.

Talbot sat up, winced as a bolt of pain shot through his head, and took in his surroundings. The room – the *cell*, he quickly realised – was made up of four windowless brick walls, a hardpacked dirt floor and a ceiling of wooden boards and joists. Built into one wall was a door of solid steel while the opposite wall featured a prison-style metal gate secured to the bricks by several sturdy hinges. The only light source was a lantern on a table in a small room beyond the gate, the block of light that fell across the floor and walls of the cell crisscrossed with the shadows of the gate's bars. Near the table a narrow, enclosed staircase rose out of sight.

Talbot heard a groan and looked over to see Henry slowly rising to one knee. "Crafty little bastard, eh?" Henry said.

"And he seemed like just a nice old man," Ambrose said as he appeared at Talbot's side and offered him a hand. Talbot took it and Ambrose helped him to his feet, his legs still a little shaky but a lot steadier now than earlier.

"I'm going to have 'Look where his optimism got him' carved on your headstone, Ambrose," Digby said as he emerged from a dark corner of the room.

On his feet now, Henry looked around the cell. "Where are we?"

"Looks like a cellar," Talbot said.

Ambrose walked to the gate, wrapped his hands around two of the bars and rattled it but the gate was securely locked. "Won't budge."

"Out the way," Talbot said.

Ambrose stepped aside as Talbot approached the gate and kicked out his left foot, the sole of his shoe slamming against the metal panel that held the keyhole, the gate rattling but showing no signs of loosening. Talbot felt the shock of the impact travel up his leg and he limped away, teeth clenched.

"Bastards!" he hissed.

Digby smiled. "Don't worry, maybe the old man will lend you his cane."

"Piss off."

Henry pressed himself up against the gate and turned his head one way then the other, trying to get a better look at the room beyond. "Doesn't seem to be much on the other side. Room looks small, just a table and a few crates and boxes. I can see the end of a lever next to the gate. Can't see where the stairs lead."

"Can anyone else smell that?" Digby said, frowning.

Talbot smelled earth. Mould. Then he caught it, faint but unmistakeable. "Blood."

From the top of the stairs came the sound of a door creaking open then closing again. Henry stepped back from the gate and the Roustabouts waited and listened to descending footsteps accompanied by the tapping of a cane.

Lucan smiled at the Roustabouts as he stepped off the stairs and approached the gate. "I thought I heard voices. You're all awake, excellent."

"What was that shite you sprayed us with?" Talbot asked.

"That wasn't 'shite', thank you. That was a concoction of my own creation, the chief ingredient of which is the extract of a rare flower that only grows in a certain part of the Huangshan mountain range in eastern China. I was sensible enough to stock up during my time there. When mixed with certain chemicals, the result is an extremely effective and fast-acting sedative, as you gentlemen discovered."

"Where's Blacklock?" Henry asked.

Lucan shrugged. "I have no idea. I've never heard of an 'Arthur Blacklock'. I purchased this house four months ago from a man named Derrick Berkshire. An architect."

"I *knew* Offal was lying," Digby said.

"Ah, now there's a name I *do* know. I assume you're referring to Offal Cromwell?"

"How do you know Offal?" Henry asked.

"I don't know him personally, only through my trade."

"Which is?"

"I offer my clients solutions to their problems via the application of disruptions. Usually to life, sometimes property."

"What's that supposed to mean?" Talbot asked impatiently.

"It means he's scum with delusions of grandeur," Digby said. "A common murderer who pretends he's something fancy. We've seen his type before."

"I don't know, the only thing this old bastard looks like he could murder is a cup of tea first thing in the morning."

"An estimation from an ignorant fool on the wrong side of a cell door," Lucan said, smiling. "You'll understand if I don't put too much weight in that."

"So you work for Offal?" Ambrose asked.

Lucan shook his head. "In opposition to him. In the service of Hubert and Charles Candle, specifically. I lived abroad for many years, but following some unfortunate business in India I decided to return to England. I purchased this house and made some necessary changes such as expanding and redesigning this cellar. Then, being a craftsman in possession of valuable skills, I sought employment."

"And the Candle brothers paid you to hassle Cromwell," Henry said. "We heard a couple of his operations were put out of business recently. That was you?"

There was pride in Lucan's smile. "Guilty as charged. The Candle brothers are very keen to remove Offal Cromwell as a competitor and expand the scale of their own operations. Hence why they were willing to meet my price. Which is a fair one given the quality of the service I deliver, I assure you."

"We also heard innocent people were killed in those attacks," Ambrose said darkly.

"Regrettable," Lucan said in the voice of a man who didn't regret a thing. "But occasionally unavoidable."

Talbot frowned as something occurred to him. "Hang on, how did you manage to carry the four of us down here?"

"Oh, Peanut assisted me with that."

Henry raised his eyebrows. "'Peanut'?"

Lucan placed his left hand on the lever next to the gate. "You see, telling you you had the wrong house when you knocked seemed like a waste of an opportunity. You all have plenty of meat on you and Peanut must be fed. I preferred to wait until you were awake, I do take pleasure in watching him play with his food."

Lucan pulled the lever down with a metallic clank. A click behind the Roustabouts made them turn around and they saw the solid metal door open inwards a few inches, although nothing but darkness could be seen through the gap.

"*Peanut!*" Lucan called out.

There was a moment of silence before a prolonged moan drifted out from the darkness of the adjoining room, the voice sounding like two voices mixed together, one deep and booming, the other a harsh hiss. This was followed by several slow, heavy footsteps, then a large hand appeared and pulled the door open further and a hulking figure filled the doorway, dipping its head to avoid banging it on the lintel as it stepped through into the cell. Standing before the Roustabouts, far from small themselves, was one of the biggest men Talbot had ever seen. He was around seven feet tall and his stained and ragged trousers and shirt strained against the thick, powerful muscles beneath, his sleeves rolled up around his bulging biceps, his feet bare and black with dirt. His wavy black hair hung down to his shoulders in matted tangles and his beard was just as unkempt. The man's skin appeared to be a shade of brown naturally although it was hard to tell given its waxy pallor and the poor light in the cell. His eyes were red orbs that flared fiercely in their sockets as they moved slowly over the Roustabouts, his slab of a jaw shifting slowly, mouth open slightly.

"Gentlemen," Lucan said, "meet my creation: Peanut."

"If that's your son then I'm the Queen of Spain," Talbot said.

"He's not my son, although I suppose I did birth him in a way."

"There's an image I could've done without," Henry said.

"Peanut is a vetala, a wraith I enslaved during my time in India. Vetalas are powerful spirits but they have no physical form of their own, instead they rely on the possession and reanimation of human corpses, whose decay ceases once a vetala begins using them as a vehicle. Given the uses I had in mind for my vetala, I needed a physically impressive host. When I found the man you see before you, I knew he was the one. He was alive at the time, but with a little preparation I was able to change that before trapping the vetala inside his body. The spirit increases the host's natural strength tenfold, it feels no pain and has no choice but to do my bidding. A most effective tool. Although bringing Peanut into the country discreetly wasn't without its challenges."

Peanut took another heavy step into the cell and the Roustabouts spread out, keeping their eyes on the undead giant.

"You don't seem particularly shocked," Lucan said with a trace of disappointment.

"We've been around," Henry said. "So that's how you destroyed Cromwell's businesses, by using this thing."

"Why 'Peanut'?" Ambrose asked.

"The vetalas themselves have no names and I didn't see the need to ask the Indian's name," Lucan said. He smiled fondly. "When I was a child, my family owned a cat named Peanut."

Talbot grunted disdainfully. "A cat person. What a surprise."

"If this bloke's dead then why does he need to feed?" Henry asked as Peanut's fingers clenched and unclenched.

"I have to admit to not being completely certain," Lucan said. "My guess is the intensity of the symbiosis means an intake of energy is still necessary for it to be sustained, despite one half of the equation being a spirit and the other a corpse. I do know that human flesh is the only thing Peanut will consume. Although I'm not certain what happens to it since he never actually excretes waste. Perhaps that might be of some comfort to you all, the fact you won't end up as…" Lucan smiled at Talbot. "'Shite.'"

Peanut lunged at Digby with a roar. Digby ducked, moved to the giant's side and threw two quick, hard punches into his ribs. Peanut swung one tree-like arm, Digby raising his forearms to block but there was still enough power behind the blow to send him flying across the cell.

Ambrose leapt onto Peanut's back and wrapped his arms around the giant's throat, trying to throw him off-balance, but Peanut bore the weight easily while Henry swung his right fist at Peanut's face only to find it swallowed by a huge left hand, the bones in Henry's trapped fist making a horrible grinding sound as Peanut squeezed.

Talbot charged forward, driving a shoulder into Peanut's midsection in a hard tackle, but although the impact was enough for Henry to free himself, Peanut's feet remained firmly planted. A forearm came crashing down onto Talbot's back and he hit the floor. His back, shoulders and neck burning with pain, he rolled aside a second before Peanut's foot pounded into the dirt where his head had just been.

Peanut reached up over his shoulders, grabbed Ambrose and swung him over his head, Ambrose's lower legs banging against a ceiling joist as he went over before landing on his back. Henry thrust both thumbs towards Peanut's eyes but the giant turned his head so only one found its mark, Henry's right thumb sinking all the way into Peanut's left eye socket with a nauseating squelch, the burning red eyeball disappearing inside his skull. Thick blood spurted from the socket, splashing onto Henry and running down Peanut's face.

Talbot heard Lucan utter a distraught gasp. Still, the old man had been right about the vetala not feeling any pain, the loss of an eye not giving Peanut pause as he clamped a hand around Henry's right forearm and flung him, Lucan flinching back a step as Henry slammed into the gate then fell to the floor.

Talbot shot out a foot at Peanut's left knee and with a loud cracking sound the giant's leg bent inwards at a horrible angle. Peanut stumbled, his left leg suddenly useless. He swung a fist at Talbot but his aim was thrown off as Digby shoulder-charged him in the back, the giant off-balance enough now that the impact knocked him forward and brought his jaw into the path of Talbot's right fist. Peanut crashed to the floor and Talbot and Digby certainly weren't above kicking a monster when he was down, so as Digby brought the sole of his shoe down onto Peanut's head, Talbot placed one foot on Peanut's right elbow, grabbed the giant's right wrist in both hands and yanked upwards. Peanut's right arm snapped, the splintered end of one of the bones in his forearm puncturing through flesh and skin, spraying blood, Peanut pushing himself up with his left arm until Ambrose scrambled onto his back, weighing him down, Digby putting his own weight on Peanut's legs.

Rushing over from the gate, Henry took a knee at Peanut's side, grabbed the bloody, eight-inch-long section of bone sticking out of the giant's forearm and snapped it off. He raised the jagged bone above his head.

"*No!*" Lucan cried.

Henry plunged the bone into the back of Peanut's neck, severing his spinal cord. The giant went limp, although his remaining red eye continued to move in its socket and a low gurgle emerged from his lips.

Paralysing a possessed corpse with one of his own bones, that's a new one, Talbot thought.

Henry, Ambrose and Digby stood up, the jagged bone making a wet sucking sound as Henry pulled it free of Peanut's neck, gouts of blood following it.

Lucan stared at his fallen creation in disbelief. "You... you..."

Henry hurled the bloody bone at Lucan but it hit one of the gate's metal bars near his face and spun away. Lucan flinched and almost lost his balance but managed to steady himself with his cane. He glared at the Roustabouts.

"You *scum!*" Lucan hissed, outraged. "Do you have any idea what you've cost me?"

Henry leaned down and took hold of Peanut's left arm. "Well, since we don't have a key for that gate, let's try a battering ram."

Talbot gripped Peanut's right arm, Ambrose his left leg and Digby his right leg, and together the Roustabouts lifted the enormous body off the floor, Peanut's drooping head facing Lucan.

"Stop that!" Lucan said. "Put him down!"

The Roustabouts carried Peanut to the gate.

"On three," Henry said. "One!"

The Roustabouts swung Peanut backwards, then forward.

Lucan banged the end of his cane against the floor. "I said stop that!"

"Two!" Henry said, and backwards and forward Peanut went again, with slightly more force now, building momentum.

"*Three!*" Henry shouted, and Peanut went backwards a third time.

Lucan's eyes widened. "*Don't!*"

The Roustabouts stepped forward with the final swing and the gate jerked in its frame, tiny fragments of brick falling from around its hinges, as Peanut's head broke open against the bars, showering the Roustabouts and Lucan with blood and pieces of flesh, bone and brain. One of Peanut's collarbones snapped and jutted out of his muscular shoulder, the tip piercing his blood-soaked shirt.

Lucan looked down at his gore-spattered body, horrified.

"One!" Henry said, and Peanut was swung again.

Lucan looked up, alarmed.

"Two!"

"*Stop, stop!*" Lucan cried.

"*Three!*"

Into the gate Peanut went again, his already ruined head and shoulders twisting further into an even more broken mass of flesh and bone, more brick fragments falling as one of the gate's hinges was wrenched partially free.

Lucan turned and hurriedly limped up the stairs as fast as he could manage, his cane tap-tap-tapping with him.

"Again," Henry said.

"I think I've got a piece of brain in my eye," Talbot said.

Lucan disappeared from view, tap-tap-tap.

"One!" Henry said.

The tapping of Lucan's cane stopped as he ascended the final step.

"Two!"

From the top of the stairs came the sound of a door handle being turned.

"*Thr–*"

Peanut only bumped into the gate with a squishy, limp thud as the Roustabouts' attention was suddenly drawn to the sounds of a door slamming into a body, a surprised cry, and then something clattering and thumping down the stairs. They watched as Lucan and his cane came tumbling into view, and there was a sharp cracking sound as the old man fell down the final few steps then rolled onto the dirt floor. He came to rest facing the cell, his eyes wide and unblinking, his mouth open.

Muffled voices drifted down from upstairs, becoming not only clearer but also familiar as those talking descended into the cellar.

"– God, oh God, I didn't know he was there, I just opened the door!" Oliver said.

"Let's just have a look," Bryn said.

"Do you think he's alright?"

"Well, if he didn't need that cane before I reckon he does now," Annie said.

The three of them stepped off the stairs and looked down at Lucan's corpse.

"Maybe he's just stunned," Oliver said without much hope.

"So stunned he's going to start turning green by tomorrow," Bryn said.

As one, Bryn, Oliver and Annie looked from Lucan to the nearby cell gate, through which they saw the blood- and gore-soaked scene of Talbot, Henry, Digby and Ambrose carrying an almost decapitated giant of a man. The two groups stared at each other. A piece of brain fell out of Peanut's shattered skull and plopped onto the floor.

"Well," Annie said. "Looks like you lot have got everything under control here."

The Role He Was Born to Play

Blacklock grinned. *Happy*.
He creased the centre of his brow. *Sad*.
He frowned. *Angry*.
He frowned in a slightly different way. *Thoughtful*.

He widened his eyes in surprise, let his mouth hang open dully, raised a lascivious eyebrow, bared his teeth in a snarl, his face a shifting mask of expressions; the character, their story, the world in which they lived, all changing from one moment to the next, an endless universe of possibilities as the audience – from the commoners in the stalls to the elite high up in their boxes – looked on in enthralled amazement and he gave their little lives meaning, even if only for a fleeting, illusory moment. They were nothing. While he could be absolutely anything. He had read about how a professional actor required extensive training in physical and emotional expressivity, mime, observation, speech skills and more, but he didn't need all that nonsense. He was a *natural*. After all, his teacher had described his performance as Birch Tree No.2 as "stiff" and "wooden", and since he was playing a tree he took that as high praise.

Blacklock stopped moving his face and stared, his expression blank. *Nothing*.

He wasn't sure how long he stood there like that but eventually he heard the sound of someone knocking on the front door downstairs. Naked, Blacklock turned away from the full-length mirror and walked to his bed, where he had neatly laid out his clothes after undressing. He slipped back into his underwear, socks, trousers, shoes, shirt, and waistcoat as the knocking repeated.

Blacklock exited the bedroom and walked along the second-floor hallway until he reached the landing that looked down on the lobby below, gloomy daylight entering through the windows that flanked the front door. He descended the stairs, passing framed paintings which, like the rest of the ornaments, furnishings, gadgets and other contents of his home, were expensive but meant nothing to him. He flaunted his wealth as much as the next gentleman because that was what a gentleman did, but it brought him no joy. He existed on a higher, more profound and creative plane than other men like him. It was one of the burdens he carried.

Another bout of knocking, more insistent now.

Blacklock wasn't expecting anyone. That morning he had telephoned Sugarfoot and Orchardson to inform them of the incident at The Bewigged Pig and his resulting plan to have Abyss-Dwellers lie in wait at Oliver's house to kill him should he return, a plan which he and Gerald had already put into action without consulting Sugarfoot or Orchardson first, Blacklock having never placed much value in their opinions.

Sugarfoot was no spring chicken but Blacklock was certain that even as a younger man he had never been any kind of clever businessman. He had just been in the right place at the right time, any fool with half a brain could make his fortune during those years of railway frenzy like Sugarfoot did. He was lucky and had coasted on that luck ever since, getting fatter, lazier and drunker. Blacklock recognised that the railways had changed the world, but Sugarfoot was little more than a red-nosed slug clinging onto the underside of a train carriage.

Orchardson was certainly sharper than Sugarfoot, with a keen eye for details, procedures and figures that made him very good at what he did, but by God, Blacklock had never met a man so utterly devoid of charisma or personality and who could kill a conversation stone-dead from twelve paces. As with the railways, Blacklock was aware of the impact of Orchardson's chosen profession, finance becoming an increasingly dominant force in the world of industry, but Orchardson may as well have been made out of cheques and banknotes himself for all the humanity he possessed.

Neither Sugarfoot nor Orchardson had any imagination, any creativity, any *presence*. They weren't artists like Blacklock. But as long as they kept doing what they were told then that was what mattered. He didn't credit either with enough nerve to betray him, although perhaps the two of them conspiring with a certain spectacled Abyss-Dweller...

Blacklock cast the thought aside. For the moment. In the end, no one, human or otherwise, was going to stop him correcting reality.

He stepped off the stairs and crossed the lobby, his shoes tapping on the wooden floor. He opened the front door then tried to hide his surprise and dismay.

Offal Cromwell smiled. "Hello, Arthur."

The other man – Caleb, if Blacklock remembered correctly – only stared. Blacklock forced a smile. "Mr. Cromwell, hello."

Blacklock glanced past the two thugs standing in their suits, hats and topcoats, towards his front garden and the street beyond, which he suddenly found uncomfortably desolate, the only movement the rustling of trees in the breeze and an elderly woman walking a small dog, the houses across the way dark and quiet in the dismal afternoon. Feeling isolated, Blacklock wished Quinn was there.

Then he caught himself. Why the hell should he be made to feel this way? He had nothing to be nervous about, he was on the brink of becoming a god. He was in control here, not a pair of common criminals whose existence would be even more meaningless in the new world than it was in this one. Blacklock considered that if he was feeling merciful, perhaps he might include Cromwell and Caleb as members of his eternal, teeming audience. *If.*

Blacklock put on a no-nonsense expression and puffed out his chest. "How did you know where I live?" he asked firmly.

"A man should know his friends, shouldn't he?" Cromwell said innocently. Then he frowned. "Are you wearing make-up?"

Shit, Blacklock thought.

He had been experimenting with various rouges, white paints and other cosmetics in front of the mirror earlier, trying to find the perfect combination for tomorrow night's performance, and forgot to clean his face before coming downstairs.

"It's… ointment," Blacklock said as he hurriedly wiped at his face with a shirtsleeve. "For my skin. I have a condition."

"Is it called being a tosser?" Caleb said.

"He's just joking, Arthur," Cromwell said, smiling again. "You look like you've been crying as well."

Blacklock thought of the drops he had put into his eyes. They burned like fire but really gave his eyes a brightness and sparkle which he knew would be utterly captivating on stage once the initial wateriness and severe bloodshot appearance had receded.

"Just lack of sleep," Blacklock said as he finished wiping his face.

Cromwell looked over Blacklock's shoulder. "Anyone else at home?"

"No. Look, can I do something for you?"

"You can start by inviting us in."

"I'm afraid I –"

"Grand."

Cromwell and Caleb stepped forward and Blacklock found himself instinctively moving aside, allowing them to enter. After a brief hesitation, he closed the front door.

"Very nice," Cromwell said as his gaze roamed over the lobby's pricey décor. He looked at Caleb. "How the other half live, eh?"

Caleb nodded casually.

"I'm in the middle of something so you'll understand I don't really have time to chat," Blacklock said.

"What's that, then?" Cromwell asked.

"Pardon?"

"What are you in the middle of?"

"Business," Blacklock said as he watched Caleb drift over to an end table at one side of the lobby. "Just paperwork."

"Maybe it's something we could help with. We're businessmen, aren't we, Caleb?"

A large porcelain vase stood on the end table and Caleb tapped it twice with the nail of his right index finger as he studied it, apparently unimpressed. "That's us."

Blacklock wished Cromwell would take the hint. "I'm sure you'd find it very bor–"

"Besides, we're going to be working together a lot in the future," Cromwell said as he took a step towards Blacklock.

"Mr. Cromwell, our business concluded with the payment I made to you for delivery of the Yaroslav Manuscript pages."

Cromwell ambled like a man with all the time in the world, although his eyes were fixed on Blacklock. "The possibility of future dealings was brought up."

"Possibility, perhaps, yes –"

"I told you I wanted to move up in the world. That I want what this city owes me. Respect. Power. You said you could help with that."

"We may have discussed something along those lines, but –"

"Promises were made."

Blacklock took a step backwards. "Now hang on, there were definitely no pro–"

All the air in Blacklock's lungs rushed out as Cromwell's right fist ploughed into his gut, deep enough that it felt to Blacklock like it went right through to his spine. He crumpled to the floor, knees drawing up, eyes watering, trying but failing to suck in air, the veins on his neck bulging.

"A man should keep his promises," Cromwell said from somewhere above Blacklock.

Just as Blacklock felt like his lungs were about to explode, he managed to start drawing in breath in small gulps.

"Help him to his feet," Cromwell said.

A pair of hands pulled Blacklock up and he found himself being dragged across the lobby, his shoes scrabbling at the floor. He was spun around and looked into Caleb's face a moment before his lower back slammed against the end table behind him, his upper body bent backwards slightly over it, the vase into which he had been pushed falling to the floor and shattering. Caleb held him there, the thug's knuckles white as he pressed his fists against Blacklock's chest, clumps of shirt and waistcoat bunched up in them, Blacklock's own hands held to his throbbing stomach. A frightening, merciless light flickered in Caleb's pale-blue eyes.

Cromwell came to stand at Caleb's side, his face wearing the kind of no-nonsense expression that Blacklock had tried to pull off earlier. It came so naturally to Cromwell, and Blacklock felt a stab of jealousy he tried to ignore.

"I've been patient," Cromwell said. "I've been polite. But now I suggest you pay attention, Arthur. Understand?"

Blacklock nodded.

"Good man. See, I've worked very hard for a very long time to get where I am, to pull myself up out of the shit and build what I have. I've done things I'm proud of and – I'm not going to lie – some things I'm not proud of. But I always did what was *necessary*. And I can promise you this: there are a lot of men in this city who wouldn't have shown the restraint and generosity I have. But do you think people appreciate any of the good I've done, any of my achievements? No, I'm always just Offal Cromwell, crime boss. But men like you, you're all bigger crooks than me except you're not treated like it, are you? You're pillars of society, the men who shape the world. Well, I've paid my dues, Arthur. It's time I take my seat at the table and you're going to help me get there. Do you have a problem with that?"

Blacklock shook his head.

"Thing is, I'm under a lot of pressure at the moment, so I need to be absolutely sure I've made my point."

It happened fast. Cromwell clamped his right hand around Blacklock's right wrist and his left hand around the little finger on Blacklock's right hand. Blacklock drew in a short, sharp breath to protest but what came out was a scream as his finger snapped and the world exploded in agony. He thrashed and cursed and hissed through gritted teeth, spittle flying, but Caleb and Cromwell held him in place. Blacklock felt Cromwell's left hand move onto the next finger along.

"*No, don't!*" Blacklock cried. "*Don't! Please!*"

Blacklock's chest shuddered, his chin wet with spit and his cheeks with tears but he didn't care, all he cared about was not being hurt again. After a moment which felt very, very long, Cromwell took his hands away.

"I think we understand each other," Cromwell said. "Let him go."

Caleb released Blacklock and took a step back. Blacklock sagged against the end table, cradling his injured hand against his stomach, his legs unsteady. He felt sick and lightheaded and he only made it worse when he looked down and saw the little finger on his right hand pointing off at a nauseating angle. Bile rose in his throat and he forced himself to keep it down.

"Like I said, I'm under a lot of pressure," Cromwell said. "I've got competitors who've decided they want to take what's mine, and I'll be buggered if I'm going to let that happen. But the Lord works in mysterious ways, doesn't he? Because the solution to my problem might've walked into my office earlier today, all on account of you. What's your connection to the Roustabouts, Arthur? Because they were very keen to find you."

Blacklock tried to think but it was hard, he just wanted to lie down and close his eyes and go far away. But he couldn't do that, he was the star of this drama so all eyes were on him, he needed to get the show back on track.

"They came to one of my factories and threatened an employee," Blacklock lied, barely thinking about the words as they spilled forth through the pain. "He'd had some kind of disagreement with them. In a pub. I can't have people disrupting my business but I didn't want to involve the police so I did some investigating of my own. They must've gotten wind of it and now they're looking for me."

Cromwell looked at Blacklock with a thoughtful frown then nodded slowly. "Sounds like them, throwing their weight around like that."

Bolstered by his convincing performance, Blacklock went on. "Listen, I'm a member of a small group of Newmuck businessmen, very rich and powerful. We can help you like you want. We'll visit you tonight, at your cooperage. To discuss your future."

Cromwell smiled. "That's more like it. Eight o'clock. But not at the cooperage, you're not the only one who'd rather avoid a possible visit from the Roustabouts right now. I own a locksmiths on Brown Ox Row, meet me there."

"I'll be there. You have my word."

"Don't be late. Or I'll start cutting things off instead of just breaking them."

Cromwell and Caleb left the house. Within seconds of Caleb closing the front door, Blacklock turned towards the end table, planted his left hand on it and vomited all over its surface, spattering his waistcoat and trousers. He stood there for a time, breathing slowly, eyes closed, putting off what he knew he needed to do. Eventually he straightened up and used a sleeve to wipe his face. He gently grasped his broken finger with his left hand – the finger and the knuckle at its base were already beginning to swell and change colour – and took several deep breaths. He stared at the wall, envisioning Cromwell's face.

Blacklock snapped his little finger back into place and let out a high-pitched, utterly miserable cry which he had never made before in his life, perhaps apart from that time he caught his gentleman's pouch in the zipper of his trousers. His forearms thumped wetly against the surface of the end table as he leaned on it, his nose full of the sour smell of vomit, his head hanging as fresh tears fell. He reminded himself he was the hero of this story. Every hero endured great hardships, and he would endure his. Everyone would understand his pain after he became a god. He would make certain of it.

Blacklock walked to the stairs, thinking of the bandages he kept in the cabinet in the upstairs bathroom, bandaging his injured finger to the adjoining finger seeming like a sensible course of action. Leaning forward so as not to fall backwards if he fainted, he climbed the stairs and walked to the bathroom.

If someone had asked Blacklock at that moment if there was anything that could take his mind off the pain even for an instant, he would have said absolutely not. But when he opened the bathroom door, all thoughts of his broken finger suddenly vanished, replaced by the surprise of finding Gerald sitting on his toilet.

Blacklock froze, his mouth hanging open as he and the Abyss-Dweller stared at each other.

"Your make-up is smeared," Gerald said.

Blacklock unconsciously touched his face with his left hand then his surprise began to dissipate, the blanket of pain settling into place once more. "What the hell are you doing?"

Gerald hopped off the toilet seat. "Never sampling Newmuck's famous eel-wrapped chilli corn again." He pulled the chain and the toilet flushed. "I felt a powerful urge to defecate. In our natural environment, Abyss-Dwellers can do so when and where we please, but I didn't think you'd appreciate me doing so in your home so I used your facilities."

The thought of Abyss-Dwellers swimming around in their own filth had never occurred to Blacklock and it certainly wasn't a mental tableau he felt up to picturing at that moment.

"And why are you *in* my home?" Blacklock asked impatiently as he walked to the wall-mounted cabinet and opened it with his left hand.

Gerald approached the sink and turned on the cold tap, running water into an upturned claw. Then he uttered a satisfied croak as he slowly poured the water over his gills, first one side of his neck then the other. Blacklock saw the gills quiver gently and he turned back to the cabinet, disgusted. He rooted through its contents until he found what he was looking for then took a seat on the edge of the bath and unrolled the bandage.

"Mr. Cromwell seemed quite displeased with you," Gerald said.

Blacklock winced as he gingerly wrapped the bandage around his broken finger and the finger next to it. "Noticed that, did you?" he said sardonically. "Wait, you saw what happened?"

"From the landing. Before my bowels demanded attention."

"Why didn't you help? You could've killed both of them easily!"

"We've already expended a significant amount of effort on your behalf, Arthur. In fact, you're costing us a great deal."

"What are you talking about?" Blacklock grumbled, returning his attention to his bandage.

"The Abyss-Dwellers you suggested I have wait in ambush at Oliver's home are all dead. My auntie had a staircase spindle jammed through her skull."

"I thought your auntie was sliced in half at The Bewigged Pig?"

"I have many aunties. My bloodline has always enjoyed particularly fruitful spawnings."

That was another mental image Blacklock was in no shape for so he focused on finishing wrapping his fingers, using a pair of scissors to cut the bandage then pinning it in place with a safety pin. It was an amateurish job but it would do.

"My fallen kin have all been removed and returned to Mother Ocean but their deaths were unnecessary," Gerald said.

"Obviously Oliver didn't kill them all by himself," Blacklock said. "He must've had help from his new friends again. But if you're implying this is my fault then forget it. I suggested a plan and you agreed to it, no one forced you. The blood of your people isn't on my hands, it's on the hands of these Roustabouts."

"I can't help but notice that while Cecil was leading The Order of the Void, no Abyss-Dweller blood was shed. Yet since you usurped him, we've lost more of our number in the space of a single day than we have in centuries."

Using the edge of the bath for support, Blacklock stood up. "You're doubting me?"

Blacklock and Gerald stared at each other, anger mixing with Blacklock's pain now. First Cromwell and his lackey, now Gerald. Blacklock was sick of being threatened and criticised by his inferiors, by thugs and monsters not fit to clean his vomit-stained shoes. He was keenly aware of the scissors next to him and the satisfaction it would give him to jam them into Gerald's throat and watch him bleed out on the bathroom floor.

But no. Not yet.

"Oliver's allies were an unforeseen complication for all of us," Blacklock said, trying to mask his pain and anger with confidence, "but one we'll resolve, along with Oliver himself. I'm a leader of industry, a leader of men and the leader of The Order of the Void. And I'm your ally in the vision we share: a world reborn with the coming of the Old Ones."

"Are you certain Thomas or Frederick wouldn't be just as capable in your role?" Gerald asked.

It would be a cold day in Hell before Blacklock took orders from Sugarfoot or Orchardson. "They have faith in me."

"For a leader of men, you didn't seem to inspire much awe in Mr. Cromwell or his colleague."

"I was just playing the part required of me at the time."

"Helpless, terrified and subservient?"

Thinking of the scissors again, Blacklock forced a sickly smile, his head pounding, hand throbbing, stomach churning. Pretending you didn't want to stab someone in the throat with a pair of scissors was hard, but it was that kind of skill that made Blacklock the gifted actor he was.

"It can be very useful to have your enemies underestimate you," Blacklock said. "And speaking of Offal Cromwell, I think we can now consider *him* a complication as well. If I don't meet him tonight then he'll come back for me. He might even know about the ritual site. So I'm sure you'll agree he represents a potential threat to us."

"And how do you intend to resolve this complication?" Gerald asked.

Blacklock smiled again, this one not requiring quite as much effort. "By keeping my word."

The Unhelpful Silence of Mr. Squirrel

"Do you reckon a man could live if you pulled off his legs and fed them to him?" Talbot asked.

Bryn scratched his beard, smoke rising from the cigarette between his lips. "I'm not sure. I once knew a bloke who sneezed so hard all the bones in his arms were sucked up into his nose and flew out of his nostrils. He survived. His juggling was never the same, though. Why do you ask?"

"'Cause that's what I'm going to do to Cromwell."

"Bastard never changes," Digby said, leaning against a tree and frowning off across the grassland.

Sitting on a wooden bench, Ambrose looked over at Digby's furrowed brow. None of the other Roustabouts, Ambrose included, knew all the ins and outs of Digby's history with Cromwell, and Digby had never been keen to go into much detail, but they knew enough. Namely, that Digby had once been a member of Cromwell's gang until he soured on that life and decided to leave it behind and turn over a new leaf, a decision Cromwell didn't take very well. There had been bad blood between them ever since, and the worst kind: the kind that could only form between two people who were once very close.

Ambrose heard high-pitched laughter in the distance and looked towards the far end of the gently sloping clearing to see a young couple walking arm in arm, the girl smiling, her free hand raised to her mouth to stifle further laughter as the man grinned at her. They sauntered along, comfortable in each other's company, worlds apart from the formal stiffness common to many Newmuck couples when out in public. Ambrose smiled. Good for them.

The Roustabouts, Annie, Oliver and Randolph had come to a clearing at the south end of Touchpudding Common, which may not have been one of Newmuck's fancy urban parks but was the largest expanse of open land in the city and, unlike so much of the increasingly overpopulated city, was protected against being built upon, although Ambrose wondered how long that would last. Money talked, after all, and rarely had anything nice to say. He liked the hustle and bustle of life in the city, he had never known things any other way, but he also appreciated having some space to breathe and a little peace amongst nature every now and then. The clouds had cleared somewhat and the trees cast long shadows as the sun sank and evening came on. The spot where Randolph had parked was quiet, the nearby dirt track that wound through the woods uneven and overgrown, the numbness in Ambrose's arse from the bumpy ride thankfully having faded by now.

They had all left Lucan's house together after Ambrose, Henry, Talbot and Digby were freed from the cell and Lucan and Peanut locked inside in their place. Both the monster and its creator were dead, Lucan's neck having broken in his fall down the stairs. The Roustabouts broke off the cell key in its lock just in case Lucan's handiness with reanimating dead flesh included his own. Bryn, Annie and Oliver were filled in on what happened at the house, and they in turn told of Orchardson's fate at the Annual Newmuck Bankers Garden Party. Although Oliver didn't really contribute, being badly shaken after inadvertently killing Lucan by opening the cellar door without realising the old man was on the other side of it.

A brief search of Lucan's house turned up a large collection of strange ingredients and formulas, several daggers and other small weapons, books on magic and various arcane practices, a small bundle of cash, and a pile of newspaper clippings spanning several decades and countries, detailing murders, arsons and other crimes which Lucan must have been responsible for.

Henry asked Randolph, who had driven Bryn, Annie and Oliver to Lucan's address after rejoining them following their flight from the party, to drive all of them to a quiet spot where they could decide upon their next course of action. Because with Orchardson dead and them being no closer to finding Blacklock, their two leads had come to nothing.

Ambrose doubted that anyone had ever accused the Roustabouts of being great strategists, even with his military background, although admittedly thirty-six hours as a private in the British Army, from the moment he signed up to the moment he sobered up, wasn't much of a military background. Still, he was confident that between the seven of them, they could come up with something. He wasn't including Randolph as the driver was currently taking a nap inside his carriage, exhausted due to a combination of working long hours and having two young children at home. Randolph was visible through the windows, his arms folded, head resting against the seat, hat tipped down over his eyes. His two horses, still hitched to the Clarence, munched contentedly on some grass.

"Cromwell must've known who was living at that house," Henry said. He sat with Bryn and Annie on one bench while Ambrose, Talbot and Oliver sat on a second identical bench, their paint peeling and faded. "That's why he sent us there, in the hope we'd kill Lucan and save him a job or Lucan would kill us. Or both."

"Cromwell knows what usually happens to people who try to kill us," Ambrose said.

"He also knows having us out of the picture will make things a lot easier for him if he's getting ambitious."

"Maybe it was more out of desperation, what with those lunatics the Candle brothers making a move against him."

"When we get our hands on him, we can ask him," Talbot said. "Before his mouth is full of his own legs, obviously."

"Exactly," Digby said, stepping away from the tree and turning towards the benches. "Why are we wasting time sitting around here? Let's go get him."

"Cromwell isn't going to be at the cooperage," Henry said, "he knew there was a chance we'd walk out of Lucan's house alive and come looking for him, and he knows that's the first place we'd look. And we don't have time to go chasing around half of Newmuck after him, not with what's at stake. He might not even know Blacklock's address anyway. You giving Cromwell a hiding won't count for much if the world ends."

"Might be worth it." After a moment, Digby looked across the clearing and sighed. "Fine, we'll save the world *then* make Offal wish we hadn't."

"So what's the plan?" Annie asked.

The Roustabouts looked at each other, each man waiting for someone else to offer a suggestion, but the closest thing to a contribution was Randolph's gentle snoring. Their attention turned to a grey squirrel as it scrambled down a nearby tree, ran a few yards then stopped and looked back at them in silence. Apparently it didn't have any ideas either.

"Lizzie gave us an address for her father," Bryn said. "We could search the place but there's no way the police won't be there after what happened at the party, so it's probably a bad idea."

There was a general murmur of agreement.

Digby gave Bryn a sly smile. "'Lizzie', is it?"

Bryn frowned. "That's what she told us to call her. What?"

Digby shrugged, still smiling. "Nothing."

Ambrose looked down and saw the message "GARY IZ A NOB" crudely carved into one of the wooden slats visible between his thighs. Following that revelation he looked over at Oliver, who was staring at the ground with a troubled frown, lost in thought.

"What about the cannery?" Ambrose said.

"What about it?" Henry said.

"Maybe Cecil Burgess kept something in his office there that might be able to help us, something to do with Blacklock or Sugarfoot or the ritual. We could break in and take a look. And there's the caves Oliver told us about. Who knows, maybe Blacklock's still planning to have the ritual there after all."

"I reckon it's worth a shot. Oliver, what do you think?"

Oliver looked up at Henry like a man awoken from a drowse. "Sorry?" Ambrose repeated his suggestion but Oliver seemed sceptical. "I don't know. The information and materials to do with the Order and the Ritual of Suth-G'nar that my father had, he always kept that sort of thing at home, never at work."

"Are you sure?" Annie asked. "You said yourself you weren't really kept in the loop."

"No, I suppose I can't say for certain. I have keys to the cannery but they don't include a key to my father's office or the cellar. The cannery's closed on Sundays but there'll still be some guards on duty. Well, that *was* the case. With everything that's happened in the past couple of days, I'm not certain of much of anything anymore."

"Life's full of surprises," Ambrose said.

"Like when Barry the greengrocer turned out to be five midgets in a coat," Talbot said.

Bryn shook his head as he dropped his cigarette butt and ground it beneath his shoe. "How his wife never realised that I'll never know."

Henry clapped his hands onto his knees and stood up. "The cannery it is. Unless anyone has any better ideas?"

No one did, and the squirrel was gone. Everyone rose to their feet.

Henry turned to Annie. "Now, I know what you're going to say –"

"That me and Burgess should go back to the Pig and stay there while you five check out the cannery?" Annie said.

Henry paused. "Alright, so maybe I *didn't* know what you were going to say."

Annie nodded in the direction of Oliver, who had resumed staring at the ground, as downcast as a drunk who had just missed last call. "He's not going to be much use to you as he is, just take his keys. As for me, I'd like to check on the pub and I think you boys can handle this one without me. I'll keep an eye on Burgess, make sure he doesn't get any sudden ideas about legging it. If any trouble shows up, I'll handle it." Henry opened his mouth to speak but Annie beat him to it. "*If* I can. If not then me and Burgess will both leg it. Don't worry, I'm not stupid."

"I know. Just be careful."

As everyone else began walking towards the carriage, Ambrose turned to Oliver. "You alright? You look like you've got the morbs."

Oliver continued staring at the ground. "I killed a man."

"A very bad one. You saw the news clippings."

"I know, but… well, you don't just go around killing people, do you? That's not how things work. That man's dead. Because of *me*. I know there was that poor worker at the cannery, but… this is different."

"Lucan was more of a monster than the thing he kept in his cellar. And now there's one less monster in the world. You've got nothing to feel guilty about."

Oliver looked up at Ambrose and managed a weak smile. "Thank you."

They rejoined the others at the Clarence as Bryn stroked the neck of the nearest horse and Henry tapped on the window next to Randolph, who jerked awake, opened the door and stepped down from the carriage.

"We need to go," Henry said. "Then we'll let you get home to your family."

"Not a problem," Randolph said. "You just tell me where."

Henry reached into his right-hand trouser pocket. "This is for you," he said as he withdrew the cash taken from Lucan's house and placed it in Randolph's hand.

Randolph frowned at the money. "What's this?"

"You've gone above and beyond for us today and we don't take that kind of thing for granted."

Randolph thumbed through the banknotes. "There's about two months' wages here." He shook his head and held out the money to Henry. "This is too much, I can't take this."

"You can and you will. That money came from a bad place, so you do some good with it, for you and your family."

Randolph hesitated then nodded. "Thank you. All of you." He pocketed the money and hoisted himself up into the driver's seat.

Digby held open the carriage door and motioned for Annie to enter. "Ladies first," he said, smiling.

"Thank you, Digby," Annie said as she placed a foot on the step.

Digby gave her a wink. "You can sit on my lap if it makes you more comfortable, you know."

"Well, it's not as if you've got much getting in the way down there, is it," Annie said innocently as she climbed into the carriage.

"What do – hey, hang on!"

An Odd-Chinned Nephew's Story Relayed

The Scotch burned Blacklock's throat as he gulped it down, emptying the glass in three long swallows.

At almost two pounds a bottle the Glengibbous was usually a drink to savour, but Blacklock was desperate to dull the pain in his hand and the Scotch was the best available option. The three aspirin in his bathroom cabinet would do nothing for a broken finger but he had washed them down with his first glass anyway.

He had also tried to distract himself with his album of little card-sized photographs which came with the first issue of a bimonthly magazine he had bought last year. The magazine focused on famous British actors of the day and each issue came with a photograph card of a different actor, the goal being to buy every issue, collect the whole set of cards and fill the album. But Blacklock only bought the first two issues before forgetting about the magazine, so only Peter Hunter and Breezy Eaves looked up at him from the otherwise empty album. It wasn't long before he realised how much he hated the sight of their handsome, smug, smiling faces, and he declared them talentless hacks as he threw the album to the floor, where it had lain since.

His bandaged right hand resting in his lap, Blacklock used his left hand to lift the Glengibbous from the table next to him and was about to refill his glass but paused when he saw he had already drunk almost a third of the bottle. He couldn't afford to get drunk now, he needed to stay in control, his appointment with Cromwell less than two hours away. But the agony in his hand had spread up his arm, his neck and shoulders ached with tension, and a bright star of pain blazed in his head. So maybe one more. Just a small one.

Blacklock poured himself a large Scotch. Sitting in his bedroom armchair, he stared out of the window. A deep orange glow bathed the horizon as the sun sank beyond it, the undersides of distant clouds an angry shade of pink. The jagged Newmuck skyline was black against the vivid colours, lights flickering into life across the city as night descended.

Blacklock had no lights on in the bedroom, preferring the darkness for now. Soon enough he would be standing before the brightest lights the world had ever seen, and there would be no more pain. Not for him, anyway.

He was alone in the house as far as he was aware, Gerald having left after their discussion earlier, the Abyss-Dweller needing some convincing on Blacklock's plan for Cromwell but eventually agreeing. Blacklock looked at his swollen and discoloured right hand, thought about what Cromwell had coming to him, and almost smiled as he took another drink.

Blacklock had briefly thought about leaving as well in case the Roustabouts came for him or Cromwell returned but he refused to flee his own home. He was fairly certain that Oliver didn't know where he lived so couldn't share that information with the Roustabouts, and as for Cromwell having a change of heart and coming back to finish the job, that was why next to Blacklock's Glengibbous lay a loaded double-action revolver. Quinn had provided him with the gun some time ago as well as taught him how to load and fire it.

So Blacklock had stayed, removing clothes damp with sweat and vomit and changing into clean underwear, trousers, shoes, shirt, and waistcoat, the process a lengthy and painful ordeal given the condition of his right hand. He washed his face, smoothed his hair, rinsed out his mouth and even cleaned up the mess in the lobby. Then he sat in his bedroom and began to drink as the room darkened to match his thoughts.

Blacklock flinched as someone hammered on the front door.

In the silence that followed he leaned forward, tense, his heart pounding. When the hammering repeated he replaced the Scotch in his left hand with the gun, stood up, took a deep breath and left the bedroom. He walked to the landing then down to the lobby floor, stopping near the foot of the stairs as whoever was at the front door pounded on it again, the noise unnervingly loud and close now. The lobby was dark except for a single light which Blacklock had left on.

Blacklock pointed the revolver at the door, trying not to think about how heavy the gun felt, how it was shaking in his hand, how he had never fired it at a living thing and how he was right-handed. In an effort to steel himself, he thought about hitting Cecil with that decanter: that frozen moment of shock and pain on Cecil's face, Cecil writhing and bleeding on the floor before him. He tried to recall that thrilling rush of savagery and power but it seemed like the memory of a different man. But of course he had had an audience then.

"*Who's there?*" Blacklock called out, blaming the unsteadiness of his voice on the Scotch.

"Arthur?" a muffled voice answered. "Is that you?"

Sugarfoot. What was he doing here?

Blacklock used the three free digits of his right hand to unlock and open the front door. Sugarfoot stood in a suit and fur-lined overcoat, his top hat held before his chest in both hands as he nervously fiddled with its brim, his eyes darting around. He was agitated, a change for a man who usually exhibited the kinetic energy of lakebed sediment.

"Arthur, thank God," Sugarfoot said as, uninvited, he shuffled past Blacklock and into the lobby.

Blacklock gritted his teeth, his left index finger tightening ever so slightly on the trigger of his revolver. He had had enough unwanted visitors for one day. Beyond his front gate he saw Sugarfoot's brougham and driver parked at the pavement. He closed the front door, making sure to lock it.

"Are you alone?" Sugarfoot asked.

"I *was*," Blacklock said. "Why are you here, Thomas?"

Sugarfoot opened his mouth to speak but then hesitated as he saw what Blacklock was holding down at his side. "What's the gun for?" he asked cautiously.

Blacklock looked down at the revolver. "Shooting, traditionally."

Sugarfoot's eyes moved to Blacklock's right hand. "What happened to your hand?"

"I caught it in a door," Blacklock said, refusing to admit the truth and appear weak in Sugarfoot's eyes.

"Must've been quite a slam. Perhaps you should see a doctor."

"I don't have time for that. Again, why are you here?"

Sugarfoot paused. "Frederick is dead."

"What?"

"I received word about an hour ago. It happened at that bankers garden party he was attending today. My nephew – horrible chap, odd chin, married an American girl – he was there, saw everything."

"What happened?"

Sugarfoot relayed the story his nephew had told him about how this year's Annual Newmuck Bankers Garden Party had been uneventful until Orchardson came barrelling through the house with a woman and two men in pursuit, the chase moving out to the rear garden as a number of guards joined in, and eventually ending with the pursuers fleeing into nearby woodland and Orchardson being found impaled on a tree, the party coming to an abrupt end and the police soon arriving on the scene.

"I thought I'd best tell you in case you hadn't heard," Sugarfoot said.

Blacklock stared at the wall with a troubled frown. He felt as much grief at the news of Orchardson's death as Sugarfoot did, but it was yet another unexpected development and there had been too many of those recently. "You could've told me over the telephone."

"I thought… well, safety in numbers and all that," Sugarfoot said.

"The younger man chasing Frederick, from your nephew's description that sounds like Oliver. And the big one with the beard must've been one of the Roustabouts. As for the woman, I have no idea. Somehow they knew about the party and went there for Frederick, probably to kill or kidnap him."

Sugarfoot started pacing the floor, shaking his head. "This is bad business, Arthur, very bad."

"Calm down," Blacklock said, trying to think.

Even when The Order of the Void had numbered five people, the Ritual of Suth-G'nar never required all of them. When Blacklock first considered having Cecil and Oliver killed, he did so in the knowledge that Sugarfoot, Orchardson and himself would still be enough to carry out the necessary steps of the ritual when the time came. But now they were down to two.

Sugarfoot was rambling now as he went on pacing back and forth. "What if I'm next? Oliver and these thugs are out for blood, they've made that clear, and they won't stop at Frederick, oh no. They'll be coming for us."

"Be quiet," Blacklock said irritably.

He and Sugarfoot would just have to fill in for Orchardson while still playing their own parts, Blacklock preferring this option to having Gerald or another Abyss-Dweller replace Orchardson. Although there would be plenty of them present at the ritual, Blacklock didn't want the Abyss-Dwellers to have any more direct involvement than they already did if he could help it. It would be a little awkward but he was confident it could be done. Orchardson's death was probably a good thing, in fact. One less potential failure or betrayal. Everything was still under control.

"I'm not afraid to say it," Sugarfoot said, "I'm starting to have doubts about this whole business, these bloody Abyss-Dwellers and Old Ones, they're all more trouble than they're worth, I'm not going to –"

Blacklock suddenly found himself striding towards Sugarfoot, whose rambling and pacing abruptly stopped as Blacklock jammed the muzzle of his revolver into the roll of fat beneath Sugarfoot's chin. Sugarfoot gasped in alarm, his eyes widening as Blacklock leaned in close, crushing Sugarfoot's hat between their chests.

Blacklock's eyes blazed. "If you think for *one second* I'm going to let you ruin this for me now after everything I've been through then you've got another thing coming! So pull yourself together and just *do as I say! Understand?*"

Sugarfoot risked a tiny nod. "Mm," he squeaked.

The two men remained like that for a moment before Blacklock lowered his revolver and took a step backwards, his pulse slowing and anger subsiding. "Good," he said.

Sugarfoot exhaled and sagged with relief. "Steady on there, old chap. No need for all that."

Blacklock knew that a little more pressure on the trigger and there would have been another mess to clean up in the lobby, namely Sugarfoot's brains. Losing Orchardson for the ritual was one thing but Blacklock didn't want to risk losing Sugarfoot as well, so for now they were still in this together.

"I'm sorry, Thomas," Blacklock said, forcing an apologetic smile. "It's just we're so close to achieving what we've worked for and I'd hate to see you lose out on what you deserve. And of course I'm shaken by the news of Frederick's passing. You understand."

Sugarfoot fondled his fat roll and looked doubtfully at Blacklock. "Of course."

Although Blacklock had made the required impression on Sugarfoot, he was sceptical as to how long it would last when they went their separate ways again. He wondered if he should keep an eye on Sugarfoot to ensure the old fool didn't entertain any more notions of abandoning his role. Also, it wouldn't hurt for Sugarfoot to personally witness what happened to people who crossed Blacklock. People like Offal Cromwell.

"Why don't you go take a seat in the study and I'll fetch you a drink?" Blacklock said, certain that Sugarfoot wouldn't be able to resist alcohol and a comfortable armchair. "I have a bottle of Glengibbous already open. We can share it until we leave."

Sugarfoot straightened out his hat and pretended to give the suggestion some thought before eventually nodding approvingly. "Capital idea." He frowned. "Until we leave for where?"

"Brown Ox Row," Blacklock said as he headed for the stairs.

"Why are we going there?"

Blacklock began to ascend to the second floor. "Because you're not the only man I know who should get what he deserves."

A Liberal Seasoning

Oliver heard a plop and looked down to see that some kind of unknown organ, rubbery and slick with black blood, had fallen out of one of the dead Abyss-Dwellers and landed on his shoe.

Oliver felt his stomach lurch. He tilted his foot, the organ sliding onto the stone floor. He glanced at the gaping hole in the gut of the Abyss-Dweller to whom the organ had belonged, then focused on the string of garlic in his hands. He plucked one of its few remaining bulbs and tossed it onto the corpse as Annie did the same next to him, the pile of dead Abyss-Dwellers already dotted with dozens of bulbs.

It had been Annie's idea. After they left Touchpudding Common she asked Randolph to make a quick stop at a greengrocer then emerged a minute later carrying armfuls of strings of garlic, intending to use them to combat the smell of the dead Abyss-Dwellers in the pub cellar, the garlic aroma overpowering inside the cramped carriage. Randolph dropped off Oliver and Annie at The Bewigged Pig, they wished the Roustabouts luck then the carriage rolled away into the night.

Oliver plucked another bulb and tossed it onto the corpse pile, trying not to let his eyes linger on any grisly details for too long, although his gaze froze when it met the eyes of an Abyss-Dweller who seemed to be staring directly at him, knowing and accusing. Just as Lucan had. Oliver shuddered and tore his gaze away.

The cellar had a stone floor and walls, a low wooden ceiling and a short staircase leading to a trapdoor connecting the cellar to the ground-floor storeroom. At one end of the cellar a wooden ramp led to a securely locked metal hatch built into the floor of the alley at the side of the building, and it was through this hatch that full barrels of lager, cider and bitter were delivered to the pub and empty barrels taken away. The barrels currently in use were connected to their respective taps upstairs by thin metal pipes that rose into the ceiling while the empty barrels had been moved from their usual corner to make room for the dead Abyss-Dwellers, the corner now occupied by a jumbled, leaking mound of pulped and torn flesh, congealed blood, exposed organs, broken bones, and the occasional severed limb or loose eyeball. The smell was bad but not as bad as Oliver had expected, the Abyss-Dwellers seemingly not decomposing too quickly. It was cool in the cellar, he imagined that helped. Not that he was an expert. He was used to being around dead sea creatures but not quite like this.

Annie threw her last garlic bulb onto the pile along with the length of raffia to which it had been attached. "Done."

With no small degree of relief, Oliver did the same then followed Annie to the stairs, where she turned off the cellar's single light, plunging the room into darkness, the corpse pile glistening horribly in what light spilled through the open trapdoor above. They climbed the stairs to the storeroom and Annie closed the trapdoor after them, the smell of garlic lingering in Oliver's nose. Most of the shelves in the storeroom were taken up by liquor bottles including various brands of whiskey, gin, rum, vodka, and more, while amongst the packaged snacks Oliver couldn't fail to notice the Burgess-brand whelks, mussels, sardines and sweet 'n' cheesy plankton.

"Let's have a drink," Annie said.

Oliver thought of those accusing eyes, both Abyss-Dweller and human. "A drink would be nice."

"Go and sit down, I'll just be a minute."

Oliver headed to the barroom as Annie went upstairs. She had lit the fire earlier and the burning logs were piled high but the room didn't get too warm as cool air drifted in through the small gaps in the barricaded windows and front door. After the oppressive and cloying atmosphere of the cellar, Oliver was grateful for it.

Oliver took a seat at the Roustabouts' table and sighed, knowing he didn't deserve fresh air or any other simple pleasures. True, he hadn't been as active in preparing the apocalypse as his father, the other members of The Order of the Void or the Abyss-Dwellers, but he did his share, always following orders, aware he was doing a terrible thing but too weak and scared to do otherwise. And although he was helping to try to stop it now, he knew he wasn't in this situation as a result of any kind of moral choice on his part. If Blacklock and the others hadn't betrayed him and his father, he would have carried on doing what he was told until the Ritual of Suth-G'nar was performed and the Old Ones came and made things very unpleasant for everyone, including Annie and the Roustabouts, strangers who had taken him in, saved his life, done the right thing. He was ashamed of himself. He had always been a coward, now he was a coward who had just happened to end up on the right side.

Not only a coward, Oliver thought. *A murderer too.*

He frowned at the memory of the noise Lucan had made tumbling down those wooden stairs: *ba-dump, ba-dump, ba-dump, crack*. He had opened a door and just like that a man was dead. He knew Ambrose was right, that Lucan had been a terrible person, a killer with blood on his hands who deserved what he got, but that didn't automatically sweep away the guilt like Oliver wished it would. Because didn't he have blood on his own hands now?

Annie entered the room carrying a bowl of water which she placed on the bar. "Wash your hands."

Oliver stared, wondering if she had read his mind. "What?"

"Get the smell of garlic off them. Plus we were just standing next to a pile of monster corpses, so it's probably a good idea generally."

"Right, of course."

Oliver stood up and walked to the bar as Annie washed her hands in the bowl then dried them on a tea-towel she had slung over one shoulder. She left the tea-towel for Oliver, who washed and dried his own hands as she went behind the bar and took two small glasses from a shelf.

Annie poured a generous measure of gin into one glass and an equal measure of whiskey into the other. She took a large swallow of gin and passed the whiskey to Oliver, who thanked her. They walked to the Roustabouts' table and sat down, Oliver grimacing as he took a drink, the whiskey burning his throat and making his mouth water unpleasantly.

Annie looked at the expression on his face. "I can get you something else."

Oliver shook his head. "It's fine, thank you. I'm not usually much of a drinker but I feel like I could do with this right now."

"It's been a busy weekend."

Oliver gave Annie a tired smile. "Somewhat of an understatement. Do you think they'll be alright? The Roustabouts, I mean?"

Oliver had handed Henry his keys to the cannery while warning the Roustabouts to be careful if they did explore beneath the property, as beyond the cave which was the intended ritual site the place became a treacherous labyrinth. Some tunnels were flooded, others blocked by cave-ins, a few ended in sheer drops into abyssal blackness while some split again and again, a network of subterranean passageways twisting and spreading like malignant, hollow roots. Oliver had never liked setting foot down there and was always glad that even his father, obsessed as he was, recognised the dangers of venturing too far into that maze, although the fact the Abyss-Dwellers had an advantage over Cecil in being intimately familiar with it grated on him.

"They'll be fine," Annie said. "You'd be amazed at the messes they get themselves into."

"You seem quite close to them," Oliver said.

"They were already regulars here when I moved in and started working for my uncle, that was years ago. They can be idiots sometimes but their hearts are in the right place and they've always been there when I needed them. I try to do the same for them."

Oliver opened his mouth to say it must be nice to have friends but caught himself as he realised how self-pitying that sounded. He didn't hold out much hope of actually impressing Annie but if he could stop himself from appearing even more pathetic in her eyes then that would at least be something.

"Well, that's good," he said instead, somewhat lamely. He sipped his whiskey. "So your uncle used to own the pub?"

Annie pointed in the direction of the nude painting of Ewan Radcliffe. "That's him up there."

Oliver followed her finger. "I, um, did wonder about the painting. Is it just me or do the nipples follow you around the room?"

Annie smiled fondly. "Ewan was a mad old bugger. When he died, he left this place to me. He'd already bought the property outright so it's been run as a free house ever since, I've never been tied to one brewery like a lot of landlords. And I already knew everything I needed to know, more or less. There's a lot of competition, obviously: fancy pubs, tiny brewhouses, chancers selling booze off casks on their backs. Then you've got the temperance lot, who won't be happy until you can't get a drop of alcohol in the whole city. They think all of mankind's evils can be put down to booze instead of just, well, people being arseholes. But at the end of the day, there are a lot worse places to drink in Newmuck. Places where you won't be halfway through saying 'Pint please, barman' before someone clubs you over the back of the head and pinches your wallet and shoes. The boys being regulars helps keep the scum out, everyone knows they drink here. Mess with The Bewigged Pig, mess with the Roustabouts." Annie gave Oliver a pointed look. "Not that I can't look after this place on my own."

"Oh, I don't doubt your capabilities one bit, Miss Radcliffe."

"Just call me Annie."

"Alright, Annie. In fact, I'm amazed at how well you and the Roustabouts have handled all this. The first time I became aware of the Abyss-Dwellers and the Old Ones I'm afraid I was... rather more rattled."

"I learned a long time ago to keep an open mind and take things in my stride. As for the boys, they've faced their share of strangeness and more. Some of the stories they've told me would blow your mind, and I know they never lie about any of it. Misremember because they were drunk, maybe, but never lie. And nothing much rattles them, they're too bull-at-a-gate for that, for good or bad."

As silence fell between them, Oliver looked around at the damage and once again reflected on the trouble he had caused Annie. He looked up at the painting of Ken Radcliffe but found no comfort there, the nipples seeming to thrust accusingly in his direction.

"I really am sorry about all this," Oliver said, gesturing at the barroom in general.

"You've already said that," Annie said. "And I believe you. Still, would've been better if it hadn't happened in the first place, eh?"

Oliver hung his head and stared into his glass.

After a moment, Annie broke the silence. "Anyway, what are you going to do when this nonsense is over?"

Oliver considered the question. "I don't know. I honestly hadn't given it any thought."

"Because you think we're all going to die?"

"Oh, only a percentage of the world's population will die when the Old Ones enter our reality. Those left will be at the Old Ones' unknowable whims, but from what I gather most people will likely be plunged into a nightmarish insanity in which every terrible second feels like an eternity and –"

"Yes, alright. You know what I mean."

"I suppose I've just never considered an alternative. My father told me what was going to happen and that was that. There was never any point in hoping for anything else."

Annie studied Oliver for a moment. "Your dad really did a number on you, didn't he."

Oliver nodded. "I can't deny that." He took a large swallow of whiskey and immediately regretted it.

"Well, he's gone now, so when this is over maybe you can finally be your own man," Annie said. "If you don't end up dead or in prison."

A smile crept cautiously onto Oliver's face. Being his own man, imagine that. It was a terrifying prospect, but also an exciting one. If the world didn't end tomorrow as he had been expecting for so long then the future beyond that was an endless horizon of possibilities he had never considered, a limitless sky undarkened by the vast, looming figure of his father. What would he be in such a future? What *could* he be?

Then he brought himself crashing back down to Earth as he thought of the Old Ones, the Abyss-Dwellers and the remaining two men who now made up The Order of the Void. Oliver didn't doubt the Roustabouts' strength and resolve but knew it was best not to hope for too much.

Then again, here he was, having drinks and conversation with a beautiful and intelligent lady, just the two of them, a young man and young woman getting to know each other. It was a new situation for him, but not an unpleasant one.

Oliver felt another smile creeping onto his face as he sipped his whiskey, which went down the wrong way and caused him to cough violently, spittle and whiskey droplets flying, Annie leaning back to avoid the spray. Oliver covered his mouth as quickly as he could and coughed several more times, then cleared his throat and tried to blink away the tears in his eyes.

"Are you alright?" Annie asked.

His hand still in front of his mouth, Oliver glanced at her and nodded as he cleared his throat a final time. Then he stood up with as much dignity as he could manage, which he knew was next to none, and said, "I'll just fetch myself a glass of milk if you don't mind."

Tough Crowd

Blacklock stepped out of the brougham and onto the pavement, followed by Sugarfoot.

"Wait here," Blacklock told Sugarfoot's driver, a chubby, middle-aged man with a neatly trimmed beard. The driver looked down at his employer, who gave him an uncertain nod in return.

Blacklock started walking, Sugarfoot pulling his overcoat tighter around himself as he fell into step at Blacklock's side. The carriage was parked at one end of Brown Ox Row, the street stretching ahead, a strip of old buildings and uneven cobbles, shadowy figures slumped in alleys and shuffling along the dirty, poorly lit pavements. Almost all of the businesses were closed at this time of night, their interiors silent and dark, while light crept out from between the window-shutters of houses and the distant sounds of a pub could be heard from an adjoining street. Blacklock and Sugarfoot passed a house inside which a couple were arguing, their voices raised but the words indistinct, although the tinkling crash of a piece of crockery shattering against a hard surface was clear enough. Sugarfoot flinched but Blacklock paid it no mind. Despite the pain, he was focused.

"You've still got that pistol on you, haven't you?" Sugarfoot asked as he glanced nervously around the street. "I really don't think it's wise, us being exposed like this when our lives are in danger."

Blacklock felt the weight of the revolver nestled inside his coat's interior pocket. "I told you, everything's in hand."

Sugarfoot frowned. "Was that a joke?"

"What?"

"You said 'everything's in hand.' I didn't know if that was a joke. About *your* hand."

Blacklock looked down at his swollen, discoloured right hand and bandaged fingers, then at Sugarfoot. "Why the hell would I joke about that?"

"I don't know, I –"

Blacklock stopped suddenly and turned on Sugarfoot. "Do *you* find it funny?"

Sugarfoot leaned away from Blacklock. "No! No, not at all! I just thought… never mind."

They continued on their way, a mangy cat watching them lazily from the top of a high wall as they passed by. Blacklock hissed at it but the cat just stared at him with its yellow-green eyes, unimpressed.

"You're looking a tad pale, Arthur," Sugarfoot said.

"I'm fine," Blacklock said firmly as his hand throbbed and head ached. "Just remember what I said: when we're inside, keep quiet and stay out of the way."

"Stay out of the way of what, precisely? You still haven't told me quite what the purpose of this visit is."

"As I said, I owe Cromwell a debt."

"I thought you'd paid him for the Yaroslav Manuscript pages?"

"It's not about the pages."

Blacklock almost followed this up with "It's about revenge", a suitably dramatic line, but Sugarfoot was his audience for this scene and Blacklock didn't want to tip his hand too early. If the audience could see the blood coming then it didn't have the same impact.

About halfway along the street, Blacklock and Sugarfoot found themselves outside Ox Locks, a terraced two-storey building and what Blacklock assumed to be the locksmiths Cromwell had spoken of. A blind was pulled down behind the glass pane set in the front door, the window next to it revealing little of the dark interior. Blacklock knocked on the glass with his left hand and a figure detached itself from the shadows within. A key turned in the lock then the door opened inward, revealing a flat-nosed, dull-eyed man in a cheap brown suit.

"I'm Arthur Blacklock," Blacklock said. "Mr. Cromwell is expecting me."

The man stepped aside and Blacklock and Sugarfoot entered the locksmiths, where a wide array of locks were displayed on shelves and stands, from simple bar padlocks to a pierce lock which would fire a small harpoon into the hand of anyone who tried to pick it. At one side of the room stood a waist-high counter, a till, a rack of hooks with dozens of keys dangling from them, and a key-cutting machine. The only light was a dim glow in an adjoining hallway at the back of the room, several coats and hats hanging from a nearby coat-stand.

Blacklock saw the apprehension on Sugarfoot's face as Cromwell's man locked the front door again, and that apprehension turned to outright dismay when Blacklock took out his gun and held it out to the man grip-first. He wouldn't need it to deal with Cromwell, although he had chosen not to mention that fact to Sugarfoot. Blacklock found himself taking pleasure in Sugarfoot's unease, visualising it as a cloth mouse on a string that he could bat around with his paws. If he was a cat, that was. And not a mangy stray like that little shit outside but a sleek, dark predator. He possessed the range to pull off the role. He could be anything he wanted to be.

The man looked at the revolver then at Blacklock, who smiled and said, "To save you searching me."

The man took the gun and tucked it into the waistband of his trousers then searched Blacklock anyway, roughly patting him down before doing the same to Sugarfoot, who appeared extremely uncomfortable throughout. When the man was satisfied, he started walking towards the hallway at the back of the room.

"Follow me," he said.

Blacklock and Sugarfoot followed, removing their hats and carrying them down at their sides. Leading off the hallway were two doors and Blacklock and Sugarfoot followed their guide through the one which stood open, light and voices emerging from the room beyond.

The room was small and simple, with painted brick walls and a single window covered by a metal grille and a pair of curtains. Around the edges of the room stood stacks of small crates, a metal filing cabinet and two workbenches covered in tools and lock parts.

In the centre of the room, sitting around a battered circular table, were Cromwell, Caleb and a third man, skinny and with an ugly scar on his neck, who Blacklock didn't recognise. They were drinking, smoking and gambling, hazy clouds of cigarette smoke hanging in the air, the table dotted with small piles of cash, a brimming ashtray, a half-empty bottle of rum, playing cards, and three liquor glasses. They were a shabby audience to say the least. But Blacklock knew a good actor could control *any* audience.

Cromwell and the scarred man had been laughing about something but stopped as Blacklock and Sugarfoot were led into the room.

Cromwell smiled and placed his cards face-down on the table. "Arthur!" He took a timepiece from his shirt pocket and glanced at it. "And right on time. See, lads, a professional attitude can get you far in this life."

The scarred man smirked. Caleb's face didn't twitch.

The man in the brown suit approached the table and set down Blacklock's revolver. "He was carrying this."

"A man can't be too careful walking the streets at night," Blacklock said.

"Very true," Cromwell said, nodding, apparently unconcerned by the revolver.

He isn't worried about the gun because he doesn't think I'd have the nerve to use it, Blacklock thought. Then he thought of what Cromwell's underestimation of him was going to cost the insolent thug, and once again Blacklock saw himself as a cat, this time toying with flesh-and-blood prey.

"I must say I can appreciate the irony," Blacklock said, looking around the room. "A criminal running a business designed to make people feel safer. I imagine it must be quite useful to know exactly what kind of security your customers use for their homes and businesses."

Cromwell shrugged. "This shop only sells quality products, but any house-breaker with a bit of skill, well, if he wants to get in somewhere then he's going to get in."

"And give you your cut of the profits afterwards, of course."

Cromwell glanced at Sugarfoot. "Where's the rest of your friends?"

"I'm afraid the others couldn't attend due to the short notice. They're very busy men. But my colleague and I speak for all of us. Rest assured, we're going to change your life tonight."

Out of the corner of his eye, Blacklock saw the utterly lost expression on Sugarfoot's face. Cromwell took a drink of rum and nodded at the man in the brown suit, who left the room.

"How's the hand?" Caleb asked Blacklock.

Blacklock forced a smile. "Fine. Thank you."

Cromwell looked Sugarfoot up and down. "So who's this, then?"

"Actually, Offal, I have a question for you first," Blacklock said.

"Fire away."

Blacklock hesitated briefly as he wondered if Cromwell's remark was some kind of mocking jab regarding him and his revolver, but the moment passed and he regained his composure.

"Do you have any regrets?" Blacklock asked as he placed his hat on top of the nearby filing cabinet and began casually pacing his end of the room, working the space, holding the attention of his audience, a small but intentional gesture here, a meaningful glance there. "Mistakes you've made you wish you could take back? Decisions that keep you awake in the dark, lonely hours of the night?"

Cromwell, Caleb and the scarred man were all staring at Blacklock. They clearly didn't know what he was getting at, and their uncertainty pleased him. The tables had already irrevocably turned and Cromwell had no idea.

"Where's this going?" Cromwell asked.

"Please, humour me," Blacklock said. "It's just that when you and your dog" – Blacklock gestured at Caleb, who didn't react – "visited me earlier today, you mentioned having done things you're not proud of. We didn't get much of a chance to discuss it at the time." Blacklock held up his injured hand. "You were keen to move on to other matters."

"Your injury seems to have clouded your judgement, Arthur," Cromwell said, his voice calm but with an edge to it which might have unnerved some men, but Blacklock knew he wasn't in the slightest bit of danger. Cromwell was already dead, he just didn't know it yet.

"I don't think it's anything to be ashamed of," Blacklock said. "I think it's a strong man who recognises his mistakes, and an even stronger man who strives to rectify them. *I* have a regret. A considerable one. But here's the difference between a man like me and a meaningless little wretch like you…"

Blacklock took a step forward and fixed Cromwell with a withering stare, radiating self-assurance and superiority, about to deliver the devastating conclusion of his speech, and that was when Cromwell lifted the revolver off the table and shot him in the leg.

The bullet tore through Blacklock's left thigh and he collapsed to the floor, screaming and clutching at the wound with both hands, blood soaking his skin and trousers, fresh agony flaring in his right hand with the sudden movement. Sugarfoot took an unsteady step away from him, staring in shock.

"I reckon I can see that difference you mentioned," Cromwell said, looking at Blacklock through the gun smoke. "I'm not bleeding on the floor with a hole in my leg."

Blacklock writhed and moaned as blood ran over his hands and pooled on the floorboards beneath him, but the attention of the other men was drawn to the doorway as the sounds of a scuffle could be heard coming from the main room at the front of the building. The scuffle concluded with a cry of pain, abruptly cut off.

Outside of Blacklock's agony, there was silence.

"Jimmy?" Cromwell called out.

From the hallway came the sound of soft footsteps – more than one pair – approaching.

Cromwell, Caleb and the scarred man rose from their chairs, Caleb withdrawing a wickedly sharp knife from inside his suit jacket while the scarred man pulled a blackjack from behind his back. Cromwell pointed Blacklock's revolver at the doorway as Sugarfoot backed up against a wall, looking like he wished he could melt into the bricks behind him.

When the squat figures appeared in the doorway, Cromwell and Caleb stood their ground while the scarred man stumbled away from the table, knocking over his chair and shouting, "*Jesus Christ!*"

Blacklock looked up at the group of Abyss-Dwellers as they entered the room. They were all armed, fresh blood on a couple of their weapons.

"*What are you waiting for?!*" Blacklock shouted at the creatures. "*Kill them!*"

The Abyss-Dwellers let out a chorus of harsh cries and croaks as they rushed forward, drowning out the squawk that issued from Sugarfoot's lips as he discarded his hat, dropped to the floor and scrambled on his hands and knees into the nearest corner. The roar of gunfire filled the room again.

Blacklock's position on the floor combined with his agony and the smoke and general chaos meant he only saw snatches of the melee that followed: Caleb tipping over the table, Cromwell shooting an Abyss-Dweller in the chest, a trident sailing through the air and into the belly of the scarred man, Caleb repeatedly stabbing an Abyss-Dweller in the throat, a machete slashing Cromwell's left shoulder, Caleb and an Abyss-Dweller crashing into a workbench as they wrestled, the room all blood and rage and smoke and noise.

Blacklock wanted to see the light fade from Cromwell's eyes when he died, to savour his realisation that he had been bested by the better man, one he should have never dared oppose. Blacklock tried to stand but a searing bolt of pain shot through his left leg, intense enough to make him squeeze his eyes shut, press his face against the rough wooden floor and whine miserably.

When he was eventually able to open his eyes again, Blacklock lifted his head and looked around to see the scarred thug and three Abyss-Dwellers lying dead on the floor and Sugarfoot huddled in the corner. There was no sign of Cromwell or Caleb. Then he saw the hatch in the wall, one previously hidden behind some crates. The hatch stood open, offering a glimpse of the alley beyond, and one of the few surviving Abyss-Dwellers was crawling through it, following his prey out into the night.

Cromwell and Caleb had escaped.

As Blacklock let his head fall back to the floor and roared in frustration and pain, the conclusion of his speech rose unbidden in his mind.

The difference between you and I, Offal, is that you're going to die... and I'm not.

Blacklock didn't know which hurt more, his leg or the realisation that he could have probably come up with a better final line.

No, it was the leg. Definitely the leg.

An Old Sailor's Trick

Hanging around in dark alleys and exchanging money with women of ill repute was a time-honoured Newmuck tradition, one the Roustabouts were currently engaged in but not for the typical reason.

"See that bobby over there?" Digby asked, pointing up and across the street towards Burgess Canning Company and the bored-looking, middle-aged constable standing before the front gate.

"Yeah?" Rita said.

"We need you to lead him away so we can get inside the cannery."

Rita looked over the Roustabouts, all gathered closely together at the mouth of the alley. "Why don't you lot just flatten the bugger?"

Digby gave her a look of mock offence. "Rita, have you no respect for our brave boys in blue?" He took her hand and pressed a couple of banknotes into it. "Take this and go brighten up his night, alright?"

Rita raised her eyebrows at the money. "For this much, darling, I'd give him a Vicarage Chimney."

Ambrose frowned. "What's a –"

Digby held up a hand. "You don't want to know."

Rita wore a long, thick shawl over her second-hand – but once expensive – dress, and the money disappeared beneath it as she tucked the banknotes into some unseen pocket before adjusting the shawl in such a way as to highlight her low neckline and the hint of cleavage there. Ever the gentleman, Digby didn't look until he was sure Rita wouldn't notice, which of course she did.

Rita ran a gloved hand through her long, dark hair. She smiled and gave Digby a wink, her face pale in the darkness with the make-up she wore. "Always a pleasure, Digby. Don't wait up."

She exited the alley and crossed the street, the heels of her boots clicking on stone. In most circumstances Digby would agree that a woman walking alone through Bryanferry at night was a bad idea, but just like the other prostitutes who worked the riverside district, Rita was no shrinking violet. Besides, the street was empty apart from the occasional passing vehicle or worker on his way to his night shift, it was Sunday night and most businesses were closed until the morning. Most, but not all, the wind carrying the clattering of a ship unloading cargo, the whistle of a locomotive transferring coal from barges to boiler houses inland, and other sounds of heavy industry along the riverbanks. There was far too high a volume of goods and materials moving through Newmuck every day for Bryanferry or any other industrial part of the Brazenbrook to shut down completely. The same went for crime, with small cargoes regularly being stolen from docks by thieves working under the cover of darkness.

"You really do know a lot of doxies, Digby," Ambrose said.

Digby turned his head to find the other Roustabouts all staring at him. "Don't give me that look, I've never paid for it in my life."

They went on staring.

"Well, not recently anyway."

They went on staring.

Digby frowned and returned his attention to Rita. "Look, let's just get on with it."

Rita approached the bobby, who had perked up at seeing her, straightening his back and puffing out his chest. They spoke, too far away for Digby to hear, but Rita's hand on the constable's chest and a whisper in his ear spoke volumes. The constable looked both ways along the street, glanced at the cannery behind him then grinned at Rita and said something. She laughed, took his arm and led him away, past the neighbouring shipbuilders, around the corner and out of sight.

"Let's go," Digby said.

The Roustabouts walked to the front gate of Burgess Canning Company, the stink of the neighbouring gasworks mixing with that of the cannery. Henry took Oliver's keyring from his trouser pocket as the others kept an eye out for guards or more police. There were eight keys attached to the ring and Henry selected the one Oliver had said was for the gate. The key turned in the lock and the Roustabouts entered the property, closing the gate behind them. No one challenged them as they crossed the yard, they had watched the cannery from across the street for a time and saw no sign of any guards. The constable at the gate must have been stationed there in case Oliver showed up, but he was at The Bewigged Pig with Annie.

The company of a beautiful woman, a warm fireplace and a fully stocked bar, Digby thought in the chilly darkness. *Lucky bastard.*

Up on the edge of the main building's roof, herring gulls uttered harsh, undulating squawks as the Roustabouts made their way around to one side of the building, passing stacks of damp wooden pallets before stopping at a locked metal door. It took Henry four attempts but he eventually found the right key and the Roustabouts went inside, the cannery dark and silent.

The Roustabouts ascended to the second floor and Cecil Burgess' office. Oliver's keyring didn't hold any of the three keys required to unlock the door but Bryn's shoulder, applied several times with enough force, did the trick. Broken lock parts and splinters of wood spun through the air as the door flew open and banged against the wall. But after a search as ungentle as that of any bitter proctologist, the office yielded nothing useful, so the Roustabouts went back downstairs and found the storeroom that contained the entrance to the cellar. The thick metal door was locked and very sturdy, in no danger of being shouldered open.

Digby looked at the brickwork surrounding the door. "There are plenty of tools in this place, we could take some crowbars to the bricks, take the whole thing out."

"It'll take too long," Talbot said, frowning thoughtfully. A few seconds passed. "Wait here a minute."

Talbot turned around and left the room. Digby looked at Henry, who shrugged. A couple of minutes later, Talbot returned with his hands full.

"You've got crabs," Digby said.

"You're one to talk," Talbot said.

"Ha bloody ha."

Talbot held up the two dead crabs, large and intact, one in each hand. "These are Atlantic Bowler Crabs. I was hoping I'd find some in the freezer and there they were."

"Why are they called Bowler Crabs?" Ambrose asked.

"To entertain themselves they grab smaller creatures on the seabed and play bowls with them, using them as the balls. Lot of wankers in the sea."

"What are you going to do with them, make us some soup?" Digby asked.

Talbot held out one of the crabs. "Hold this."

Digby took the dead crustacean, letting it dangle by one of its hefty claws, its body cold from the freezer. Talbot gripped his remaining crab in both hands and cracked it open with one swift, powerful turn then dug his fingers around inside, making thick squelching sounds.

"See, what most people don't know about the Atlantic Bowler," Talbot said as his fingers, slick and spotted with tiny pieces of gore, shifted and probed, "is that its stomach has a peculiar property." His fingers eventually emerged holding a dark, spongy and very small organ. He tossed the crab onto the floor, walked to the cellar door and pushed the organ into the keyhole. "It's very volatile."

Talbot took the other crab from Digby and repeated the process, pulling out an identical organ and adding it to the one already inside the keyhole. "Anyone got a match?" Talbot asked.

"Here," Digby said as he reached into one of his trouser pockets and pulled out a box of matches. He opened the box and handed Talbot a match.

Talbot struck the match against the door, turned it around and placed the unlit end inside the keyhole. "Stand back."

The Roustabouts stepped back from the cellar door and watched as the match burned down.

Digby looked at Talbot with a sceptical expression. "Crab stomachs? Really?"

A compact but powerful explosion blew open the cellar door, rattling the items on the storeroom shelves and causing everyone but Talbot to flinch. Acrid smoke drifted from the door, the metal around the keyhole blackened and warped.

Henry wafted the air in front of his face. "Nature, eh? It's bloody weird."

Beyond the doorway was a set of stone steps leading down into darkness. Two paraffin lamps hung from hooks in the wall and Henry and Ambrose took one each and turned them on. With Henry at the front of the group and Ambrose at the rear, the Roustabouts descended.

They stepped off the stairs and into a short, narrow hallway, the floor, walls and ceiling all bare stone, the darkness beyond the edges of the lamplight complete and oppressive. They passed an open doorway leading to a room filled with rusty and cobweb-covered tools and small machinery, then at the end of the hallway found themselves confronted with another metal door. This one wasn't locked, however, and Henry opened it to reveal a tunnel dug directly into the bedrock, one that sloped downwards into further blackness, crude steps carved into the floor at irregular intervals. The Roustabouts descended again, the curving tunnel silent apart from the dripping of water, the creaking of the lamps and the Roustabouts' footsteps, the rock around them gradually becoming paler and wetter.

Oliver had explained how most of this network of caves and tunnels was natural, the rest of it having been carved out by the Abyss-Dwellers many centuries ago, although this particular tunnel leading up to the cannery was only dug after the creatures allied themselves with Cecil Burgess.

A fat drop of water plopped onto Bryn's head and he glanced upwards. "We must be under the Brazenbrook by now. That's a lot of water above our heads."

"We've been in worse places underneath the city," Digby said. "Two bloody days we spent lost in those sewer tunnels looking for Mrs. Clubber's gerbil. At least this place smells better."

Ambrose smiled. "But remember how happy she was when we brought little Fernando back to her? And she gave us some lovely felt."

Digby shook his head. Ambrose could be as soft as semolina pudding sometimes.

Eventually the sloping floor evened out and the tunnel came to an end at the mouth of a cave. The Roustabouts stepped out into the space beyond, Henry and Ambrose raising their lamps in an effort to better illuminate their surroundings, the cave large enough that its edges remained dim, the light only reaching so far. Unlike the cannery tunnel, the cave was a natural formation, roughly circular in shape, its walls curving inwards until they became the high ceiling from which an inverted forest of stalactites hung, the uneven floor dotted with puddles of water. The cannery tunnel wasn't the only point of access, as two more tunnels led away into darkness. The cave walls were covered with strange symbols carved into the rock, a tapestry of no recognisable images, patterns or languages.

Digby gestured at the carvings. "What do you think all that's about?"

"Maybe the Abyss-Dwellers got bored one day and started writing on the walls," Talbot said. "Can't be any worse than what's written on the walls of some pub toilets."

Oliver had told them that the first cave they would come to was the intended ritual site, but apart from perhaps the wall carvings, Digby could see no signs that this place was going to be used for a ritual or anything else. "There's nothing here," he said, stepping around a puddle of stagnant water.

"We knew there was a chance they might've changed the location," Henry said as his eyes roamed over the walls and ceiling.

"Or Oliver's been lying to us."

"I don't think so. Either way, it doesn't look like anything here is going to lead us to Blacklock or Sugarfoot."

"Gentlemen, a pleasure to finally meet you," croaked a strange voice.

The Roustabouts turned to see a number of Abyss-Dwellers emerging from one of the other tunnels, their damp skin glistening in the lamplight. They formed an uneven row and stood facing the Roustabouts, Digby counting seventeen of them.

The Abyss-Dweller at the centre of the group took a step forward. He was the only one not carrying a weapon and, more noticeably, the only one wearing spectacles. A drop of water ran down one of the lenses as his mouth twisted into a disturbing expression that Digby assumed was meant to be a smile.

"My name is Gerald," the Abyss-Dweller said, his voice wet and thick. "I believe we've gotten off on the wrong foot."

"We've heard of you," Ambrose said.

"The friends of yours we've met haven't been as talkative as you," Bryn said.

"Only a small number of us are chosen to learn your languages and act as representatives in our dealings with mankind," Gerald said.

"Seems you've changed the venue for your big party tomorrow night," Henry said. "Mind giving us the new address?"

Gerald smiled that horrible smile again. "You'll understand that just because I can talk to you doesn't mean I don't know when not to."

"How did you know we'd be here?" Digby asked.

"We've been watching the surrounding streets for sign of you or Oliver Burgess. When I received word of your arrival in Bryanferry, I came as quickly as I could. I wanted to meet you personally."

"That doesn't seem too clever after what we did to your mates," Talbot said.

"That is precisely why I'm here, to put unnecessary violence behind us and come to an understanding. We need not be enemies, not when we would all benefit so much from being allies."

"Like your ally Cecil Burgess?" Henry said. "Or Oliver?"

"The Burgesses were weak. You five are different, your strength deserves respect. You should be rewarded in the paradise to come, not consumed."

"And you're going to make that happen, are you?"

"I could. As far beyond you and I as the Old Ones are, they are not without appreciation for those lesser beings who serve in their names. Their true designs are unknowable, but the tiny slivers of insight which have been grasped have guided my race since long before your ancestors learned to walk upright. And over the millennia, many humans have also recognised the Old Ones' majesty and dedicated their lives to fitting worship."

"If you're expecting us to get on our knees and pray then you're in for a disappointment," Bryn said. "We're not really the religious type."

"You wouldn't even need to do that. All you need do is cease your interference in the Ritual of Suth-G'nar, nothing more. A small price to pay for immortality, wouldn't you agree?"

"And what do Blacklock and Sugarfoot have to say about this?" Henry asked. Gerald's reaction was very slight, but enough, and a sly smile appeared on Henry's lips. "They don't know you're here, do they? Haven't you already promised them what you're offering us? They don't strike me as men who like to share."

"They'll do what's necessary, as will we all," Gerald said. "The gifts that will be bestowed upon them in the new world can just as easily be bestowed upon all of you. You have my word."

"I've got a word for you: piss off!" Talbot said.

Gerald frowned. "That's two w–"

"If you think we're like Cecil Burgess or Arthur Blacklock or any other arsehole willing to step on everyone else just to get a leg up then you're barking up the wrong tree," Henry said. "The human race may have its share of problems but we'll be damned if we're going to let a bunch of monsters come in here and kill everyone or drive them mad or whatever else, no matter how old and powerful they are. Since you're so keen to be our friend, let me give you some friendly advice: go back to the sea, forget about your gods and find a new hobby. Or this won't end well for you."

There was silence as Gerald stared at Henry, expressionless. When he finally spoke, Gerald's voice was matter-of-fact. "The veil between realities will be torn asunder. The Old Ones will come. And mankind's delusion of significance in the unending cosmos will be at an end. So, I extend my offer one final time: join us."

"Or what?" Bryn said. "We've already turned plenty of you into fish paste, you think we can't do the same to you and your friends here?"

"What I think is that not every obstacle can be overcome with your fists. And that Mother Ocean is ever hungry for those who do not belong in her depths."

Gerald took the conch shell from his seaweed bandolier and blew into it, the discordant droning echoing around the cave and through the connecting tunnels. He reattached the shell as the sound gradually faded into silence. The Roustabouts looked at each other then at Gerald.

"Was that supposed to frighten us?" Digby asked.

"No," Gerald said. "That was the signal."

"Signal for what?" Ambrose asked.

Then Digby heard it. A low rumble, faint and distant but growing louder. Something was coming, something powerful enough that he quickly realised he not only heard the rumbling in his ears but felt it beneath his feet as well.

There was a soft *plip* as a drop of water fell from a stalactite onto Digby's shoulder. When the water hit him, so too did a realisation. "The river," he said.

The Roustabouts looked at each other.

"Shit," Talbot said as Gerald smiled his ugly smile.

Twin torrents of river-water exploded out of the two tunnels that didn't lead to the cannery, surging into the cave and washing over the Abyss-Dwellers, who slipped gracefully into the rushing water.

The Roustabouts were swept off their feet as the foaming wall of water crashed into them, Digby taking a quick breath an instant before the incoming wave swallowed him and sent him tumbling, no idea which way was up or down, his ears filled with the muffled, burbling roar of the water. His back scraped along stone, a body slammed into him before spinning away again, his head broke the surface and he opened his eyes and tried to take a breath but swallowed water and he coughed and choked, then he was back under, the chaotic water pulling at him savagely, something hard hit his head, darkness.

A Brief Interlude for Dramatic Effect

As the churning fury of the Brazenbrook was being unleashed upon the Roustabouts in an effort to condemn them to watery graves in that subterranean labyrinth beneath the river, Peckish Booth sat staring at the wall in the small, largely bare single room in which he lived, having drifted aimlessly through another day in what had so far proved to be an aimless life.

Peckish softly cleared his throat in the dim light of a candle.

If you had told Peckish that a snapshot of his unremarkable character and uneventful life was being used solely as an interlude in a much more interesting situation for no other reason than to potentially create a degree of tension, first he would have asked what a snapshot was, then he would have asked what an interlude was, and finally, having no strong feelings on the matter either way, would have said, "Fair enough."

Peckish shifted his weight on his rickety chair.

The most interesting thing about Peckish was his name, and that wasn't especially interesting. He didn't even have a good story behind it, his parents having both died when he was two years old, before he ever had the chance to ask them about it. The best he could do with it was on the very rare occasions when a stranger would ask him, "Are you Peckish?" and he would answer, "No, I just had my dinner." No one had laughed at that to date but he was only forty-six years old, he reckoned it was bound to happen soon.

Peckish thought about scratching his leg but then decided against it.

He saw a frog once, that had been mildly interesting. He couldn't think of anything else off the top of his head.

Peckish looked towards his room's curtainless window. Still night. He looked back at the wall.

As a seven-toed, unemployed apprentice grubber – his master, a veteran grubber, had decided that Peckish didn't have what it took to scavenge from drains for a living – Peckish probably should have given a little more thought to his future, but he didn't, neither to that nor anything else. He assumed that tomorrow would just sort of happen to him, as had today and all those yesterdays.

Peckish scratched his leg. Well, time for bed.

Peckish settled down on his thin, lumpy mattress as more exciting things were happening to more interesting people elsewhere.

Peckish Booth died in 1928 at the age of ninety-four. He never saw another frog.

Missing, Presumed Annoyed

Henry leaned against the wall in the cellar hallway, doubled over, his breathing slow and ragged. He looked at what little he could make out of Digby in the darkness, Henry's lamp having been lost to the water, the only light in the cellar a faint glow cast on the stairs from the ground-floor storeroom above.

"Are you alright?" Henry asked.

Digby, conscious again after being knocked out briefly inside the cave, rubbed the back of his head. "I feel like I've been sealed inside a barrel of rocks and rolled down a hill, but apart from that I'm fine. Thanks for dragging me out of there."

Henry didn't say anything, he didn't need to, they had all saved each other's lives more times than any of them could remember.

"*Bastards!*" Bryn cursed, then he coughed and spat.

The three of them had been tossed around, battered and soaked by the raging river, their hair and clothes plastered to their skin, the water up to their knees in the flooded hallway, making soft lapping sounds but no longer rising. There was no sign of Talbot or Ambrose.

"We've got to go back down," Bryn said.

"We can't," Henry said.

He didn't want to say it but the facts were the facts. The tunnel that led down into the cave – the one which Henry, Digby and Bryn had just scrambled and swum up, jostled and swept along by a torrent of river-water – was flooded, its ceiling sloping downwards until it disappeared beneath the surface of the water. As far as they knew, every cave and tunnel down there was flooded now. The Abyss-Dwellers hadn't followed them, Henry guessed they either thought the Roustabouts were dead or they didn't want to try their luck against him, Digby and Bryn outside of the water. Either way it didn't make him feel any better about Talbot and Ambrose still being down there somewhere.

Henry stood up straight and wiped water from his face. "If the Abyss-Dwellers let in the Brazenbrook then that means the cave we were in connects to it, right? So Talbot and Ambrose might've made it out into the river through one of the other tunnels. You know what Talbot's like, a little water to him is like, well, water off a duck's back."

"We can check the banks of the river, see if they washed up somewhere," Digby said.

"Croker Bridge isn't far from here, we'll split up there and work our way downstream."

Henry, Digby and Bryn waded along the hallway, emerging from the water as they climbed the steps to the storeroom.

"I'm going to kill that little shit in the glasses," Bryn said, the Roustabouts leaving trails of water behind them, their feet squelching inside their shoes. "Drop a river on *us*, will he?"

"The fact they tried making a deal shows they're scared," Digby said.

"They should be," Henry said.

They left the cannery through the same door by which they had entered, Henry feeling his skin prickle with goosepimples as the chilly night air hit his wet clothes. The police constable remained absent from his post at the front gate.

"Bloody hell, what's she doing to that bobby?" Henry asked.

"Rita's a talented girl, she can hold his attention for a while," Digby said, thankfully recognising Henry's question as a rhetorical one.

The Roustabouts crossed the yard behind the main building and came to a wide pair of gates set in the fence at the rear of the property. The river-water hadn't stolen Oliver's keys, and Henry unlocked the gates and the Roustabouts passed through. A stretch of concrete led to the river's edge, ending in a sheer drop of several metres to the surface of the water below, two timber jetties spattered with bird-shit jutting out into the river. The lights of the far bank glowed hazily through the mist rising from the Brazenbrook and there was still traffic on the river at night, from small rowboats with lanterns hanging at their prows to huge steamships whose horns blew out long, mournful blasts.

Henry, Digby and Bryn walked out onto the nearest jetty and looked around at the black water but saw no signs of life besides a trio of ducks. They called out for Talbot and Ambrose, waited, called out again, waited some more.

Nothing.

The Roustabouts began following the Brazenbrook downstream, staying close to the water, trespassing when necessary while other stretches of the riverbank were open to the public. They kept an eye out for any sign of Talbot and Ambrose and regularly called out to them, but apart from an unfamiliar, slurred voice somewhere off in the darkness telling them to shut up, they received no reply.

They reached the old, stone structure that was Croker Bridge, its road wide enough to accommodate two vehicles, its single pavement lined with streetlights, although the far end of the bridge remained indistinct in the mist.

Croker Bridge connected Bryanferry to the district of Croker, and despite the two districts being very similar, the mere fact that a river separated them had long acted as an excuse for Bryanferry residents to hate Croker residents and vice versa. Up until the early 1870s, gangs of youths from opposing sides of the river would occasionally engage in mass brawls in the centre of Croker Bridge, bringing traffic to a standstill, before local businessmen put enough pressure on the Newmuck Police Force to force them to crack down on it.

Not long after that, the Candle brothers took over most of the crime in Croker through a combination of extreme violence, absolute ruthlessness and a dash more extreme violence just to be sure. The district remained their turf today, the majority of its criminal element smart enough not to do anything that might be bad for business, as if you were bad for the Candle brothers' business then that was often bad for your chances of leaving this world in the same number of pieces as when you came into it.

Henry looked towards the far end of Croker Bridge. "You two cross over and search that side of the river, I'll check this side. Gallows Bridge is the next one along, we'll meet up on there."

Digby and Bryn walked onto Croker Bridge as Henry continued downstream, following an unlit dirt path that ran between a row of run-down houses and a short stretch of grey, pebble-strewn sand that sloped down to the river's edge, which was marked by a build-up of unpleasantly thick and suspiciously coloured foam. Although the Brazenbrook was certainly cleaner than it used to be, plenty of riverfront businesses still dumped whatever they could get away with into the river.

Henry came across a pair of mudlarks, the two teenage boys standing ankle-deep in the river as they scavenged amongst the sand, mud and pebbles for anything of value. They were barefoot, their trousers rolled up around their skinny calves, their dark clothing well-worn and stained, each of them carrying a damp sack over one shoulder.

"Excuse me, lads," Henry said. The boys had been stooped over but now stood upright and looked at him with flat expressions. "You haven't seen two blokes come out of the river, have you? Both big, about my age?"

The mudlarks looked at each other then back at Henry, and one of them shook his head. He thanked them anyway but they had already returned their attention to their work.

Henry continued following the Brazenbrook but there remained no sign of Talbot or Ambrose. Still, he wasn't overly concerned. He was sure they would be fine.

The Summoning of the Watchman

Talbot was no doctor but he knew that Ambrose being dead wasn't a good sign.

He placed his hands on Ambrose's chest, one on top of the other, and began pressing down firmly at quick, regular intervals, mentally counting the presses as he went. When he reached thirty he leaned down, placed his mouth over Ambrose's mouth, and exhaled twice.

Nothing.

One, two, three, again to thirty, two breaths.

Nothing.

"Come on," Talbot muttered.

Thirty presses, two breaths.

Nothing.

Another round. This time, as Talbot blew his first breath into Ambrose's mouth, Ambrose shuddered and gave a choked cough, turning his head to one side and spraying river-water onto the sand.

Talbot let out a relieved breath and moved from his kneeling position to a sitting one. "There you go."

Ambrose lay on his side, leaning on one forearm, getting his breath back. He frowned at the sand, drool dangling from his lip, strands of wet hair across his face. After a few dazed seconds he focused on Talbot. "What happened?"

"You died," Talbot said. "Drowned. I brought you back to life."

"How?"

"Something I learned from a surgeon I was at sea with."

"Thanks. If I'd died, my nan would've killed me." Ambrose sat up and nodded at the prone figure nearby. "Is *he* dead?"

The Abyss-Dweller named Gerald lay on his back on the sand, unconscious, black blood running from his snout and down the sides of his face. His spectacles lay next to him, their string still around his neck, one of the lenses cracked.

"No," Talbot said. "He was struggling when we came onshore so I popped him one."

Soaked and covered in sand, Talbot and Ambrose got to their feet, brushed their hands against their trousers and wiped their faces. Talbot looked around the curving stretch of shoreline, the Brazenbrook lapping against the pebble-dotted shore of dirt and sand, which gave way to grass followed by a line of trees and overgrown foliage that ringed the whole island on which they had washed up, hiding the land within from passing vessels and people on the riverbanks. A tall chain-link fence ran through the woods, parallel to the shore and stretching off into darkness in both directions.

Ambrose looked out over the misty river then turned his attention inland. "We're on Pilgrim Island."

"Aye," Talbot said, having recognised it as well.

Situated in the centre of a wide section of the Brazenbrook, Pilgrim Island was an eight-acre piece of land which didn't get its name from being any kind of sacred site but rather from Timothy Pilgrim, the larger-than-life entrepreneur who bought the island in 1818 and turned it into a popular leisure spot, its previous name now largely forgotten. Pilgrim lived on the island, building homes for himself and his closest staff as well as an inn, a theatre and a shop, while also turning a large part of the island into a park. A footbridge on the north side of the island connected it to the riverbank, Pilgrim wanting to make the place easily accessible to visitors.

Pilgrim died of a heart attack during a poker game in 1834, and although business on the island continued under a succession of new owners over the next several decades, by the late 1860s the place had fallen into disrepair and the visitors stopped coming, and in the end the island was abandoned and left to rot, home only to vagrants.

Then, last year, an unknown party bought Pilgrim Island, cleared out the vagrants, fenced off the entire island and demolished the footbridge. Also, most of the short piers where visitors travelling by river used to disembark were dismantled, leaving only a single pier with a large "NO TRESPASSING" sign on it. The Roustabouts heard a rumour in The Bewigged Pig that the buyer intended to revitalise the island and reopen it to the public, but there had been no news of any developments since then. Anyway, pub rumours were hardly reliable, like that one about the government introducing a new law banning people from looking left on Wednesdays.

"We're quite a way downstream from the cannery," Ambrose said. "How did we end up here?"

"When those bastards flooded the cave, me and you got swept into the tunnel connected to the river," Talbot said. "You swallowed water but I grabbed onto you and kept swimming. Gerald came after us so I grabbed him too, thought he might come in useful. When I reached the surface, this was the closest shore so I swam for it."

Ambrose rubbed his throat, frowning. "I remember now."

"Drowning's a bad way to go."

"So you swam all the way up here while carrying me and Gerald? How did you manage that?"

"When you're a sailor, being a strong swimmer and being able to hold your breath for a long time are skills worth learning. Just in case."

"What about Henry, Digby and Bryn?"

"I saw them get swept into the cannery tunnel we came down. The force of the water probably pushed them all the way back up there, they'll be alright. Even if the Abyss-Dwellers went after them, the lads can handle them."

"What shall we do with him?" Ambrose said as he and Talbot walked over to Gerald.

"I thought we'd wake him up then beat him until he tells us where Blacklock is and where they're holding this Ritual of Soft Granville," Talbot said.

"I think it was 'Suth-G'nar.'"

"Whatever." Talbot nudged Gerald with his shoe. "Oy. Wake up." There was no reaction. Another nudge, harder this time. "*Oy.*"

"Are you sure he's not dead?" Ambrose said. "Maybe you hit him a bit too hard."

"Look, his gills are moving."

Talbot and Ambrose stared at Gerald as the Brazenbrook sloshed and burbled, and the breeze rustled grass and leaves. Gerald didn't stir.

Ambrose turned to Talbot. "What about Dennis?"

"Dennis who?" Talbot said.

"Dennis Johnson, the mind-reader. He lives in Gallowside, so he's not far from here. If we can get off the island, it's only a ten-minute walk from the river. Dennis could read Gerald's mind even if he's unconscious and find out where Blacklock and the ritual site are."

"The man's a fancy con artist. And I doubt he'll want to do us any favours."

"We'll just have to convince him what's at stake. It's worth a shot, unless you've got a better idea."

Talbot sighed. "Alright. But it's your turn to carry him," he said, pointing at Gerald.

Ambrose lifted Gerald effortlessly and slung him over his right shoulder.

"We need to find a boat," Talbot said, first looking up and down the empty shoreline then towards the dark, crowded woods and wire fence. "We'll cut across to the other side of the island, Gallowside's over that way anyway."

Talbot and Ambrose approached the fence. It was around eight feet tall, a mesh of steel wires topped with clusters of nasty-looking metal prongs and strung between thick wooden poles planted in the earth at regular intervals.

"What do you reckon?" Ambrose asked.

"Pass him here a second," Talbot said, reaching out and taking Gerald off Ambrose's shoulder.

Talbot adjusted his grip, holding the limp Abyss-Dweller before him like a shield, then charged at the chain-link fence. Gerald was crushed between Talbot and the wire mesh, which toppled forward with the impact and the combined weight of Talbot and Gerald. The nearest wooden poles fell with it, grass and earth being churned up at their bases as they were uprooted. The fence, Gerald and Talbot hit the ground, the wire mesh and wooden poles flattened for metres in both directions.

Talbot stood up, lifting Gerald with him, the Abyss-Dweller still unconscious and now with a diamond pattern of indentations across his face and torso. Talbot passed him back to Ambrose.

"I don't know how much luck Dennis will have reading Gerald's mind if his brain's been squashed," Ambrose said.

Talbot shrugged. "Thought I'd save wear and tear on my shirt."

Ambrose looked at Talbot's shirt and trousers then his own, their clothes equally wet, torn and stained. "I think it's a little late to worry about that."

They headed inland, stepping over the fallen fencing and entering the ring of woodland, the long grass brushing their legs as they passed bushes and trees. They walked carefully, the darkness thick around them, what little moonlight there was barely penetrating the tree canopy overhead.

They emerged at the edge of the park. Talbot had only visited Pilgrim Island once, when he was a teenager and before the decline had set in, but he remembered the park: the flat expanses of neatly trimmed grass, the clear water of the layered stone fountain, the flowerbeds, the bright white paint and polished metalwork of the large bandstand where a brass band played, the croquet lawn, the ornamental stone flowerpots and columns, the lamppost-lined gravel paths, and the sounds of laughter and easy conversation in the air as people relaxed in the afternoon sunshine.

Now the grass was overgrown and obscured the paths, the fountain was dry and covered in moss, its top layer broken off, the flowerbeds were choked with weeds, the flowerpots and columns were chipped and cracked or outright shattered, and the metal of the bandstand was rusted, its wooden roof collapsed. The park was dead and silent and empty, a shadow of its former self.

"This used to be a nice place," Ambrose said.

At the far end of the park and off to the east, partially obscured by a stand of trees, was a short, paved street on which stood the island's inn, theatre and shop, the shop serving as a tobacconist, confectioner, toy store and more.

Built apart from these structures were the three bungalows in which Timothy Pilgrim and a handful of his staff had lived, each bungalow occupying its own small plot of land amongst the trees on the east end of the island, close to the shore. Two of them had burned down and were nothing but shells of partially collapsed walls and charred wood, but the third bungalow, which looked out onto the river, was still standing. Not only that but there was a light coming from inside, the soft glow visible through a window.

Talbot pointed at the bungalow. "Someone's at home."

"Maybe they can give us a lift over to Gallowside," Ambrose said.

"I don't know, Pilgrim Island doesn't seem to welcome visitors like it used to."

Talbot and Ambrose and the unconscious Gerald crossed the park, Talbot cursing as his shoe crunched through a glass bottle discarded in the grass, eventually arriving at the cracked and rubbish-strewn paved street. Although none of the businesses on the street had burned down like the two bungalows, their neglect was obvious, the front door of the shop standing open while the inn's front door was missing, the windows in both buildings almost all shattered, their paint peeling, signage faded.

At four storeys, Pilgrim Theatre stood taller than its two-storey neighbours and its architecture was of a more ornate design, although the effect was diminished by the building's current condition. Its formerly colourful paint was drab, scraps of old posters advertising long-ago acts clinging to the damp stone walls, and the rusted metal letters which had once spelled out the theatre's name above the front entrance now only managed "PI GR M THE RE", two of the letters lying in the street while the others were nowhere to be seen. Whatever grandness Pilgrim Theatre had once boasted, whatever joy and entertainment it brought to its customers, was long gone. Unlike the inn and shop, the theatre had no windows that could be smashed, and its front entrance, a pair of double-doors, was not only still intact but also securely locked, its handles held together with a thick metal chain and hefty padlock. Although Talbot only glanced at the door, the chain and padlock seemed newer than the other metal on display.

Ambrose looked up at the theatre's sad façade. "My grandparents brought me here when I was a boy. We saw dancers and a singer and an escape artist. I never thought a man could escape from inside a lion, but there we go. The place was packed, everyone clapping, laughing and cheering." He smiled wistfully. "It was a good day." He turned to Talbot. "Did you ever go in there?"

"Maybe," Talbot said. "I came here once but the last thing I remember is ordering my twelfth pint of ale at the inn. The next morning I woke up on the roof of a church two miles away." He smiled wistfully. "It was a good day."

Talbot and Ambrose left the street, passed the two ruined bungalows and approached the final, standing bungalow from the side, the stone-and-wood structure looking to have been kept in decent condition. A wooden porch extended from the front of the building, the ground in front of that sloping gently down to the water's edge. Around halfway along the slope was the chain-link fence that circled the island except here the fence had a gate set in it, one granting access to the short pier outside it. Moored to the pier were two rowboats, each covered with a dark tarpaulin.

Talbot couldn't see the front wall of the bungalow or much of the porch but he knew the front door must have been open because of the light that spilled out from there. When an unseen figure coughed from that direction, Talbot and Ambrose stopped in their tracks and looked at each other.

Ambrose pointed towards a large tree near the closest ruined bungalow. "We can get a better look from over there," he whispered.

Ambrose led the way quietly and Talbot followed begrudgingly. "Softly softly catchee monkey" had always rubbed him the wrong way, he had never hunted a monkey but he was confident that stealth wasn't the only way to go about it.

They concealed themselves behind the tree and looked towards the occupied bungalow. Talbot could see the porch clearly now along with the source of the cough: a man was sitting on a wooden chair on the porch, running a rag over a double-barrelled shotgun he cradled in his lap. He coughed again then turned his head and spat. He looked to be in his thirties or forties, with a lean build and wavy, shoulder-length brown hair, and was wearing trousers, boots, braces and a shirt, the sleeves rolled up over his forearms. Next to him the front door stood open, giving him enough light to see by as he turned the shotgun over, giving it a thorough cleaning. His face was lined, his jaw covered in stubble, and he frowned in concentration as he stared at the gun.

"Must be a watchman working for whoever owns the island, keeping an eye on the place," Ambrose whispered.

"Whoever he is, he's got one more boat than he needs," Talbot whispered.

"*Blargh!*" Gerald cried out suddenly in a confused, half-conscious croak, his eyelids fluttering.

Talbot punched Gerald in the head, knocking him out again. Talbot looked back towards the bungalow to see the watchman had risen to his feet and was looking in their general direction, his face in shadow, shotgun pointed at the ground but held at the ready.

"*Who goes there?*" the watchman called out.

Talbot and Ambrose hid themselves completely behind the tree and waited, listening. The floor of the porch creaked beneath several slow, steady footsteps before the unexpected, shrill ringing of a telephone suddenly cut through the night, the noise coming from inside the watchman's bungalow.

"A telephone?" Ambrose whispered. "A bit fancy for a deserted island, isn't it?"

Talbot and Ambrose looked again to see the watchman enter the bungalow, disappearing from view then briefly appearing again as he passed a window. The telephone cut off mid-ring as he picked it up and said something, Talbot unable to hear him clearly from this distance. The conversation was brief, the watchman saying little, then he was moving around inside the bungalow, apparently with some urgent purpose. Eventually the light went out and the watchman reappeared on the porch wearing a topcoat, his shotgun wrapped in cloth and slung over one shoulder. In one hand he carried a satchel and in the other a ring of keys, one of which he used to lock the front door.

Moving swiftly but not rushing, the watchman walked to the gate, unlocked it and passed through the fence, then locked it again from the other side. He walked to one of the rowboats, removed the tarpaulin and stowed it on the remaining boat, then climbed into the uncovered boat and untied it. He pushed off from the pier and the boat began drifting out into the river. He set the oars in place, took his seat and began to row towards the south bank. When he was eventually out of sight, Talbot and Ambrose stepped out from behind the tree.

"Good timing on that phone call," Ambrose said.

"Saves us the bother of dealing with the bloke," Talbot said.

They walked to the gate in the fence and Talbot kicked it open. He uncovered the remaining rowboat and he and Ambrose stepped into it, Ambrose setting Gerald down between them.

"Best we keep him covered if we're going to be carrying him through Gallowside," Ambrose said as he lay a tarpaulin over Gerald. He nodded towards the oars. "I'll let you do the honours, captain."

Talbot set the oars as Ambrose pushed the boat away from the pier, then they took their seats opposite each other. The veins in Talbot's arms stood out as he worked the oars, turning the boat north and rowing towards Gallowside.

"You were probably right about Dennis, I doubt he's going to be happy to see us," Ambrose said.

"As long as he does as he's told, he can be as unhappy as he likes," Talbot said. "He won't need to be a mind-reader to know we're not messing about."

Silk and Lead

"*Of course I'm not alright, you idiot!*" Blacklock shouted. His head swam with the outburst and he sagged in his chair. He took a deep breath and closed his eyes until the feeling passed.

"I only asked," Sugarfoot said in a somewhat offended tone.

Blacklock gave Sugarfoot a withering look before turning his attention to the shirt wrapped around his left thigh, his left hand pressing it against the bullet-wound beneath, the shirt taken from the scarred man killed by the Abyss-Dwellers at Ox Locks. Once grey, the shirt was now red from the blood it had soaked up from both the scarred man and Blacklock.

Apart from Blacklock's breathing and occasional wincing, the manager's office was silent. The silk factory wasn't open on Sundays and Blacklock and Sugarfoot were the only people in the building, Sugarfoot's driver having remained outside with his carriage since bringing them here.

Blacklock felt the terrible pain radiating from his left leg and right hand, confident that no one had ever suffered for their art the way he was suffering. He had been so sure he had everything under control. Cromwell surprised him, that's all, used a dirty, underhanded trick typical of his kind. It was certainly no mistake on Blacklock's part. And Sugarfoot was useless, as expected. It was the audience and venue – Blacklock belonged in a several-thousand-capacity theatre, not some dingy back room – that let Blacklock down, not his performance.

A fat lot of good the Abyss-Dwellers had turned out to be as well. They may have killed two of Cromwell's men but what did that matter when they allowed Cromwell and Caleb to escape? Blacklock wondered if any more of Gerald's aunties were among the three Abyss-Dwellers who fell at the locksmiths. Either way, Gerald wasn't going to be happy that another of

Blacklock's plans had led to more Abyss-Dweller deaths. Not that Blacklock gave a damn, he would walk over a mountain of their corpses to reach his new reality if that was what it took.

There was still a chance the Abyss-Dwellers who had set off in pursuit of Cromwell and Caleb had killed them but Blacklock wasn't going to assume that. The hole in his leg meant he left the locksmiths in a hurry, although with no intention of going to the hospital. He trusted Quinn to fix him up just as well as any doctor, he just needed somewhere familiar, private and safe – and with a telephone – where he could wait until Quinn arrived. And the silk factory, one of three which Blacklock owned and located less than a mile from Brown Ox Row, was ideal. Sugarfoot reluctantly assisted, getting Blacklock's blood all over his own suit and the inside of his brougham in the process.

Now here they were in the manager's office, Blacklock sitting in a padded leather armchair behind the desk while Sugarfoot occupied a second armchair nearby, the room illuminated by wall-mounted gas lights. The interior windows looked out onto the rows of power looms lining the factory floor that took up most of the high-ceilinged brick building, the cavernous space loud and bright during work hours but quiet and dark now. The office's exterior window, which faced the enclosed yard at the rear of the property, was shuttered and bolted.

This wasn't Blacklock's office, he rarely spent time at his factories, instead employing managers to oversee their day-to-day running, hence why he had decided not to pay to have a fireplace installed in the room. It was a decision he regretted now as a chill went through him. He wondered how long he and Sugarfoot had been waiting. Maybe he should take a quick nap, just until Quinn arrived. His eyelids felt heavy and the wooden surface of the desk looked surprisingly comfortable. There were silk samples lying on a nearby chest of drawers, from a simple ribbon to an intricately embroidered handkerchief, he could rest his head on those soft, makeshift pillows, close his eyes and just drift off...

Blacklock squeezed his left thigh and the resulting stab of pain immediately cleared his head and caused him to gasp.

No, he thought. No sleep. He needed to stay focused.

Sugarfoot rubbed at some dried blood on his shirtsleeve, drummed his fingers on an armrest, cleared his throat. "How much longer do you suppose he'll be?"

"I don't know," Blacklock muttered.

"Are you sure you wouldn't rather visit a hospital? Your man Quinn has always seemed, well, a rather rough sort. No offence intended, of course."

"Quinn can fix people as expertly as he can break them," Blacklock said pointedly.

Sugarfoot studied the carpeted floor for a moment then stood up. "Perhaps I should be going. You seem… stable now. My driver can take me home. Once Quinn has patched you up, you can visit me and –"

Blacklock glared at him. "*Sit. Down.*"

Sugarfoot sat down. "No rush, I suppose." He gave Blacklock a strained smile. "At least you can forget about Cromwell now, eh? He must've had the shock of his life, I wager he's still running now. And Oliver and his friends, we can keep our distance from them, no need to –"

Blacklock closed his eyes. "Thomas, I swear, one more word and bullet-wound or no I'll drag you out onto the factory floor, feed you into one of the looms and make a parasol out of you."

Blacklock and Sugarfoot both flinched as the door to the office swung inward and a figure stepped into the room.

"Quinn," Blacklock said with relief.

"Sir," Lionel Quinn said.

Quinn set down his satchel, removed the wrapped shotgun he was carrying on his back and leaned it against the wall. He took off his topcoat and hung it on the coat-stand next to the door, picked up his satchel again, walked over to Blacklock and got down onto one knee. He glanced at Blacklock's right hand and said, "You didn't mention your hand."

"The leg seemed more pressing," Blacklock said.

Blacklock moved his left hand away as Quinn reached for his left thigh and removed the bloody shirt. He looked at the hole in Blacklock's trouser leg then stood up and began clearing the telephone, stationery, paperwork and other items off the desk.

"I need to cut away that trouser leg to get to the wound," Quinn said. "Lie on the desk."

Quinn helped Blacklock up from his chair and onto the desk. As Blacklock stared up at the ceiling, Quinn placed his satchel on the desk, opened it and withdrew a pair of scissors. He carefully cut away the trouser leg and took a close look at the wound, his hair hanging around his face.

"The bullet was small-calibre," Quinn said. "It went in the front and out the back, didn't hit your femur or any arteries. You were lucky."

"Oh yes, I'm positively blessed!" Blacklock snapped. "Can you fix it?"

Quinn took more items out of his satchel. "I'll do what I can."

"What does that mean?"

"I'm going to clean and dress the wound and you're going to need to stay off that leg. Barring infection and with enough rest, you should be more or less back to normal within a few weeks, perhaps even without a limp."

Blacklock clutched Quinn's nearest shirtsleeve. "I can't rest. I just need to last until tomorrow night. As soon as the ritual is done, none of this will matter."

"Alright. But you're risking aggravating the wound and you'll need a crutch or cane if you want to get around."

"Fine."

Quinn lifted Blacklock's head and held a metal canteen of water to his lips. Blacklock took several swallows, unable to remember a time when water tasted so good, then Quinn placed his head back down on the desk and got to work. Blacklock kept his eyes on the ceiling, not wanting to see what Quinn was doing. But he had faith in the man's skills, not to mention his loyalty, Quinn having proven both during the four years he had been in Blacklock's service.

Quinn had picked up his medical training during his years in the British Army, although he never claimed his knowledge was much more than rudimentary. He saved some lives while he was a soldier, although that number was outweighed by the number of lives he took, Blacklock having seen Quinn's military record (following a donation made to a cooperative Army lieutenant): the Second Opium War, the Indian Rebellion of 1857, the New Zealand Wars... Quinn had seen a lot of horror and shed a lot of blood for his country and even been decorated more than once. According to his record he was loyal, obedient and dangerous, the exact qualities Blacklock was looking for.

Quinn's arrival in Newmuck marked the first time he had returned to his homeland in over a decade, his return preceded by several years drifting around Europe, that preceded by his two decades of service in the British Army. He moved to the capital in search of work and by chance was brought to Blacklock's attention. Blacklock was impressed by Quinn, who carried out every task he was assigned with the same uncomplaining dedication and efficiency, whether he was moving furniture or garrotting a troublesome business rival. Of course the real test was Blacklock's revelation of the Old Ones, the Abyss-Dwellers and The Order of the Void and their plans. But he was pleased to discover Quinn was unfazed by it all, claiming that as far as he was concerned nothing had changed: he remained Blacklock's employee and would continue to follow whatever orders he was given, admitting that he had never found the world particularly appealing as it was anyway. After Blacklock's purchase of Pilgrim Island and given its importance to his plans, he had Quinn act as a live-in watchman there the majority of the time. Although Blacklock missed his presence at home, Quinn was only a telephone call and a short boat ride away should Blacklock need him. In the event of being shot in the leg, for example.

And of course Quinn would be suitably rewarded for his years of loyal service when Blacklock made him a member of his eternal audience. He felt very magnanimous about that.

But part of Blacklock despised Quinn at the same time. Because Quinn wouldn't have gotten himself shot or had his finger broken or allowed himself to be threatened by Offal Cromwell or anyone else. Quinn would have handled things. But Blacklock always reminded himself that the battlefields were littered with the corpses of soldiers, the true power belonged to the men who sent those soldiers to their deaths.

Less than ten minutes later, Blacklock was once again sitting behind his desk, his leg wound cleaned, covered with dressing soaked in carbolic acid as an antiseptic, and bandaged. Quinn had even rewrapped Blacklock's two fingers on his right hand, doing a tidier job than Blacklock himself had done. Blacklock took another drink of water from Quinn's canteen then handed it back to him. Quinn poured a little water over his blood-covered hands, rubbed them together thoroughly then wiped them on a rag taken from his satchel.

Sugarfoot sat up in his chair and looked hopefully at Quinn's satchel. "I don't suppose you've got a canteen of brandy or anything in there, have you? Medicinal alcohol, even?"

"No," Quinn said.

Sugarfoot slumped back down, disappointed.

Quinn turned to Blacklock. "I can give you something for the pain if you'd like."

God, please, yes, Blacklock thought. "Will it dull my senses?" he said.

"If it's going to have any real effect, yes."

Blacklock looked at the satchel, hesitated, then looked away. "No. I need to stay alert."

Quinn placed his bloody rag inside his satchel then rolled down his shirtsleeves and buttoned the cuffs. The office door opened and in one smooth motion Quinn's right hand moved to the small of his back then reappeared holding a revolver which he pointed towards the doorway. Blacklock was reminded of his own revolver, which Cromwell had taken with him in his escape.

In the light of the office, the shabby hooded cloak worn by the visitor did little to hide the fact it was an Abyss-Dweller. The creature stood just inside the room and stared at Quinn and his gun. Quinn stared back.

"It's alright, Quinn," Blacklock said.

Quinn returned the revolver to the small of his back without taking his eyes off the Abyss-Dweller. Blacklock had no idea which of the creatures this one was, except for Gerald they all looked the same to him.

"Yes?" Blacklock said to the Abyss-Dweller.

The creature glanced at Sugarfoot before turning his attention to Blacklock and approaching the desk, lowering his hood at the same time. He spoke a string of guttural croaks that Blacklock knew were words in their language, but as to what those words meant, he had no clue.

"*I don't understand you*," Blacklock said slowly and condescendingly.

The Abyss-Dweller held up two fingers on his right claw.

"Two?" Blacklock said. "Two what?"

"Two words?" Sugarfoot suggested. "I'll have you know I'm no slouch at charades."

"We're not playing charades, Thomas."

"Two people," Quinn said.

The Abyss-Dweller nodded and croaked in the affirmative.

"Two people," Blacklock said. "Do you mean Cromwell and Caleb? Were you one of the Abyss-Dwellers at the locksmiths?"

Another nod and affirmative croak.

"Did you catch them?" Blacklock asked eagerly.

But that eagerness dissipated as Blacklock, Sugarfoot and Quinn spent the next ten minutes slowly dragging meaning out of the Abyss-Dweller's croaks and gestures, Blacklock having never thought he would see the day he wished Gerald was present. God, why couldn't these things learn a proper language like English?

This Abyss-Dweller had indeed been one of the three who followed Cromwell and Caleb as they fled the locksmiths, the creatures tracking the two men through streets and alleys until eventually arriving at The Bewigged Pig, Cromwell and Caleb having taken shelter inside the barricaded pub. There were also two other people present, Oliver Burgess and a woman. Blacklock wondered if it was the same woman who had been with Oliver at Orchardson's last party. The pursuers didn't enter as Gerald had previously said that no Abyss-Dwellers were to attack the pub unless specifically ordered to do so by him. So the three Abyss-Dwellers simply turned around and left, this one coming to update Blacklock.

Blacklock fumed. The Abyss-Dwellers had had Cromwell and Oliver in their grasp but let them slip away thanks to Gerald's cowardice. Also, Gerald had neglected to tell Blacklock his little rule about the Abyss-Dwellers not attacking The Bewigged Pig again. What else was the slippery bastard hiding from him? Who the hell did Gerald think he was dealing with?

Blacklock glared at the Abyss-Dweller. His chest felt tight and the knuckles of his left hand were white as he squeezed the accompanying armrest. "You lot think you're so clever, don't you?"

The Abyss-Dweller said nothing, his bulging eyes expressionless. But not really. Because Blacklock saw what was truly there: arrogance, condescension, dismissal. And Blacklock would be damned if he was going to be looked down on by this monstrosity.

"You live at the bottom of the bloody *sea*," Blacklock said. "You're animals, *abominations*."

The Abyss-Dweller croaked something then turned to leave.

Blacklock leaned forward, pain flaring in his thigh. "*Don't you walk away from me!*"

The Abyss-Dweller ignored him and walked towards the open office door.

Blacklock winced as he rose to his feet. He held out his left hand to Quinn. "*Give me your gun!*"

Quinn placed his revolver in Blacklock's waiting hand.

"Arthur –" Sugarfoot said before he was cut off by the deafening blast of a gunshot, the bullet from Quinn's pistol passing through the Abyss-

Dweller's cloak and penetrating his back, just to the left of his spine. The creature took an unsteady step to the side and uttered a wet grunt then Blacklock fired again, twice, the first bullet hitting the Abyss-Dweller in his upper back while the second pierced the back of his skull and emerged from his left eye socket, bursting his eyeball and spraying black blood into the air. The Abyss-Dweller toppled forward and lay still, blood pooling around his head.

His ears ringing, Blacklock stared at the corpse, gun smoke heavy in the air. This was Gerald's fault.

Blacklock looked at the revolver in his hand then held it out to Quinn, who took it and tucked it back into his trousers.

Sugarfoot looked from the Abyss-Dweller to Blacklock with an uneasy expression. "I don't think Gerald's going to like this, Arthur."

"I don't care what he likes or doesn't like!" Blacklock snapped. He sat back down. "Besides, he's not going to find out. Now make yourself useful and close the door, it's letting in a draught."

Sugarfoot pushed himself up from his chair and moved to the door, being careful to keep his distance from the Abyss-Dweller and the spreading pool of black blood.

Blacklock tried not to show how tired and lost he felt as he looked at Quinn and said, "Given where we stand at the moment, what would you suggest our next course of action be?"

"You said yourself all you need to do is make it to tomorrow night and you win, so you shouldn't expose yourself to unnecessary danger in the meantime," Quinn said. "As for Cromwell, Oliver or the Roustabouts, you don't need to kill them to stop them interfering. You could have them arrested."

Blacklock frowned. "Involve the police? Frankly, Quinn, I hoped you'd suggest something more... final."

"I'm just suggesting what I think gives you the best chance of coming out on top, sir. I'm sure the police would be interested in speaking to all of them, especially if you tell them that Oliver, the Roustabouts and Cromwell were all involved with the deaths of Cecil Burgess and Orchardson. If the police took them in for questioning, they wouldn't be released before tomorrow night. They'd be out of the way. Cromwell and Oliver might still be at that pub now and it's the Roustabouts' local, so maybe they could even be rounded up all at once."

"Sounds like a solid plan to me," Sugarfoot said. "It would be nice to not be looking over our shoulders and worrying about ending up like Frederick."

Blacklock thought about it. Quinn's idea did seem sound, if not as satisfying as he would have liked. Still, as Quinn reminded him, soon he would have the power to do whatever he wanted to Cromwell, Oliver, the Roustabouts and anyone else. Why settle for a moment of agony on Cromwell's face when Blacklock could stretch that agony out for eternity instead?

Blacklock stood up, intending to approve Quinn's plan, but then wondered why Quinn and the room around him were tipping to one side. As he lost feeling in his legs and his vision blurred, Blacklock realised it wasn't Quinn tipping but him, then that realisation and everything else went away.

A Meeting of Minds

Ambrose studied the tattered poster stuck to the front door of Dennis Johnson's flat.

"'Dominic Joyeux,'" Ambrose read aloud. "'Psychic and spiritualist. Master of the mystical, the occult, the strange and all else beyond human comprehension. Curses removed, deceased loved ones contacted, minds and fortunes read. Book four sessions and your fifth is half-price. Enquire within.'" He looked at Talbot. "'Dominic Joyeux'?"

"As long as he's not putting on a silly accent, because I am not in the mood," Talbot said.

Ambrose knocked on the door.

Dennis' flat occupied the ground floor of a two-storey back-to-back house on a shabby residential street, his front door opening onto an alley at the side of the building, a metal staircase granting access to the flat above. The alley was dark and there were heaps of rubbish piled up along both it and the adjoining street, the local council having apparently not bothered with refuse collection for some time. The building of new back-to-back housing had been banned decades ago, and while the city was gradually demolishing and replacing these hastily and poorly constructed buildings, they could still be found in poorer parts of Newmuck.

The last time Ambrose came here, Dennis was adamant it was only a temporary situation and that he would soon be packing theatres all over Newmuck once again with his act, a polished display of magic, mind-reading and other mental feats, all performed with confident showmanship. But that was seven months ago, and judging by the poster it looked like Dennis – or Dominic now, apparently – was still here. Ambrose knew he and the other Roustabouts weren't really responsible for Dennis' fall from grace but still he couldn't help feeling a twinge of guilt over their involvement in what happened.

Talbot shifted his right shoulder, resting on which was Gerald, still unconscious and now wrapped in the tarpaulin from the rowboat they had taken from Pilgrim Island. Two large, dishevelled men openly carrying a grotesque monster through the streets of Gallowside at night was the kind of thing that would draw attention from people. Whereas two large, dishevelled men carrying something suspiciously body-shaped wrapped in tarpaulin through the streets of Gallowside at night, now that was the kind of thing people had the sense to avoid.

It hadn't taken long to sail from Pilgrim Island to Gallowside, and Ambrose and Talbot left their stolen boat moored to an empty pier next to a derelict pub before making their way to Dennis' flat, sticking to side-streets and alleys as much as possible. They didn't see any bobbies but never expected to, no policeman with a lick of sense would wander these streets alone after dark.

Ambrose knocked on the door again but still no one answered.

"Oh, bugger this," Talbot said. He turned the handle but the door only rattled in its frame, so he leaned back then threw his left shoulder at it, the interior bolt which had kept the door shut breaking off and hitting the wooden floor inside with a dull clang.

"*Dennis!*" Talbot called out as he and Ambrose entered the flat.

They followed a dimly lit, L-shaped hallway of faded wallpaper and scuffed floorboards, passing an open doorway leading to a cramped and grimy kitchen, the hallway ending at a closed door that Talbot now opened, striding into the room beyond.

It was clear that the parlour was the room Dennis wanted his customers to see. On one hand the parlour was clean and neat, with a large, patterned rug covering much of the wooden floor, the furniture and glass all polished, a small fire burning cosily, well-padded chairs, and more doilies than any one man should own. But amongst this pleasant, typical décor were some very untypical inclusions such as framed photographs of what appeared to be tiny, winged fairies fluttering around flowers, a full-length mirror with a star-dotted black cloth partially draped over it, a crystal ball, a stuffed raven staring glassily from the perch to which it was glued, a shelf of dusty tomes bookended by two human skulls, and an oversized "gold" scarab which Ambrose reckoned could be traced back to a cheap Newmuck workshop rather than some ancient Egyptian tomb.

Ambrose recognised the scene for what it was: a fake, tawdry display designed to impress the gullible. Dennis had manipulated his audiences with some theatrical flourishes back when he was on the stage, but nothing as blatant or lazy as this. The intended mood was emphasised by the low light, the parlour illuminated only by the fireplace and some scattered red candles.

"There you are," Talbot said, and he walked towards the circular table that stood at one end of the room.

Sitting around the table and staring at Ambrose and Talbot in open-mouthed shock were Dennis and three other people, the four of them all joining hands in a circle. Dennis' guests were two women and a man in their fifties or sixties, well-groomed and formally dressed, the man in a stiff grey suit while the women wore heavy, layered dresses, their hats, shawls and coat hanging from a coat-stand next to the hallway door.

Dennis looked ridiculous in an ostentatious black suit with a golden medallion around his neck, a puffy red cravat, an elaborately patterned waistcoat, black leather gloves, an unnecessarily tall hat, and a waist-length cape. Ambrose could see that even the pointed goatee beard Dennis wore on his face was fake.

Talbot slammed the tarpaulin-wrapped Gerald down on the table and Dennis and his guests flinched and released each other's hands, one of the women gasping in alarm. As Ambrose approached, Dennis looked at the Roustabouts and Gerald, his shock turning to anger.

"What the *hell* are you doing?" Dennis demanded. He frowned at Gerald. "What's this?" He paused. "And why is it moving?"

Dennis was right, the tarpaulin was shifting in places as Gerald writhed lazily inside, regaining consciousness. Talbot took hold of one end of the tarpaulin and yanked it, the material unravelling until Gerald spilled out onto the table, his eyelids fluttering and a low moan issuing from his throat.

"This is Gerald," Talbot said.

Dennis' customers screamed and bolted from the table, tipping over their chairs, running out of the parlour and into the hallway.

"*Mr. and Mrs. Plowman, Miss Lancaster!*" Dennis called after them, rising to his feet. "*Please, wait!*"

But the terrified screams only receded until eventually there was silence.

Dennis gave Ambrose and Talbot a venomous look. "Well, thank you *very much*. It's fine, it's not like I was planning on *eating this week!*"

"Don't be so dramatic," Talbot said. He nodded in the direction of the coat-stand and the forgotten clothing that hung there. "You can probably get something for those down the market. Anyway, what was that, a séance? You can't talk to the dead."

"It's not about talking to the dead."

"I think that's generally what a séance is about," Ambrose said.

"I give people closure, tell them what they want to hear."

"And get paid for it," Talbot said. He looked around the parlour. "Look at this place, you're a cheap charlatan."

"I am *not* a charlatan, I provide – why am I trying to justify myself to you?" Dennis angrily pointed towards the hallway. "*Get out!*"

"Sorry, but we need your help," Ambrose said.

A look of outraged astonishment appeared on Dennis' face. "*You* need *my* help? After what you did?"

"Saved your life?" Talbot suggested.

"You ruined my career!"

"We're not the ones who hired an evil hag as an assistant."

"I didn't know what Magda was when I hired her! You saw her, she didn't look like a two-hundred-year-old witch!"

"You're just lucky we got to her before she had your soul as a snack."

"*You cut off her head in front of four-hundred people!* No venue in Newmuck would have me after that show!"

"The world's at stake, Dennis," Ambrose said.

"I've got enough problems of my own. I told you before I don't want anything to do with you lot." Dennis straightened his fake goatee. "And it's not 'Dennis' anymore, it's 'Dominic.'"

"Why?"

"The punters like a more exotic name."

"Give me that," Talbot said, and his right hand whipped out, pulled off Dennis' fake facial hair and tossed it aside. "Now listen, Deirdre –"

"*Dominic.*"

"Never mind that. Listen, you can't talk to the dead but we know you *can* read minds, and we need you to read this thing's mind and tell us what you see. If you don't then tomorrow night you and us and Newmuck and the whole bloody world goes down the toilet."

Dennis looked at the half-conscious Gerald then gave Ambrose and Talbot a sceptical frown. "You're serious."

"As a cricket ball to the plums," Ambrose said.

Dennis sighed. "Alright, I'll help. But not for free."

"You always were a greedy sod," Talbot said.

"In case you hadn't noticed, I'm not exactly rolling in it. I'm still stuck here in this hovel and I'm sick of it. A man has to make a living, so if you and the world want my help, you can pay for it."

Ambrose reached into his trouser pocket. "Here, I've got..." He pulled out two pennies, looked at them then placed them on the table. "Sorry, I had more but we took a dip in the Brazenbrook earlier, most of my money must've fallen out then."

"What about you?" Dennis asked Talbot.

Talbot reached both hands into his trouser pockets and pulled them inside-out, revealing them to be empty, and thankfully not following that up with an elephant impression.

"Look, we're in a bit of a rush," Ambrose said, "but once this is all sorted out, we'll come back and make things right. You have our word." Ambrose looked at Talbot. "Right?"

"It'll be top of our to-do list," Talbot said sarcastically.

Dennis shook his head, took off his hat and smoothed back his brown hair. "Come on then, what exactly is going on?" He put the hat down on the table with one hand and loosened his cravat with the other, then took off his gloves and placed them on top of the hat. "You can start by telling me who your friend is."

Gerald began groggily pushing himself up onto his elbows until Talbot planted one hand on his chest and shoved him back down onto the table, pinning him in place.

Ambrose did the talking, giving Dennis a condensed account of the past two days, Dennis taking it in his stride as Ambrose suspected he would. Despite the tacky façade, Dennis possessed a genuine gift and some experience with the supernatural, and not just when his lovely assistant Magda revealed her not-so-lovely true colours.

Even so, Dennis remained sceptical. "This all sounds pretty unlikely to me."

"That's because your primitive brain refuses to comprehend the truth," Gerald said, fully conscious now and not looking pleased about his situation. "But soon your eyes will open and you will look upon the Old Ones and know that your entire species is nothing but an accident, a pathetic, meaningless flicker of noise and light in the infinite void. A void into which you will soon be fed while my kin and I, the Old Ones' chosen children, bask in their glory for eternity."

Dennis looked at Ambrose and Talbot. "He's a charmer, this one."

"Can you help or not?" Talbot asked.

"I can try. The only non-human mind I've ever read was my dog's when I was nine years old. I never tried again after that."

"Why?" Ambrose asked.

"Back then I didn't have the same control over my power that I do now. I was… impressionable. My mother caught me dragging my bare arse across the living room floor and chased me around the house with a carpet-beater." Dennis looked at the expressions on the Roustabouts' faces. "It's *not* funny. So, what am I looking for inside this thing's head?"

"We want to know where they're planning to hold the ritual," Ambrose said, "but anything else you can dig up about stopping the Abyss-Dwellers and Blacklock might be useful."

"Alright, let's get on with it. Hold him down."

Ambrose moved to stand near Gerald's feet and gripped his ankles, pinning his legs, while Talbot did the same to Gerald's wrists, the Abyss-Dweller struggling in vain.

"You have no idea what powers you are trifling with, human!" Gerald snarled at Dennis. "The sights I've witnessed, the knowledge I possess, even a glimpse of the truth will shatter your mind beyond repair!"

Dennis placed his hands on the sides of Gerald's head. "I just spent the last forty-five minutes listening to Miss Lancaster bang on about what kind of biscuits her dead husband preferred, you'll be surprised at what my mind can take."

Looking ahead, Dennis closed his eyes and took several deep breaths. For a few seconds nothing happened, then he winced, frowning.

"What do you see?" Talbot asked.

"The ocean…" Dennis said, his voice distant, his eyes remaining closed. "All around. So deep. Down into the blackness… spires of stone and coral…

a city. Vast… and so old. Older than us. Touched…" Dennis winced again, more intensely this time. "Touched by… the Old Ones. So long ago… the womb of Mother Ocean… I can't… I…"

"Concentrate, Dennis," Ambrose said. "Where are they holding the ritual?"

Dennis' muscles tensed. "The great alignment! The great alignment draws near!"

Gerald's eyes rolled up into their sockets as Dennis' arms began to tremble and tears ran down his cheeks. Ambrose was starting to get a bad feeling about this.

"Focus on the ritual," Ambrose said. "Where are they holding the ritual?"

"They will come from the void between the stars!" Dennis said, his voice rising. "*Their gaze will turn to us and we will be unmade!*"

Gerald's eyes began to glow a deep, swirling shade of purple, and then Ambrose saw that Dennis' eyes were now wide open and had the same glow. Ambrose and Talbot looked at each other. They had both seen Dennis read minds in the past and it was never like this.

"We should stop this," Ambrose said as the parlour began to fill with a constant, unsettling hum that didn't seem to have a specific source.

"He hasn't told us anything yet," Talbot said.

Dennis' back arched as his hands also began to glow and the strange humming sound steadily rose in pitch and volume. Gerald's entire body began to vibrate against the table.

"*The Old Ones will come!*" Dennis shouted rapturously. "*The Old Ones will come! Ghr-klu'up! Ro-fhal g'hn ras-tep! Ghr-klu'up!*"

The hum had become a horrible, high-pitched whine that hurt Ambrose's ears and felt like it was crawling into his brain, and he had to shout to make himself heard. "*Something's wrong! Dennis is in trouble!*"

The purple glow was also emanating from Dennis' mouth now as he continued ranting in that alien language, the veins on his forehead and neck standing out, his body trembling.

Talbot released Gerald's wrists and pulled Dennis' hands away from the Abyss-Dweller's head. The world exploded in a deafening scream and blinding purple light.

Dennis' New 'Do

Digby thought he recognised the building before him as the home of Dennis Johnson although he couldn't be completely sure since much of it had been reduced to rubble. The front of the two-storey building had been blown apart from within, the interiors of both flats exposed beneath the overhanging remains of its roof, chunks of stone and other debris strewn across the street and alley outside. People were emerging from nearby buildings, wary but curious.

There was no smoke or fire, but then it didn't seem to have been a typical explosion.

Digby and Bryn had searched the north bank of the Brazenbrook, following the river from Croker into Gallowside. Not that there was any noticeable boundary separating the two districts, the waterfront around that way being an uninterrupted jumble of damp and dingy docks, factories and warehouses. But there was no sign of Talbot or Ambrose, and Henry reported the same when Digby and Bryn met him on Gallows Bridge. As they began to discuss their plan B, or rather lack of one, from somewhere in Gallowside a jagged column of purple light suddenly shot up into the sky and through the clouds, illuminating the surrounding streets, the light accompanied by a sound like the crack of thunder but more high-pitched, a sharp and unpleasant noise that made the three Roustabouts wince. The light vanished as abruptly as it had appeared while the high-pitched noise gradually faded. Having no better ideas, Digby, Bryn and Henry ran towards the source of the light.

"Over there," Henry said now, pointing at an arm sticking out of the rubble.

Digby and Bryn followed Henry as he ran to the building, stepping over what little remained of the front wall and clambering over the debris within.

"Digby, give me a hand," Henry said. "Bryn, see if you can spot anyone else."

Although nothing could be seen of the buried figure beyond the one limp arm, Digby recognised the shirtsleeve rolled up around the forearm, and he and Henry hurriedly tossed aside chunks of masonry and pieces of broken furniture until they uncovered a familiar face.

"I'm starting to lose my patience now," Talbot said somewhat groggily, looking up at them through narrowed eyes.

Digby and Henry helped Talbot to his feet. He was covered in dust and his clothes were ripped in places, but he didn't seem to be injured apart from some cuts and bruises.

"*I've found Ambrose!*" Bryn called out.

Henry stayed with Talbot as Digby walked over to Bryn, debris shifting beneath his feet. He did a double-take when he saw the head of a raven staring up at him from the rubble, then realised the bird was stuffed. He and Bryn cleared the wreckage that Ambrose was trapped beneath then helped him up. Ambrose was dazed and coughing but like Talbot didn't seem to be seriously hurt.

Bryn slapped Ambrose on the back, sending up a small cloud of dust. "Can't leave you two alone for five minutes."

Ambrose looked around. "Where's Dennis?"

"Dennis Johnson?" Digby said.

"We brought Gerald to him. They were both with us."

"We'll find him."

And less than a minute later they did, the Roustabouts searching for Dennis as onlookers gathered in the street, watching but not going so far as to actually help. Digby expected that most of them were just waiting for a chance to pick over the ruined building for anything worth looting. Dennis was alive but unconscious as Digby and Henry lifted him from beneath some debris and carried him to the pavement, where they lay him down and took a knee on either side of him.

Henry leaned in towards Dennis. "Dennis? Can you hear me?" He gave Dennis' cheek a soft slap. "Dennis?"

Digby and Henry flinched as Dennis' eyes snapped open and he abruptly sat up.

"*Ghr-klu'up!*" Dennis shouted. "*Ghr-klu'up! Ghr-klu–*"

Henry slapped Dennis again, harder this time. "Get a hold of yourself, man!"

Dennis fell back to the pavement, eyes wide as he blinked several times, slowly coming back to his senses. Digby and Henry moved him into a sitting position.

Dennis stared at nothing, his brow furrowed. "I'm... Dennis."

"Yeah, we know that," Digby said.

"I... *saw* things... *knew* things... but it's all fading now..."

"Are you hurt?" Henry asked. "Anything broken?"

Dennis looked down at himself. "I don't think so. No. No, I'm alright."

Digby and Henry helped Dennis to his feet as Bryn, Talbot and Ambrose joined them.

"Dennis, was there anyone in the upstairs flat?" Ambrose asked.

Dennis looked towards the second floor of the building, where the shattered remnants of a living room and bedroom could be seen, the rooms bare and impersonal. He shook his head. "No, it's been empty since last week."

"Anyone see any sign of Gerald?" Talbot asked.

"He's gone," Dennis said.

"How do you know?"

"I was... inside his head. The connection's been cut and it's fading fast, but I know he's not here anymore." Dennis looked at what remained of his flat, its condition suddenly sinking in, a distraught expression appearing on his face. "Look what you've done to my home!"

As if to emphasise Dennis' point, another damaged section of the ground-floor ceiling collapsed with a crash.

Digby turned to Talbot and Ambrose. "What happened?"

Ambrose explained about Talbot saving his life and grabbing Gerald, about Pilgrim Island, and about their visit to Dennis and the explosion of purple light that occurred when Dennis tried reading Gerald's mind.

Digby gestured at the rubble. "If the Abyss-Dwellers have got magical powers that can do this, why didn't they use them before?"

"It's not like that," Dennis said. "The explosion wasn't magic, not as we know it anyway. And it wasn't some intentional attack. I think it happened because of Gerald's connection to the Old Ones, and our reality and theirs brushing up against each other. They can't coexist without terrible things happening, even with Gerald acting as a conduit. Me trying to tamper with his knowledge and those memories triggered something, like a spark."

"Hell of a spark," Bryn said.

"Whatever it was, it did a number on your building," Ambrose said. "I'm surprised we're not in pieces as well. We were lucky."

"So you couldn't find anything useful while you were rooting around inside Gerald's head?" Bryn asked Dennis.

"I've looked into some strange minds before but nothing like that," Dennis said. "I was lost in there. Centuries upon centuries of memories, forbidden knowledge never intended for the human mind... The few details I saw didn't make up the tiniest fragment of it all, but still, if the connection had stayed in place any longer I would've gone insane." Dennis squeezed his eyes shut and pinched the bridge of his nose. "I don't want to think about it. I *can't*. If the door to this world is opened for the Old Ones..." Dennis shuddered as he trailed off.

Henry clapped Dennis on the shoulder. "Don't worry, those bastards can knock all they like but they're not getting in. We'll see to it."

"It's not as if anyone else is keen to take the job on, apparently," Digby said.

Dennis wandered away from the Roustabouts and into the ruins of his flat, looking around at the devastation.

"I'd stay out from under what's left of that roof if I were you," Ambrose called out to him.

"Looks like we're back at square one," Bryn said.

"Well, the Abyss-Dwellers flooded the place so we know they're not going to hold the ritual underneath the cannery," Ambrose said.

"So that's one place crossed off our list," Digby said. "Shame there are a thousand others they could use."

"Let's head back to the Pig," Henry said. "There's no point us wandering the streets with our tally whackers in our hands, if we're going to decide what to do next then we might as well do it over a pint. We can check on Annie and Oliver at the same time."

"*What the bloody hell?!*" Dennis cried.

The Roustabouts turned to see Dennis holding in one hand a large shard of broken mirror-glass which he had apparently picked out of the debris. He was staring at his reflection in the shard with a shocked expression, his other hand grasping strands of the white streak that ran through his brown hair.

"What's *this*?" Dennis demanded of his reflection, which apparently didn't have an answer.

"That's your hair," Bryn said.

"The, um, white streak wasn't there before the explosion," Ambrose said.

Dennis glared at the Roustabouts while pointing at his hair. "So blowing up my flat wasn't enough, you have to do *this* to me as well?"

"It can happen sometimes during a traumatic experience," Henry said.

"Oh, so you're a doctor now, are you?"

"I actually think it suits you, Dennis," Ambrose said. "Makes you look more mysterious."

Dennis hesitated, an uncertain frown on his face. "Really?"

"Yeah. Don't you think it's a good look for 'Dominic Joyeux'?"

Bryn turned to Talbot. "Who the hell is Dominic Joyeux?"

"I'll tell you on the way to the pub," Talbot said.

Dennis studied his reflection then smoothed back his hair and nodded. "You know, I think you're right. It *does* suit me. The punters will lap it up."

"You can tell them you were bitten by an enchanted skunk," Digby said.

The Roustabouts stifled laughter as Dennis looked at Digby, unimpressed. He dropped the mirror shard, which shattered on a chunk of stone, then said, "I've still got nowhere to live because of you bastards."

"Sorry, Dennis," Ambrose said. "It was my idea to bring Gerald to you."

"Why don't you come with us?" Henry suggested. "There's room at The Bewigged Pig, you can stay there tonight."

Dennis shook his head. "Oh no, I don't want to be within ten miles of you lot, you've already done more than enough damage."

"We'll make things right," Ambrose said. "We gave you our word."

"Forget it. Just go. And stay away from me." Dennis gestured at the surrounding ruins. "I need to see what I can salvage from this mess. Then I'm getting out of here before my landlord shows up."

"That's a point. I hope he's got insurance."

"This place should've been knocked down years ago," Digby said. "Sod the landlord, we're doing the city a favour."

"If you change your mind, Dennis, you know where the pub is," Henry said.

The Roustabouts began to leave but then turned to look back at Dennis as he spoke.

"I barely remember anything of what I saw," Dennis said, his expression grim. "But I know the Old Ones aren't a problem you can just hit until it goes away."

Digby smiled. "You don't know how hard we can hit."

Drinks with Friends (and Offal Cromwell)

When the Roustabouts entered The Bewigged Pig, Bryn was glad to see Annie and Oliver, less so Offal Cromwell and the younger man with him.

The four of them were sitting at the Roustabouts' table and Cromwell and the younger man looked like they had seen some trouble, their clothes spattered with blood, Cromwell's right hand holding a bloody tea-towel against his injured left shoulder. On the table before him was a revolver, his left hand resting on the gun. Bryn didn't recognise the younger man but assumed he was one of Cromwell's bunch.

Digby strode towards the table, fists clenched at his sides. The younger man rose to his feet, smiling at Digby as his right hand moved then suddenly had a knife in it.

"Digby," Cromwell said.

Digby kept walking, the other Roustabouts following him now.

"Digby, wait!" Cromwell said.

But Digby didn't wait, and the smiling knifeman stepped forward, feinted with the knife then thrust it at Digby's gut. Digby sidestepped, grabbed the knifeman's right wrist in one hand and his head in the other, and slammed one side of his skull into the Roustabouts' table, rattling the four glasses and bottle of whiskey on the table's surface. The knifeman's weapon fell from his hand as his unconscious body slid off the table and onto the floor.

Digby turned his attention to Cromwell, who had risen from his chair, his revolver pointed at the floor between them. Digby took a step towards him but stopped when Annie stood up, slammed the palm of one hand against the table and shouted, "*That's enough!*"

The Roustabouts and Cromwell looked at Annie, who glared at them.

"This is *my* pub and I'm *not* putting up with any more fighting, understand?" No one spoke. "*Well?*"

The Roustabouts murmured agreement. All except Digby, who said, "Annie, this arsehole –"

"I know what this arsehole has done and I don't want him in my pub any more than you do."

"Charming," Cromwell said.

"Shut up," Annie told Cromwell before turning back to Digby. "He said he's here because he wants to talk to you, and by the sound of it I think it's worth you hearing him out. After that, if you still want to kill him then you can do it outside."

"No wonder I don't drink here," Cromwell said.

"You don't drink here because I don't *want* you here. And don't think this changes that. Now put the gun on the table and sit back down."

Cromwell looked at Digby for a moment then did as Annie said.

"Grab yourselves some glasses," Annie told the Roustabouts.

Bryn didn't need to be told twice when there was a free drink involved. "I'll get them."

The other Roustabouts took their seats at the table with Cromwell, Annie and Oliver, Digby rolling the unconscious knifeman aside with one foot before picking up the fallen knife and placing it on the table. The Roustabouts had mostly dried off by now but Bryn still appreciated the warmth of the lit fireplace as he passed it, heading for the bar. He took five liquor glasses off a shelf, grabbed a nearby chair and joined everyone else at the table.

Cromwell glanced at the man on the floor. "You gave Caleb's head a good rattling, Digby. You haven't lost your touch. He's not dead, is he?"

"No," Digby said. "But the night's young."

Bryn picked up the bottle on the table and poured whiskey into the five glasses. He ignored Cromwell's and Caleb's glasses, saw Annie had gin in hers, and Oliver's was half-full of milk. He resealed the bottle and set it down.

Annie looked at Ambrose and Talbot. "You're all a mess, but you two look like someone dropped a building on you."

"Funny you should mention that," Ambrose said.

The Roustabouts recounted what happened at Burgess Canning

Company and the events that followed. The story didn't take long and neither did the first round of whiskeys, Bryn refilling the glasses as soon as they were empty.

"Looks like you two had a run-in with Blacklock's fishy friends as well," Bryn said to Cromwell, having noticed that some of the blood on him and Caleb wasn't red but black.

Cromwell glanced at his wounded shoulder. "It was a surprise to me, let me tell you," he said, then went on to explain what happened at his locksmiths.

Cromwell drank the remaining whiskey in his glass, set it down and reached for the bottle only for Digby to grab it and move it out of his reach. Cromwell frowned at him but sat back without complaint.

"That's why I came here," Cromwell said. "I've been around the block, I've seen some weird things in my time but not like you lot, I know you've dealt with plenty of stuff like this over the years."

"I understand why you came," Henry said. "What I don't understand is why you think we'd help you after you lied to us."

Cromwell sighed. "Right. Lucan. Look, I'm sorry, but Blacklock still owed me so I couldn't let you get your hands on him until I got what was coming to me. So I lied."

"You didn't just lie, you tried to kill us," Digby said.

"Now hang on, that's not true. I knew you were never in any danger, that you could handle that bastard the Candle brothers set on me. I only found out his name and address a few hours before you three showed up. Just thought I'd kill two birds with one stone, that's all."

"Do you know what Lucan was, exactly?" Bryn asked.

"A pain in my arse. He did some real damage to my business. Must've cost the Candle brothers a pretty penny. I suppose I should feel flattered." A hint of a smile appeared on Cromwell's lips. "You said 'was'. Does that mean he's dead?"

Oliver frowned and stared into his milk.

"He's dead," Talbot said. "So's his friend."

"His friend?" Cromwell said.

The Roustabouts told Cromwell what happened at Lucan's house.

"I give you my word, I didn't know anything about there being two of them," Cromwell said. "Or the big bloke being some kind of monster or demon or whatever you reckon he was."

Bryn usually trusted Cromwell about as much as he trusted a hypnotist with an erection, but in this case he thought Cromwell was telling the truth.

"But let's put all that behind us, eh?" Cromwell smiled. "I understand you're upset, but let me make it up to you and we'll go back to business as usual."

"And how are you going to do that?" Henry asked.

"The way I see it, we share a common enemy. You want to stop Blacklock and these Abyss-Dwellers, and since the bastards tried to kill me, so do I. I can help you."

"We don't need your help," Digby said.

"You sure about that? Because it sounds to me like you're out of ideas. *I* know where Blacklock lives."

"We're not falling for that one again," Talbot said.

"No bullshit this time, I promise. Cross my heart."

"And hope to die?" Digby said.

Cromwell ignored that. "I'll even come with you this time, so you know I'm telling you the truth."

Digby looked around at the other Roustabouts. "We can't trust him, you all know it."

"He's right, though," Henry said. "We *are* out of ideas. And he's not going to pull a fast one again if he's with us because he knows what we'll do to him." He gave Cromwell a meaningful look. "Don't you, Offal?"

"Henry, I'll be on my best behaviour," Cromwell said.

Bryn shrugged. "A human shield's always handy."

Digby's expression was hard as he glared at Cromwell. "I swear, if you –"

"Save your breath, Digby," Cromwell said. "I get the message. I'm not going to give you that excuse you're looking for."

Henry looked around the table. "Any objections?" When none were raised, he finished his whiskey and set down the empty glass. "Drink up then, lads. Time to go."

"No," Annie said.

Henry paused. "No?"

"Have you seen yourselves? You're all bloody and bruised, your clothes are falling apart, you haven't eaten and I know none of you got much sleep last night. You're all exhausted." Annie leaned to one side to get a better look at something. "Ambrose, you've got a trout sticking out of your pocket, for God's sake."

Ambrose looked down and saw the fish head staring blankly up at him from his right-hand trouser pocket. He pulled out the dead trout and set it down on the table. "Didn't even realise he was in there. Poor bugger." Ambrose frowned as something occurred to him. "Hang on, I checked my pockets after being in the river…"

Bryn didn't like to admit it but Annie was right, it had been a long weekend and it was catching up to them, he could feel it in himself and see it in the others.

"I know you're all tough as nails, but you're still human," Annie said.

"I'm not sure about Talbot, we never had him tested," Bryn said.

"Piss off," Talbot said.

"You've still got until tomorrow night to stop Blacklock and the Abyss-Dwellers, and you'll have a better chance of doing that if you're fit and fresh," Annie said. "Get some rest, even if it's just a few hours. Then I'll sort you out some food and clean clothes and those bastards can get what's coming to them."

Henry smiled. "Annie, what would we do without you?"

"Die horribly, I imagine."

"So what's all this about some ritual and a deadline tomorrow night?" Cromwell asked.

"We can fill you in on the details in the morning," Henry said. "But basically, if we don't stop Blacklock and the Abyss-Dwellers by tomorrow night then the world ends. So like I said at the cooperage, it's in your best interests to help us do that."

"No pressure, then." Cromwell smiled at Annie. "So, darling, I assume the bed-and-breakfast offer extends to me and Caleb as well?"

"I'll be damned if I'm going to feed you but if you're helping the boys then you can stay," Annie said. "In fact, I've got the perfect room picked out for the two of you. If your friend dies during the night then just chuck him on the pile."

Cromwell frowned. "What pile?"

An Early Start for the Apocalypse

Henry swallowed his last mouthful of egg and fried bread, set his cutlery down on his plate and sighed contentedly. Annie would be the first to admit she wasn't much of a cook, but she could whip up a hearty breakfast. Alright, the eggs had started out fried but ended up scrambled when she got annoyed, but they tasted fine.

"Thank you, Annie," Henry said. "That really hit the spot."

"You're welcome," Annie said, having already finished her breakfast.

The Roustabouts were sitting at their table with Annie and Oliver while Cromwell and Caleb sat on stools at the far end of the bar, unfed and muttering to each other and occasionally throwing hard looks towards the Roustabouts' table. Caleb had survived his blow to the head, waking up in the early hours of the morning in a pub cellar that stank of death and garlic, with a pile of Abyss-Dweller corpses for company. He and Cromwell weren't thrilled about the sleepless night they spent locked in the cellar, although Cromwell was in a less murderous mood than Caleb, who eyed Digby in particular with real venom.

Henry caught Caleb's eye, raised his cup of tea in a toast and gave him a smile and a wink. Caleb glared for a moment before turning back to the bar.

Wunker, Henry thought as he took a sip of sugary, milky tea.

From somewhere up the street he heard the faint tapping of a baton on front doors as a knocker-upper made his rounds, rousing the people inside so they could get ready for work, the sun beginning to rise. The lights were on in the barroom as the barricaded door and windows allowed in little of the dim natural light, although the sky was clear and the gentle breeze that drifted through the gaps in the barricades was cool and bracing. Henry felt it was going to be a good day to save the world.

The Roustabouts had all washed, had their cuts disinfected by Annie, got a few hours of sleep, and changed into clean shirts and trousers where necessary, Annie raiding the last of the suitable spare clothes before putting on a clean skirt and blouse and brushing her hair. The Roustabouts had taken turns keeping watch during the night but there was nothing to report, Abyss-Dweller-related or otherwise. Now it was time to settle this Old Ones business.

Oliver was the last to finish his breakfast and he thanked Annie as he picked up his tea but then almost spilled it when an unexpected voice called out, "Morning, Miss Radcliffe!"

Everyone turned towards the hallway entrance at the rear of the room to see Martin "Mog" Deering looking around with an amused expression. "Blimey, busy weekend?" he said.

One of the boys employed by *The Newmuck Post* to deliver copies of the newspaper to its subscribers around the city, Mog was a cheerful young lad with an infectious smile who could be seen lugging his bag of papers across Wealdbury every weekday morning come rain or shine. Henry knew Mog was sharper than he often let on, the boy spent a lot of time on Wealdbury's streets and amongst its people and knew them well.

Annie rose from her chair and walked towards the bar. "Something like that, Mog. How did you get in here?"

"I saw the front was all boarded up so I used the back door," Mog said.

"The back door's locked."

Mog took a lockpick out of his trouser pocket and smiled as he waggled it in the air. "A professional delivery boy doesn't let locked doors stand in his way, miss. I never miss a customer."

"That's a worrying level of dedication you've got there," Annie said as she opened the till, withdrew some coins then closed it again.

Mog returned his lockpick to his pocket and adjusted the cap that sat atop his thick mop of blonde hair. "Morning, gents!" he said to the Roustabouts, who greeted him in return. Mog then glanced at Cromwell and Caleb and with noticeably less enthusiasm said, "Sirs." The two men said nothing as they turned back to the bar.

Annie approached Mog, who reached into the large bag slung across his right shoulder, withdrew a copy of today's paper, held it out to her and said, "Here you go." Annie took the newspaper, thanked him and handed him the money. He looked at the coins in his palm. "There's too much here, miss."

"The payment for the paper is right," Annie said. "The rest is yours."

"Very kind of you, thank you."

"Just promise me you won't spend it wisely."

Mog winked. "You have my word."

Smiling, Annie flicked the brim of Mog's cap. "Now go on, bugger off."

Mog headed for the hallway, bidding everyone goodbye before he disappeared from sight.

Annie returned to her seat and set the newspaper down on the table. Oliver was sitting next to her, and a worried frown appeared on his face as he saw the front page. "Oh," he said.

"What is it?" Ambrose asked.

"'Big Business Bigwigs Burned and Barked,'" Annie said, reciting the front page's headline.

"Eh?" Talbot said.

"It's an article about the deaths of Cecil Burgess and Frederick Orchardson."

"What does it say?" Henry asked.

"'Tragedy struck in Fondle Green on Saturday evening when fire raged through the home of canned seafood magnate Cecil Burgess, whose body was discovered by authorities in the charred ruins of his house the following morning. Three other bodies believed to be employees of Mr. Burgess were also found on the scene. Police are treating the fire as suspicious and are keen to speak to Mr. Burgess' son, Oliver, who was seen in Fondle Green on the night in question. Anyone with any information on Oliver Burgess' whereabouts is advised to come forward.'"

"Is there a reward?" Digby asked.

"That's not funny," Oliver said. He turned to Annie. "Does it say anything about Blacklock or the others? Or the Abyss-Dwellers?"

"It mentions Orchardson," Annie said, her eyes moving over the article. "It says police have refused to comment on a possible connection between his death and your father's, but that a man fitting your description was seen chasing Orchardson in the moments before he died." Annie looked up from the paper. "As well as two other people who apparently look a bit like me and you, Bryn."

"Funny, that," Bryn said.

Talbot frowned. "Hang on. 'Barked'? What's that supposed to mean?"

"I assume it's because Orchardson was technically killed by a tree," Henry said. "As in tree bark?"

"That's stupid."

"That's British journalism for you."

Everyone looked towards the hallway entrance again at the sound of footsteps, only this time it wasn't a cheerful delivery boy who appeared there but a procession of police constables. The Roustabouts, Annie and Oliver rose to their feet and Cromwell and Caleb climbed off their stools as over a dozen uniformed policemen fanned out around the room.

A figure in a dark suit, knee-length overcoat and bowler hat stepped through the line of constables and approached the Roustabouts' table. "Watch those two," Jeremy told his colleagues, pointing at Cromwell and Caleb.

"Sorry, but we're not open yet," Annie said.

Jeremy frowned at the faces at the table, his eyes briefly meeting Henry's before looking away again. "You're coming down to the station for questioning. All of you."

"You sure you brought enough men with you?" Digby asked.

"I doubt it," Talbot said.

"What's this about, Jeremy?" Henry asked, not wanting this situation to go the way it might.

"You know what it's about," Jeremy said, all business. "People are dead, Henry, and you and the current company you're keeping are all mixed up in it together somehow. I want to know what's going on."

Cromwell smiled as he took a step towards the table. "Inspector Alabaster, I'm sure this is all some sort of misunderstanding."

"Save it, Cromwell. You can do your talking at the station."

"Jeremy, listen to me," Henry said. "I know this looks bad but you don't understand what's at stake here."

"Then enlighten me."

"You won't believe me. But I need you to trust me. To trust *us*. We've got something very important we need to do. As soon as that's done, I'll explain everything, I promise."

"The promise of a criminal," said a man's voice from the direction of the hallway. "As if that was a thing of any worth."

The speaker had entered the room flanked by two other men, the three of them walking towards the Roustabouts' table. Despite his expensive suit, overcoat and top hat, the speaker looked like he had been through the wringer: his right hand bore a large, ugly bruise, two fingers bandaged together; his skin was pale, with dark bags beneath his eyes; and he was limping on his left leg, his left hand gripping the head of a polished wooden cane which he obviously needed. He was trying to appear confident but the pain and exhaustion were clear on his face.

The man on the speaker's left wore similar, equally expensive-looking clothing but was older, shorter and fatter, with nervous eyes darting around beneath bushy eyebrows.

The final man looked to be the youngest of the three and showed neither pain nor nervousness, his expression flat, eyes calm but alert. Unlike the speaker, his confidence was quiet and natural, and his longer hair, plainer clothes and harder appearance helped set him apart even further from his companions.

Jeremy gave the speaker an annoyed look. "I told you and your colleagues to wait outside, Mr. Blacklock."

"Sorry, inspector," Arthur Blacklock said as the three men came to a stop at the table. "I'm sure you can appreciate I'm simply eager to see justice served after all the terrible things these villains have done," he added, speaking like a man who enjoyed the sound of his own voice.

Henry turned to Oliver. "This is him, then."

Oliver nodded nervously, only glancing at the three men. "And Sugarfoot. And Quinn. Blacklock's man."

Henry looked at Blacklock and Quinn. "Oh. Well, nothing wrong with that."

Blacklock's confident smile slipped. "What?" A moment later, realisation dawned. "No, not like *that*, Quinn is my employee."

Ambrose shrugged. "No judgement here."

"No, look, we're not –"

"But what we *are* going to judge you on is everything else you've been up to, you colossal twat," Bryn said.

Blacklock regained his composure. "I'd be more concerned in cooperating with the police than flinging around any spurious accusations, if I were you. I'm not the one in very serious trouble here."

"What's he told you?" Henry asked his brother.

Jeremy didn't seem keen on Blacklock himself but hid his contempt better than the Roustabouts, which admittedly wasn't difficult. "Mr. Blacklock and Mr. Sugarfoot came to the station earlier. I was on duty at the time and when they claimed they had information on the deaths of Cecil Burgess and Frederick Orchardson, I took their statements. They also claimed attempts were made on their lives, resulting in Mr. Blacklock's current injuries. They accused all of you of being co-conspirators in these crimes and said they knew where to find you. And here you all are."

Blacklock looked at Oliver with a heavyhearted expression. "Even taking into account your murderous intentions towards me, Oliver, I still truly hope your father can forgive you from Heaven. For a man to die at the hands of his own son…"

"You're lying!" Oliver snapped, outrage overcoming nervousness. "*You* killed him! You and Sugarfoot and Orchardson and the Abyss-Dwellers!"

Jeremy looked at Blacklock, who sighed and shook his head. "I'm afraid the weight of the boy's crimes may have taken its toll on his wits, inspector. It's sad, really."

"Oliver's telling the truth," Annie said defiantly. She pointed at Blacklock. "*He's* the one behind all this. Him and his friend there."

Sugarfoot averted his eyes from Annie's accusing glare. "Nonsense. Bloody nonsense."

"They're right," Henry said to Jeremy. "Blacklock is using you to stop *us* from stopping *him*. If what he's planning comes to pass then something terrible is going to happen tonight."

"All I know is I've got more than enough reason to take you all in for questioning and no reason to suspect Mr. Blacklock of any crime," Jeremy said. "You'll have the chance to tell me your side of things at the station. Don't make this harder than it has to be, Henry."

Henry looked at Blacklock. "Like I told your mate Gerald, we're not going to let you do what you're planning to do."

Blacklock's smile faltered. "I'm, uh, afraid I don't know any 'Gerald'."

"Oh, I think you do," Bryn said. "Short bloke, glasses, bad skin. He tried to make a deal with us. Behind your back, looks like."

Blacklock kept smiling but it was strained now. "As I said, I don't know who you mean."

"Close friends keeping secrets from each other," Ambrose said. He shook his head and tutted, turning to Talbot. "You hate to see it, don't you?"

"A crying shame," Talbot said.

"Well, this has all been very exciting," Cromwell said with a pleasant smile, Henry only now noticing that he had gradually moved closer to the table. "But I'm afraid there's a problem, inspector."

"And what's that?" Jeremy asked.

Cromwell stepped behind Annie, his left arm wrapping around her waist as his right hand appeared at her throat with a knife, the blade pressed against her skin but not deep enough to draw blood. "I don't like police stations," Cromwell growled, his smile gone.

"*Bastard!*" Annie hissed as Cromwell started backing towards the hallway, taking her with him. Caleb joined them, the two men keeping their eyes on the police and the Roustabouts.

"Nobody move or I'll open her throat, understand?" Cromwell said. "Inspector, any more of your boys outside?"

"No," Jeremy said.

"Smashing. The three of us are leaving now. Anyone follows us and the girl dies."

Jeremy held out a placating hand. "Cromwell, put down the knife."

Digby stared at Cromwell. "I'm going to kill you for this."

Caleb disappeared into the hallway and Cromwell was about to do the same when Annie drove the heel of her right shoe down onto his right foot. He cried out but didn't release his hold on her, instead leaning in towards her nearest ear and angrily whispering something, the words too quiet for Henry to hear. But he noticed the expression that flashed briefly across Annie's face. Henry looked at Cromwell, who held his gaze and gave him the tiniest nod before rushing through the doorway with Annie.

Ambrose turned to the other Roustabouts. "We've got to go after them!"

"You're not going anywhere," Jeremy said, but none of the Roustabouts were paying him any attention.

"Let them go," Henry said.

Digby frowned. "What are you on about? We're not just going to let that bastard take Annie!"

"What are you waiting for, inspector?" Blacklock said. "Go and get them!"

Jeremy turned to him. "Mr. Blacklock, please –"

"Just trust me," Henry said to the other Roustabouts, hoping he was right about this. They looked at him for a long moment, Digby glancing towards the hallway.

"Alright," Bryn said eventually. And that was the end of it.

"You're *not* going after them," Jeremy told the Roustabouts.

"We know, we just decided," Talbot said.

"*You* decided? Right, I've had enough of this. We'll handle Cromwell, you five go outside and get in the Black Brenda out there. You too, Mr. Burgess." Jeremy turned to Blacklock, Sugarfoot and Quinn. "Mr. Blacklock, Mr. Sugarfoot, with Cromwell on the loose I suggest you both go home and stay there for now, just to be on the safe side. An officer will be in touch as soon as we have news."

Blacklock slammed the end of his cane against the wooden floor, grimacing as his bad leg took the weight for a moment. "You were supposed to take them all in, not allow two of them to waltz out scot-free! Do your damn job, inspector!"

Jeremy bristled, and Henry recognised that look. His brother very rarely lost his temper but his patience still had its limits, and he fixed Blacklock with a stern stare. "The more time I waste listening to your complaining right now, Mr. Blacklock, the less time I spend *doing* my job. So take my advice and go home. Or don't. Either way, my men and I have work to do."

Blacklock glared at Jeremy, furious, his nostrils flared and a slightly unhinged glint in his eyes. His left arm was trembling and sweat ran down his pale forehead. Henry thought he didn't look right at all.

"*Come on!*" Blacklock snapped at his companions as he stormed towards the hallway.

Henry thought about how easy it would be to end all this right now. It didn't matter how many bobbies Jeremy had with him, it wouldn't be enough to stop the Roustabouts. But although the Roustabouts' relationship with the law was a rocky one at best, Henry knew that murdering two outwardly innocent men in front of over a dozen police officers was crossing a line that could never be uncrossed.

"Be seeing you," Henry said to Blacklock, who looked back briefly with a hateful expression before he, Sugarfoot and Quinn passed into the hallway and out of sight.

Jeremy turned to the constables. "Half of you come with me, I want the rest to escort these men to headquarters. Make sure they all get there and *stay* there. Shift that stuff blocking the front door and take them out that way."

Jeremy and half of the policemen disappeared into the hallway while the remaining constables cleared the barricade from the front door and escorted the Roustabouts and Oliver out onto the street.

There was no sign of Cromwell, Annie or Caleb on Mulligan Avenue, and the early time of day meant there were only a handful of curious onlookers scattered around the street. A brougham rolled by, driven by Quinn, the shadowy shapes of Blacklock and Sugarfoot visible through the window. The Roustabouts and Oliver watched it for a moment as it continued down the street, then at the urging of their police escort they turned to the Black Brenda parked at the pavement, a team of two horses attached to the front of the black-painted police wagon. They walked to the rear of the wagon and opened the door, climbed up onto the step and ducked their heads as they entered, then sat on the two wooden bench seats inside, a constable closing and locking the door behind them. It was gloomy inside the wagon, the only light coming through two narrow slits high up in the side walls and a square, barred hole in the door.

"I hope my nan doesn't hear about this or she'll be worried sick," Ambrose said.

"At least something good came out of it," Talbot said, and he and Ambrose looked at each other.

"Blacklock's man," Ambrose said. "Quinn."

Talbot nodded.

"What about him?" Henry asked.

"We know where the ritual's going to be," Ambrose said.

A Very Exclusive Venue

Blacklock gasped in pain as the brougham hit a pothole in the road, jolting his injured leg. *"Watch where you're going, Quinn!"*

Sugarfoot flinched at the outburst but made a point of not looking at Blacklock, instead continuing to stare out of the window at the passing streets as Quinn drove. Still, like a lot of things, Sugarfoot was grating on Blacklock's nerves. Blacklock didn't know the specifics of what would happen immediately after the ritual was performed, but if an opportune moment arose, he was sure the Old Ones wouldn't mind if Sugarfoot happened to fall onto a dagger. What kind of paradise could the new world be with that buffoon as a god, anyway?

Blacklock looked at his pocket watch and frowned when he saw it was only half past ten. The morning was dragging. He supposed the few hours he had spent unconscious after passing out at his factory counted as getting some rest, but he felt no better for it. Everything ached and burned and throbbed and just generally bloody hurt. He had never wanted to cast off this fragile, mortal husk so badly.

Blacklock was glad Quinn had been present when he passed out as he was certain Sugarfoot would have turned tail and run otherwise. But Sugarfoot was up to his neck in it and Blacklock wasn't going to let him forget that. He ordered Quinn to kill Sugarfoot's driver at the factory mainly because now that Quinn had arrived, the driver was unnecessary and a loose end, but it also didn't hurt as a reminder to Sugarfoot of who was in charge. Sugarfoot protested, claiming the man had served him faithfully for years, but his complaints ceased when Quinn's garotte slipped around the driver's neck. In fact, Sugarfoot hadn't said much of anything since, which Blacklock didn't mind one bit.

Quinn dropped the corpses of the driver and the Abyss-Dweller into a manhole outside the factory, and Blacklock and Sugarfoot discarded their bloody clothing and changed into clean suits taken from the factory's storeroom. As Quinn drove them in Sugarfoot's brougham he secured a cane for Blacklock by taking one from a drunk gentleman who had made the unwise decision of walking a deserted street alone in the early hours of the morning. Following that, they visited the nearest police station to direct the law's attention to The Bewigged Pig.

Not that events had gone smoothly at the pub, what with Cromwell and Caleb escaping and the Roustabouts' claim regarding Gerald. Blacklock told himself not to worry, Cromwell had no idea where Blacklock was going so shouldn't be a threat, especially since his current priority would be staying one step ahead of the law.

But Gerald... now that was different.

Because Blacklock believed the Roustabouts. Yes, Oliver probably told them about Gerald, but why would they lie about meeting him and being offered a deal? For one thing, the Roustabouts were common thugs who Blacklock didn't credit with enough intelligence for mind games, and for another it was just the kind of betrayal Blacklock expected from the underhanded Abyss-Dweller. He *knew* he had been right not to trust him. Well, if Gerald thought he could stab Blacklock in the back now then the little shit was in for a surprise. Abyss-Dwellers may live long lives but they weren't immortal.

Blacklock let his mind wander, visualising his confrontation with Gerald, playing it out in his head, piecing it together, thinking of the most clever things he could say and the most dramatic gestures he could make, putting words in Gerald's mouth, conjuring fear and regret in the Abyss-Dweller's eyes followed by realisation a moment before Blacklock delivered the final, victorious blow...

The brougham came to a stop, rousing Blacklock from his satisfying reverie. He turned to Sugarfoot. "Out."

Sugarfoot exited the carriage as Blacklock picked up his cane. Then he reached for the plain wooden box next to him but hesitated at the thought of the grotesque object that lay inside, wrapped in black velvet. Even now, just thinking of the Idol of the Silent King was enough to bring him out in goosepimples. He doubted it would concern him once he had been made a god, but for now he hoped he would never meet the Silent King face-to-nightmarish-face. Blacklock forced himself to pick up the box and, cradling it in his right arm, stepped out of the brougham with the aid of Quinn, who had descended from the driver's seat with his satchel and wrapped shotgun.

The carriage was parked next to the building on the riverside property Blacklock had purchased at the same time as Pilgrim Island. The small, isolated property was some distance from the wharfs, factories and other busy areas that lined much of the Brazenbrook's banks in this part of the city, being nothing more than an empty, run-down brick warehouse slumped on a patch of neglected, weed-covered wasteland. But it possessed three qualities Blacklock sought: it was on the river, it was close to Pilgrim Island, and it was private.

When Blacklock bought Pilgrim Island with the intention of using it for the Ritual of Suth-G'nar after getting rid of Cecil and Oliver, he did so with as much secrecy as possible as he knew the purchase would draw attention and he didn't want anyone – particularly Cecil – connecting him to the island. This riverside property was part of that secrecy, offering a spot for private travel between the island and the riverbank. A vagrant had snuck onto the property last year, looking for shelter, but Quinn swiftly dealt with that potential problem, which now rested at the bottom of the Brazenbrook.

Quinn reached into the brougham and took out a bag containing the masks and robes Blacklock and Sugarfoot had collected from their homes after leaving that grotty pub, all of the other ritual items besides their Order of the Void clothing and the Idol of the Silent King already on Pilgrim Island. Sugarfoot wanted to bring along a bottle of something as well but Blacklock refused, having little faith in his competency sober, let alone drunk. The thought of dulling his own pain with alcohol was sorely tempting, but the crestfallen look on Sugarfoot's face almost made up for it.

Blacklock and Sugarfoot followed Quinn as he walked towards the river, the brougham and horses abandoned. The small, one-storey warehouse was off to their side, its walls damp and crumbling, roof sagging, windows boarded and doors chained shut. Quinn kept a few emergency items inside but Blacklock had no other use for the building, it was the pier behind it that mattered.

They rounded a rear corner of the building then walked down the muddy slope that descended to the water's edge and the short pier, tied to which was the rowboat Quinn had taken from Pilgrim Island the previous night. Unlike the warehouse, which Blacklock had been happy to leave to rot, he had Quinn repair the half-collapsed pier after purchasing the property.

Blacklock's cane tapped against the wooden planks as he and Sugarfoot followed Quinn onto the pier. Quinn climbed into the boat and set down the bag and his satchel and shotgun then helped the two men onboard, Blacklock cursing the pain in his thigh. Blacklock and Sugarfoot sat side-by-side on one of the bench seats, Blacklock holding the idol's wooden box in his lap. Quinn untied the boat, pushed it away from the pier and sat facing Blacklock and Sugarfoot as he took hold of the oars and began to row.

As Pilgrim Island gradually grew larger up ahead, Blacklock looked downriver, the Brazenbrook snaking into the distance before eventually disappearing from sight, obscured by waterfront buildings and the ships docked at them. Across the city, numerous columns of black smoke rose into the blue sky.

Blacklock wondered if the sky would be a different colour after the Old Ones came. Or if there would even be a sky as humanity knew it. For the first time he realised that, when he got right down to it, he didn't actually know much about the new reality he was helping to usher in. But ultimately the details didn't matter. What mattered was he was finally going to get what he deserved.

A large, iron-hulled steamship sailed along nearby, far enough away from the rowboat so as not to be a hazard but close enough that its wake caused the small vessel to bob gently. Blacklock looked down at the surface of the water, not liking the thought of Abyss-Dwellers swimming around down there in the darkness. The creatures had always used the Brazenbrook to access the cannery, Pilgrim Island and other parts of the city and it had never bothered Blacklock in the past, but now he couldn't help but wonder what other treachery Gerald might have cooked up in that alien mind. Was he down there right now with others of his kind, staring up at the boat with those horrible, bulging eyes, grinning with those sharp teeth, rusty weapons at the ready?

Blacklock looked up to find Sugarfoot staring at the box in his lap with a troubled frown. Sugarfoot glanced at him then looked away.

"I don't like being around that thing," Sugarfoot said. "Gives me the heebie-jeebies."

"It's just a statue, Thomas," Blacklock said dismissively. "Show some backbone."

In truth, Blacklock couldn't blame Sugarfoot, the idol just had that effect on people. Even Quinn was uncomfortable around it. Trying not to think about the Silent King, Blacklock focused on Pilgrim Island as the shore drew closer.

"Something's wrong," Quinn said.

"What is it?" Blacklock asked impatiently as Quinn brought the boat to a stop at the pier.

"The other boat is missing and the gate's open. It was locked when I left."

"Just help me off this damn thing."

Quinn tied the boat to the pier then helped Blacklock and Sugarfoot onto the walkway, the movement once again bringing fresh, searing pain for Blacklock, who leaned heavily on his cane, breathing hard, eyes squeezed shut and head throbbing. He felt hot and cold and sick and he just wanted to sleep. Eventually he stood up straight again to find Sugarfoot staring at him.

"*What?*" Blacklock snarled.

"Nothing," Sugarfoot said innocently before walking towards the gate in the chain-link fence.

Quinn unwrapped his shotgun and held it in one hand down at his side, the satchel and bag in his other hand, and he and Blacklock followed Sugarfoot. When they reached the gate, Quinn looked at the broken padlock on the ground.

"Someone's been here," Quinn said. "It might not be safe for you, sir."

Blacklock felt his chest tighten, terrified at the prospect of someone having stolen or destroyed the ritual items on the island but also furious at another problem, another delay, more interference. He had had *enough.* "This is where I need to be, Quinn," he said firmly. "You *know* that."

"If there's an intruder present –"

"*If there's an intruder then do your fucking job and kill them!*" Blacklock shouted, spittle flying from his mouth. "*I am sick of having to deal with other people's incompetence! I'm going to set this world right! And no one is going to stop me, do you understand?!*"

Quinn's expression hadn't changed. "Yes, sir."

Blacklock stormed through the open gate, Sugarfoot hurriedly stepping out of his way. He walked at a quick pace that did his leg no favours but his anger was stronger than his pain and it didn't take him long to pass Quinn's bungalow then the two ruined bungalows. When the paved main street came into view, Blacklock felt his anger begin to subside, and when he saw Pilgrim Theatre it dissipated entirely. He stepped around the rusted metal "L" that lay in the street then stood facing the theatre, almost smiling now as his eyes roamed over the building and Sugarfoot and Quinn approached.

Blacklock would have liked to restore the building's exterior to its former glory but knew that doing so would risk drawing attention to the island, so he told himself that the façade wasn't important, what mattered was what lay beyond those doors and on that stage, that blank canvas on which anything and anyone could be brought to life through his will, his creativity, his *performance*.

Blacklock stared at Pilgrim Theatre, the cocoon from which he would be reborn. "Quinn, unlock the doors. We have a show to prepare for."

Making Amends via the Reckless Application of Explosives

Oliver waited.

Nothing happened.

He pushed. He jiggled. He thought about heavy rain, a flowing river, a running tap. Nothing.

"Just don't think about it," Ambrose said behind him.

Oliver knew Ambrose was only trying to help but he was only making it worse. Oliver didn't reply as he stared into the corner of the room.

He waited.

"Forget we're even here," Ambrose said.

Oliver closed his eyes, more aware than ever that there were five large men behind him and here he was standing with his little gentleman in his hand and all he wanted to do was pee and he couldn't even do that and he was going to die tonight and –

Oliver sighed with relief as nature finally won out over his anxiety, the base of the metal bucket on the floor rattling with the stream that flowed into it. A complaining policeman had already emptied it once, Bryn asking him what he expected keeping six men locked in the same cell for hours.

Feeling ten gallons lighter, Oliver finished, tucked himself away and sat back down on one of the two beds, each nothing more than a creaking metal frame covered in a dirty blanket. The light in the cell was dim, the only window being a small, barred opening high in the exterior wall, the door a solid slab of steel.

"What's the time?" Digby asked, leaning against a wall.

Oliver looked at his pocket watch. "Twenty past four."

It had been less than half an hour since the last time Digby asked.

Oliver and the Roustabouts had been locked inside the cell since being brought to Lemton Police Station – one of several stations across the city and the one which served as the headquarters of the Newmuck Police Force – that morning. Henry's brother was keen to question them but was called away on other urgent business, and since then no one else had questioned them or given them any indication as to how long they might be held for. Oliver imagined there would be a lot of questions, especially if the police discovered what was in the cellar at The Bewigged Pig.

Like the Roustabouts, Oliver was worried about Annie. Although he was certain she still didn't think much of him, she seemed to have slightly less contempt for him now than when they first met, and that was a big win in Oliver's book on women. It was a very small book. More of a large-print pamphlet, really.

And it wasn't just Annie they had on their minds: the Ritual of Suth-G'nar was fast approaching. But like Bryn, Digby, Ambrose and Talbot, Oliver was putting his faith in Henry.

During the ride from the pub to the police station, Henry had explained his reasoning for not wanting to pursue Cromwell and Annie. He believed Cromwell faked the kidnapping to get away from the police with Annie so that they could later rescue the Roustabouts and Oliver rather than be locked up alongside them. As such, Annie was never in any real danger. Henry reckoned Cromwell wasn't doing it out of the goodness of his heart but in the hope it would make him and the Roustabouts even over the Lucan incident. Cromwell was simply betting on the Roustabouts coming out on top in this conflict with Blacklock. Henry mentioned Cromwell whispering into Annie's ear, the look of realisation that then crossed her face, and the subtle nod Cromwell gave him. Although the other Roustabouts – particularly Digby – remained slightly sceptical, they agreed to go along with the idea.

On the bright side – not that Oliver really saw it as one, the thought of hiding in this cell and hoping everything would just turn out alright holding a definite appeal – they now had a good idea where the ritual was going to take place, Talbot and Ambrose revealing that Quinn was the man they had seen on Pilgrim Island. As a likely site it made sense. It was a very private spot, its current owner had gone to a lot of trouble to hide his identity and keep people away, and it was right on the Brazenbrook, meaning the Abyss-Dwellers could come and go as they pleased. Blacklock had never mentioned purchasing the island to Oliver or his father as far as Oliver knew, but given his scheming, why would he?

The Roustabouts had asked Oliver what he knew about Quinn, which was very little beyond him being an experienced and unnerving ex-soldier. Blacklock never really spoke about him in detail and Quinn himself was a man of few words.

"I spy with my little eye –" Ambrose began.

"Is it 'cell'?" Talbot asked.

"Yeah."

Something clanged against one of the metal bars of the window then landed on the ground outside with a quiet thud.

"Shit!" a female voice whispered from the alley beyond the window. "Bloody bars!"

A moment later, Oliver and the Roustabouts watched as a small object sailed between the bars and landed on the floor of the cell. They looked at each other then Talbot walked to the object and picked it up. It was a rock, tied around which was a scrap of paper.

Talbot removed the string, unfurled the paper and looked at it. "It says, 'Move away from the wall and cover your ears.'"

Henry smiled. "Alright, you heard the rock."

Oliver and the Roustabouts moved to the wall opposite the window and stood with their hands pressed to their ears as they waited for something to happen.

When nothing did, Oliver turned to Digby. "What do –"

Oliver recoiled and bumped into the wall behind him as the far wall suddenly exploded inwards, showering the cell and its occupants with dust and small chunks of debris. After a few seconds of darkness he dared to open his eyes again, checked himself and was relieved to find he was still in one piece. Then, coughing at the dust and smoke, he peered through the grey haze at a large, jagged hole in the far wall, standing outside which was a familiar figure.

"Come on, we haven't got all day!" Annie said through the ringing in Oliver's ears.

Oliver smiled then followed the Roustabouts as they passed through the hole and out into the alley behind Lemton Police Station, where Annie and Cromwell were waiting.

"I knew you wouldn't let us down," Henry said.

Cromwell spread his arms and smiled. "When have I ever?"

Digby frowned at him. "Not you."

"You can all tell me how amazing I am later, right now we need to move," Annie said.

She was right, Oliver could hear raised voices and general sounds of alarm and confusion from the police station and the street beyond the mouth of the alley. Police whistles were blown. Oliver knew it was serious when there was whistling.

Turning away from the street, Annie and Cromwell ran, Oliver and the Roustabouts following them into a tangled network of alleys, the rears of terraced houses and other buildings passing by in a blur.

"I knew the kidnapping was a feint!" Henry said.

"I went along with it when Cromwell told me what he was doing!" Annie said. "But I told him what I'll do to him if he ever puts a knife to my throat again!"

"It was very detailed!" Cromwell said, breathing heavily. "So we're even now, yeah?"

"Don't get ahead of yourself!" Digby said.

"Where's your right-hand arsehole?" Bryn asked Cromwell.

Cromwell was panting now, his words coming in bursts between ragged breaths. "Caleb's taking care of things for me! While I'm doing this nonsense! For you!"

They rounded a corner, Oliver almost charging into a pair of startled women taking a cigarette break behind a small workshop of some sort as the fugitives hurtled past, Oliver shouting an apology back over his shoulder. They emerged onto a narrow side-street busy with pedestrians and wagons, and darted between the traffic as they ran across the road and into the mouth of an alley on the opposite side, that in turn leading to even more alleys and cul-de-sacs with multi-storey buildings looming on both sides, a gloomy warren of brick and stone.

"How did you know which cell we were in?" Ambrose said.

"I've got a few friends on the force!" Cromwell wheezed. "I found out! From one of them!"

"Up here on the left!" Annie said a moment before she passed through an arched gap in a wall.

The men followed her into a courtyard surrounded on three sides by leaning and crumbing old buildings with shuttered windows. The floor of the courtyard was made up of broken and uneven paving slabs, weeds sprouting from the gaps between them, and there was a second entrance in the form of a wide, high-ceilinged tunnel that led through one of the buildings and out onto a street. Standing in the courtyard were five saddled and bridled horses, and sitting on one of them, reins in hand, was Randolph.

"Randolph, what are you doing here?" Henry asked.

Randolph smoothly dismounted his horse and frowned at Cromwell, who was leaning forward with his hands on his thighs as he got his breath back. "You can thank *him* for that," Randolph said.

Cromwell stood up straight and wiped his sweaty forehead with a shirtsleeve. "With how you lot saved poor, innocent Randolph here from my boys, I thought he might be willing to help us break you out. The dynamite was mine, by the way. I won't charge you for it."

"We can't thank you enough," Ambrose said to Randolph, "but you shouldn't put yourself in danger for us like this."

Randolph made a dismissive gesture. "Happy to help." He glanced at Cromwell. "Shame about the circumstances, though."

Cromwell smiled at Randolph. "Come on, we've put that little misunderstanding behind us, haven't we? We're all friends here." He looked at the faces around him then shrugged. "Well, close enough."

Bryn had approached one of the horses and was now stroking its neck whereas Oliver maintained a wary distance. He didn't have much experience with animals and certainly wasn't comfortable being around one that could kick his head off his shoulders if it felt like it.

"What's with the horses?" Digby asked Randolph.

"When Annie and Cromwell came to the stable they said you'd need a fast getaway," Randolph said, "but I was in the middle of fixing my Clarence after one of the wheels came loose this morning so it was no good. But I still had my horses."

"I borrowed the other three from a livery worker I know," Cromwell told the Roustabouts. "You're welcome."

Talbot frowned at the horses then Randolph. "Hang on, are you expecting us to ride these things?"

"This is better than the Clarence, really," Randolph said. "You'll be quicker, you can get through spaces a carriage can't, and if you need to split up then you can do. Have you ever ridden a horse?"

"Not *sober*, no."

"We've all ridden before," Henry said, taking the reins of a shiny black mare. "We'll manage."

"So which one of you am I riding with?" Cromwell asked.

"You're not coming with us," Digby said.

"If you want me to take you to Blacklock's house then –"

"We don't," Henry said. "We're going to Pilgrim Island."

Annie frowned. "Why are you going there?"

"We've got good reason to think that's where the ritual's going to be held. But Offal, you go to Blacklock's house in case we're wrong. If he *is* there, kill him."

"And if he's got more of those monsters with him?" Cromwell said.

"Take your men with you," Henry said. "*All* of them. Blacklock has to be stopped."

"So much for you lot giving me a hand then, even after what I just did for you." Cromwell sighed. "Alright, I'll round up the boys and pay Blacklock a visit, show him that my friends are even nastier than his."

Police whistles and urgent shouting could be heard again, distant but drawing closer.

"We should go," Bryn said.

The Roustabouts mounted the five horses, Talbot and Digby doing so with noticeably less grace than the others.

Henry held out a hand to Oliver. "Oliver, you can ride with me."

Oliver looked into the dark, impassive eyes of Henry's horse and saw nothing there. It could want to kill him or cook him a slap-up Sunday dinner with treacle pudding for dessert, it was impossible to tell.

"Come on!" Henry said.

With Henry's help, Oliver climbed up onto the horse. He sat behind Henry and the saddle, directly on the horse's back, his hands gripping the saddle.

"Bryn, I'll ride with you," Annie said.

"I don't suppose me arguing it's too dangerous for you would make any difference?" Henry said.

"None at all," Annie said pleasantly as Bryn helped her up onto the back of his horse and she placed her hands on his hips.

"Shouldn't you be riding side-saddle, love?" Cromwell said, smiling suggestively at Annie. "You know what they say."

"Oh, shut up," Annie said. She turned to Henry. "How are we going to get onto the island? The footbridge is gone and I don't think the horses will fancy swimming the Brazenbrook."

"We'll think of something," Henry said.

The pursuing policemen were closer now, although it was hard to pinpoint how far away they were or exactly what direction they were coming from due to their voices and whistling echoing through the alleys, bouncing between buildings.

"Are you going to be alright?" Henry asked Randolph.

"I'll be fine, they're not looking for me," Randolph said. "Good luck with... whatever it is you're about to do. If you need to leave my horses then don't worry, they can find their own way home."

Cromwell looked over the people on horseback. "If I find Blacklock, I'll tell him you said hello. Do the same for me, yeah?" Then he left the courtyard by the way they had entered.

Randolph stepped aside as the Roustabouts turned their horses towards the mouth of the spacious tunnel. Oliver's grip tightened on Henry's saddle and he prayed horses couldn't run as fast as he suspected they could.

A wide grin appeared on Bryn's face. "*Let's ride!*"

The Roustabouts Ride!

With his horse beneath him, Annie at his back and the wind in his beard, Bryn rode.

It had been a long time since he had done so, living neck-deep in the overcrowded urban hive that was Newmuck not allowing for many opportunities to ride with wild abandon. But with the world at stake and the Newmuck Police Force snapping at their heels, today was an exception, and Bryn couldn't be happier as the Roustabouts raced through the streets in the direction of the Brazenbrook, accompanied by the thundering rumble of twenty shod hooves clashing against cobblestones and asphalt. They weaved their way around carriages, omnibuses, carts, wagons, and foot-traffic, the startled cries of alarm and angry curses quickly fading behind them as the city rushed past.

Bryn glanced over at Henry, who was focused on the road ahead while behind him Oliver's eyes were squeezed shut, his teeth clenched. Behind Bryn and Henry were Ambrose, Talbot and Digby, while further back again were their pursuers, three mounted police officers and a horse-drawn wagon carrying around a dozen more constables, the bobbies shouting, waving their truncheons and blowing their whistles. While the Newmuck Police Force still had somewhat of a reputation for laziness, blowing a hole in their headquarters was apparently a good way to get them moving.

Still, Bryn couldn't help but smile. He could see the image in his mind now as clearly as when he saw it for the first time ten years ago: the man in the hat firing a pair of six-shooters at some unseen target as he rode his majestic horse across a vast, dry landscape before a setting sun, a trail of dust billowing out from behind him, a steely-eyed look of determination on his face. A *cowboy. The American West.*

The painted image graced the cover of a tattered magazine titled *Two-Gun Tales* which Bryn found discarded at The Bewigged Pig. It fascinated him immediately and since then he had read a lot about the United States of America, specifically the western frontier: the landscapes, natives, settlers, outlaws, lawmen, gold and silver rushes, railways, cattle drives. Whether books, newspaper articles or magazine tales, Bryn devoured them all. It was another world, similar in some ways but so very different in others. He would love to see it for himself, and while that had initially seemed a fanciful notion, he knew the world was becoming a smaller, more connected place all the time thanks to international cable lines and innovations in travel. Maybe one day.

"*On your left!*" Annie shouted.

Bryn looked left to see Henry veering towards him, forcing Bryn to pull hard to the right, almost clipping a line of carriages parked at a kerbside cab-stand.

Henry had been made to swerve by the sudden appearance of Winthrop Pollock-Seymour's penny-farthing, the leader of the Penny Dreadfuls accompanied by the four other members of his gang, all of them pedalling their gigantic bicycles frantically as they sped out of an adjoining street and joined the chase.

"*I told you we'd meet again, you foul commoner!*" Winthrop shouted down at Henry.

"*Not now, Bollock!*" Henry shouted back.

"*It's POLLOCK, you bastard!*"

Winthrop tried to sideswipe Henry again, forcing him right once more. Bryn pulled on his reins, dropping back and sweeping around to Winthrop's left side, the other Penny Dreadfuls mixed in amongst the Roustabouts now, trying to force them into traffic or run them off the road, ignoring the pursuing policemen.

Ambrose reached out and snatched a stovepipe hat from the head of a shocked pedestrian then jammed it between the spokes of the front wheel of the penny-farthing next to him. Both bicycle and rider were abruptly launched into the air, somersaulting end over end before crashing back down to the ground in front of the police, who swerved to avoid the ensuing explosion. Bryn wondered what kind of penny-farthings these were if they could explode like that, but he knew that sometimes things just exploded – his uncle Hywel, for example – and it was best to not ask questions.

Movement on Bryn's right caught his eye and he glanced up into the haughty face of a Penny Dreadful as he swerved close to Bryn's horse, urging him towards the kerb.

"*Hyah!*" Bryn shouted, giving his horse his heels, speeding up and pulling ahead of the Penny Dreadful just in time to avoid a parked wagon and the two men unloading crates of vegetables from it.

The chaotic, high-speed chase continued through the streets of Newmuck, the Roustabouts and Penny Dreadfuls weaving this way and that, the two sides trading insults – the Roustabouts clear winners on that front – and the Penny Dreadfuls losing another of their number when Talbot kicked a rider into a lamppost. With their slow horses, overloaded wagon and difficulty navigating traffic, the police fell far enough behind that Bryn lost sight of them, although all they had to do was follow the trail of swearing, startled and curious pedestrians.

Bryn was riding at the rear of the commotion now, another Penny Dreadful at his side, the gang member with one hand on his handlebars and the other holding a whip which he snapped down at Bryn, who leaned away from it, its crack loud in his ear. A moment later there was another crack and Annie cried out as she was wrenched off the horse, Bryn looking back to see her tumbling across the asphalt, thick patches of manure cushioning her fall slightly. The end of the whip was grasped in her hand, yanking the rider off his penny-farthing, the bicycle clattering to the ground.

When Bryn looked forward again he saw the side of a newsstand rushing towards him an instant before his horse skidded to a stop and threw him from the saddle. Bryn smashed through the wooden planks of the newsstand, his ears filled with the squealing of his horse, the snapping of wood and the fluttering of paper.

When the world stopped spinning, Bryn found himself lying amidst a pile of newspapers, magazines and wooden planks. Apart from a papercut on his right thumb – *Typical*, he thought – he seemed to be unhurt. He swept aside copies of *The Newmuck Post*, *Like Adults but Smaller: A Magazine for Boys and Girls*, *Fudge!* and *Discreet Gentleman's Photography*, and rose to his feet. He was surrounded by shocked faces, including that of the newsstand owner, who luckily hadn't been inside his newsstand but standing on the pavement nearby, and who now stared at Bryn with a newspaper in one hand and a sausage roll in the other, one cheek bulging with half-chewed meat and pastry.

"Sorry," Bryn said.

He looked up the street and saw Annie standing in the road, smeared with horseshit and angrily raining blows down upon the Penny Dreadful she had pulled off his bicycle, the half-conscious man on his knees, his collar bunched in one of Annie's fists. Her teeth were bared and her hair was wild as she punctuated her words with punches. "*Knock! Me! Off a horse! And into the shit! Will you?!*"

Bryn smiled but only briefly as the policemen who had been chasing them appeared from around a distant corner, their number having grown to two wagonloads of men and six on horseback. They were approaching fast and would reach Annie before Bryn could, but that wasn't going to stop him going back for her. He mounted his horse as Annie looked from him to the police then back again.

"*Go!*" Annie shouted. "*Stop the ritual!*"

"*I'm not going to leave you!*" Bryn shouted.

"*I'll be fine! Just come and get me when it's done! Now go!*"

Several of the mounted constables brought their horses to a stop near Annie and the dazed Penny Dreadful while the rest of the police sped past her, heading for Bryn, who hesitated before reluctantly turning his horse and racing on. There was no sign of the other Roustabouts or the remaining Penny Dreadfuls ahead, he needed to catch up.

An old man pulling a handcart stepped out into the road, and with no time to go around him, Bryn leapt his horse into the air, the animal neighing loudly as it cleared the handcart before landing smoothly on the other side and running on without a pause. Knowing these streets and their shortcuts well, Bryn turned sharply into an alley, the police wagons behind him too slow to make the turn and too wide to fit anyway while only two of the mounted policemen reacted quickly enough to follow. He sped along the alley, which was narrow enough that the constables had to ride single-file, and empty of life apart from some rats which scurried out of sight. Bryn leapt his horse over a fallen length of guttering then leant to one side to avoid a window-shutter that dangled by a single hinge, jutting out into the alley.

Bryn made another sharp turn into an adjoining alley, his horse skidding on the slick and dirty cobblestones but keeping its balance, unlike the police horse directly behind him, which crashed into the wooden fence at the corner where the two alleys met, horse and rider tumbling into the courtyard beyond.

Bryn heard the remaining constable make the turn and continue his pursuit. Up ahead a washing line with long-forgotten items of clothing hanging from it spanned the alley about a foot above Bryn's head, and as he passed beneath it he reached up a hand and snatched from the line a pair of mouldy and generally foul-looking underpants, reminding himself to scrub that hand with bleach – or perhaps fire – later. He threw the underpants into the air behind him and turned his head to see the loathsome item sail right into the face of the mounted policeman, who clutched his face with both hands and uttered a blood-curdling scream then fell from his horse and bounced along the cobblestones.

With no other police in sight, Bryn emerged from the alley onto Rib Lane, avoiding a tram that almost filled the road as it rumbled along on its rails, the surprised faces of passengers looking out at him from behind its windows. Then, after navigating a few more streets, alleys and other shortcuts, Bryn finally caught up to the other Roustabouts and Winthrop, the only remaining Penny Dreadful. Despite being alone, Winthrop continued to be a threat, his penny-farthing snaking between the four horses as he targeted one then another, trying to dismount the riders or force the horses into traffic. Winthrop may have been a pompous arse but he knew how to ride that stupid bicycle, Bryn had to give him that.

They were on Orson Row, a street of crumbling, drab buildings and a general air of defeat and misery, just one of many such streets in the poor district of Dredger's End, a district Bryn was familiar with but which he was certain Winthrop wouldn't be. And that gave him an idea.

Bryn urged his horse onwards, its breathing heavy as it galloped to the front of the group, passing the other Roustabouts and Winthrop. Bryn caught Henry's eye and shouted, "*Follow me!*"

Bryn turned onto another street, the other Roustabouts and Winthrop following close behind. Up ahead on his left, Bryn spotted the next turn that he wanted, a pedestrian side-street set back from the pavement. Still leading the way, he moved closer to Winthrop.

"*Oy, Bollock!*" Bryn shouted up at Winthrop, who glared down from his high perch, the spokes of his massive front wheel a blur as his thin legs pumped furiously. "*What do you call a stuck-up English wanker on a penny-farthing being insulted by a Welshman on a horse?*"

"*What?*" Winthrop shouted, outraged.

"*Do you want me to tell you?*"

"*You're all going to get what's coming to you, do you hear me?*"

"*Alright, I'll tell you!*"

Bryn turned onto the pedestrian side-street and the other Roustabouts and Winthrop turned with him, Bryn glad to see Winthrop's attention was still focused on him.

Bryn smiled at Winthrop. "*Distracted!*"

Winthrop's angry frown turned to one of confusion. "*Wh–*"

The brick arch that spanned the mouth of the side-street was in poor condition but still sturdy enough that it didn't budge when Winthrop slammed into it at high speed, his penny-farthing rolling on without him as he fell to the ground, unconscious.

Bryn looked back at Winthrop and laughed as the other Roustabouts passed beneath the arch, giving the riderless penny-farthing a wide berth as it wobbled then crashed into a wall. Henry rode up alongside Bryn as Digby, Ambrose and Talbot closed in behind, the side-street containing little foot-traffic.

"You knew that was there, didn't you?" Henry said, smiling.

"And I knew Bollock didn't!" Bryn said.

Henry noticed the empty space behind Bryn and frowned. "Where's Annie?"

Loudly enough for everyone to hear, Bryn explained what had happened to Annie. None of the Roustabouts were happy about the situation but, reluctantly accepting it, they rode on until they reached a public footpath that ran alongside the Brazenbrook, a concrete embankment sloping down to the water. They reined in their horses and looked downriver at Pilgrim Island in the distance, overgrown and fenced-off with no signs of life, not looking much like an origin point for the apocalypse. But Bryn had once seen a chocolate macaroon transform into a seven-foot-tall umbrella – that shapeshifter had been *so drunk* – so knew not to put too much stock in appearances.

Henry glanced over his shoulder. "You can open your eyes now, Oliver."

Oliver slowly opened one eye then the other. He looked around with a dazed frown. "My testicles hurt and I can't feel my hands."

"Well, we're not there just yet."

"So how are we getting onto Pilgrim Island?" Bryn said, patting his horse's neck as the animals caught their breath.

Talbot nodded towards the river and the vessels sailing along it. "We catch a lift." He pointed upriver at Saint Wiggler's Bridge, initially a stone structure which had been repaired and rebuilt several times over the centuries until eventually being demolished and fully reconstructed from cast iron, its arches large enough to allow modestly sized vessels to pass through them. "We'll use the bridge."

"How?" Oliver asked suspiciously.

"We jump off it onto a boat."

Oliver groaned unhappily.

The Roustabouts rode along the footpath in the direction of Saint Wiggler's Bridge, the pedestrians in their path moving aside, the only police presence a red-nosed, middle-aged bobby whose gut bulged against his jacket and who only needed a brief look at the Roustabouts to decide he was fine where he was, namely sitting on a wooden bench with a hip flask in hand.

The Roustabouts turned onto Saint Wiggler's Bridge, rode to a spot almost halfway across then stopped and dismounted on the upriver side, the horses partially blocking the road. The driver of an approaching carriage began to loudly object, but when the Roustabouts all turned to look at him he settled for muttered grumbling and driving around the horses.

Bryn stroked the side of his horse's face, the mare snorting softly. "Thank you, girl."

The Roustabouts and Oliver walked to the waist-high wall that ran along the edge of the bridge and looked at the handful of vessels sailing in their direction. The closest was a rowboat, too small and flimsy for their purpose, but the next was a steam-powered barge, old and battered but sturdy-looking, with a windowed cabin near its bow and a small rowboat secured to the stern. At the wheel inside the cabin was the captain, the only person onboard, while behind the cabin a number of large crates covered much of the deck. Tied to each other and the deck itself to prevent them moving, the crates had no lids and seemed to be filled with fabrics or something similar.

Talbot pointed at the barge. "That one."

They jogged along the bridge to the spot where the barge would pass directly beneath them, then crossed the road. Oliver watched as the Roustabouts climbed up onto the wall and sat on its edge, their legs dangling over the side as they looked down at the water, waiting for the barge.

"Move it!" Digby told Oliver.

Oliver reluctantly joined them on the wall. "It looks a lot higher up from here, doesn't it?" he said nervously.

"You'll be fine," Bryn said. "Just go limp."

"Does that make it hurt less?"

"Not if you land awkwardly and shatter a hip," Talbot said.

"Here it comes," Henry said, and he inched forward.

They all kept their eyes on the water until the barge's bow appeared, followed by the roof of the cabin.

"*Now!*" Henry said.

The Roustabouts and Oliver pushed themselves off the edge of the bridge and they plunged towards the deck of the barge below, landing in several of the open-top crates with six soft thumps, the contents breaking their falls. They all sat up to see the captain looking over his shoulder at them through the open doorway at the rear of his cabin.

"*What the bloody hell?*" the captain said in a Cornish accent. He released the wheel and stormed out onto the deck, reaching his right hand to his belt and grabbing the large wooden cudgel that hung there.

The captain was a short, wiry man who looked to be in his early sixties, although he might have been younger but just very weathered, as one look told you here was a grizzled sailor, the kind of man who chewed seashells and pissed brine, Bryn hoping for his sake it wasn't the other way around. His white handlebar moustache was accompanied by stubble, and wavy white hair flowed out from beneath his mariner's cap. He wore sturdy boots and a thick, waist-length coat over a shirt, braces and trousers, his clothes as weatherworn as his skin.

"What's this about?" the captain demanded, brandishing his cudgel. "If you lot are marauders, you picked the wrong barge to raid, I can tell you that."

"These are jumpers," Oliver said as he lifted an arm of one of the thick woollen jumpers that filled the crates in which he and the Roustabouts sat, the jumpers varying in colour and size.

"Aye," the captain said. "Chester Nesbit's Extra Comfortable Jumpers, to be precise. Winner of Most Comfortable Jumper three years running at the Jumpies."

"'The Jumpies?'" Ambrose said.

"Annual awards ceremony for the British jumper industry." The captain shrugged. "So I'm told. I just get paid to transport them."

"Why are there no lids on the crates?" Bryn asked.

"It's how Mr. Nesbit insists on them being transported," the captain said. "Reckons it 'lets the wool breathe' or some rubbish. Mad bugger. It's a pain in the arse when it starts raining, that's what *I* know."

Ambrose rubbed a jumper between the fingers of one hand. "They really are *very* comfortable…"

"Come on," the captain said impatiently, gesturing with his cudgel. "Out of there, the lot of you."

The Roustabouts and Oliver climbed out of the crates and stood on the deck.

"We're sorry for the intrusion, captain," Henry said, "but we need you to drop us off at Pilgrim Island. The fate of the world depends on it."

"'Fate of the world' my arse," the captain said, and he pointed his cudgel at Henry. "*Your* fate is to either piss off into the river right now or have your brains loosened."

Talbot stepped forward. "What's your name, captain? And the name of your vessel?"

The captain straightened, a hint of pride creeping into his bearing as he lowered his cudgel. "I'm Captain Hesketh Fry and this is the Isabela Dawn. What's it to you?"

"I'm Talbot Ashmole, former able seaman of the Jolly Gamble and veteran of the South Pacific Prawn War of Eighteen-Sixty-Three."

"A fellow seadog, eh? Royal Navy?"

Talbot shook his head. "Private prawning ship, just doing our bit."

"Don't see many old hands around nowadays."

"I haven't served onboard a ship for a long time, but it never leaves you."

"Aye, for good and bad. Dark days, down there in the South Pacific back in sixty-three. Where were you?"

"A few hundred miles off the coast of Chile."

Fry nodded grimly. "So you saw the worst of it. I was captaining a frigate around there for a time, a little further north, near Ecuador. Lost a lot of good men to those damn prawns."

"They will be remembered."

"Any chance we can move this along?" Henry said.

"Captain Fry, we need to get to Pilgrim Island as a matter of urgency," Talbot said. "If you could –"

Fry held up his free hand as he returned his cudgel to his belt. "Say no more, lad. You and I share the saltwater bond, and a true sailor doesn't turn his back on that. The Isabela Dawn's no clipper but I'll get you to the island quick as I can."

Talbot gave Fry a nod then the captain turned and headed for his cabin. The Roustabouts were about to follow him but paused as Oliver, an uncharacteristically determined expression on his face, took off the suit jacket Annie had given him, letting it fall to the deck, then reached into the crate he had climbed out of. He took out a thick, patterned, bright-red wool jumper and pulled it on over his head. When he had finished adjusting it, he looked at the Roustabouts.

"Bugger it," Oliver said. "If I'm going to die then I'm going to die *comfortable*."

Blacklock's Mask, or Lack Thereof

Blacklock's gaze roamed over the dust and cobwebs, the chipped stonework and torn carpeting, the peeling paint and battered seats, the patches of mould and puddles of water, the dirt and random debris, and the length of rope from which a chandelier had once hung.

But although Blacklock had never visited Pilgrim Theatre when it was open, the current condition of its auditorium couldn't disguise the fact it had once been an impressive establishment. The cavernous space was split into two tiers, the raised seating platform that was the balcony – "the gods", how apt – at the rear of the auditorium, overhanging some of the seats below, the room's total capacity close to a thousand people. Two boxes, one at each side of the room, offered excellent views of the stage. The walls boasted sculpted columns and detailed paintings while the decorated ceiling and surrounding cornice were elegantly designed. And all of this wonderful décor would have been illuminated by the chandelier and the numerous gas lights that lined the auditorium, although only those lights closest to the stage were lit now, leaving the back of the room dim.

The unseen rooms behind the stage – dressing rooms, costume wardrobe, manager's office, a storeroom for props and scenery – were as dilapidated as the auditorium. As for the stage door at the rear of the building, Blacklock had had that bricked up as a security measure.

Yes, time and neglect had taken their toll and now the interior of Pilgrim Theatre was a mess.

Except for the stage. Blacklock had seen to that.

Curtains of thick, burgundy velvet held in place by gold-coloured ropes flanked the expanse of polished and perfectly level oak floorboards while at the rear of the space hung a large tapestry of white stars scattered across a black sky, the whole scene framed by the proscenium arch. The stage was bathed in the light of several suspended spotlights and the gleaming golden footlights that ran along the curved front of the stage, Blacklock having replaced the old, somewhat volatile stage lights – many theatres in Newmuck had burned down at least once over the years – with fancy new carbon arc lamps. He didn't really understand the difference but they were expensive and apparently used by the top theatres in the city, so he assumed they were good.

A glorious sight unsullied by the surrounding decay, the stage was a fitting scene for Blacklock's rebirth and the creation of a new kind of theatre with which he would be fundamentally, inseparably intertwined. There would be no need for writers or directors or scenery or stagecraft or lighting or any other such superfluous trivialities, and there would *certainly* be no need for any other actors. Every aspect of the unending performance would belong to and be born from Blacklock, no one else.

His first thought had been to revitalise the theatre's whole interior in preparation for the Ritual of Suth-G'nar, but then he realised only the stage mattered. *That* was where the eyes of the universe would be looking when the planets aligned. At *him*. Who cared about the plebs out there in the darkness beyond the footlights? Although his audience tonight wouldn't be your typical theatregoing crowd. He didn't imagine there was much treading of the boards at the bottom of the ocean.

From where he stood in a rear corner of the auditorium, Blacklock could see all of the two-dozen or so Abyss-Dwellers present, the majority standing guard around the edges of the room or near the stage.

Three particular Abyss-Dwellers were recognisable by the strangely patterned robes and hats they wore, these being the priests who would lead the other Abyss-Dwellers in the proper chanting and worshipping when the Ritual of Suth-G'nar began. The priests were onstage, moving between the various relics required for the ritual, the objects lined up in a row along the front of the stage, resting on barnacle-encrusted stone plinths the Abyss-Dwellers had brought from their aquatic home via the Brazenbrook. The priests treated the relics with extreme reverence, bowing their heads, murmuring prayers and making meaningful gestures with their claws.

Resting on its own separate plinth at the rear of the stage, set apart from the relics, was the Red Scripture, an ancient tome of yellowed pages covered in hellish illustrations and writing of no human language, yet Blacklock would be required to read aloud select passages from it during the ritual. Gerald had previously coached him on how to speak the text in question, although Blacklock soon grew tired of those sessions and ended them early, insisting he was ready. It was only line delivery, after all, and what was that to an actor like him?

The relics at the front of the stage were an odd assortment: the Tower of Dust, a rough and angular column-like sculpture; the Exile's Heart, a desiccated internal organ taken from no creature born of this world; the Shattering Tide, a glass vial of liquid whose unnamed colours glittered and shifted, the vial encased inside a metal cage; the Word of Gub Nubbins, a smooth, dark stone with a weird symbol carved into it; the Seed of the Eaters, a rugby ball-sized seedpod, the contents of which lazily but constantly writhed; and the Book of Harold, another incredibly old tome similar to the Red Scripture.

One of the seven relic plinths currently stood empty, however: the one reserved for the Idol of the Silent King.

Blacklock had hidden the idol in a secret floor compartment in one of the dressing rooms hours earlier, before the Abyss-Dwellers arrived on Pilgrim Island via the subterranean tunnel that connected the Brazenbrook to a small pond inside the island's perimeter fence. Thanks to Quinn, the compartment was fitted with a small explosive device that would detonate if the compartment wasn't opened in just the right way, so any Abyss-Dweller who tried to get his claws on the Idol of the Silent King would find those claws suddenly replaced with bloody stumps. The idol remained Blacklock's insurance, something to lessen the likelihood of betrayal.

But then, he had already been betrayed, hadn't he?

Blacklock stared at Gerald, who was talking to another Abyss-Dweller near the stage.

Look at him, Blacklock thought. *Shifty, grotesque, duplicitous monster. Even now he's probably telling his friend to stab me in the back as soon as the opportunity presents itself. Well, not today, "Gerald", or whatever your real name is in your vile language. I don't care how long you and your kind have been waiting, today doesn't belong to you. Today is mine. This is the day I fix things.*

Gerald – wearing different spectacles today, Blacklock noticed – had arrived with the other Abyss-Dwellers and asked Blacklock for the Idol of the Silent King as the other relics were moved from where they had been stored in the theatre's securely locked cellar to the stage, but Blacklock insisted on producing the idol only when absolutely necessary and not a minute before.

Since then Blacklock had kept an eye on Gerald while the Abyss-Dweller oversaw the ritual preparations. Gerald said nothing about meeting the Roustabouts or offering them a deal, even with some subtle prodding from Blacklock, who didn't mention the incident at The Bewigged Pig. Gerald's secrecy was the final straw for Blacklock, definitive proof that the Abyss-Dwellers intended to betray him. It was just a question of when.

Beneath his Order of the Void robes, Blacklock felt the weight of the sheathed knife against his left hip. Any Abyss-Dweller who made a move against him would be in for a surprise. An actor should be prepared, after all. The knife had come from the small arsenal Quinn kept – neatly arranged and in pristine condition – inside a locked cabinet in his bungalow. Sugarfoot had asked for a weapon as well but Blacklock denied the request. As for Quinn, he carried a knife in his right boot, a revolver at the small of his back, a shotgun in his hands, and a bundle of extra shells in a pocket of his coat. Quinn was no actor but he was certainly prepared.

Blacklock watched Quinn calmly stroll around the auditorium, expressionless but always alert. After they had arrived on Pilgrim Island, Quinn carried out a search but found no further evidence of intruders apart from a damaged section of fencing. Since then Blacklock had kept him close, Quinn being the only one present who he trusted not to betray him.

Blacklock grimaced as he shifted his weight on his cane, briefly wondering if it was too late to have Quinn give him something for the pain after all. The constant, terrible throbbing in his left leg and right hand had left him exhausted and his skin was clammy even though his robes were hot and smothering. His stomach churned in a way that might have been a sign of nervousness if he were a lesser man. A lesser *actor*. He had applied his make-up to his face earlier, wanting to look the part even though he and Sugarfoot would be wearing their masks during the ritual, but now his face felt greasy and his eyes stung. He had tried some voice exercises but soon gave up as they just made the pounding in his head worse.

Blacklock turned to see Sugarfoot approaching, dressed in his voluminous robes and holding his mask in front of his stomach. Blacklock's own mask lay on a nearby seat, and he tried not to think about having that stifling thing over his face for the duration of the ritual.

Sugarfoot stood at Blacklock's side and there was a moment's hesitation before he said, "Won't be long now." He sounded like a man talking about an upcoming appointment with a firing squad.

Blacklock gave him a sideways glance. "Just play your part, Thomas. And don't mess it up."

"I was thinking, when we become gods… well, how exactly is that going to work? It's not going to hurt, is it? Will it be quick? Will we keep our bodies or just… float up into the sky or something?"

Blacklock opened his mouth to deliver a cutting, dismissive reply but closed it again when he realised he didn't know the answer. The talk surrounding the godhood process had always involved reassuring words like "ascendance" and "glorious" and "blessed" without ever actually going into detail. Considering the physical pain he had suffered over the past two days, the question gave Blacklock pause now as he suspected that becoming a god would likely either not hurt at all or be unbelievably, indescribably agonising. He doubted there was much middle ground when it came to something like godhood. Not that he was going to admit any of this to Sugarfoot.

"It'll be fine," Blacklock said. "We're being rewarded, rewards don't hurt."

"I suppose," Sugarfoot said, clearly unconvinced. "So what's the first thing you're going to do once –"

"Be quiet."

Blacklock was watching the Abyss-Dweller who had just entered the auditorium from the foyer and was now striding along the central aisle in the direction of Gerald. The creature was wet all over, fresh from the Brazenbrook. Gerald and the new arrival exchanged some words then Gerald began walking towards the foyer alone. Something was going on.

Blacklock looked at Quinn, and the look that passed between them told him that Quinn had just seen the same thing he had. Blacklock brushed past Sugarfoot and limped along the aisle at the rear of the auditorium, heading for the foyer entrance, intending to intercept Gerald, while Quinn moved to intercept Blacklock at the same time.

When they came together, Blacklock leaned towards Quinn and whispered, "I'm going to see what Gerald is up to, keep an eye on these bastards. And make sure Thomas doesn't go anywhere."

Quinn nodded and Blacklock continued on his way, hurrying despite the pain it caused, eventually meeting Gerald at the foyer entrance.

"Everything alright?" Blacklock asked.

Gerald didn't stop or slow down to accommodate him, instead continuing through the open double-doors and into the foyer beyond at the same speed, Blacklock forced to maintain his painful pace to keep up. He thought of the Abyss-Dweller he shot at the factory and hoped the thing had been another of Gerald's aunties.

"I've been informed of a disturbance offshore," Gerald said. "I'm going to deal with it."

A number of Abyss-Dwellers patrolled the waters around Pilgrim Island, staying beneath the surface to avoid being seen, ordered to prevent any intruders making it to shore. The creature who just visited Gerald must have been one of them.

"What sort of disturbance?" Blacklock asked as they crossed the foyer's ruined carpeting.

The foyer was in the same condition as the rest of the theatre, one half of its double staircase leading up to the balcony seats and boxes partially collapsed, the ticket counter and tables smashed and splintered, the armchairs torn and mouldy. Old posters advertising entertainments from decades ago, from a classic tragedy to a satirical ballad opera, drooped from walls or lay on the floor, the lustre long gone from their golden frames. With the front entrance closed, the windowless foyer was gloomy and would have been gloomier still if not for the two lit paraffin lamps Quinn had placed in the room.

"A vessel is approaching the island," Gerald said as he pushed open the double-doors at the front of the building. After the dimness of the theatre interior, Blacklock winced at the afternoon daylight as he and Gerald stepped out into the street.

"Boats pass by here all the time," Blacklock said.

"This one is on a direct course. And is carrying the Roustabouts and Oliver Burgess."

Blacklock frowned. "That's impossible."

Gerald looked at him. "Why is that, Arthur?"

Blacklock didn't answer and silence fell between them for a brief time as they left the street and entered the park, heading for the far side of the island.

"It *can't* be them," Blacklock said eventually, frustration boiling within him. He wouldn't allow it. Gerald, Cromwell, the Roustabouts, even that pathetic worm Oliver, everyone was trying to stop him fulfilling his destiny, stop him achieving the goal a cruel universe had always dangled just out of his reach. He was tired and hurt and he was supposed to be an actor and it wasn't *fair*.

"It's them," Gerald insisted calmly, adjusting his spectacles. "The time for subtlety is over."

Blacklock stopped and glared at Gerald, unable to hold his tongue any longer. "What are you going to do, offer them a better deal?"

Gerald stopped and turned to face Blacklock. "The deal I offered those men was no detriment to you. I didn't tell you because they turned it down. You see betrayal where there is none."

"I'm seeing clearer than I *ever* have."

Blacklock was breathing heavily, the knuckles of his left hand white as he squeezed the head of his cane. He felt a bead of sweat run down one side of his face. There were scattered clouds in the sky and a cool breeze blew through the park but still everything was too bright and he was too hot, the noise of ships and waterfront activity distant but buzzing aggravatingly in his ears like a fly he couldn't swat. Gerald looked him up and down and Blacklock could swear he glimpsed a sneer flash across the Abyss-Dweller's face.

"I somewhat doubt that," Gerald said. He turned away and continued walking. "Focus, Arthur. Our priority is safeguarding the ritual."

After a moment spent grinding his teeth and staring at Gerald's back, Blacklock followed, and they eventually entered the narrow but dense woodland that ringed the island and hid the park from the Brazenbrook. When they emerged again, the ground gently sloped away from them until it met the river, the chain-link perimeter fence separating them from the shoreline.

Blacklock and Gerald stopped before the fence and looked through it at the approaching barge, the vessel distant but close enough that Blacklock could just about make out six familiar figures – one in a bright-red jumper – gathered at the bow, facing the island. Another wave of sickening frustration rolled through him.

"What are you going to do?" Blacklock asked, ignoring the desperation in his voice.

"I'm going to order an attack," Gerald said, and he untied the conch shell from his seaweed bandolier.

"They've killed every Abyss-Dweller you've sent after them!"

"I'm well aware of that. But this time my kin will have help. I'd hoped this wouldn't be necessary, but desperate times call for desperate measures."

"What are you *talking* about?"

Gerald tilted his head up, put the thin end of the conch shell to his lips and blew into it, Blacklock grimacing at the unpleasant sound that filled the air and drifted out across the water. When he was finished, Gerald lowered the shell and the sound gradually faded.

Blacklock watched the barge but the blowing of the conch shell seemed to have done nothing. He was about to say something when he saw them: multiple trails in the water marking things swimming rapidly just beneath the surface, all converging on the barge. The Abyss-Dwellers patrolling Pilgrim Island were answering Gerald's call.

Then something else caught Blacklock's eye.

At two separate spots several dozen feet from the shore, two large shapes began to emerge from the Brazenbrook.

Blacklock's eyes widened as the shapes grew larger. And larger.

Barging In

"Oh God," Oliver said as the two enormous shapes slowly rose from the water. "Deepthralls."

The Roustabouts stood with Oliver at the bow of the Isabela Dawn and watched the figures rise to their full height from whatever hunched positions they had been in beneath the surface of the river, both ahead of the barge, one off to the left and the other the right.

Talbot estimated the two towering humanoid creatures to be around twenty feet tall, although it was hard to tell exactly with the water being up to their thighs. They had flat, slab-like heads, squat necks, broad backs, and limbs as thick as tree trunks, with hands ending in four large fingers. Their hairless skin was sickly pale with a grey-green hue and barnacles attached here and there, although more numerous were the scars the creatures bore, the welts of even paler skin criss-crossing their arms, legs and torsos. Beneath oozing nostrils were wide mouths large enough to swallow a man, their few teeth yellowed and broken. Their eyes were small and round and jet-black and they only had three between them, one of the creatures having a twisted mass of scar tissue where its left eye used to be. Four thick manacles of rust-spotted, strange-looking metal were clamped around the creatures' wrists, each manacle featuring a loop through which a chain could be run, although their hands were currently free. There was no flicker of intelligence in their beady eyes, only dull, bestial rage.

Henry turned to Oliver. "You know what those things are?"

"They're called Deepthralls," Oliver said. "They're an ancient species like the Abyss-Dwellers but not as intelligent. I don't think Gerald ever mentioned them but I read about them in one of my father's books, apparently they're almost extinct. They come from the sea as well, the Abyss-Dwellers enslaved them thousands of years ago."

Gerald and Blacklock remained behind the fence on Pilgrim Island, watching, the Roustabouts and Oliver having seen the fast-moving trails in the water after the conch shell was blown and as such were ready when the first of the Abyss-Dwellers climbed up onto the bow of the barge and appeared at the metal railing before them, a harpoon raised in one claw as he uttered a guttural cry. Talbot stepped forward and punched him in the face, the creature's cry now a pained gurgle as he fell back into the river. But more armed Abyss-Dwellers were already boarding the front half of the Isabela Dawn, growling and cursing as they clambered over the railings.

As the Roustabouts and Oliver fanned out to intercept them, Fry laughed inside his cabin and shouted, "*Looks like we've got ourselves a right benjo here! Give those buccaneering bastards hell, lads!*"

Fry wasn't fazed by the appearance of the Abyss-Dwellers or Deepthralls and Talbot suspected it had less to do with the Roustabouts' warning of potential monstrous resistance on Pilgrim Island and more with how much it took to rattle a veteran sailor like Fry.

Talbot approached an Abyss-Dweller as the creature's feet hit the deck with a wet slap. He swung his machete but Talbot dodged the first blow and swatted away the second, grabbed the Abyss-Dweller by his shoulders and headbutted him three times. The creature went limp, his mouth hanging open and one eye crossed, and Talbot hurled him overboard.

The front end of the Isabela Dawn swarmed with a chaotic tumult now as the Roustabouts fought the other Abyss-Dwellers who had climbed onto the deck while even more appeared at the railings, the rush of the barge cutting through the water of the Brazenbrook a steady background noise to the violent din.

Even Oliver had found the courage to chip in, whirling around the deck in his red jumper, screaming and swinging wildly with the razor-sharp cutlass Fry had given him earlier. He had his eyes closed much of the time and wasn't actually hitting anything with the weapon, but Talbot gave him points for enthusiasm.

Talbot noticed the Deepthralls had started to slowly wade towards the Isabela Dawn, the giants looking powerful enough to send the barge to the bottom of the river. Talbot ran to the front of the cabin, looking at Fry through the glass as the captain stood at the wheel.

"Captain, start turning –" Talbot began, only to be interrupted by the cry of a charging, sword-wielding Abyss-Dweller. Talbot shot out his right foot, the sole of his shoe slamming into the creature's gut and sending him spinning across the deck. Talbot turned back to Fry. "Start turning the barge around before those big bastards get here or you beach her! When you're a bit closer to shore we'll disembark and you can get out of here!"

"I may not know you and your friends, lad," Fry said, "but I know arseholes from the deep when I see them! I'll be fighting by your side!"

"I appreciate that, captain, but you've done enough! We'll see to the rest!"

Fry hesitated before nodding. "Alright, if that's how you want it! I'll turn the old girl as close to shore as I can!"

Talbot turned to see Ambrose yank a squirming Abyss-Dweller off his back and slam the creature onto a railing, the limp body then sliding overboard. Other fallen Abyss-Dwellers lay scattered around the deck, broken and bleeding and dead. Henry picked up a fallen machete and hurled it at an Abyss-Dweller rushing at Bryn, who was busy pummelling another attacker, the machete sinking into the running creature's neck, knocking him off his feet and into the path of Digby, who stepped over him and threw several vicious punches into the face and gut of an oncoming Abyss-Dweller before grabbing him by the back of the head and driving his face into the deck. As for Oliver, his blind whirling saw his cutlass slice off the left arm of a nearby Abyss-Dweller who wasn't paying enough attention, black blood spurting from the wound as Talbot charged at one of the remaining Abyss-Dwellers, breaking his jaw with a punch before placing him in a headlock and snapping his neck.

The Isabela Dawn was drifting to port, the shore of Pilgrim Island not far now, although neither were the Deepthralls as they waded towards the barge, lumbering but purposeful.

"*Here's where we get off!*" Talbot shouted. "*Everyone over the starboard side and onto shore!*"

Oliver wasn't listening. "*AAAAAAAA!*"

"*Burgess!*"

"*AAAAAAAA!*"

"*BURGESS!*"

"*AAA-*mm?"

Oliver stopped spinning and opened his eyes, blinking and stumbling and almost losing his balance. His jumper was spattered with black blood and he had a dazed expression on his face as he looked at his bloody cutlass then the surrounding carnage then finally Talbot. "Sorry?" he said.

"We're leaving!" Talbot said, and he headed for the bow as Henry and Bryn finished off the final two Abyss-Dwellers, one falling to the deck with a trident impaled in his chest, the other with his skull caved in.

Digby, Henry and Bryn joined Talbot and the four of them looked back at Ambrose, who wasn't following.

"Just a second," Ambrose said to them before turning to Fry. "Captain! What's the story behind your barge's name?"

"Is this really the time for that?" Digby said, annoyed, the starboard side of the Isabela Dawn almost parallel to Pilgrim Island now, the shore only a short swim away, the Deepthralls closing in on the barge.

Ambrose smiled at Digby. "Come on, he's a grizzled old sea captain who's seen and sailed the world, you just know there's going to be a good story behind it! 'The Isabela Dawn', doesn't it make you think of exotic romance and adventure?"

"It makes me think you're an even bigger idiot than I thought!"

Ambrose turned back to Fry as the captain looked off into the distant sky with a wistful smile. "Ah, I remember it like it was yesterday," Fry said. "There she was, Princess Isabela Saracco, the most beautiful and sought-after woman in all of Italy, and me, a simple, shipwrecked sailor with nothing to my name but a letter that could bring down the entire monarchy..."

Ambrose grinned at Digby. "See? I told you!"

Talbot had approached Ambrose, who sighed disappointedly now as Talbot placed a hand on his shoulder and walked him towards the bow.

Oliver held out his borrowed cutlass to Fry. "Oh, captain?"

"Keep it," Fry said. "I think you'll need it."

Oliver smiled nervously and thanked him before joining the Roustabouts.

"Good luck, lads!" Fry called out. "Oh, and Ashmole! If we never meet in this world again, I'll see you in Fiddler's Green!"

"If you're ever in Wealdbury, stop in at The Bewigged Pig!" Talbot said. "Rum's on us!"

Talbot turned to the railing and looked down into the shallow water, the barge dangerously close to being beached.

"They're getting closer!" Oliver said, eyes moving from one Deepthrall to the other.

Talbot saw Oliver was right, the giants looming large. He also spotted more Abyss-Dweller trails in the water, all converging on the Isabela Dawn. It was time to take this fight onto land and away from Fry.

As the Roustabouts and Oliver climbed over the railing, Ambrose looked at Talbot and said, "Back into the river, then."

"We keep this up and you'll have to start bringing your rubber duck with you," Talbot said.

"He has a name and it's Mr. Quackington," Ambrose said defensively.

The six men leapt off the barge.

A Gutsy Manoeuvre

Drenched by the murky water of the Brazenbrook for the second time in less than a day, Digby swore the next time he took a dip anywhere outside of his bath, it would be at that nude beach up in Scarborough he had heard about.

"They're coming!" Oliver cried as he and the Roustabouts waded towards the shore of Pilgrim Island and the Deepthralls turned to follow them.

The Isabela Dawn continued turning away from the island, the barge ignored by the Deepthralls and the scattered Abyss-Dwellers swimming through the water, their attention focused on the Roustabouts and Oliver.

As he walked onto the pebble-strewn shore, Digby saw Blacklock and Gerald still standing on the other side of the chain-link fence, although they had moved back to the treeline now.

"*We're coming for you, you bloody, buggering... buggers!*" Oliver shouted at the two figures, his chest rising and falling, his cutlass wobbling as he pointed it in their direction.

"That told them," Digby said.

Blacklock and Gerald spoke briefly but were too far away for Digby to hear. He turned around as the two Deepthralls and over a dozen armed Abyss-Dwellers emerged from the river, their eyes fixed on the Roustabouts and Oliver as the men spread out along the shore. Digby had never been a big fan of the sea and the past few days had only further convinced him he was right in that opinion.

"I'm no fisherman but I reckon we should throw these ones back," Digby said.

"Not before we've given them a battering," Ambrose said.

"You've already used that one," Henry said.

"Shit."

The Abyss-Dwellers and Deepthralls charged forward, the ground trembling with the giants' footfalls. The Roustabouts stood ready while Oliver started screaming and swinging his cutlass again. Remembering the Abyss-Dweller who had lost an arm to that blade on the Isabela Dawn, Digby made a mental note to keep a safe distance.

Digby stepped forward to meet an oncoming Abyss-Dweller and kicked out his right foot into the creature's left knee, resulting in a loud crunch and the Abyss-Dweller collapsing with a howl of pain. Digby stamped on his head and turned to face the next attacker, avoiding the creature's thrusting trident before yanking the weapon from his claws. He slammed the pommel into the Abyss-Dweller's face, stunning him, then spun the weapon around and rammed the prongs deep into his stomach before kicking the flailing creature away.

Digby hurled the trident at the one-eyed Deepthrall, the weapon hitting it in the chest. The prongs didn't pierce the tough skin, however, and the trident spun uselessly away as the Deepthrall stomped towards him, bellowing angrily. Digby darted forward, trying to close the gap between them, but the giant was faster than he expected and swatted him with one huge forearm. The breath exploded from Digby's lungs, his neck jerked painfully, his feet left the ground and the world spun around him briefly before he crashed into something.

As the stars in his vision faded, Digby found himself lying on the ground, or rather on the section of chain-link fencing he had knocked over after being flung into it. He rose to his feet, wincing as his neck clicked, and looked inland to see Blacklock and Gerald retreating through the trees. With Blacklock on that cane, Digby could catch him easily. One twist of Blacklock's neck and all this could be over. But the other Roustabouts were fighting in the opposite direction so that took priority. A man stood by his friends until the end. And that included the end of the world.

On the shore, Oliver had fallen over and was scrambling backwards on his arse, retreating from an Abyss-Dweller trying to impale him with a harpoon, until Talbot shoulder-barged the creature and sent him bouncing back into the Brazenbrook. Talbot helped Oliver to his feet a moment before they were attacked by two more Abyss-Dwellers, Talbot dropping one with a haymaker to the face while Oliver, with more reckless swinging of his cutlass, managed to deflect the other's sword before slashing his throat, the Abyss-Dweller clutching his wound and falling to his knees, blood pouring over his claws. Oliver stared at him with wide, disbelieving eyes and barked a slightly unhinged laugh.

Four Abyss-Dwellers had surrounded Ambrose, who was using a dead Abyss-Dweller as a shield, black blood and pieces of pale flesh scattering into the air as Ambrose's attackers slashed and jabbed at him with their weapons, the corpse being cut to ribbons.

The two-eyed Deepthrall swung its fists and stamped its feet in an effort to crush Henry and Bryn as they punched and kicked its ankles and shins, the blows powerful but not enough to bring down the giant. A couple of Abyss-Dwellers harried Henry and Bryn at the same time, the creatures being careful to avoid the Deepthrall's indiscriminate attacks, and beyond them Digby could see more Abyss-Dwellers emerging from the Brazenbrook, there seemingly being no end to the bastards.

Digby took all of this in quickly because the one-eyed Deepthrall stomping in his direction really did deserve to be the focus of his attention. The Deepthrall swung its boulder-like right fist down towards his head but Digby dodged aside and the fist ploughed into the fallen fencing instead, crumpling it even further. Digby leapt onto the giant's right forearm and hurriedly clambered up its arm as it tried to shake him off, its frustrated roaring booming in his ears. Although his hands and shoes slipped on the Deepthrall's wet, leathery skin, Digby managed to gain enough purchase to land a punch on its chin. The giant grunted and Digby swung again, this time aiming for its remaining eye, but missed when the giant thrashed its head and upper body around. Digby lost his grip and the momentum of the Deepthrall's swinging right arm threw him through the air and into the woodland beyond the fence. He felt leaves and branches whipping at him until he hit the trunk of a tree and fell to the ground.

Digby heard the Deepthrall crashing through the undergrowth and rolled across the dirt and fallen leaves a second before the giant's fist slammed into the ground where he had been lying. Rising from the roll, he saw the Deepthrall's other fist coming towards him and ducked, the punch missing his head by inches. Digby was getting annoyed now, he didn't like being on the back foot.

They were at the treeline bordering Pilgrim Island's park, the Deepthrall having thrown Digby almost all of the way through the woodland, the giant leaving a trail of trampled foliage behind it as it followed him. As the Deepthrall lunged at him with its arms outstretched, Digby leaned down, grabbed a handful of dirt and threw it into the giant's eye. The Deepthrall roared, squeezing its eye shut and pawing at it, stumbling out of the trees and into the open space of the park.

Digby followed, spotting Blacklock and Gerald in the distance as they retreated from the fighting, heading for the far end of the island.

Digby heard a commotion amongst the trees before a nearby spot along the treeline burst apart in an explosion of foliage and branches as the second Deepthrall came charging through into the park. One of its hands was wrapped around a tree which it had uprooted and was now swinging like a club as it tried to dislodge a screaming Oliver from the end of the tree, the blade of his cutlass embedded in the trunk, his hands wrapped around the grip as he hung on for dear life. The Deepthrall was also trying to remove Bryn from the top of its head as he pounded on the giant's skull with his fists.

More figures followed the Deepthrall: Ambrose had stolen a sword and was engaged in a fight with three Abyss-Dwellers, two armed with swords and the other a harpoon, the sound of clashing metal ringing through the air; an Abyss-Dweller whose face had been pulped came flying out of the trees and hit the ground, followed by Talbot flicking black blood and gore off the knuckles of his right hand; and a mass of several angry, squirming Abyss-Dwellers turned out to be clinging to a running Henry, who skidded to a halt and threw open his arms, the hangers-on squawking as they tumbled off him.

Henry smiled at Digby, strands of black hair hanging down over his forehead. "Nothing like a nice afternoon in the park."

"If I'd known, I'd have made sandwiches," Digby said.

A red blur rolled across the grass between them, Digby and Henry watching it go and only recognising it as Oliver when he came to a stop a few yards away. Oliver's eyes were closed as he groaned, alive but dazed and now unarmed, his cutlass still embedded in the tree the Deepthrall was using as a club.

As he ran towards the tree-wielding Deepthrall and Bryn, Henry turned to Talbot and said, "I'll give Bryn a hand, you and Digby deal with the other one!"

As Ambrose comfortably parried and riposted incoming attacks from the remaining two Abyss-Dwellers, the third creature he had been fighting now lying dead on the grass, Talbot ran to Digby's side. Blinking, the one-eyed Deepthrall finished wiping the dirt from its eye then turned to look at them and roared furiously, thick spittle flying from its gaping mouth, mucus oozing from its nostrils.

"Ugly bastards, aren't they?" Digby said.

"You've had worse," Talbot said.

"That's no way to talk about your own mother."

Digby and Talbot rushed at the Deepthrall as it came charging at them, the soles of its massive feet stamping down grass and crunching gravel, a violent swing of its left arm shattering an already crumbling stone column in its path.

Digby was on Talbot's left, and as the Deepthrall swung its right arm towards them, Digby rolled beneath it and came up next to the giant's right ankle, which he hammered with fast, hard punches, his fists thudding wetly against the thick skin.

Over at the Deepthrall's left foot, Talbot grabbed one of its toes in both hands and wrenched upwards. Digby heard the toe break, and the Deepthrall roared. It shot out its hands and clamped them around Talbot's torso, his arms trapped at his sides. It began to squeeze, Talbot grimacing as he struggled.

Digby ran to a nearby wood-and-metal bench, picked it up and threw it, the bench hitting the Deepthrall's nearest hand, causing it to flinch and loosen its grip enough that Talbot was able to break free.

"*Talbot!*" Ambrose called out, and Digby turned to see him sprinting towards Talbot, a bloody sword in each hand, the three Abyss-Dwellers he had been fighting all lying dead behind him. "*Give me a boost!*"

Talbot braced himself and when Ambrose got close enough and leapt into the air, Talbot squatted, placed both hands beneath Ambrose's right shoe and pushed up with enough force to boost him higher. The Deepthrall bellowed at Ambrose, a bellow abruptly cut off when he flew headfirst into its mouth, up to his waist. The Deepthrall gagged and grunted as with some difficulty it swallowed Ambrose, his kicking legs gradually disappearing down its throat. Digby and Talbot looked at each other then back at the giant as it stared ahead, groaning, seemingly stunned at the size of what it had just swallowed.

The Deepthrall placed a hand on its stomach and frowned, then threw back its head and howled as two sword blades suddenly thrust out from just below its ribcage, black blood running down its skin in thick trails. The swords moved downwards, cutting through flesh, the Deepthrall collapsing to its knees as blood pooled on the ground before it. Then the blades turned inward, and just as they were about to meet, the Deepthrall's stomach burst open, depositing a flood of blood, intestines and other organs onto the grass. The giant's roar of agony faded and it toppled to one side, the ground shaking with the impact. The Deepthrall's mouth was slack, its one eye open and unblinking.

The glistening mound of entrails shifted, and with a horrible slurping sound a figure rose from the gore.

"I thought it might be easier to cut out than in," Ambrose said, smiling at Digby and Talbot through a coating of blood, his swords in his hands as he opened his arms wide, a thick rope of intestine draped across one shoulder. "Who wants a hug?"

Oliver appeared, frowning and rubbing his head and keeping a wary distance from Ambrose. "Are we winning? I killed one. I think."

Talbot walked to the dead Deepthrall's head, planted one foot on its lower jaw, leaned down, gripped one of its large teeth in both hands and began to pull. A few seconds later the tooth popped free and Talbot stood up straight again, turning the tooth to hold it by the narrow end. He swung it once like a club then nodded approvingly to himself.

Accompanied by more slurping sounds, Ambrose stepped out of the pile of entrails.

Digby nodded at the fallen Deepthrall. "I know how he feels, your jokes always give *me* indigestion as well."

The Brutal Truth

"I said, where are you going?" Blacklock said. "*Gerald!*"

But Gerald continued to ignore him as they walked across the park and towards the theatre at a brisk pace, Blacklock's left leg burning fiercely as he limped after the Abyss-Dweller.

Blacklock glanced back over his shoulder and saw Oliver and three Roustabouts rushing to join their two companions in fighting the one remaining Deepthrall. Blacklock had read about Deepthralls but Gerald never mentioned he had two of them hidden beneath the surface of the Brazenbrook. When they rose from the water, Blacklock was suitably impressed. The Deepthralls would crush Oliver and the Roustabouts and that would finally be the end of them.

Only that didn't happen.

Instead, Blacklock and Gerald had fallen back and watched, Blacklock's confidence steadily dwindling, as the Roustabouts killed every single Abyss-Dweller from the river and one of the Deepthralls. Even that bumbling fool Oliver somehow managed to stay alive. When the eviscerated Deepthrall hit the ground, Gerald turned and headed for the theatre.

They were almost at the edge of the park now and Blacklock had had enough. He lunged forward, leaning on his cane while placing his right hand on Gerald's shoulder and turning the Abyss-Dweller around, the pain caused by the movement fuelling his anger.

"*Get back here!*" Blacklock shouted.

"It's over, Arthur," Gerald said.

"What do you mean?" Blacklock asked. But he knew.

"Those men cannot be stopped. Not here, not today. They killed that Deepthrall, they killed all of the Abyss-Dwellers I sent against them, soon they will kill the remaining Deepthrall and then they will come for us. The Ritual of Suth-G'nar will not take place this night. We'll return to Mother Ocean with the relics and wait for the next alignment."

"No. No, you can't. Everything's ready, the next alignment is eight-hundred years from now!"

"Which is of no concern to my kin and I with the lifespans and patience we possess."

"Alright, listen to me," Blacklock said desperately, "we don't need to stop the Roustabouts, just delay them. We can perform the ritual now, the Abyss-Dwellers in the theatre can keep them busy while we do it!"

"The planets aren't in alignment. The ritual would fail."

"*It's a few fucking hours!*"

"We're leaving, Arthur. You won't see us again."

Blacklock stared at Gerald, his breathing heavy. "I won't let you do this."

Gerald began to turn away.

"The Silent King idol!" Blacklock said. "*I* have that! And *you* need it, so you need *me!*"

Gerald turned back to face Blacklock. "I'm aware of the hidden compartment beneath the dressing room floor. And the trap. I'll be taking the idol. Even if I was to leave it in your inept hands, the Idol of the Silent King cannot be destroyed, and the tides of time would wash it back to us eventually. The Old Ones aren't just eternal, but inevitable." Gerald fixed Blacklock with a look of contempt. "You're not as clever as you think you are, Arthur. And you're a terrible actor."

Gerald continued walking towards Pilgrim Theatre but had only taken a few steps when Blacklock discarded his cane and, with a hoarse roar, launched himself onto Gerald's back and plunged Quinn's knife into the Abyss-Dweller's chest. They fell to the grass, Blacklock stabbing and slashing while Gerald clawed and kicked, both grunting and hissing and cursing, black blood and red blood running, Gerald's spectacles being torn loose. They rolled and thrashed, Blacklock screaming when Gerald raked a claw across his face, narrowly missing his eyes. Blacklock held the knife in his left hand, both hand and weapon slick with blood, and after jamming the blade between Gerald's ribs up to the guard, he lost his grip on the knife when he tried to pull it free again. Gerald snapped his teeth, Blacklock slapping and kicking frantically as he scrambled away, his robes shredded and soaked.

Blacklock crawled towards his cane as Gerald slowly rose to one knee, streams of blood running down his body, his breathing ragged as he looked down at the knife in his torso. Blacklock picked up his cane and stood, panting and swaying as he turned to face Gerald.

Blacklock gripped his cane in both hands and tried to think of something clever to say, a fittingly triumphant line of dialogue that a heroic lead might deliver at the climax of a play while smiting his enemy in the name of righteous justice. But his head was swimming and everything hurt and he was hot and sticky and clever words seemed complicated and far away and unimportant compared to the one simple, savage thing he wanted to do at that moment.

So Blacklock said nothing as he limped over to Gerald, raised his cane above his head and swung it down with as much force as he could manage, the cane slamming across Gerald's forearm as the Abyss-Dweller raised it to shield his face. Blacklock swung again and again, battering Gerald's head, arms and upper body until the cane finally snapped with a loud, splintering crack.

As Blacklock looked at the broken cane in his hands, Gerald wrapped both claws around the grip of the knife impaled between his ribs and cried out as he yanked it free, blood gushing after it. He leapt at Blacklock, who stepped back but not quickly enough, the knife sinking into his left hip. Blacklock screamed and, without thinking, thrust the broken cane towards Gerald, the jagged end penetrating the underside of the Abyss-Dweller's jaw and plunging up into his skull.

They stood there like that for a moment, bleeding and swaying and glaring at each other, then they separated, Blacklock losing his grip on his cane while Gerald hung onto the knife, Blacklock screaming again as the blade slid free.

Pressing his left hand against the wound in his hip, Blacklock watched as Gerald, a confused frown on his face, slowly raised the knife, then his claw opened and the weapon fell from it, his other claw reaching shakily for the cane buried in the underside of his jaw. He uttered a brief grunt then toppled backwards to the ground.

Blacklock stared at Gerald until blood trickled into his left eye and he winced and wiped it away. He approached the Abyss-Dweller slowly, partly out of caution and partly because every awkward step was agony, and without taking his eyes off Gerald he picked up the knife in his right hand and held it at the ready as best he could. But Gerald was definitely dead, his body and the ground around it wet with blood from his numerous wounds, his bulging eyes staring up at the sky.

"I'm a *great* actor," Blacklock told the corpse.

His face hurt when he talked but everything already hurt anyway. The pain didn't matter. Gerald didn't matter. And he certainly didn't give a damn about the Old Ones. He just wanted what he was due and he hadn't come all this way and suffered so much just to be stopped now, not by anyone or anything.

Perform the ritual, Blacklock silently told himself. *Become what you were always meant to be.*

Leaving a bloody trail behind him, Blacklock – the hero, the leading man, the star – limped towards Pilgrim Theatre and what he knew would be his defining role.

Chester Nesbit Knows His Business

The grass surrounded Henry as he lay on the ground, his back pressing hard into the earth and his arms burning as he pushed against the sole of the Deepthrall's foot, the giant attempting to crush him beneath it.

The calloused skin unpleasantly close to Henry's face reminded him of a new beauty trend that Murray – not exactly the height of self-maintenance – had mentioned in The Bewigged Pig a few weeks ago, one in which a person placed their feet in a bucket of water and had any dead skin nibbled off by fish. Murray said his wife tried it only to lose two toes to a haddock with a bad attitude. Henry had been sympathetic, but now, as the massive, dirty foot pressed down on him, he was beginning to see things from the haddock's point-of-view.

The pressure abruptly eased as the Deepthrall roared and removed its foot. Henry quickly rose from the ground and saw that Digby, Talbot and Ambrose were now attacking the Deepthrall, Digby and Talbot going for its ankles and feet while Ambrose – covered in blood and God knows what else – dangled from two swords he had jammed into the Deepthrall's back. The giant swung its tree as it tried to dislodge Ambrose from its back and Bryn from its face.

Oliver had joined in as well, ineffectually poking at one of the Deepthrall's ankles with a trident. His red sweater was streaked with dirt and black blood but Henry thought it still looked damn comfortable. It seemed those Jumpies awards were well-deserved.

Bryn lost his grip on the Deepthrall's face and fell to the ground while Talbot hit one of its feet with the huge tooth he was using as a club. The giant bellowed and swung its tree into him, Talbot flying through the air and into a large stone flowerpot which shattered with the impact, spilling loose earth.

"*Ambrose, Digby!*" Henry shouted. "*Go for its knees, bring it down! Bryn, give me a hand!*"

The Deepthrall swung its tree again, low enough to the ground that Henry was able to punch its wrist, and with enough force to cause it to release the makeshift club. Ambrose dropped to the ground and threw one of his two swords in Digby's direction, Digby catching it by the grip as the Deepthrall put its fists together and swung them at Henry, who dived out of the way. The Deepthrall raised its arms again but then howled as Ambrose and Digby sank their swords into the backs of its knees, the skin thinner there. The Deepthrall's legs buckled and it fell forward onto its hands and knees a moment before Talbot strode up to it and slammed his massive tooth against its temple.

Henry moved to the base of the uprooted tree and lifted that end off the ground. As Bryn approached, Henry nodded towards a point halfway along the tree and said, "Lift it there!"

Holding the tree like a battering-ram, Henry and Bryn ran at the dazed Deepthrall, which looked in their direction an instant before several feet of tree-trunk plunged into its right nostril then its brain, killing it instantly. Blood poured from its nostrils as its body went limp, its head suspended in place by the tree until Henry and Bryn released their grip and both tree and head hit the ground.

The Roustabouts gathered and looked at the dead Deepthrall.

"Reminds me of my great-uncle Norman," Ambrose said. The other Roustabouts looked at him, waiting for elaboration. "Couldn't keep his fingers out of his nose. He lost his wedding ring up there once."

Henry looked around. "Where's Oliver?"

A muffled squeak caught the Roustabouts' attention and Henry spotted a red arm waving frantically from beneath the Deepthrall's left thigh. He and Bryn lifted the leg to reveal Oliver lying on his stomach beneath, his face pressed sideways against the grass. Coughing and sucking in deep breaths, he crawled out from beneath the leg.

"You alright?" Henry asked Oliver as he helped him to his feet.

"I think so," Oliver said as he wiped dirt off his face and got his breath back. "Thank you."

"Doesn't look like they've got anything left to throw at us," Talbot said, and the Roustabouts and Oliver surveyed the carnage in the park.

"One thing's for sure," Bryn said as he nudged the nearby Deepthrall with his shoe, "a lot of people on the river and along the banks will have spotted *these* things. If Blacklock wanted to keep this place inconspicuous until tonight then I think he's ballsed that up."

Digby pointed towards the far side of Pilgrim Island and the buildings that could be glimpsed through a stand of trees. "Blacklock and Gerald were heading that way."

"Did anyone see Sugarfoot?" Henry asked.

No one had.

"Should we expect any more surprises like the Deepthralls?" Digby asked Oliver.

"I don't know," Oliver said. "None of this is really playing out the way I expected it to."

Bryn slapped Oliver on the back and smiled. "Welcome to life, Oliver."

The Faithful Are Rewarded

Blacklock stumbled into the auditorium, the room tilting queasily around him. Where his body wasn't numb, it was agony.

Sugarfoot sat in an aisle seat in the back row, fiddling with his mask until he saw the haggard and blood-soaked Blacklock, at which point his hands stopped moving and his eyes widened.

Blacklock stepped forward and placed a hand on the back of the aisle seat across from Sugarfoot, leaning on it. Quinn was off to one side of the auditorium but already striding in his direction. He drew in a breath to shout but something wet rattled in his throat and he coughed, spraying blood and spittle. He tried again.

"*Outside!*" Blacklock shouted, waving his knife at the foyer behind him.

The eyes of every Abyss-Dweller in the room focused on him, including the three priests on the stage. *His* stage.

"*The Roustabouts are here!*" Blacklock shouted, hoping the Abyss-Dwellers at least got the gist of what he was telling them. "*They're coming, you have to stop them! They killed Gerald!*"

The Abyss-Dwellers looked around at each other and murmured amongst themselves.

"*Go!*" Blacklock shouted.

He sagged but then felt a hand take hold of his upper arm, helping to keep him on his feet, and found Quinn standing at his side.

The Abyss-Dwellers walked quickly towards the foyer, some of them staring at Blacklock as they went. He was sure he saw suspicion in those eyes, but as long as the bastards left him to do what he needed to do then he didn't care. Soon they had passed through the foyer and exited the theatre, closing the double-doors behind them. There were three who hadn't joined the others, however: the priests remained onstage, conversing in their native language while occasionally glancing at Blacklock. He couldn't understand what they were saying but they were clearly agitated.

"Follow my lead," Blacklock whispered to Quinn, and with some effort he took his hand off the seat next to him and limped down the central aisle, Quinn releasing his arm but remaining at his side.

The priests barked what sounded like questions and demands at Blacklock as he and Quinn approached the stage, walked around to one side of it and – Blacklock needed Quinn's help again here – climbed the short flight of steps there. The pain, exhaustion and numbness didn't go away when Blacklock set foot on the stage, but just being up there, in the glare of the lights where he belonged, made him feel a little better, stronger, and he took a deep breath and a moment to let it sink in.

Then the moment passed and the grating chatter of the three priests came into full focus again. Blacklock fixed his eyes on the nearest priest, walked up to him and stabbed him twice in the side of the neck, two quick thrusts that sent the priest stumbling backwards, croaking and reaching for his wounds as black blood poured forth.

The other priests had little time to be shocked as Quinn stepped forward, raised his shotgun and shot them both in quick succession, knocking them off their feet, their torsos exploding in blood and shredded cloth, the booming of the shotgun echoing around the auditorium.

The stabbed priest gurgled angrily as he lunged at Blacklock, claws outstretched, but Quinn kicked him in the side, sending him tumbling towards the front of the stage. Quinn reached into his coat pocket and took out two more shells, reloaded his shotgun, and looked at Blacklock.

"Finish it," Blacklock said.

The stabbed priest was lying on one side, choking and bleeding, as Quinn calmly walked over to him, aimed his shotgun and fired. The upper half of the priest's head disappeared in a thick black mist, his ruined hat flying off and landing on a front-row seat.

Blacklock looked at the three corpses, annoyed at the necessity of making a mess on the stage, although he supposed it could be considered a bold, transgressive touch, something that made this production and his starring performance more real and visceral: *true* theatre, the kind only fit for an artist like him.

Blacklock spotted Sugarfoot standing in the central aisle, facing the stage. The dim light at the back of the auditorium meant he couldn't see Sugarfoot's face clearly, but he could easily imagine the gormless expression on it.

"Come here, Thomas," Blacklock called out, a little thrill running through him at the enhancing effect the room's acoustics had on his voice while he was onstage.

Quinn looked Blacklock over and said, "Sir, your wounds –"

"There's no time for that," Blacklock interrupted. "I want you to lock the front entrance and barricade it as best you can. The Roustabouts are coming and I don't want them or those Abyss-Dwellers getting in here. If they do, I need you to protect Thomas and I while we perform the ritual."

Quinn nodded. "Sir."

Quinn leapt down from the stage and headed for the foyer, passing Sugarfoot, who came to a stop near the front of the stage and looked up at Blacklock.

"Perform the ritual?" Sugarfoot said, glancing at the dead priests. "Now? But… isn't it too early?"

"Go and fetch the Silent King idol," Blacklock said. "Lift the floorboard just a fraction, unhook the thread to disarm the trap, *then* lift it the rest of the way. I don't need you having your arms blown off right now."

Blacklock wasn't sure if Sugarfoot suddenly turned paler or if he just imagined it.

Sugarfoot looked at Blacklock's robes, soaked with blood both red and black, and the knife in Blacklock's hand. "Where's Gerald?" he asked, although his expression suggested he already knew the answer.

Despite the pain it caused, Blacklock smiled grimly. He felt a drop of blood fall from his chin. "With his gods, perhaps. *Now move!*"

He Had a Good Innings

No self-respecting bird would have taken a dip in the stagnant, scum-filmed rainwater that filled the cracked stone birdbath, but it was still a step up from Deepthrall fluids so Ambrose didn't hesitate as he gripped the edges of the basin and dunked his head into the water. Then he stood up straight again and ran his hands through his hair and over his face and neck, wiping off most of the mess.

"Well done, now you're only covered in shit up to your neck," Digby said.

"At least I can't taste it anymore," Ambrose said.

He picked up his swords and the Roustabouts and Oliver continued on their way. They had crossed most of the park, leaving behind the dead Abyss-Dwellers and Deepthralls as they made their way towards Pilgrim Island's main street, following the gravel paths that cut through the overgrown grass. Despite the smell of what he was covered in and the uncomfortable way in which his shirt and trousers stuck to him, Ambrose felt pretty good about how this whole escapade was going, perhaps because he didn't arrive on Pilgrim Island dead this time.

"There's something up ahead," Henry said.

Ambrose followed Henry's gaze and through the grass glimpsed something off to one side of the path they were on. As the Roustabouts and Oliver got closer, they saw what it was.

"Gerald," Oliver said.

The Abyss-Dweller was dead, his bloody body cut and stabbed multiple times, the end of a cane protruding from the underside of his jaw. His spectacles lay broken nearby.

Talbot prodded the corpse with the Deepthrall tooth he was carrying. "Looks like him and Blacklock had a falling out."

Ambrose was about to say something when Oliver stepped forward and plunged the blade of his cutlass into Gerald's chest. He pulled it free and stood in silence, glaring at the Abyss-Dweller. When he eventually looked up again he found the Roustabouts staring at him.

"Just making sure," Oliver said.

"Does this mean Blacklock and Sugarfoot can't perform the ritual now?" Ambrose asked him.

"Technically, Gerald isn't required for it, but if Blacklock killed him then the Abyss-Dwellers aren't going to be happy with him."

They returned to the path and followed it through the trees at the edge of the park, stepping onto the paved street as the front doors of Pilgrim Theatre swung shut behind a large crowd of Abyss-Dwellers exiting the building. The men and the creatures faced off in the street.

One of the Abyss-Dwellers stepped forward, pointed his sword at the Roustabouts and Oliver and shouted some words in their language.

"I hope for your sake that means 'We surrender,'" Henry said.

The Abyss-Dwellers howled and surged forward with murder in their eyes.

"I didn't think so."

Sugarfoot Takes a Bow

The Red Scripture was heavy in Blacklock's hands as he read aloud from its rough pages, the thick tome bound in some kind of ugly, warped leather. The strange, flowing text scrawled within was hard to follow at the best of times, let alone through his current pain and dizziness, and the harsh, alien words hurt his throat as he spoke. And whereas just minutes ago the bright lights shining upon the stage gave him strength, he had quickly come to find them far too hot and bright, and now narrowed his eyes against them. So Blacklock did his best to hurry through the passages required for the ritual, the muffled din of the fighting in the street outside the theatre acting as further incentive for haste.

He glanced towards the foyer and saw Quinn standing in the doorway, the same spot he had occupied since padlocking the front entrance and barricading it with furniture and assorted debris. Quinn's shotgun was held against his right shoulder, the muzzle pointed at the double-doors.

Blacklock returned his attention to the Red Scripture. He stood in the centre of the stage, facing the seven relics on their plinths – Sugarfoot having managed to retrieve the Idol of the Silent King without blowing himself up – and the auditorium beyond them. The dead priests had been rolled off the stage although their blood remained, as did the blood trails left by Blacklock, whose wet robes clung to him like a crimson shroud. He and Sugarfoot weren't wearing their masks, Blacklock insisting they had no time to waste on anything nonessential, not admitting that the thought of placing his mask over his face made him feel even more like fainting.

"Do you think it's working?" Sugarfoot asked, interrupting Blacklock.

Blacklock looked up from the Red Scripture. "*What?*" he said, irritated.

"I just thought perhaps we might see something happening by now, you know. We *are* early, Arthur, the writings say the moon needs to be up, after all, and it's still afternoon."

"Thomas, I can promise you one thing that's going to happen if we don't hurry up and complete the ritual, and that's *me feeding you every single one of these bloody relics!*"

Dark spots appeared in Blacklock's vision and he tried to ignore the tremors in his legs and the invisible iron weights attached to his eyelids as Sugarfoot turned away and resumed doing both his part and what should have been Orchardson's part.

Sugarfoot's role was to repeatedly walk from plinth to plinth while holding aloft a metal censer which was to be passed through the air above each of the relics, with the same brief chant – the alien language of the Red Scripture again – being spoken each time. The material burning inside the censer was a stiff lump of grey flesh, the exact nature of which Gerald had never divulged, but the dark, oily smoke it produced through the censer's holes was chokingly foul.

Finally, while Blacklock read from the Red Scripture and Sugarfoot swung his censer, Orchardson was to light the twelve black candles arranged in a semi-circle of metal dishes at the sides and rear of the stage, each lighting accompanied by another brief chant. But with Orchardson dead, this task had fallen to Sugarfoot. Blacklock would have done it himself but right now even just remaining on his feet was a struggle. So this resulted in Sugarfoot waddling between plinths and candles, coughing and crying from the censer's smoke and fumbling his way through the chant required for the candles, having never learned it himself, instead working from the vague memory of a meeting of The Order of the Void during which Orchardson had practiced the chant with Gerald. Using a box of matches, Sugarfoot had lit three candles so far and Blacklock was fairly certain he said the chant wrong every time, but it was too late to worry about that now.

A loud crash at the front of the building drew Blacklock's attention and he saw Quinn fire his shotgun into the foyer, the muzzle flash momentarily illuminating the gloom at the rear of the auditorium. The chaotic racket of the street battle was louder now and although Blacklock couldn't see much through the foyer doorway, he knew the fighting had spilled into the theatre.

Quinn fired again then snapped open his shotgun and reached for more shells only to be knocked off his feet when a bloodied Abyss-Dweller was hurled into him. The two tangled figures tumbled to the floor, Quinn's shotgun falling from his hands.

Sugarfoot stood frozen before the Word of Gub Nubbins, staring at the foyer doorway.

"*Thomas!*" Blacklock shouted. Sugarfoot flinched and turned towards him. "*Keep going or I swear I'll kill you!*"

Sugarfoot's eyes were wide, his face pale apart from his blotchy red nose. He turned back to the Word of Gub Nubbins and carelessly swung the censer over the dark stone, his chanting panicky and even messier than before.

The Roustabouts, Oliver and the Abyss-Dwellers came into view as the fighting moved through the foyer and into the auditorium, fists and feet and weapons swinging, blood flying, the cursing and grunting and shouting of both men and Abyss-Dwellers echoing around the room.

Quinn had fallen back to a spot about halfway along the central aisle, where he now took cover behind an aisle seat and withdrew his revolver, having lost his shotgun. He aimed at the melee and fired but the Roustabout he was targeting – the Welsh one, Blacklock remembered – saw the danger in time and grabbed a nearby Abyss-Dweller to use as a shield, the creature crying out as the bullet hit him in the back.

Sugarfoot had been heading for the next unlit candle when he stopped suddenly and looked over at Blacklock. When Blacklock saw the expression on his face, he knew what Sugarfoot was about to do.

And sure enough, Sugarfoot dropped the censer and box of matches and ran for the side of the stage.

"*Bastard!*" Blacklock hissed as he limped hurriedly towards the front of the stage, carrying the Red Scripture with him.

Sugarfoot slipped on Abyss-Dweller blood and landed heavily on the floorboards with a pained grunt, an outstretched arm knocking over one of the lit candles, its metal dish rattling as the candle rolled towards the curtain on that side of the stage. As Sugarfoot scrambled to his feet, Blacklock took the Idol of the Silent King from its plinth and put the Red Scripture down in its place then hurled the idol across the stage. It hit the back of Sugarfoot's head with a clonk and he fell forward and lay still.

Leaning on the plinth for support, Blacklock's eyes moved from Sugarfoot to the curtain near him as flames appeared at its base where the lit candle had come to a stop, the burgundy velvet charring as it began to burn.

The fighting at the rear of the auditorium was painfully loud to Blacklock's ears, his head pulsing and buzzing with the cacophony. Everything was chaos and fire and blood and it was all falling apart around him.

No, he thought, clenching his teeth. *This isn't where it all falls apart. This is where it all comes together. This is your moment, Arthur. And then it will be your eternity.*

Blacklock found his place in the Red Scripture and rapidly spat mispronounced, inhuman words through bloody lips as he gripped the edges of the plinth, a frenzied gleam in his eyes.

Somewhere in time, a young boy stood silently at the rear of a small stage, grin beaming from amongst a shoddy costume of green and brown. He was a birch tree.

An Unwelcome Enlightenment

Even with his heart pounding in his chest and his blood rushing in his ears, Oliver felt somewhat guilty when he stabbed the Abyss-Dweller in the back, although that guilt evaporated when the cutlass was wrenched out of his hand as the creature spun around and howled at him in pain and rage, the weapon protruding from his back.

Oliver took a step backwards. "Right, now, hang on…"

The Abyss-Dweller raised his machete but then from out of the surrounding melee rushed Henry, who punched the creature in the side of the head, sending him sprawling, his machete clattering away.

Henry's eyes flicked towards the stage then focused on Oliver as he shouted, "*Get down!*"

Oliver instinctively looked towards the stage and halfway along the central aisle saw Quinn pointing his revolver in their direction. Two gunshots boomed as Oliver threw himself to the floor and he and Henry moved into cover behind the back row of seats.

"Thank you," Oliver said, sitting with his back pressed up against the seat behind him while Henry was down on one knee. Oliver noticed Henry's upper left arm. "You're shot!"

Henry glanced at the wound. "Bullet just grazed me. I've been shot in worse places. Like Nottingham."

Oliver looked around at the chaos that was the battle between the Roustabouts and the remaining Abyss-Dwellers, dead creatures scattered across the street outside, the foyer and the rear of the auditorium. Despite their dwindling numbers the Abyss-Dwellers fought fiercely, but no more fiercely than the Roustabouts.

Henry raised his head enough to see over the top of the seat next to him, his attention focused on the stage. "Have Blacklock and Sugarfoot completed the ritual?"

"If they have, they're hours too early," Oliver said. "Gerald always told us the ritual had to be performed at exactly the right time or it would fail. The writings all said the same thing."

"Right." Henry nodded towards the stage. "So what's *that*, then?"

Oliver reluctantly took a peek, expecting a bullet in the forehead, but Quinn's attention was elsewhere. Onstage, Sugarfoot lay limp, seemingly either dead or unconscious, while spreading flames had begun to consume the curtain near him. Blacklock stood before a plinth on which rested the Red Scripture, his face and arms raised to the ceiling.

"*Yes!*" Blacklock shouted, laughing. "*Yes!*"

But what Henry was really drawing Oliver's attention to was the crackling, spinning sphere of churning purple energy which had formed in the air above Blacklock. It was roughly three feet in diameter and floated about twenty feet above the stage, purple sparks popping off it, the air around it shimmering as if with a heat-haze. And only now did Oliver's ears pick up the constant, low drone which accompanied the sphere but seemed to come from everywhere around him, not just the direction of the stage.

"I – I don't know," Oliver said. "The ritual shouldn't have worked. Gerald said there could be unforeseen consequences if it failed, maybe this –"

With a harsh cry an unarmed Abyss-Dweller leapt onto Henry, quickly followed by another, the three thrashing figures tumbling over the back row of seats as they fought while Oliver scurried away on his hands and feet, terrified but aware there might not be any time left to lose. The Roustabouts were occupied with the Abyss-Dwellers and Quinn, and what if he was wrong and the Ritual of Suth-G'nar *was* going to succeed if someone didn't stop it right now? Ideally someone strong and brave, but since they were all busy, that just left him.

Oliver crouch-walked along the back row of seats, heading towards one side of the auditorium. When he reached the end of the row he turned the corner and made his way down the aisle, staying low.

As Oliver moved towards the stage he realised that although he was scared, there was more to it than that. It was a largely unfamiliar emotion but he was *angry*. He had felt flashes of it earlier during the fighting but that had been instinctive, primal, now it was directed, a righteous anger aimed at Blacklock for everything he had put Oliver through. Blacklock hadn't been working alone, of course, but he was the one pulling the strings. He had killed Oliver's father (alright, so Oliver wasn't *too* upset about this), burned down his family home (or this) and tried to kill Oliver, Annie and the Roustabouts (now *this* wasn't on). Blacklock needed to pay for what he had done and Oliver wanted to be the one to make him, not just to punish Blacklock but to try to atone for his own part in this whole mess. He pictured Annie's face. It was a fleeting image but one that gave him heart.

He saw the dead Abyss-Dweller priests when he reached the front row, and Blacklock seemed no less oblivious to Oliver's presence than they did as he continued to stare raptly at the sphere above him, trembling arms still raised to it.

Oliver looked back towards the rear of the auditorium to see Bryn tear a seat loose from the floor and hurl it at Quinn, who was knocked over by the projectile. Digby ran down the central aisle, Quinn returning to his feet and firing his revolver but not before Digby charged into him, the bullet going wild as the two men clashed.

A deep, horrible cracking sound turned Oliver's attention to the strange sphere as it began to spin faster and churn more violently, lightning-like bolts of purple energy arcing from it.

Oliver hurried towards the steps at the nearest side of the stage. He was sweating and his jumper was torn and covered in mud and grass and black blood so he – slightly reluctantly, it really was *very* comfortable – pulled it up over his head and threw it aside. He climbed the steps to the stage, feeling the heat of the flames as they spread up the nearby curtain. Sugarfoot lay on his stomach, the Idol of the Silent King a few feet away.

Oliver focused on Blacklock, took a deep breath, and proceeded across the stage. He didn't realise it, but he was striding.

"Arthur!" Oliver called out.

The constant drone became louder and more pervasive the closer Oliver got to the sphere, not just an unpleasant sound in his ears but an unnerving feeling in his bones, while its unnatural, shifting shades of purple both fascinated and repelled the eye.

"*Arthur!*" Oliver shouted, loud and forceful, when there was no reaction from Blacklock. "*This is over!*"

Blacklock blinked but his smile didn't falter as he lowered his arms and turned to look at Oliver. His face was a ravaged, bloody mess and there was an unsettling glint in his eyes.

"Oliver," Blacklock said in a faraway voice. "I've done it. *I've done it!*"

"I don't think so," Oliver said, and he gestured at the surrounding chaos. "Look around you. Does any of this look right? You've failed, Arthur."

The smile finally fell from Blacklock's face, replaced with an ugly snarl. "You're just jealous! Your father was the same! Thomas, Frederick, Gerald, Cromwell, *all* of you, always trying to hold me down, prevent me from fulfilling my destiny!" Blacklock stabbed at his chest with an index finger. "Well, I'm a *god* now! And what are *you?*"

Oliver frowned at the blood-soaked madman before him and felt his fists clench. "A better man than you."

Oliver charged forward, shouting wordlessly, as Blacklock picked up the Red Scripture and threw it, the book striking Oliver's right forearm as he raised it to shield his face, then he ploughed into Blacklock and they fell to the floor, limbs flailing. Oliver punched and kicked while Blacklock did the same, the two men thrashing around until Blacklock ended up on his back with Oliver awkwardly straddling him. A punch connected with Oliver's mouth but he kept fighting. Or at least he believed he was fighting, it was all very messy and confusing.

Already badly injured, Blacklock quickly began to weaken, Oliver managing to keep him pinned down while punching him several times in the face. It began to dawn on Oliver that he was winning. *Him*, winning a *fight*. It was a surprise.

As was Blacklock suddenly driving a knee into Oliver's balls.

A high-pitched cry emerged from Oliver's throat and he toppled to one side and curled into a foetal position, his hands between his legs and his eyes squeezed shut. He may have never had much use for his balls but that just made it seem even more unfair, that something so underutilised could still cause him so much agony.

He didn't know how long he lay there like that, wanting to vomit and die, preferably in the reverse order, but when he eventually opened his eyes again he saw the fire had climbed all of the way up the curtain and was now spreading across the nearby wall and the arch above the stage, glowing orange embers peeling off and drifting through the air, Sugarfoot lying perilously close to the flames. The roar of the fire was louder now as well but still partially drowned out by the noise of the sphere.

Oliver craned his neck to see Blacklock lurching to his feet, struggling to stay upright as he took a few unsteady steps to once again stand beneath the sphere. With what looked to be the final reserves of his strength, he raised his eyes and open arms to it.

"*Old Ones!*" Blacklock cried. "*I, Arthur Marigold Blacklock –*"

'*Marigold*'? Oliver thought.

"*– summon you from beyond! Hear my call, Suth-G'nar! Lead your kind forth through the black halls so you may bestow upon me your gifts! I give you your freedom! And I am ready to receive what is mine!*"

The sphere shuddered and its numerous shades of purple pulsed and swirled hypnotically as the horrible drone loudened further. As much as Oliver's brain was screaming at him to look away, he found he couldn't do so, and he stared unblinking at the sphere, everything else – the pain, the noise, the theatre, everything – fading until there was nothing but the colours.

No, not just the colours. Also what lay behind them.

The sphere wasn't just a ball of cosmic energy but a portal to somewhere else, a place beyond. And for less than a fraction of a second, the barest instant, a tiny speck of that place was revealed behind those shifting shades of purple, and Oliver Burgess looked into that pinprick of truth... and his mind shattered.

Arthur Blacklock's Star Turn

This was it. The moment Blacklock had been waiting for all his life.

All those years of dashed hopes, painful regret and artistic genius yearning to be unfettered were finally behind him. How he had suffered, carrying his terrible burden with courageous stoicism all the while, but now he had eternity to revel in his craft and create his own realities like a true actor did. Realities into which his audience would be drawn, seeing what he made them see, feeling what he made them feel.

Blacklock stared up into the sphere in rapturous triumph, his ruined mortal shell a distant thing of no importance now, just like everything and everyone else around him. There was only this, his time in the spotlight. And it was only just beginning. Admittedly he hadn't expected the appearance of the sphere and had no idea what it was, not to mention that the Ritual of Suth-G'nar hadn't actually been completed, but what else could it be but proof he had succeeded?

Blacklock watched as numerous black spots began to form across the sphere's surface, each one blossoming lazily like a drop of blood falling into water before quickly thickening, taking on a more viscous form.

Blacklock blinked as something hit his left cheek.

He touched the spot with his left hand and frowned at the oily black smears he found on his fingertips. Then he gasped as the substance suddenly sank into his skin without a trace and he felt a cold, invasive sensation fill his left hand and begin moving up his forearm.

Blacklock felt a drop land on his head, then another. Fear gripped his heart.

"No," he said in an unsteady voice. He rubbed at his hair but felt the two drops sink into his scalp then spiderweb across his skull. "*No, stop!*"

Blacklock looked up at the sphere again an instant before a shower of black droplets rained down on him. He closed his eyes and sputtered, frantically wiping at his face and neck as he stumbled and fell to his knees. He screamed as the ooze sank into him, and there was no rapture or triumph now, only terror at the ghastly writhing sensation spreading throughout his entire body with terrible speed.

Unspeakable agony followed as bones snapped, flesh tore and organs burst. Blacklock threw back his head and opened his mouth wide to scream but no sound came out, and he would have collapsed but the substance now transforming and puppeteering his body kept him on his knees.

Tears streaming down his face, Blacklock looked into the sphere, its blackness disgorged. In there, he saw the stars.

Then he saw the void between the stars and the beings that inhabited it, and Arthur Blacklock was no more.

Show's Over

Bryn stood in the central aisle of the auditorium, hands gripping an Abyss-Dweller's head as he repeatedly slammed the creature's face into the seat next to him. Nearby, Digby and Quinn bounced around the aisle as they fought, hitting hard and fast with fists, knees, elbows and heads. Quinn obviously knew how to fight, keeping a cool head and displaying more skill than your typical brawler, enough to keep Digby on his toes.

Bryn was about to bring the limp Abyss-Dweller's head down on the seat a final time and move to help Digby when a horrific, ear-splitting roar filled the auditorium and made everyone left on their feet, both human and Abyss-Dweller, stop what they were doing and look towards the stage. The source of the roar was Blacklock, although no human voice could have made the monstrous sound coming from him. He was on his knees below the levitating sphere, face raised to it, body twitching violently, robes shifting and flapping as if there were numerous things beneath trying to get out.

Then Arthur Blacklock burst like a ripe peach in a careless shot-putter's fist.

Blood sprayed and skin and flesh and robes tore as the thing inside Blacklock broke free, rending and consuming the human body around it, the pieces of Blacklock sinking into the dark mass of the thing replacing him.

Where Blacklock had been kneeling there was now a chaotic, pulsating mound of oily black flesh. It was as big as Blacklock himself had been and was quickly expanding outwards and upwards, the thing seeming to bubble up from inside itself. A number of tentacles sprouted from it, their undersides the colour of curdled milk and covered with angry-red suckers, while in random places the flesh parted to reveal numerous large, alien eyes and gaping mouths lined with uneven rows of pointed teeth, each maw adding another voice to the thing's monstrous roar. A human face emerged from within the writhing mass: Blacklock's face, although he was barely recognisable, the face mutilated and grotesquely stretched, one eye missing and the mouth yawning wide in a scream.

Tentacles flailed, mouths snapped and eyes flicked this way and that as Blacklock's new form grew to around fifteen feet in height, his weight enough to break some of the floorboards beneath him, the stage partially collapsing. Not that the stage – or the entire theatre – would be standing much longer with the fire raging out of control, the roar of the flames mixing with Blacklock's inhuman howling.

Oliver and Sugarfoot lay unmoving on the stage while above Blacklock the purple sphere crackled and spun. Bryn noticed it was now sucking in the air around it, its pull strong enough that nearby drifting embers were being drawn into it and disappearing beneath its swirling surface.

The clatter of metal at the rear of the auditorium drew Bryn's attention and he saw that the few surviving Abyss-Dwellers had all dropped their weapons and fallen to their knees, their eyes fixed on Blacklock as they raised their claws and chanted in their native language, seemingly in worship.

Quinn went for his revolver lying in the central aisle and Bryn rushed towards him, releasing the Abyss-Dweller he had been holding, the creature crumpling to the floor. Digby was already moving but neither Roustabout reached Quinn in time to stop him picking up his gun and firing at Digby, although his aim was thrown off as a harpoon came sailing through the air and slammed into his chest.

Quinn lay on his back, blood spreading quickly across the front of his shirt as Digby kicked the revolver out of his hand. Frowning up at the ceiling, Quinn gripped the harpoon and tried to pull it free but then his arms went limp, his face slackened and he died without a word.

Bryn and Digby looked towards the rear of the room and saw Talbot smiling at them.

"I could hit a prawn in the eye from fifty yards," Talbot said. "You never lose it."

Ignored by the Abyss-Dwellers, the Roustabouts gathered in the central aisle and looked at the monstrosity onstage as one of Blacklock's thrashing tentacles knocked over two plinths and the relics resting on them.

"So is Blacklock one of these Old Ones now, then?" Talbot said.

"I don't know," Henry said. "Oliver said even just seeing an Old One is supposed to drive a man mad. But it just looks bloody ugly to me."

"Well, if Blacklock *has* performed the ritual then I'm glad his reward is turning into a massive pile of shit," Digby said.

"Whatever the case, he obviously didn't like this world the way it was," Henry said. "So let's do him a favour and send him out of it."

As the Roustabouts charged down the central aisle, one of Blacklock's longer tentacles swung outwards in a sweeping arc, powerful enough to tear up several seats and scatter them into the air, the Roustabouts ducking the tentacle and flying furniture before leaping onto the stage and surrounding Blacklock. Bryn could feel the heat of the spreading fire and the insistent tug of the sphere as it continued to suck in air. Blacklock roared, eyes swivelling madly as the Roustabouts hammered on his tentacles and body. Bryn grabbed one of the stone plinths and jammed it into Blacklock's nearest mouth, breaking off several large teeth, dark-purple blood spewing forth as Bryn shoved against the plinth's base, forcing it in deeper.

Something flew past Bryn's head and just before it disappeared into the sphere he saw it was the large, strange seedpod which had been resting on one of the plinths, the sphere's pull becoming more powerful all the time.

A tremendous pressure suddenly encircled Bryn's waist as one of Blacklock's tentacles wrapped around him, and he was yanked off his feet and swung around above the stage, air rushing in his ears, the auditorium a blur. He pounded on the tentacle with his fists as it tried to crush him, then Blacklock screamed in agony and the vice around Bryn's waist slackened as the tentacle released him. He fell to the floorboards, landing on his back with a painful thud.

Bryn saw the source of Blacklock's pain: Henry had wrenched a football-sized eyeball out of its socket, blood pouring from the aperture. He threw the eyeball aside a moment before a tentacle struck him and sent him tumbling across the stage while Digby and Ambrose pummelled Blacklock's body with thunderous punches and Talbot wrestled with two more tentacles.

Bryn rose to his feet and saw more ritual relics and Blacklock's torn-out eyeball fly into the air and disappear into the sphere. If it kept this up then he and the other Roustabouts would soon be getting a first-hand look at what lay beneath those swirling shades of purple. A loud creaking sound was followed by a burning section of wall breaking loose and collapsing onto the stage, the heat uncomfortable now, the air harsh with smoke.

Bryn had never been one to run from a fight but only an idiot stood on the beach swinging his fists as the tide came in and drowned him.

He ran across the stage, smacking aside an incoming tentacle before reaching Henry, who was on his feet again.

"We can't stay here much longer!" Bryn said, raising his voice to be heard over the chaos, the sphere tugging at his and Henry's hair and clothes. "Not unless we want to be cooked or sucked up into that ball!"

"Oliver might be right about the ritual failing but what about Blacklock and that thing?" Henry said, looking at the sphere. "We can't assume the fire will take care of them!"

"I was thinking we could try using Blacklock to plug that drain!"

Henry smiled as he intuited Bryn's suggestion. "He's a big bugger, but we've lifted bigger!"

Bryn and Henry ran towards the other Roustabouts and Blacklock.

"*Everyone grab a tentacle and gather together!*" Bryn shouted.

Ambrose frowned as his eyes roamed over Blacklock's misshapen body. "*I don't know if he's got any!*"

"*Tentacle!*" Talbot said emphatically.

Realisation dawned on Ambrose's face. "*Oh, I thought he said – never mind!*"

The Roustabouts grabbed the ends of five struggling tentacles then came together to stand in a group.

"*Now pull!*" Bryn shouted.

They all pulled and Blacklock's mouths cried out in protest as he toppled over and crashed to the floor.

"*Keep going!*" Bryn shouted.

The Roustabouts turned in unison and dragged Blacklock, floorboards snapping beneath his bulk, until he tumbled over the edge of the stage. He hit the floor below but only briefly, the momentum that the Roustabouts had built up lifting him and bringing him up above stage level again as they continued turning in a circle, swinging the roaring Blacklock through the air around them, picking up speed, teeth clenched and veins bulging with the weight. They swung him in a complete circle once, twice...

"*Now!*" Bryn shouted, and the Roustabouts released Blacklock's tentacles.

As soon as Blacklock came into contact with the sphere, its pull was inescapable, and he dangled in the air as he was slowly sucked into it, his massive body rupturing as it was forced to contract to fit inside the sphere, gouts of dark-purple blood spilling only to be instantly sucked up again. Blacklock screamed, his mouths vanishing one by one, eyes twitching frantically. His human face stretched until it split apart, his single human eye staring at the Roustabouts until it, like the rest of his body, was gone, consumed by the sphere.

"*There's your mate, you bastards!*" Talbot shouted at the sphere. "*And if any of you ever think about showing your faces over here, you'll get worse!*"

If anything beneath the sphere's surface heard Talbot's warning, it gave no sign, and the absorption of Blacklock had made no difference to the sphere's continually increasing pull, the Roustabouts forced to lean away from it and steady themselves while the flames engulfing the stage and surrounding walls whipped in its direction, accompanied by a meteor shower of embers.

"*We've done what we can!*" Bryn shouted. "*We should go!*"

Henry glanced at the two unmoving bodies on the stage. "*Alright, let's grab Oliver! Sugarfoot too, if he's alive! He might come in useful!*"

Bryn hurried over to Oliver, who was unconscious but breathing, lifted him up and slung him over his right shoulder, Oliver's head and arms dangling behind Bryn's back. Ambrose did the same with Sugarfoot and the Roustabouts climbed down from the stage and hurried up the central aisle, the sphere tugging relentlessly at their backs. Some loose seats flew into the air and hurtled towards the stage, Talbot cursing as one of them clipped his right arm.

At the rear of the auditorium the Abyss-Dwellers continued to chant on their knees, staring at the sphere. The Roustabouts ran past them and into the foyer, Bryn looking back as the Abyss-Dweller nearest to the stage was snatched into the air. The unresisting creature disappeared into the sphere, his remaining companions making no move to stop the same thing happening to them. Spotlights and footlights were torn loose, floorboards snapped free, the heavy stone plinths were lifted as if weightless, and huge cracks appeared in the walls.

Moving around debris and Abyss-Dweller corpses as the foyer floor rumbled beneath their feet, the whole theatre coming down around them, the Roustabouts ran out through the front entrance and across the street. The ground shook and trees bent towards the sphere, the Roustabouts being pelted with a shower of loose leaves and grass as they passed through the trees and into the park on the other side.

Bryn looked back to see the sphere still hanging in the air and Pilgrim Theatre gone, the structure and its contents completely consumed, its foundations and the earth on which they were built now following it, as were the nearby buildings and land, the sphere sucking in that entire end of the island.

The Roustabouts once again passed Gerald's corpse as they headed for the far side of Pilgrim Island, benches and debris rolling and bouncing past, the long grass pulled almost flat, rustling furiously. They reached the far side of the park, the dead Abyss-Dwellers and Deepthralls lying where they had fallen, the treeline and the shore beyond up ahead as Bryn and Henry ran side-by-side at the rear of the group with Digby, Talbot and Ambrose just ahead, Bryn's breath burning in his lungs while the roar of the sphere filled his ears.

Henry cried out as he slipped and tumbled backwards, scrabbling at the ground before being lifted into the air.

"*Henry!*" Bryn shouted, then he was yanked off his feet as well, holding Oliver tight against his shoulder as he went head over heels.

Bryn's left arm suddenly jerked, sending a stab of pain through his left shoulder, his legs flapping in the air behind him, pointing towards the sphere. Henry's right hand was clamped around his left wrist, Henry, his own legs in the air, having managed to grab onto the top of a low stone wall with his left hand, and this was now the only thing stopping him, Bryn and Oliver being sucked into the sphere.

A dead Abyss-Dweller crunched into the far side of the wall before sliding over the top and flying past Bryn, and he turned his head to watch the creature sail through the air towards the distant sphere. That whole end of the island had disappeared, the Brazenbrook rushing in to fill the gap left by the missing land only to be pulled up into the sphere in turn, the water swallowed as quickly as it could surge in.

Seeing the strain on Henry's face, Bryn shouted, "*Let me go!*"

"*Sod off!*" Henry shouted back.

Bryn looked past Henry and saw Digby, Talbot and Ambrose standing up ahead, and he realised the sphere's pull must have finally stopped expanding as although it was still ruffling their hair and clothes, it wasn't pulling the three Roustabouts off their feet.

Ambrose jammed the unconscious Sugarfoot between the branches of a tree to keep him in place then he, Digby and Talbot ran to the disembowelled Deepthrall lying nearby. Digby reached into the pile of spilled guts and picked up the severed end of a length of intestine before throwing it into the air, the sphere's pull catching it, yard after yard of the thick, lumpy tube unfurling in the direction of Henry, Bryn and Oliver until it snapped taut just above them, the far end still connected to the corpse. Digby, Ambrose and Talbot took hold of the intestine, gripping it like a tug-of-war rope.

Henry looked at the intestine flapping in the air above him then at Bryn, who gave him a nod.

Henry let go of the wall.

Still joined together, Henry, Bryn and Oliver were pulled into the air as Henry reached up with his free hand. He grasped the intestine but it was soft and slippery and his hand slid along it until he managed to get a proper grip. The three men remained suspended like that as Digby, Talbot and Ambrose reeled the length of intestine in, pulling it hand over hand, leaning back with their feet firmly planted. Henry grimaced, his grip slipping again by inches as they were slowly but surely hauled forward.

There was a deafening crack and Bryn saw the sphere had begun to shine incredibly brightly and crackle more violently than ever as the air around it warped and vibrated for dozens of yards in every direction, its already loud roar rising to a painful volume, drowning out the world.

Bryn squeezed his eyes shut and unleashed his own roar, meeting the sphere's fury with his own.

The pull of the sphere and its terrible noise both suddenly stopped as if with the flick of a switch, and Bryn grunted as he fell to the ground face-first.

His ears ringing, Bryn rolled aside the unconscious Oliver and pushed himself up as Henry slowly rose to one knee, having released Bryn's wrist and the Deepthrall's intestine, which now lay limp on the grass. Bryn and Henry stood and looked at each other, then smiled as Bryn clapped Henry on the shoulder.

Digby, Ambrose and Talbot came running over, Sugarfoot left dangling from the tree.

"Nice one, boys," Bryn said to them. "Quick thinking there."

The Roustabouts turned to face the end of the island from which they had come, except that end of Pilgrim Island didn't exist anymore and there was no sign of the sphere, which had ended up consuming over half of the island. The Brazenbrook had already claimed the new space, water lapping at the earth where the land now abruptly ended, not far from where the Roustabouts stood. There was no suggestion that Pilgrim Island had ever been any larger than what remained of it. All of the Abyss-Dweller corpses which had lain scattered across the park had been swallowed by the sphere, the two Deepthralls still present thanks to their enormous weight.

"What the hell just happened?" Ambrose said.

Talbot shrugged. "Probably some cosmic bollocks."

Letting It Lie

Henry checked himself in his mirror, smoothed his hair and moustache, and left his flat, locking his door and heading for the stairs.

In the ground-floor hallway, the widow Mrs. Reynolds was opening the door that led to her flat. She wore a plain blue dress that was snug on her plump frame, most of her long brown hair hidden beneath a bonnet. She had a sweet smile, which she gave Henry as he stepped off the stairs and they bid each other good morning. Henry said he was on his way to the butcher's and asked if she needed anything, but she politely declined and thanked him.

Henry walked out of the building, the brightness of the day and the hubbub of the busy street washing over him as he descended the three stone steps that led from the front door to the pavement.

"Henry!" called a familiar voice, and Henry turned to see his brother walking along the pavement in his direction.

"I was just on my way to see you," Jeremy said as he approached.

"I'm going to pick up some meat for the weekend," Henry said. "Walk with me if you like."

"Alright."

The brothers fell into step beside each other as they made their way along the street, the pavements bustling with people while vehicles clattered past in the road. It was Friday morning and the approaching weekend was in the air, along with the omnipresent smell of horseshit. Up ahead, Henry saw a defeated-looking man emerge from a pawn shop, look at the few coins in his hand, sigh, and shuffle off.

"So to what do I owe the pleasure?" Henry asked. "Are you delivering my compensation for my wrongful arrest?"

Jeremy gave him a sidelong frown. "Don't push your luck. I was in the area and just thought I'd check in on you."

"Didn't bring a Black Brenda this time, then?"

Jeremy let that pass and they walked in silence for a time. Henry was happy to needle his younger brother occasionally but knew not to overdo it at the moment, Jeremy's patience having been sorely tested by the recent business with The Order of the Void and Oliver.

"I hope you didn't come to tell me Sugarfoot's had a change of heart," Henry said.

"No, he's sticking to his story," Jeremy said. "Apart from complaining about not being able to get a drink, he's behaving himself. A date should be set soon for his trial."

"Trial shouldn't take long, what with you already having a full confession."

"He'll be going away for a long time. He seems to be quite looking forward to it, strangely enough."

"What about Blacklock?"

Jeremy shrugged. "What about him? His body's probably never going to be found since Sugarfoot threw it into the Brazenbrook. His house and possessions burned to the ground, as far as we know he had no friends or close family, and I suppose his business interests will be carved up by investors or the bank or be bought by competitors. All in all, I imagine he'll be forgotten in time."

Jeremy had told the Roustabouts about the arson of Blacklock's home at the police station on Tuesday, and Henry imagined that with no suspects and Blacklock being dead, it wouldn't be long before that particular investigation was side-lined and forgotten as the police moved on to other cases. Despite his brother's inherent urge to uncover the truth of things, Henry knew the Newmuck Police Force had bigger problems to deal with than the burning of a dead man's house.

"Sounds like everything's sorted, then," Henry said.

"Mm," Jeremy said noncommittally.

Taking the unconscious Sugarfoot and Oliver with them, the Roustabouts had left what remained of Pilgrim Island soon after the sphere vanished by getting a lift with a small sailboat whose curious captain came to investigate. They left behind the Deepthrall corpses and the Abyss-Dwellers they had killed on the shore after disembarking the Isabela Dawn.

Since they were fugitives, the Roustabouts holed up in an abandoned boathouse and when Sugarfoot woke up they told him what he had missed. He had no explanation for the sphere or Blacklock's transformation beyond the warnings that the Ritual of Suth-G'nar must be performed at exactly the right time and in the right manner, that such chaotic, cosmic forces were not to be mishandled. It seemed Blacklock had paid for ignoring those warnings. The Roustabouts also recalled Dennis Johnson's claim that this reality and that of the Old Ones couldn't coexist without terrible things happening.

The Roustabouts laid things out simply for Sugarfoot: if he didn't want to end up at the bottom of the Brazenbrook, he would need to confess to the murders of Cecil Burgess and his house guards, Frederick Orchardson, and Arthur Blacklock and Quinn – oh, and kidnapping the Roustabouts and Oliver from police custody – while clearing the names of Oliver, Annie and the Roustabouts in the process. Sugarfoot agreed, claiming he had had more than enough excitement for the rest of his days and that a quiet prison cell sounded appealing. He did fret briefly about the possibility of execution, but the Roustabouts reassured him he could afford a lawyer skilled enough to keep him from the gallows.

They got Sugarfoot's story straight, his crimes having been motivated by greed and suitably vague business rivalries, nothing more. Nothing was to be said about The Order of the Void, the Old Ones, the Abyss-Dwellers or Pilgrim Island. They needed his confession to be convincing, and the truth was far too ridiculous for that.

After getting rid of Sugarfoot's robes, the Roustabouts escorted him to Lemton Police Station, where Henry insisted they would only speak to Jeremy so they would be properly heard out. Locked up with Annie and Oliver for the better part of a day, the Roustabouts waited while Sugarfoot made his confession. Then, after lying their way through some follow-up questioning, everyone besides Sugarfoot was released. Somewhat reluctantly, it had to be said. And that was that.

Ahead of Henry and Jeremy, a crowd of people suddenly popped into view as they ascended the stairs that connected the Burrows station below to the street-level pavement, while the clanging of metal on metal rang out from a nearby blacksmith's workshop and two suited men standing outside a teahouse engaged in a loud, jovial conversation in German.

"How's Burgess doing?" Jeremy asked. "Any less... distracted?"

"No change," Henry said. "You'll get the same amount of sense out of him now as you did the other day, so if you're planning to interrogate him again, I wouldn't waste my time if I was you."

"That's not why I asked," Jeremy said, a touch defensively. "I hope Annie knows what she's doing."

"They'll be fine."

Henry and Jeremy turned a corner and almost bumped into a woman in a filthy apron selling toffee apples from a tray hung around her neck, their glaze marred by the struggling flies mired in the sticky substance. Despite the hawker's insistence that the flies were just friskily fresh raisins, the brothers passed her by.

"Strange happenings recently," Jeremy said. "That purple light shooting up into the sky in Gallowside and the explosion that went with it, and of course the Pilgrim Island business."

"Very strange," Henry agreed without looking at his brother.

"Especially Pilgrim Island. Half an island just disappearing like that. It's a mystery. I expect you've heard some of the rumours flying around."

"Ambrose read in the paper that it was stolen by the Dutch. I heard someone else say it sank under the weight of the secret subterranean sex-labyrinth the royal family had there."

Henry had also heard several other explanations over the past few days, none of which were anywhere near the truth.

"We've heard it all down at the station," Jeremy said. "Monsters in the Brazenbrook, an angel descending from Heaven and blowing a holy trumpet that vaporised the island..." He shook his head. "Gossip. Never changes. Anyway, it's no longer a police matter."

"Why's that?" Henry asked.

Jeremy frowned. "Apparently some... unusual discoveries were made on what was left of the island, and within a day the higher-ups told us the investigation was being handed over to some men from the government. They closed off Pilgrim Island to everyone, police included. No idea what they're up to, but orders are orders and this one came right from the top." He glanced at Henry. "I don't know who these government people are but they're a serious bunch. Very cloak-and-dagger. So if I knew anyone who might've been involved in whatever happened on Pilgrim Island, I'd warn them to be careful. Even if that person probably wouldn't listen."

Henry nodded. "Sounds like good advice."

A familiar Clarence came rolling up the road and when Henry saw the driver he smiled, raised a hand in a wave and called out, "Morning, Randolph!"

"Henry," Randolph said with a smile and a tip of his hat as he drove past, a smartly-dressed couple visible behind the windows of his carriage.

Henry and Bryn had checked in with Randolph yesterday and were glad to learn the horses he had lent them made it home safely and that he hadn't been visited by the police.

Not wanting Jeremy's attention to linger on Randolph now, Henry turned to his brother and said, "Any word on Cromwell?"

"No, him and his man Caleb are still on the loose," Jeremy said. "But he'll turn up soon enough, he always does. The problem is he always gets away with everything as well."

"Cromwell's a survivor, you've got to give him that."

"What I'd like to give him is a twenty-year stretch. Not to mention a bill for the damages caused to the station, I'm *sure* he had something to do with that."

"It was only a hole in a wall."

Jeremy looked at Henry with an annoyed frown. "In that case, maybe I should just give the bill to the prisoners who escaped *through* that hole, then."

"Sugarfoot explained all that."

"In a very frustratingly vague way, yes," Jeremy said, his voice rising.

Henry stopped walking and turned to face his brother, and Jeremy did the same. "Jeremy, why did you want to see me? Because if you're not going to arrest me, I've got things to do."

Jeremy looked away down the street and sighed. He removed his hat, smoothed back his hair then put it back on his head. "I'm sorry, Henry. I came because we wanted to invite you over for lunch on Sunday."

"You're not cooking, are you? Because if so, I'd rather you arrest me."

Jeremy smiled. "No, Jane refuses to let me interfere when she's in the kitchen."

"I always said she was a clever woman."

"Robert and Emily would love to see you, so we thought this would be a good idea."

Henry smiled. "It's an excellent idea. I'll be there. Thank you both."

Jeremy nodded. "Well, I'll leave you to it. I assume you'll be at The Bewigged Pig later?"

"I will. Refurbishment's starting properly tomorrow but Annie's opening up again today. She wants everyone to know it's business as usual, or will be soon."

"I hope she's freshened the place up. It stank of garlic the last time I was there."

Old Habits

"You really have been in the wars, haven't you?" Alma said, and she lightly kissed the dark bruise on Digby's chest. Her eyes – and a single soft fingertip – roamed over the other bruises and cuts across his bare torso and arms. "What on Earth have you been doing, darling? One of your other female companions playing too rough?"

Digby smiled. "You know I've only got eyes for you, Alma."

It was a lie and they both knew it but he said it all the same.

A lock of dark-brown hair fell across Alma's face as she gave Digby a playful smile. "It's not your eyes I'm worried about."

He winced as she gently – but not too gently – prodded one of his bruises before laying her head down on his chest again.

The mattress and pillows were thick and comfortable beneath Digby as he stared up at the ceiling of the spacious second-floor bedroom. This was the only room he had seen of the upmarket, terraced, three-storey house but he assumed the rest of the interior was just as impressive and tasteful. Alma's wealthy husband, Albert, had fine taste in his choice of both wife and home, and not for the first time Digby thought him a fool for never being around to appreciate either.

Not that Digby was complaining. Albert Robson had some kind of job in the hotel industry which saw him away on frequent business trips, which for the past several months had allowed Digby to share the occasional morning, afternoon or evening with Alma, Albert's beautiful and criminally unsatisfied wife. Her husband had at least one mistress Alma knew of, so she considered it only fair she seek out entertainments of her own, and handicrafts simply weren't going to cut the mustard. And ever since their first chance meeting, Digby had been happy to entertain her.

Sunlight streamed in through the windows and across the four-poster bed, the room quiet apart from the background sounds of the city, muffled and distant, and the crackling of the small fire in the fireplace. Digby looked down at the soft skin and fine hairs of Alma's right forearm as he stroked it with his left hand. He breathed in the smell of her hair, felt the warmth of her naked body against his, the duvet pushed down around their waists. It had been a good morning. But he had other commitments.

Digby looked at the clock on the bedside table then kissed the top of Alma's head. "I've got to go."

Alma propped herself up on one elbow and caressed his stomach. "Are you sure?"

"Not when you stroke me like that. But I have to."

Alma smiled and patted him on the chest. "Go on, then."

She rolled onto her back as Digby pulled the duvet off himself and got out of bed, the carpet soft beneath his bare feet. His clothes lay scattered in a rough line between the bed and a window which opened onto the alley below and acted as the access point for his visits. Albert Robson may have been away but there were always live-in servants present, so the front door wasn't an option.

Digby followed the trail of clothes, putting on his underwear, socks, trousers, shirt, braces, shoes, and suit jacket. Despite the bedroom's wide wardrobe full of dresses and other garments, Alma hadn't been wearing a stitch of clothing when he entered through the window earlier, hence the hurried removal of his own clothes. He walked to the mirrored stand where she kept her washbasin and a selection of cosmetics, although as far as he was concerned her beauty needed no enhancing. He dipped his hands into the washbasin, splashed water onto his face then dried it with a towel. He saw Alma's dark, sharp eyes reflected in the mirror, watching him, and he turned and walked to her side of the bed.

Digby leaned over her. "Always a pleasure."

"Oh, I know," Alma said, and she pulled his head down and they kissed deeply.

Digby walked to the window and slid it open, gave Alma a final smile, then climbed out onto the concrete ledge outside and closed the window behind him. He lowered himself onto the sturdy slate roof of the brick shed below then climbed over the wall surrounding the rear of the property, dropping into the alley on the other side.

"Dipping your wick with a married woman, Digby?" Offal Cromwell said as he stepped into the alley, emerging from a narrow path between two houses. "Shame on you."

"Offal," Digby said.

Cromwell looked down at himself. "And here I thought my disguise was perfect. But then you and me know each other too well for that, eh?"

His disguise consisted of heavy work boots, ragged trousers, a long coat with the collar pulled up, gloves, an unlit pipe in his mouth, and a cap pulled down tight on his head. It wasn't much up-close but would do the job from a distance.

They were alone in the alley, which was bright and clean as alleys went, lined as it was by the rears of expensive, well-maintained properties like Albert Robson's house, this area being one of the nicest parts of Elmswick. At one end the alley opened onto a pedestrian path that ran alongside a park while the other end led to a street of equally expensive homes and overpriced businesses.

"What are you doing here?" Digby asked.

"Waiting for you," Cromwell said, taking the pipe from his mouth. "I didn't want to interrupt you while you were making your house call."

"Don't test my patience. How did you know I was here?"

"I keep tabs on people I'm interested in, you know that. I've known for weeks you've been knocking off this Robson bird."

"Stay away from her. I'm warning you."

"I've got no interest in her. She's a stunner, though, isn't she? You've done well there. Although I should probably be telling her husband that, I suppose."

"Her husband's an arsehole. Not that it's any of your business either way."

Cromwell shrugged. "Whatever you need to tell yourself."

"I've got places to be, so say your piece or piss off."

Cromwell gestured at his disguise. "Obviously me and Caleb are staying one step ahead of the law at the moment, but I've still got my ear to the ground. I heard Thomas Sugarfoot confessed to murdering Blacklock, not to mention a few other things. Me and my boys would've done the job ourselves if Blacklock had been at home on Monday but there was no sign of him, so we settled for robbing the place and burning it down."

"I heard."

"We didn't run into any more of those fish bastards, either. In case you were worried about us."

"I wasn't."

"Strange about Sugarfoot, though. Didn't seem like the killer type to me, and I've known more than my share. I might go so far as to say he was put up to it. The confession, I mean. Because it worked out nicely for you lot and Annie and Oliver Burgess, all getting off scot-free like that."

"The point, Offal. Get to it."

Cromwell frowned. "Just seems to me it wouldn't have hurt for him to put in a good word for me and Caleb at the same time, get us off the hook for that business at the Pig, or at least try to make things easier for us."

Digby and Cromwell had spent many late nights together drinking and talking, and just one of the countless subjects they covered was Cromwell's vow that he would never end up in prison, a promise stemming from the time he spent in a workhouse as a boy, entering with his parents as a frightened son and eventually leaving alone as a hardened orphan. Even with his numerous misdeeds in the years since, it was a vow he had managed to keep so far.

But as far as Digby was concerned, all that was in the past.

The Roustabouts hadn't mentioned Cromwell or Caleb when they planned out Sugarfoot's confession with him as while they might have left things on even terms with Cromwell after their escape from police headquarters, that didn't mean they were interested in doing him any favours.

Digby gave Cromwell a thin smile. "We thought you could handle it."

Cromwell sighed. "Well, it would've saved me some time and money but never mind. The right amounts have already gone into the right pockets and the right people have been shown the right incriminating evidence. By Monday it'll be back to business as usual."

"Just be sure not to get any more ideas about expanding beyond your shitty little kingdom."

"I hate to hear you talk about your old stomping ground that way, Digby, I really do. But no, lesson learned there. Besides, I've got other priorities."

"The Candle brothers?"

Cromwell nodded, a hard glint in his eyes. "I've let those two nutcases slide for too long. But they took their shot and they missed. Now they're finally going to get what's coming to them."

"Well, hopefully you'll end up killing each other," Digby said, and he turned to leave.

"Hang on," Cromwell said behind him, and Digby turned back. Cromwell's eyes narrowed in a conspiratorial manner. "What happened on Pilgrim Island that day? Everybody's talking about it. Come on, you can tell me, I won't say a word."

"I've got nothing else to say to you, Offal."

"Alright. I was just curious. See you around, Digby."

Cromwell popped his pipe back into his mouth and began walking away.

Digby watched him for a few seconds then frowned and muttered, "Bloody hell."

"Offal," Digby called out, and Cromwell stopped and looked back at him. "Don't trust Caleb. You're not the only one who's known his share of killers, remember? There's nothing behind his eyes. Watch yourself."

Cromwell smiled. "Careful, I might think you wouldn't be glad to see him cut my throat and throw me in the Brazenbrook. I trust Caleb to do his job, but beyond that? Of course I don't trust him. I'm not an idiot, Digby."

Cromwell turned away again and continued walking. "I haven't trusted someone with my life for a long time," he said without looking back.

Nothing Gets Abyss-Dweller
Blood Out of the Carpet

"Oooh no," Dennis Johnson said, shaking his head. "No, no, no."
He tried to close the door but it thudded against Talbot's shoe.
"Yes, Dennis," Talbot said.
"*It's not Denn–*"
Dennis stopped himself and sagged, sighing. "Why won't you leave me *alone?*" He released the door and walked away from it. "Well, come in, why don't you? It's not like I can stop you."

Talbot pushed open the door and entered the room, its musty, damp smell the same as that which pervaded the gloomy hallways of the small rooming house to which he had tracked down Dennis. The place was a dump, a squalid terraced building of peeling paint, warped floorboards and black mould.

Dennis was dressed in shoes, trousers and a creased shirt with the sleeves rolled up and the topmost two buttons undone. He hadn't shaved in days and there were dark bags beneath his eyes. It was a far cry from his usual well-kempt appearance, although the white streak in his hair remained a striking detail.

He stood by the room's single narrow window, the glass grimy and cracked, a length of faded grey curtain hanging from one end of a lopsided curtain pole. On the windowsill stood a half-melted candle, next to which were numerous cigarette butts and an empty bottle of cheap gin. The room had no fireplace and contained no furniture besides a battered chest of drawers with three of its five drawers missing and a metal bedframe with loose springs that looked lethal enough to pierce a rhinoceros' skin. Judging by the pile of sheets next to it, Dennis had been sleeping on the floor.

Dennis saw the expression on Talbot's face and smiled grimly. "And to think I once demanded the concierge at the Grand Duchess bring softer pillows to my room."

"I met your landlord downstairs," Talbot said. "He looks like the only thing he'll be bringing you is smallpox."

"He's something, isn't he? That combination of hateful scowl and crusted drool at the corners of his mouth?"

"The half-naked bloke passed out on the stairs with an opium pipe seemed happy enough, anyway."

"Yeah, it's quite the collection of colourful tenants here. There's a reason I drag the bed in front of the door at night. Not that I sleep much." Dennis looked around the bare room. "Or have anything left to steal. But this room is the best I could get on short notice and with the pittance I made selling what little I salvaged from my last place."

"I'm surprised you don't just go to a fancy hotel and work your magic on them so they let you stay for free."

"You know my powers don't work that way. I can't just click my fingers and control people's minds." There was a pause before Dennis added as an afterthought, "And it would be morally wrong, obviously."

"Obviously."

Talbot reached into his right-hand trouser pocket, pulled out what was in there and tossed it underarm towards Dennis, who caught it.

Dennis frowned at the set of keys in his palm. "What's this?"

"The keys to your new home," Talbot said. "The previous owner's moved out. It's in a bit of a mess so you'll need to do some cleaning, but it's a lot better than this shithole."

The mess inside Oliver's house consisted of the damage and bloodstains left over from the fight with the Abyss-Dwellers. When Talbot and Bryn had checked the place last night they found all of the actual corpses had been removed, assumedly by other Abyss-Dwellers given the lack of any signs of police presence.

"You're just *giving* me a house," Dennis said with some suspicion.

"Me and Ambrose agreed we owed you one after what happened the other night," Talbot said. "We had a chat with the other lads and we thought this would be a good way to make us even, give you a chance to get back on your feet."

Dennis laughed, abrupt and bitter. "You throw a set of keys at me and everything's fixed just like that?"

"It's a nice house. Fancy enough to impress gullible rich people while you scam them out of their money."

"I'll ignore that. Where is it?"

Talbot gave Dennis the Fondle Green address.

Dennis looked at the keys again, frowning thoughtfully. "Nice part of town."

With little patience left and somewhere to be, Talbot held out a hand. "Look, take it or leave it. If you don't want the house then give me those back."

Dennis closed his fist around the keys and lowered them to his side. "I suppose there's no harm in taking a look at the place."

"Right, so we're sorted."

Talbot turned and opened the door, the loose handle rattling in his hand.

"I've forgotten the things I saw inside that Abyss-Dweller's head," Dennis said, staring out of the window. "But I do know even if you saved the world, the Old Ones are still out there."

"Don't worry," Talbot said. "They've been told."

He stepped out onto the landing, closing Dennis' door, then left the building.

Talbot headed for the Brazenbrook, it was only a slight detour and he had a little time before he needed to meet the other Roustabouts. He made his way across Gristle, these being rough streets even in broad daylight, but even the boldest pickpockets working the pavements and the hardest thugs watching from shadowy alleys recognised the strapping northerner as an unwise target and left him alone.

Talbot liked how the sounds of the riverfront gradually came to his ears as he neared the Brazenbrook, eventually arriving at a pedestrian path next to the river. He leant on the metal railing that guarded the edge of the short drop to the water below. A skein of honking geese flew overhead and out across the river, Talbot watching them until they were just dark specks in the distance.

He looked downriver and visualised the spot many miles distant where the Brazenbrook met the sea, where the water and air were clearer, cleaner. The soothing waves, the sunlight sparkling on the water, the horizon nothing but a flat line stretching into eternity. The sea was full of cruelty and rage, true, but by God it could be a thing of beauty.

A sailor's life was a hard one, what with the danger, disease, terrible food and cramped conditions, but even so Talbot had a lot of fond memories of his time at sea. It was onboard the Jolly Gamble he had learned to play piano, and trying to play an octave glissando while hammered on rum with the ship pitching and rolling in rough seas was a real test of skill. His newfound knowledge that the Abyss-Dwellers lurked in the ocean depths didn't faze him one bit, he had always known the sea was as much home to monsters as the land was.

From time to time he thought about going back out there, of just signing up on a ship and setting sail, but the notion always passed soon enough. Newmuck was his home and the lads and Annie were his family.

Talbot took a deep breath then continued on his way, the siren call of the sea fading into silence behind him.

The Coming of Madness and Biscuits

"Left a bit," Beryl Parish said.

Ambrose pushed the table left.

"No, that's too far," Beryl said.

Ambrose pushed the table right slightly.

Beryl frowned thoughtfully. "Oh, I'm not sure now, maybe it was better off where it was."

Ambrose shook his head, smiling, and released his grip on the dining table. "Have a think about it and let me know when you're sure."

Fancying a change, Beryl had asked Ambrose to move some furniture around for her, and he was not only happy to do it but glad she had the sense to ask him rather than his grandfather, who would have done it even with his bad back. But Wilbur was currently at his allotment and the furniture repositioning wouldn't take long. If Beryl ever made up her mind, that was. Ambrose didn't mind, he tried to help out how he could. Not that he could ever hope to pay back his grandparents for everything they had done for him, having raised him since he was a boy.

Ambrose occupied the second floor of their terraced two-storey house while the elderly Wilbur and Beryl lived on the ground floor so they wouldn't have to use the stairs so much. This living arrangement worked well, the house large enough to afford Ambrose and his grandparents their respective privacy while allowing him to be close in case they needed him and allowing Beryl to make sure her grandson was eating enough, had clean clothes, was staying out of trouble, and so on.

Beryl's eyes moved from the dining table to the armchair to the potted plant, all of which Ambrose had already moved and put back again more than once. "Maybe the plant would look better in the hallway after all," she mused.

Movement outside the window that looked out onto the small patch of lawn in front of the house caught Ambrose's eye. Two figures were walking up the paved path towards the front door, although the embroidered netting that hung across the window meant he couldn't properly make them out. He told his grandmother they had visitors then entered the adjoining hallway as someone knocked on the front door a few seconds before Ambrose opened it.

"The flesh-moons of Ulkoom shudder in anticipation as they gaze upon the frenzied dancing of nightmares on the shores of the still lake!" Oliver declared.

"Morning," Ambrose said.

Annie frowned at Oliver as she nudged him with an elbow, then she turned back to Ambrose. "Morning. Are you busy?"

Ambrose stepped aside, motioning for them to enter. "No, of course not, come in."

Annie glanced at Oliver, who stared ahead blankly. "I thought we'd go for a walk, get some fresh air, so we were passing. I wasn't sure about calling in with you, though, I didn't know if you'd want your grandparents meeting this one," she said, tilting her head towards Oliver.

"It's fine, my grandad's down at the allotment anyway and you know my nan, she'll get along with anyone."

"Alright."

Annie and Oliver entered the house and Ambrose closed the front door. Oliver placed a hand on the hallway's floral-patterned wallpaper and stared at it until Annie patted him on the shoulder and said, "Come on."

Ambrose led them into the dining room. "Annie's here, nan."

Beryl smoothed her already tidy grey hair and straightened her simple long-sleeve dress as she beamed at Annie. "Oh, I wasn't expecting company. Hello, love, I haven't seen you in ages."

"Lovely to see you, Beryl," Annie said with a smile, and the two women hugged briefly.

Beryl looked at Oliver, who was dressed in a casual suit the Roustabouts had paid for, a bowler hat perched on his head and a wispy beard growing on his face. His eyes roamed the room but looked through everything, his gaze distant.

"Who's this, then?" Beryl asked.

Oliver approached Beryl without looking at her. Ambrose noticed Annie tense slightly but he wasn't worried, Oliver had been generally harmless before the events of Pilgrim Island and he remained so now, just with a… different perspective on things.

Oliver took Beryl's hand and shook it politely, his eyes finally meeting hers. "The stars will offer no solace after they are devoured by the void."

"That's nice, dear," Beryl said pleasantly.

Annie gently manoeuvred Oliver away. "This is Oliver, he's a friend of ours. He's started working for me at the pub. He doesn't get out much."

"Right," Beryl said. "So how are you, Annie?"

"I'm fine." Annie glanced at Ambrose. "Bit of a hectic week. But better than it being boring, I suppose."

"Not always, love. Do you know I had the police knocking on my door on Monday, asking after Ambrose? Wouldn't tell me why, either."

"I told you that was just a misunderstanding, nan," Ambrose said. "It's all sorted now."

Indicating Annie and Oliver, Beryl said, "So, you two aren't courting?"

"Oh, no," Annie said. "No, not at all."

Beryl gave Ambrose a familiar smile. She had been telling him for a long time that he and Annie would make a wonderful couple, despite his insistence that they were just friends.

Beryl looked at the clock on the wall. "It's a little late for elevenses, but never mind. Oliver, would you like to help me prepare some tea and biscuits for the four of us?"

"I am insignificant noise and dust," Oliver said as he walked to Beryl.

"Don't go to any trouble, Beryl, please," Annie said.

"Yeah, I told you I'd be heading out soon," Ambrose said.

"Nonsense, there's always time for a cup of tea," Beryl said, "and it's no trouble at all. It'll give you two some time to chat."

As Oliver followed Beryl out of the room, Ambrose looked at Annie and rolled his eyes. She smiled, recognising Beryl's matchmaking attempts as well as he did.

"I see there have been some new additions since the last time I was here," Annie said, looking at the sideboard and the twenty-three ceramic figures lining it.

"She can't get enough of the things," Ambrose said.

All produced by the same manufacturer, the figures were a collection of young boys and girls engaged in various wholesome activities, from a mop-haired boy hooking a fish from a pond to a girl with a ribbon in her hair playing a harp. Beryl loved collecting the figures whereas Ambrose wasn't keen on them, finding them unnervingly jolly with their delighted eyes, rosy cheeks and permanent grins.

Ambrose and Annie took seats at the dining table, each of its four places marked with a pristine white doily, a small vase of tulips standing in its centre, Annie adjusting her dress as she sat.

"How are you doing?" Ambrose asked.

"Alright," Annie said. "Refurbishment starts tomorrow. I asked Sam Gaskell."

"You said you were going to. I hear Sam and his boys know their trade, I'm sure they'll do a good job."

"He's not cheap, but the money from Oliver's house and what your professor friend paid me is more than enough to cover it."

Professor Bracegirdle had indeed been generous in his offer for the Abyss-Dweller corpses piled in the cellar of The Bewigged Pig when he came to view them two days ago, even with the terrible condition they were in. He had a group of his most loyal students come at night to collect the bodies, saving the Roustabouts the job of carting them over to the University of Newmuck, and Annie then set about removing the aroma of death and garlic which remained inside the pub, starting with a thorough bleaching and scrubbing of the cellar.

Before arranging the sale, the Roustabouts had discussed whether it was a good idea to give Bracegirdle or anyone else access to the Abyss-Dwellers, eventually deciding there was no risk of any dangerous eldritch secrets being gleaned from the mangled and decomposing corpses. Besides, Bracegirdle was one sandwich short of a picnic already.

As for whatever living Abyss-Dwellers were still out there, the Roustabouts agreed that the creatures retaliating for the failure of the Ritual of Suth-G'nar was unlikely given so many of them had already died at the Roustabouts' hands. Still, they would keep their eyes peeled just in case and they told Annie to do the same.

"Any visits from the police?" Ambrose asked.

Annie shook her head. "No. Most policemen want as little to do with female troublemakers as possible if you know what you're doing, trust me. When they arrested me I blamed it on female hysteria, and between Sugarfoot's statement and me talking about water retention and sexual discombobulations, they couldn't get rid of me fast enough. What about you?"

"I tried passing for a woman but they didn't believe me."

Annie smiled. "You know what I mean."

"No visits since the one my nan mentioned. I'm just glad they didn't tell her anything." Ambrose looked towards the hallway as muffled voices and teamaking sounds drifted through from the kitchen. "Oliver seems alright."

Annie raised an eyebrow.

"Well, not any worse, anyway," Ambrose said.

"No, I suppose he's no madder than he was a few days ago," Annie said. "He's still absolutely barking, though."

Oliver's new state of mind was apparent from the moment he woke up after the Pilgrim Island incident and would only speak strange, disconnected sentences concerning the cosmos, the Old Ones, the void and all that other stuff the Roustabouts had heard so much about recently. Sugarfoot suggested perhaps Oliver had been exposed to some kind of terrible cosmic truth contained within that mysterious sphere which drove him insane.

Whatever its cause, it didn't take Jeremy Alabaster long to be convinced of Oliver's insanity when the Roustabouts escorted him and Sugarfoot to the police station. Later, after Jeremy told them Sugarfoot had been charged and the rest of them were in the clear, he recommended Oliver be left with the police so he could be transferred to a suitable facility such as Newmuck Asylum for the Mentally Aberrant. But having heard stories over the years about the asylum's wretched conditions and mistreatment of patients, the Roustabouts refused. Oliver may have been madder than a sackful of stoats and softer than a blancmange left out in the rain, but in the end he had tried his best to make amends and do the right thing, so he deserved better.

When the Roustabouts suggested Oliver move into the spare room at The Bewigged Pig and work for Annie, her initial response rhymed with "luck cough". But they made their case, pointing out how he was harmless and needed a roof over his head while she – as much as she hated to admit it – could do with an extra pair of hands running the pub. Annie didn't want to see Oliver out on the street or wrapped in a straitjacket any more than they did, so reluctantly agreed to the idea.

"Are you finding him useful at the Pig?" Ambrose asked.

"He's actually been quite helpful with the cleaning," Annie said. "When he's not distracted. He does what he's told and works hard, and you get used to the rubbish he spouts. Opening up today will be the real test. If he starts chewing on customers or pissing in drinks then he's out. Are you lot coming over later?"

"We'll be there. We've got the Slippery thing first."

"Alright, I'll see you afterwards."

An approaching rattling drew the attention of Ambrose and Annie to the hallway doorway. Beryl and Oliver appeared, Beryl carrying a large plate of assorted biscuits while Oliver carried a tray bearing a teapot, cups, spoons, saucers, milk, and sugar.

Oliver smiled. "*Ghr-klu'up!* Behold the dreadful splendour of the feast of worlds!"

"Biscuits, dear," Beryl said.

"Biscuits!"

A Newfound Appreciation of the Arts

"What do you think?" Lizzie Orchardson asked.

"It's… nice," Bryn said.

"Experiencing art shouldn't be *nice*, Bryn. What do you *see?* How does it make you *feel?*"

Bryn stared at the random splotches and spatters of paint that covered the canvas in a riot of colour. Nothing discernible leapt out at him, it was like trying to force yourself to see something in a particularly shapeless cloud. Still, he felt he should make the effort. "I see… a one-legged wizard playing an accordion. And I feel peckish."

He ate another sausage-and-cheese-on-a-stick off the plate in his hand. He had eaten over a dozen since entering Warblesworth Gallery, the bare sticks piled on his plate like the scene of a mysterious disappearance of a squad of tiny javelin-throwers. He was a sucker for nibbles, but truth be told he was eating because he was nervous. He had even drunk several free glasses of red wine when normally he couldn't stand the stuff. Also, free booze was free booze. Bryn was nervous not because he was out of his element in the gallery but because Lizzie was nice and interesting and funny and pretty and he didn't want her to think he was a twat. He was also partly responsible for her father being impaled on a tree, so there was that.

When Bryn had spoken to the other Roustabouts and Annie about it yesterday, they were mostly in agreement that him attending the opening of Lizzie's exhibition was probably a bad idea, but Bryn argued that if Lizzie had a score to settle with them then they might as well find out now, and that she deserved some kind of truth regarding her father's death even if not the whole truth. He also simply wanted to see her again, although he kept that to himself. Lizzie had made an impression on him and it had been a long time since a woman caught his eye.

Still, doubt hit him hard when he entered the gallery in his clean suit and he might have turned around and walked right back out if Lizzie hadn't spotted him, thankfully greeting him with a warm welcome rather than an accusation of murder. She was wearing a simple but flattering dress with a squared neckline, her wavy black hair done up tidier than when they first met, the same silver necklace around her neck. She was every bit as easy-going as before, and Bryn smiled when he noticed on one of her hands a small drop of paint she had apparently missed while washing.

Bryn looked away from the painting and at Lizzie. "Is that right?"

"What, the wizard?" Lizzie said. "That wasn't what I had in mind when I painted it, but that doesn't matter. What matters is what *you* get from it."

Lizzie suggested they sit down as she had been on her feet all morning, so she and Bryn walked away from her paintings and sculptures set up in one of the two spacious adjoining rooms that made up the public section of Warblesworth Gallery, the white walls adorned with paintings and drawings by various artists while sculptures of all kinds stood on pedestals around the rooms. Each room featured a skylight that let in plenty of natural light, and the gallery was quiet apart from the murmured conversation of a few visitors and occasional footsteps on the floorboards. Lizzie had told him that Warblesworth Gallery was one of the smallest galleries in Newmuck but also the boldest, being unafraid to exhibit "outsider art", because apparently that was a thing.

Bryn's eyes once again roamed over the art on display but he found no more meaning in any of its randomness now than he had earlier. But Lizzie's company was of more interest to him than his surroundings anyway.

She led him to one of the four wooden benches in the centre of the room and they sat next to each other, Bryn putting down his plate while Lizzie nursed an almost empty glass of wine.

"So did you go to art school?" Bryn asked.

Lizzie chuckled. "Oh, I doubt I'd last long in one of those. On the whole the art world is very conservative and that goes double for art schools. Heaven forbid an artist should be free to express themselves in whatever way feels most natural and creative to them, no, you'll do what everyone else is doing. And how is that art, I ask you? But things are slowly changing for the better. You've got places like this, more artists outside of the mainstream are being recognised and appreciated, and even photography is starting to be used in interesting, artistic ways." She smiled at Bryn. "Sorry. I'm probably boring you to death."

"No, not at all," Bryn said. And it was true, she wasn't.

Silence fell between them but it was comfortable rather than awkward and Bryn enjoyed the moment. But he knew he was only delaying the inevitable.

Eventually he said, "Lizzie, about your father –"

"My father was a terrible man," Lizzie interrupted, staring ahead with a thoughtful frown. "He made my childhood a misery and he was a monster to my mother. In the end he had her committed to an asylum. She died in there. He never loved her or me and he never gave me a reason to love him. The truth is, I'm glad he's dead and I hope he's burning in Hell. If that makes me a bad person then frankly I couldn't give a damn."

Lizzie turned to look at Bryn and her eyes were deep and dark and without sadness or accusation, only strength. "The police told me about this Thomas Sugarfoot person claiming responsibility for my father's death. But I also heard about the three people chasing him at the party when he died. Of course I recognised the descriptions. Not that I said anything to the police. Whatever business you had with my father, I'm sure you had good reason to be doing what you were doing. From what I gather, ultimately it was an accident anyway, but either way it doesn't matter. The only thing I feel over that man's death is relief, and the world's a better place without him." She placed her free hand on Bryn's nearest forearm. "I'm no great thinker or studier of humanity but I know what cruelty and evil look like. And I don't see them in you."

"Well… thank you," Bryn said.

Lizzie moved her hand up towards his face. "But what I do see…"

Bryn swallowed.

"…is a piece of cheddar," Lizzie finished, smiling, as she pulled a crumb of cheese from Bryn's beard and showed it to him.

Smooth, Bryn thought. *Idiot*.

"Sorry," he said lamely as he ran a hand over his beard. Thankfully a sausage didn't fall out.

Lizzie set the crumb of cheese and her wine down on the bench. "Everyone who attended my exhibition opening was gone by the time you arrived. Do you know why I waited around?"

Afraid of making an even bigger fool of himself, Bryn kept his mouth shut and just shook his head.

"Because I was hoping you'd turn up," Lizzie said. "I know we didn't talk for long the other day but I thought you were interesting and that it would be nice to see you again. So I'm glad you came."

"I'm glad too," Bryn said. "Thank you for inviting me. I liked your art."

"No you didn't. But it's sweet of you to say so. It's alright, in the end I do it for myself, not anyone else. And look, if you feel the need to tell me about what happened between you and my father then I won't stop you. Just not today. That is, if you'd like to see me again, of course."

"I would. Definitely."

Lizzie smiled. "Excellent. A writer friend of mine has a play running for the next two weeks and I promised him I'd go and see it. Maybe we could go together? His work can be on the self-indulgent side, but having you with me should make for a more entertaining evening. Or maybe we could just go for a walk in the park one day."

"The park sounds good. I've had enough theatre for a while."

"Alright, you know where I live, stop by sometime and we'll arrange something."

Bryn said he would then stood up and excused himself, explaining that he'd like to stay longer but he had somewhere to be. He and Lizzie said their goodbyes, Lizzie going to speak to the gallery's director while Bryn headed for the exit.

Bryn passed an abstract painting in which he had seen nothing earlier, but now amongst the patchwork of shapes and colours there appeared an image roughly resembling a man's face. He looked happy. Bryn knew how he felt.

Secrets Stolen and Kept

Digby pulled open the loose section of chain-link fencing and stepped through the gap and onto the T. W. Chemicals property.

The ground was dotted with flourishing weeds, the two-storey brick building's doors and windows boarded up, the business having been shut down by the authorities months ago following some kind of large-scale chemical spill. The property was deemed unsafe and sealed off and people had tended to give it a wide berth ever since, which was why the Roustabouts chose it for their meeting with Slippery, any dangerous chemicals which might have once been present having long ago soaked into the ground or evaporated as far as they could tell.

A pair of pigeons ambled around, pecking at the ground and cooing, as Digby walked to the yard at the rear of the building where he found Henry, Bryn, Talbot and Ambrose sitting on a set of steps leading up to a waist-high concrete platform that ran along the rear wall. They greeted each other and Digby leaned against a rusty metal drum near the steps, he and Bryn smoking cigarettes as they all brought each other up to speed on their respective mornings.

The fencing surrounding the T. W. Chemicals property was itself surrounded at the sides and rear by overgrown, stony wasteland, a rise obscuring the nearest industrial buildings but not the black smoke that billowed from their chimneys, so the yard was private enough that the Roustabouts didn't see anyone until Slippery appeared from around a corner of the building, awkwardly carrying a heavy, bulging suitcase in both hands.

"Do you need a hand?" Ambrose asked.

"I've got it," Slippery said. "Bloody carriage driver didn't even offer." He walked the last few steps towards the Roustabouts, set down the suitcase and exhaled with relief, then pressed a hand against his back as he arched it. "I'm getting too old for this nonsense."

"You've been saying that for years, Slippery," Ambrose said as Slippery removed his hat, took a handkerchief from his waistcoat pocket and dabbed at his forehead.

Henry withdrew his timepiece from his trouser pocket and looked at it. "And you're still on time. One o'clock on the dot. There's plenty of life left in you yet."

Digby silently agreed. Benjamin "Slippery" Hill was sixty-three years old and looked fit and strong, having kept his athletic build, his blue eyes still keen. He also still had a full set of teeth, even if they weren't actually his originals but rather dentures consisting of human teeth set into hand-carved walrus ivory. He wore a smart lounge suit and his white hair and moustache and the lines in his face lent him an air more of dignity than decay.

A well-known figure in certain circles, Slippery had been a burglar for almost fifty years and was very good at what he did, his focus having almost always been the homes and businesses of the Newmuck rich and powerful, preferring to steal from those who could afford it.

Slippery was only ever caught once, in his early days, and the only close call since then was an incident thirty-five years ago which also led to the birth of his nickname. He was robbing a factory one night when police, acting on a tip, arrived on the scene. Slippery was surrounded but managed to escape by immersing himself in a vat of animal fat then making a run for it, literally slipping through the fingers of the pursuing bobbies, his identity hidden by the mask he wore. Slippery never spoke of the incident in public but of course word has a way of getting around, and so "Slippery" he became.

"I'm supposed to be retired," Slippery said. "I should be sitting in a rocking chair out in the countryside with a glass of brandy and a pipe."

"You'll never retire, you'd get bored," Digby said.

"True enough. But I'm an old man, I'm allowed to complain. Hopefully I won't need to worry about it and I'll die on the job, slipping on a loose roof tile or getting shot by a watchman."

"That's the spirit," Henry said.

Bryn looked at the suitcase. "So this is it?"

Slippery nodded. "Everything I could find that more or less fit the description of what you said you were looking for."

"Was it hidden?" Henry asked.

"Secret room behind a false door in his study. Amateur-level stuff. And no sign of trouble, house was empty."

Talbot picked up the suitcase and placed it on the waist-high platform at the rear of the building, the other men gathering around him as he opened it to reveal the items stolen from Frederick Orchardson's house: almost two-dozen books along with other documents and a few relics, all connected in some way to the Old Ones or Abyss-Dwellers.

After leaving Pilgrim Island, the Roustabouts agreed that while the immediate threat had been dealt with, the less Old Ones-related materials there were in the world the better, as there were plenty more power-hungry bastards like Cecil Burgess, Blacklock, Orchardson and Sugarfoot out there. So before the Roustabouts took Sugarfoot to the police, they made him lead them to his home and his own stash of Old Ones-related items, which they burned. Sugarfoot swore he didn't know where Blacklock and Orchardson kept their own collections but he assumed at home, so when the Roustabouts learned about Blacklock's house burning down, that just left Orchardson.

And that was where Slippery came in, the Roustabouts hiring him to break into Orchardson's home, steal anything that looked incredibly old or unusual or which mentioned monsters, gods, rituals or anything similar, and bring it to them. They trusted Slippery to heed their warning not to tamper with any such items or even examine them too closely, and they knew they didn't need to ask him not to keep any for himself, Slippery may have been a thief but he was also a professional and a man of his word.

Slippery looked around at the Roustabouts. "This what you were after, then?"

Digby reached into the suitcase and picked up a yellowed scroll. He unrolled it to reveal alien writing and strange patterns and a sketch of some kind of monstrous, swollen, vaguely insectoid creature that had more legs on show than a three-mile line of can-can dancers. One of the Old Ones, no doubt, and probably the one with the largest sock drawer.

"Looks about right," Digby said.

Bryn picked up what looked to be a human femur except for the spots where coral-like growths erupted from it. He looked it over with a distasteful expression then dropped it back into the suitcase.

Taking a wad of banknotes from his trouser pocket, Henry turned to Slippery and said, "Here you go."

"Thank you, lads," Slippery said as he accepted the cash that was the remaining half of his fee and stashed it inside his suit jacket. "Although my back doesn't thank you. Anyway, I need to get home to the wife so she can tell me I'm an old fool who should know better. And she's right, bless her."

"Do you want the suitcase back?" Ambrose asked.

"Keep it, I was going to throw the old thing out anyway."

Slippery told the Roustabouts to look after themselves and they said their goodbyes before he disappeared around the corner of the building, heading back the way he had come.

"Right," Talbot said, sliding his hands beneath the open suitcase and lifting it off the platform. "Let's get this done."

He set the suitcase down on a patch of bare dirt and the Roustabouts stood around it as Digby took a box of matches from his trouser pocket.

"Hang on," Bryn said, and he repeatedly brought his shoe down hard on the malformed femur until the bone, the sturdiest item in the suitcase, lay in splintered pieces. Then he nodded, satisfied. "Alright."

Digby took a match from the box, lit it and dropped it into the suitcase. It landed on an ancient book whose brittle pages caught fire quickly, and smoke began to rise as the Roustabouts watched the flames spread and the materials burn, the forbidden knowledge contained within disappearing almost as unremarkably as drivel from yesterday's newspaper, the only thing of note being the flames briefly turning purple at one point.

Eventually the fire died out, leaving only ashes and charred fragments of suitcase and bone.

Digby pushed some ashes around with one shoe then looked at the other Roustabouts. "Pint, then."

Another Round

Henry walked from the bar to the Roustabouts' table without spilling a drop of the five pints he was carrying. He set down the glasses, their third round, and Ambrose, Digby, Talbot and Bryn thanked him as he took his seat.

"What do you think, Henry?" Ambrose asked.

Henry took a swallow of lager and thumbed foam from his moustache. "About what?"

"The Old Ones," Digby said as he tapped ash from his cigarette into the ashtray. "Ambrose said if they're out there and as godlike as Oliver reckoned then does that mean they're watching us all the time."

"If they see some of the things you get up to they'll go blind soon enough," Bryn said to Digby.

"Well," Henry said, "if they are all-knowing then they know how much the hiding we'll give them will hurt if they ever show up."

It was only late afternoon but the sky had clouded over and the interior of The Bewigged Pig was turning gloomy, so following Annie's instructions, Oliver began switching on the lights around the barroom, their pale yellow light blending with the deeper orange glow of the fireplace. He had his shirtsleeves rolled up and an apron tied around his waist and seemed quite content in his new job. Henry had no idea what was going to happen to Burgess Canning Company but Oliver certainly wasn't going to return and take the reins of the family business. His condition hadn't stopped him learning the ropes at the pub, however, and over the past couple of hours the Roustabouts had seen him clean tables and glasses, pour drinks, change barrels and generally make Annie's life easier. Henry noticed she kept a close eye on Oliver while they worked but seemed happy enough with how he was doing.

Annie had reopened The Bewigged Pig around lunchtime and as word spread the regulars started to trickle in, George and Murray unsurprisingly being the first, the pair settling into their usual spot at the bar. All of the customers – apart from Gambro, who treated everyone he met like a cherished friend – were initially wary of Oliver's occasional cryptic utterings and general strangeness, but soon got used to him. Some people asked about the Abyss-Dweller attack the previous weekend but Annie brushed it aside and wouldn't elaborate, the Roustabouts doing the same. They just wanted to relax and get drunk.

So far so good.

The Bewigged Pig remained in its damaged state, although the Roustabouts had spent some time yesterday helping Annie and Oliver get the place in at least good enough condition to reopen. The people who drank there were used to no airs and graces anyway, so a rogue splinter in someone's arse wouldn't be the end of the world. The Roustabouts offered to help with the work being done over the weekend but Annie refused, accusing them of just wanting to be around to make sure she didn't make any changes to the pub, an accusation they only half-heartedly denied.

But all in all, Henry was glad things were settling down again. Now there was nothing for the Roustabouts to do but what they always did: take things in their stride and deal with life's next bag of nonsense whenever the universe decided to throw it at them.

"Annie said the Sugarfoot story was in the paper this morning," Henry said.

"What did it say?" Ambrose asked.

"Apparently it was the intensive and untiring efforts of the Newmuck Police Force that led to Thomas Sugarfoot being identified and apprehended, all under the expert guidance of the police commissioner. That's what the commissioner reckoned in the statement he made, anyway."

Digby smiled cynically and shook his head. "Typical."

"He didn't give the date of the parade they'll be putting on for us, then?" Bryn asked.

"Probably still ordering all the banners," Talbot said, and the Roustabouts chuckled and sipped their drinks.

"Did you double-check with Annie about the weekend?" Bryn asked Henry. "That she's not going to make any big changes?"

"I did," Henry said. "And she said if we don't shut up about it, she'll turn The Bewigged Pig into tea rooms."

"Bloody sacrilege!" Talbot said, outraged.

Bryn frowned at the painting above the bar. "Don't listen to her, Ewan."

"Look who it is," Ambrose said.

The other Roustabouts followed his gaze to see Dulcet Jones walking in their direction, looking dapper as ever in a top hat, leather gloves, smart suit and overcoat, carrying his polished cane at his side.

"Afternoon, gentlemen," Dulcet said as he arrived at their table, the Roustabouts greeting him in return.

"Pull up a chair," Talbot said.

"I appreciate the offer but I'm afraid I can't stay, I have a prior engagement. I was just passing so thought I'd say hello."

"How did the thing in Brighton go?" Henry asked.

"Well, the jade aubergine turned out to be a red herring and the blind milkman was actually a mute postman who was in truth a Prussian assassin, but I managed to unravel the mystery and see the conspirators brought to justice."

"Been busy," Bryn said.

Dulcet looked around the damaged barroom. "Not as busy as all of you and Annie, from what I hear. Apparently I missed all the excitement while I was away, including some prominent deaths and" – Dulcet glanced at Oliver, who was talking to a bottle of gin behind the bar – "other changes. Then there's the Pilgrim Island mystery, of course."

"Reckon that's a mystery you're looking to solve?" Digby asked as he stubbed out his cigarette.

"I've not been hired to do so. Besides, even I'm aware that not all enigmas need to be laid bare. I'm sure those involved did what was best in the circumstances."

"I'm sure," Henry agreed.

"I also heard about Winthrop Pollock-Seymour and his friends ending up in the hospital," Dulcet said with a hint of a smile. "Apparently they're in bad shape. But then those penny-farthings are notoriously dangerous."

"Accidents happen," Bryn said.

"And we should certainly appreciate the happy ones. Well, I best be on my way. You gentlemen enjoy your evening."

Dulcet touched the brim of his hat as he gave the Roustabouts a nod, and they bid him goodbye. On his way to the front door he smiled at

Annie and raised his free hand in a wave, Annie returning the gesture with a smile and a nod, her own hands busy pouring a pint.

The sky darkened as the evening came on, the bustle of the busy pub a familiar and comforting background noise as the Roustabouts sat at their table and drank and laughed and talked about the big things and the little things – some of which mattered more than the big things – and the things in between, as they had countless times before and would do so again.

Henry looked around at his friends. His brothers. The simple wooden chair on which he sat wasn't particularly comfortable but he was where he belonged, surrounded by the people he belonged with. He couldn't have been more comfortable anywhere else.

Henry held out his pint. "Cheers, lads."

Ambrose, Digby, Talbot and Bryn looked at him.

"What are we toasting?" Digby asked.

Henry smiled. He didn't have the words, but then he didn't need them. "This."

Five glasses clinked.

The End

www.ingramcontent.com/pod-product-compliance
Lightning Source LLC
Chambersburg PA
CBHW020642030726
47498CB00002B/323